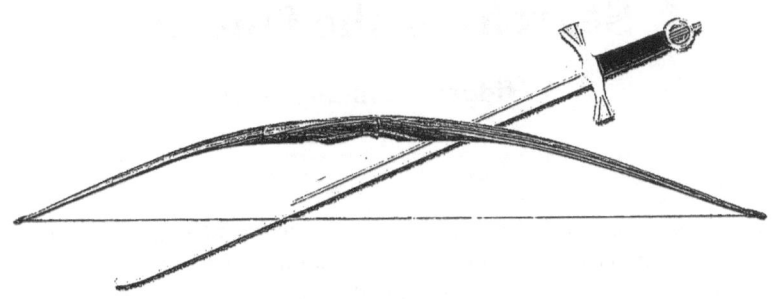

Search for the Queen

A Hidden Shaman Novel

I0679751

Gary Wedlund

Loconeal Publishing
Amherst, OH

Search for the Queen

A Hidden Shaman Novel

Copyright © 2012 by Gary Wedlund
Cover Art © 2012 by George Peyton
Interior Image Art © 2012 by Nathanial Stewart
Edited by Barbara Taft Verducci

Cover art models from left to right:
Sarah Jean Fultz (Batya), Paige Peyton (Abi).

Loconeal books may be ordered through booksellers or by contacting:
www.loconeal.com
216-772-8380

Loconeal Publishing can bring authors to your live event. Contact Loconeal Publishing at 216-772-8380.

Published by Loconeal Publishing, LLC
Printed in the United States of America

First Loconeal Publishing edition: September, 2012

Visit our website: www.loconeal.com

ISBN 978-0-9850817-5-1 (Paperback)

Hidden Shaman

The Shaman Within
Search for the Queen

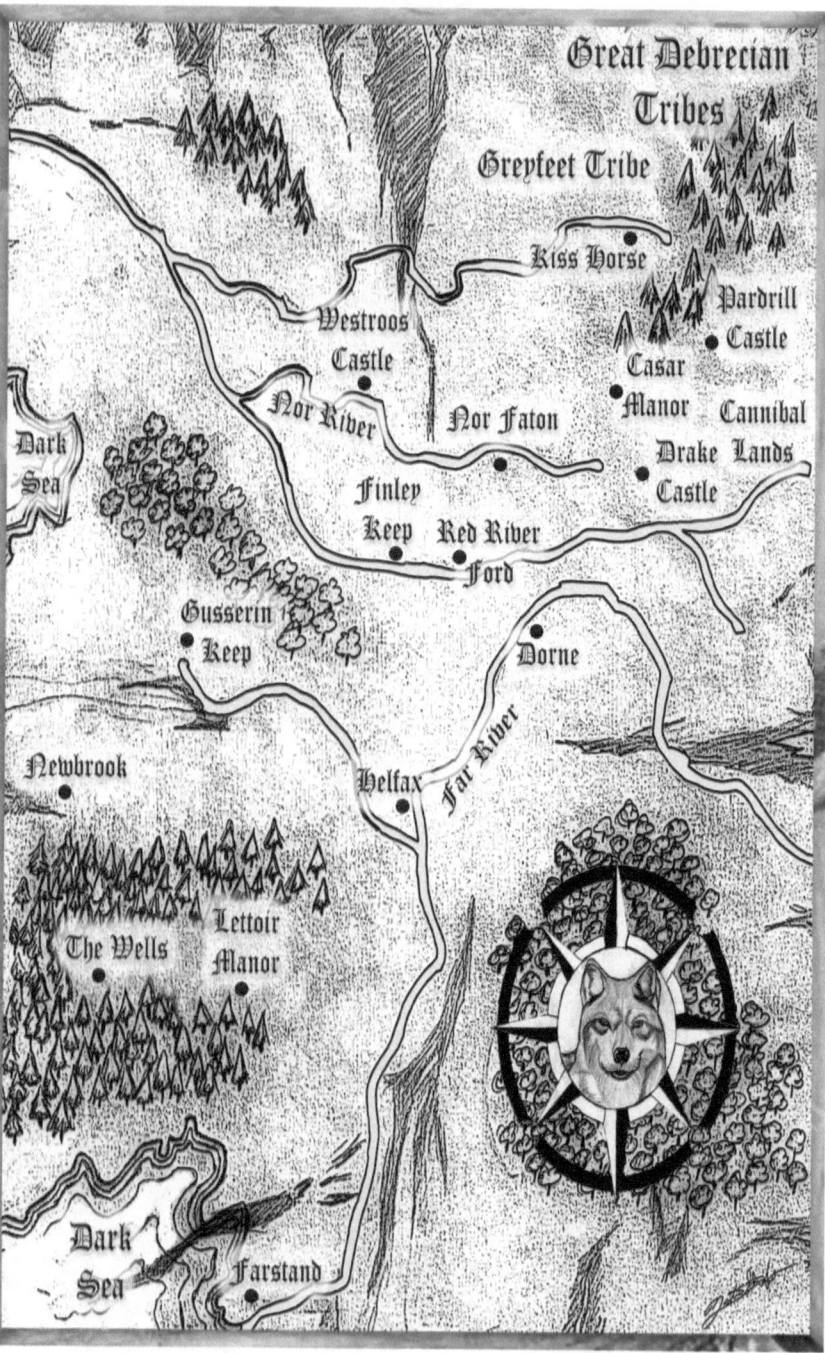

Table of Contents

I was yet a virgin
Against all odds
And though I longed
I'd been too busy to miss it
As much as a good woman should.
The only thing I truly missed was fear.
It was soon made apparent
What those two things had made of me.

Prologue

I had tunics with only minor blood stains and boots the nobles had barely worn. These were the winnings of war. Though it was illegal for me to read, I'd started a collection of four books. The last two I'd taken from the duke's ravaged train as his army had been overrun. Our loss in that battle no longer mattered to me, for I'd quit the duke's army when I'd murdered him. It seemed the right thing to do, though it hadn't even slowed the war for me.

Beef was salted away with a whole round of cheese. Two half-full sacks of grain draped my horse.

Copper, silver and even golden coins were fastened about my person and hidden within my saddlebags. I tried my best to spend them out, but each place I went in Farstand I gathered more from the fallen than I could waste.

The town before me promised no exception.

The first place I went was the posting board.

Again I found my picture, looking nothing like me. The drawing was terrible. My jaw wasn't square, as drawn. My eyebrows didn't continually scowl. My lips were much fuller than depicted. They'd colored a red spot marking a demon in my eye. Perhaps my long disguise as a man had shaded their perception?

Even the colors were faulty. My true hair was light, with tints of red and slowly turning waves, not russet and straight. I had green eyes instead of brown. The biggest insult of all was the description of my breasts as flat and like that of a boy. I nearly wished it so. I'm tall; that they had right, as did they the description of my strong body.

It was a good thing the peasants couldn't read, for none would have ever recognized me from the script.

The existence of my horse always pointed me out. Few who weren't of noble blood had horses, let alone saddles, and even fewer had saddlebags that overflowed with spoils. When it was a peasant woman on such a horse's back, even the village idiot figured it out.

I'd had to dye the elk saddle the same brown peasant color that I'd dyed all my clothing. The colors of the guards of Lettoir weren't well known, but I drew nearer to Lettoir's holdings, and my clothing remained finer than those on any other peasant in Farstand.

I would not dye Ella; it's an insult to each of us to hide so completely that we forget who we are deep inside. I'd learned this from my last mistake of being someone other than myself for too long and too completely.

Neither the poor description nor the dyeing of clothing helped. From the moment I went into any village, it was only a matter of their courage, not their discernment.

I reached down and tore the parchment off the posting board, in plain view of the curious who passed. I rode my horse on the main street, staring down every soul I met. Even the old women and small children were not spared my challenge, though sometimes I saw one look back and, of all things, smile.

When I went into the newly-planked tavern, I sat at a corner table and ordered the whole house chicken, not mutton or nibbles with beans.

Whispers passed from lips to ears. The one with the most eager ear waited until he thought I wasn't looking. Then he escaped through the doorway, in search of assistance.

One man barely looked up, almost seeing my face, clearly mistaking me for someone in need of instruction. His eyes were on his fellows when he said, "Houses of drink are meant for men."

I ignored him, saving it for the main battle. It was time to eat at a table, and I had little enough time to spare on the chore.

The chicken had been whittled down to bones by the time the two town guardsmen came in to arrest me. I pulled out my sword and killed them quickly without much tinkering. Next I killed the man who'd done the whispering and finally the man who'd told me the tavern was only for men. Everybody else fled the twirling splatters of blood. I note this quickly, for it cost me nothing in time, sweat or sympathy. My telling of it is as fleeting as the consciousness I paid it.

More than enough copper was found in the dead men's pockets to pay the tavern master for the chicken and to add two jugs of ale that I draped across my saddle horn. It seemed the whole town watched me slowly ride out. They'd been frozen by both the grandeur of my myth and the witness of my blade.

I couldn't spend all the leavings from this war and grew heavy from the collections. Too much success can leave a person empty. I found myself asking for the first time: What more is there to my life's new direction than treasures?

I didn't question that the shaman princess inside of me raged out of control and with no direction. Discerning war from peace is not the duty of a warlord. No, the wisdom needed to temper my violence was the duty of the unknown Queen, who remained lost, in spite of my every effort to track her down. Not that I didn't feel her near every place I went, and thus nowhere at all, for she'd been rendered as invisible as my life had been before becoming an outlaw.

That night I made camp on a rise within a swamp where the dogs couldn't find my scent, and the trackers were dissuaded by their beliefs in evil spirits rising out of water. I ate spiny fish and made flat bread over a raging campfire.

Sorting through my bags, I came upon my four books. I opened them one by one and read passages of poetry, battles or spells I dared not cast.

One book haunted me. I'd not touched it since before the battle that had killed the duke and baron's brother, for it was warded against anybody opening it. Many nights in the White Shirt camp I'd tried to break the spell holding it tight. I wondered who in that Debrecian cabin had carried it and about how easily I'd taken the treasure from the cabin wherein it had been placed in such plain sight. Did the former Debrecian owner miss it? Was she magical? Could she and no other open it?

Did she leave it specifically to taunt me?

Was she the Queen?

Have I been riding in the direction meant for my life?

Not even the spells in the book of shaman magic had helped break the bonds protecting the mysterious Debrecian book from prying eyes. I laid awake nights, wondering about the powerful magic that defied the shaman spells. It fiercely fueled my curiosity, knowing the book's forbidden knowledge was so close and yet untouchable.

I picked it up for the first time since the final battle separating me from Farstand's iron fist, and as easily as can be, opened it to the very first page.

I couldn't believe I'd done it until it was open. The ward had vanished, though I could still sense its presence, ready to keep unworthy hands from the book's secret passages deep within.

At first there were no words, but, as I watched, letters appeared as if an invisible hand inked the page that very moment. I was startled to find the script turn into a warning:

None may read these words, save the Queen.

Chapter One

Dead soldiers floated in the fog as I shrank away from the memory of a thousand wailing widows. This vision shifted with the lifting of the mist and the shimmering of crimson and ochre leaves abandoning the trees. I'd become transfixed between dreams, regrets and those things inches from reach.

I sat on Ella, my horse, considering this burden, content to know that, even after all the slaughter, I at least owed nothing but the space I borrowed. That was the brief moment in my life when I could afford such selfish thoughts, having liberated myself from the Lords through the act of murder.

Underneath it all, however, I felt spring buds, six months out of season, twitching to blossoms in my heart. It was a surprise to feel such a pretty emotion wiggling for space. I was no longer young, but an old maid, an unlikely virgin of eighteen. Still, the charitable feelings of hope, beginning in the first of those elderly years, arrived with the wink of new light over the foothills: minutes old and far from fully revealed.

At that moment, mourning doves flew over a slight rise, singing surprise upon seeing me meditating so still. *"Mercy, mercy, mercy,"* they seemed to peep. Their voices sent a shiver, as if the Goddess whispered into my ear.

I felt that in order to show mercy, a warrior needed someone worth giving it to. Such were few among my recent acquaintances.

On the other hand, I recalled an old woman's words: "Mercy can only be given to the sinful and by the empowered."

Did the Goddess require yet another test? Was the mastery of battle not all she intended for me? Might a test of mercy finally lead me to the unknown Debrecian Queen?

Nights before, I'd seen the first page of the Queen's book. The words were a warning that only the Queen should read it. The Goddess obviously was telling me who to return it to. Perhaps there was a meaning to my life in this newly envisioned quest?

As I contemplated, Captain Barker's men came steadily closer. Now, their arrows fell within yards of Ella's hooves. Again, running seemed prudent. I turned my horse to the west, where I'd scouted an outcrop. Seconds later, we flew over the gorge. Ella, a horse used to my joy for leaping over things, and restored to her youth by one of my favorite spells, landed solidly, though with mere inches to spare.

Captain Barker and his company of White Shirts charged, possibly unable to see the chasm because of the brush and slightly lower far side. Some of his men I'd helped harden in battles. Others bore the look of bounty hunters and highwaymen. Such probably cared little for Barker's god Sho, but they were easily converted for a few silvers.

Ella galloped to the peak of the rock hill, out of arrow range again.

This had become our pattern these past few months. I grew tired of the sport, thinking I should surrender. It wasn't a practical idea, but it might have broken the monotony.

The notion vanished the moment I remembered the penalty for witchcraft, not to mention heresy, treason and murdering the duke. And those do not even include poaching and stealing, knowing how to read, not bowing to nobles and pretending I was a man. The penalty might be the talk of the kingdom, to be sure: raping, binding, stretching, breaking, branding, the pit that comes to a narrow end so there's no place for feet, followed by drowning tests to see if I floated, burning tests to see if I cooked, and then the public stocks so I could be poked and tickled by the children. By then I'd be eager for the hanging, spitting and flaming, each to its own measure so I might linger.

Most importantly, I'd fail in my mission to find the Queen and return her book.

As I contemplated this, the soldiers of Sho dodging trees, brush and boulders without good discipline, obviously thought me too close to escape so many determined men.

Captain Barker nearly broke his horse's neck, calling him to a stop. His troops were sharp enough to follow his lead, incurring no losses over the edge. They'd winded their horses, and it was unlikely that any had the skill to jump as far as Ella anyway.

"Archers, prepare!" They fired more arrows, but I knew the range, backing Ella another few paces.

"God's curse upon all witches!" Captain Barker jumped off his horse. He paced before his soldiers. His anger appeared to only increase with time, for, on the last day when we'd both stood for Farstand in battle, we'd spoken to one another's hearts.

On this occasion, I yelled as loudly as I could: "My name is Abi, Sir Barker, not witch. Witches are harmless! I am no woman of peace!"

"Witches and murderess are all the same!" he yelled back.

Another volley of arrows struck a few paces in front of my horse's hooves. The rocky ground played havoc with the nice iron arrowheads, causing them to split the straight shafts and even ruin the fletching because of the sudden jarring. I'd collected many of their arrowheads, each worth several times their weight in coppers, though I owned no bow. These observations always found their way into my senses. The management of battles is no more than attention to many such details.

He stopped his pacing and held up his hand, signaling the archers to quit wasting their arrows.

"May we speak under truce, Sir Barker?"

He took a moment, but nodded, waving to his men. They moved back a short distance. I rode forward an equal amount to that yielded by the archers. "Abi! I am Abi, Sir Barker, not a witch. I am also a princess of war. Beckli Kahnsa, great ambassador to the Debrecians, says that I am a shaman. It is not better than a witch, I suppose, but different, in that I have no qualms about killing the enemy that is set before my blade. I remain untutored regarding the rest of the meaning, for my Debrecian heritage remains a mystery to me, but I think you will not be my teacher."

He kicked at the rocks, casting them my direction. "Abi or Abe, your name will be erased from all heavenly record the moment your flesh is burned and sent to hell. Imagine yourself burning, foul witch, and then upon death, and thinking the suffering at an end, awakened to more burning for all of eternal life. The only course for witches is repentance. Do you not see the favor I offer you by asking you to kneel?"

I laughed at him from up on my little rise where my voice carried, and I hoped, struck terror into the hearts of his soldiers. "What God worth serving demands service at the point of eternal torment? Is there any good in such a beast? When I met and came to know Sho, I realized even he laughs at such notions, and he's not one to shy away from your attention. Make my death a good one, Sir Barker, for when I die, the Goddess will take care of my soul, and I shall not burn. Instead, I shall return to you twice-fold. Know, it is the mother who tends you first, and it is the mother who tends you last. Do not make her angry while you sup."

"The twisted words of a witch!" His face reddened. Even his horse scampered to the side, avoiding him.

I smiled. "A shaman, however, can be quite dangerous. Even I wonder how dangerous, and I am far too eager to find out. Thus I've determined to give myself a difficult challenge. I shall not kill any man for a whole day, and I shall not kill you and your soldiers for as long as there is a truce between us. Enjoy the last of this fall season. Visit your homes. Get the rest you need. Let us settle this some other time."

"None of my men are weary. We'll find our way across this chasm."

Debrecian warriors did not bother with Farstand modesty, and I'd found myself increasingly at ease with the fashion. Sir Barker's men seemed fascinated by my loosely fastened tunic. I thought up a spell that took advantage of this weakness.

"Is that true, Sir Barker? Do you and your men no longer desire the company of your women? Do you not dream of their bodies at home, waiting? All women are subject to the cycle of the moon, and thus the Goddess's servants, made for seduction. But, then again, perhaps all women are witches in your eyes?"

I cast my spell:

> *"The Goddess sees you in your sleep,*
> *And the Goddess hears you in your dreams.*
> *As she lies at your side,*
> *She brings the night, the moon,*
> *And the slow caress of lips.*
> *She wraps you in her arms,*
> *And holds you to her breasts.*
> *As she pleases you in your sleep,*
> *She drives away all your fear.*
> *Tpunwvw Own."*

I twirled my whole hand in the air, and then flared my fingers in his direction while blowing a kiss.

He regained his horse in one leap and yanked his reins futilely.

As soon as he waved his arm to move south, many miles around the chasm, one of his men fell to the ground. Several slid from their mounts. Even the horses walked as if they'd had too much ale. Men fought to hold on. One of the horses fell over, spilling his man. The remaining men slumped over their horses' necks.

"Demon!" screamed Sir Barker.

"It is peace, Sir Barker. It will take you most of the day to raise your men from their slumber. Another day around this chasm. I'll be a week removed from your trail, hiding all my signs in magic, and you'll be months catching me. Swear in the name of Sho, and we'll have a truce for two months. Go see your family and bed your women. Then you may kill me if you can. I will not be so far that you can't find me."

"Ah, I see that too many of these men are not sound with God, having been rendered useless by your puny spell. I will take you up on the offer, only so I may return with better men who have longer fasted. In that time you'll agree to murder no more." He said this while brandishing his sword at me.

"I will kill any man who crosses my path with malice in his heart. I swear only to kill no man this day and to kill no more than necessary thereafter. If you live in my boots, Sir Barker, you know it is a good offer."

"Ah, this is an evil bargain, but I have sworn and am weary of your witch's voice." He turned from me and poured the contents of a water skin over the faces of several of his men. One of the sputtering men's eyes opened. He remained weak and fell back after an effort.

I turned away and soon found the back side of the small rise. It hid the rest of my departure. It wasn't a moment too soon, for the spell I'd cast had drained me like nothing previous. No doubt a spell on two score men had a serious price.

I doubted I'd even make it into the shelter of the first good patch of junipers. The experience informed me that such a trick would be useless in battle, for I'd be in no condition to fight the enemy if I put too many men to slumber. Captain Barker had only swooned, meaning that true converts to Sho might be immune from my spells entirely. There seemed clear limits to my magic.

I did make it into the forest though and then slid off Ella's back onto a soft layer of juniper needles. I worked my book of shaman spells out of my pocket and mumbled a passage that I hoped would wake me if an enemy came near. Others beside Captain Barker tracked my every movement. Each time I slept, I did it knowing that I slept in peril.

The rest of my preparations I don't remember, for I fell into sleep even before my blankets were properly straightened.

* * * * *

Hours later, I startled out of a deep slumber when half of a chewed and spit-drenched rabbit plopped across my head. The rabbit fell into my lap as I sprang up. Someone laughed and scampered at the fringes of the darkness.

I drew my sword, but the smell on the furry meat struck my nose, and I realized that I'd heard the laugh in my head, and not my ears.

I put my sword away. Wolves are not known for such generosity, preferring instead to eat the best of any catch and leave the bones and fur to those caught napping. They only gave charity when the member of the pack was hurt, young, and appreciated by a sponsor. Meals are serious matters of politics to their species.

I smelled Yellow Eyes on the rabbit! His skills at hiding were excellent, but I knew his tricks and kept my eyes pointed downwind until my sheer diligence convinced him he'd been spotted, though he'd actually been nearly invisible. He crawled out from behind a rock-footed cluster of trees. A smile blossomed on his face as he crawled forward. His tongue hung well out of his mouth, resting on his paws as if he'd been winded by a long run.

I laughed with him. I did so out of pure joy. Joy, what a thing! I'd not thought I'd feel it again. Just feeling it while looking at him made the hovering, year-long clouds disappear. My mind drifted to other joyful moments in my life as we looked at one another. I was a little girl again, splashing away the day in the creek on the last day of the old crone's life—before that disaster.

Ah, but then the curse of my warrior gift returned to me when I thought of that old woman. She bled wisdom inside of me still. "You must always be prepared, my child," the crone's words echoed from within. The White Shirts of Sho had come to her, declaring her a witch. They'd cut her head off and stuck it on a pole.

Yellow Eyes sensed my returning tension and snarled while crawling closer. The anger and hurt inside of me wasn't a good smell in my friend's nose, I suppose. I imagined the wise Beckli Kahnsa whispering this wisdom to me.

I tried to smile. "I am troubled by men who stalk me."

He got up, looked around, and then made a circle around my camp, showing a slight limp. As he circled, my eyes adjusted further to the darkness. A wound marred an upper rear leg. I caught many glimpses of it as he scouted the perimeter. The tear was ugly. Gnats ate at the open gash that was clearly not healing. Indeed, the rabbit had not been a gift, but a sacrifice, for Yellow Eyes had troubles, and perhaps feared that none would know it.

Ella wasn't so happy about seeing Yellow Eyes again. Speaking directly into my brain, she said that she didn't trust wolves, even if they were old friends, and particularly if they are hurting. Not only that, but she told me she was hungry for oats and thirsty for water, and she wasn't pleased to have been left waiting for these under a tree with no apples on it for all of a day and half of a night. Then she started in on old complaints about not having had a good crib ever since the war started. I replied into her head, thanking her for the grumpy reminder, for I'd not had a good crib since it had started either.

All that talking between our brains got me thinking of home. If Captain Barker could go to his home during this time of truce, why couldn't I go to mine? That's when I realized I'd been heading there all along, though in loops and circles, as I endlessly worked to dodge my pursuers. If I rode in a line for a change, I'd be there in two or three days.

There I hoped to both save and confront my mother. She was still under the rule of the evil man she called a husband, who, unfortunately, was the same man I called a father. As well, she was the only person I knew who could tell me any of the secrets of the Queen. If I were Debrecian, then she was as well; she did bear what I'd learned to be the mark of an enslaved Debrecian warrior, a gash across her lower leg that had crippled her and driven her to her knees in front of the man who had broken her. Now that I knew some of the secrets to my heritage, I was eager to amend a thing or two, including screaming at my mother for never having told me any of it.

I wasn't sure why my mother kept all of her past from me, but I was pretty sure the Goddess was involved somehow. The Goddess was my sponsor, but like all of the gods, I knew her to have no end to her list of plots. Surely my mother and the crone had been party to the gigantic drama the Goddess had designed for me. So far, the Goddess had led me into the life of a fugitive, little better off than when I'd left my home out of fear of being caught for the murder of young Bullor Rangleson. He'd been one of four brothers who'd betrayed the crone. It wasn't a good defense for the crime of killing so small a man. As before, there seemed to be walled off knowledge in front of me as well as behind.

I could count the walls, or I could count my blessings, I decided, as I loaded my things onto Ella and led the three of us to a nearby creek. There, I hung Ella's oat bag. She drank and plucked at some water lilies after a few mouthfuls of oats. I gathered some sticks, and with a flint and a small spell, sparked a fire for our fat rabbit.

I'd put half of the rabbit aside while the other half cooked.

Yellow Eyes wasn't fond of fire, nor did he want his meat ruined by it. He'd have to wait for me for his share though. If I fed him his share too soon, he'd want half of my share later. After swallowing that quickly, he'd want the next half of my remaining part and then half of the smaller part of that, down to the point of his wondering why I'd not shared the only bite I'd managed to actually eat before all of the begging started.

"Here, have some jerky while we wait," I told Yellow Eyes when he came close, showing impatience. He was full of anticipation as he sat to the side of me that was farthest from the fire. He didn't like flames much, but he was eager to be friends with the hand offering the dried venison. He ate a few strips without chewing, undoubtedly thinking better of the rabbit sacrifice the more he got of that.

He looked embarrassed about his wound, so I didn't ask him how he'd gotten it, but with some coaxing I managed to see the damage. I told him, "The insects are keeping the bite from healing. This means I'll have to clean it with a rough cloth. Then I'll sear it with stinging fire. After that, I'll close it with stabbing bone needles and thread before anointing it with herb medicine that will stink so badly it'll wake you up at night for thinking everything foul smelling in the forest has fallen upon you. You'll not be able to lick it off, for I'll fasten a bandage around you so tight every wolf will think you've gotten into the brambles and come away all tangled up in branches."

Yellow Eyes got up from where he was sitting by me and started whining like a pup. Then he walked in a tight circle, looking at his rump and clearly thinking that if he could just walk a little closer to it he could maybe lick it and fix it himself. The walking in a circle went on for some time, but it was getting him nowhere. I sensed he wasn't even thinking about food, which meant he was much distressed indeed because the smell of it cooking was even making my own stomach do flips.

I turned the cooked half of the rabbit upside while I waited for him to sort it out. Then I said, "If you don't let me do these things, the gnats will never leave you be, and soon your leg will go numb. You'll get hot with the sleeping illness. You'll forget how to eat and how to run. Your leg will make you into nothing but meat for the bears or worse—the bugs will cover you up and crawl into your nose. They will enjoy eating all of you up in tiny little bites as you lay there watching."

He said in my head he didn't think that would happen because it had never happened to him before. I pointed to the rabbit, and told him. "The rabbit has never been eaten before either. Imagine his surprise!"

I got out my herbs and mixed the right healing potions with my wee flask of boiled water. He also needed my ready potion of ground limestone, clove oil and garlic oil to dissuade the insects. I took one brave whiff of my tiny bottle of that, and found the hateful smell still ripe. Yellow Eyes sneezed, though he was much farther away from it than I was and hadn't even put his nose close. Rosemary oil was my own preference when in the presence of minor infestations, but Yellow Eye's bugs were formidable, claiming his wound as their home. A course burlap rag was soaked with ale and strong lye soap, ready for the cleaning. Then I threaded a bone needle, setting it on a rock. The last thing I did was pull a stick out of the fire for a second to see how the tip of it was doing. The glowing ember put sheer terror into the mind of the wolf. He even stopped circling just to stare at it.

I could see he was going to be a baby about being healed with fire, stitching and herb magic, so I had to say the sleeping words, even though I was still not fully recovered from having abused the spell so mightily the previous morning.

Once mended, Yellow Eyes worked his way through a small fever, which I tended extra special with a fever spell. By the time the spell worked and the fever broke, the morning was up. I'd saved us three good days by saying magic words over his wound. Yellow Eyes even forgot about his bandages when I reintroduced him to his share of the rabbit. We were ready to go find my mother by the time the sun touched us fully.

Much to my surprise I realized I'd managed the previous day without killing a single man. This I told my friend as we started out for the lands of Lady Lettoir. He didn't think much of it, for he'd never understood so many of our habits that he couldn't make sense enough of it to even start an opinion. All he seemed to know and all that seemed to matter to him was that he was no longer hurting, no longer hungry, and no longer a lone wolf without a pack.

"Yes we are a pack, though mighty small, Yellow Eyes. We'll find others; my mother next. Once I've freed her from the hold of my thieving father, we'll be three and better disposed to find the Queen, for I now know my mother's visions were more than my childish mind could previously fathom. The Queen that my mother mumbled about so often is a mighty warrior who is as wise as the mighty Beckli Kahnsa. It will be something special to speak to such a woman, don't you think, my friend?"

He was uncertain, but asked, Can she hunt?

I told him, "She has hundreds of hunters who hunt for her and who bring whole beasts to her tent in hope she'll simply speak to them."

He told me in my head that I was mistaken. Then after he'd thought some more, he said, it's fine if I'm wrong about such things because everybody is mistaken from time to time. He added that he'd feel even better about having a crazy wolf in his pack if we chased down another rabbit.

Chapter two

Kitchen smoke lifted above the cottage chimneys. It whitened as it touched sunbeams streaming above the foothill.

I'd crawled over the rise from which I spied down upon the small town and pike-walled grounds of the lady's manor. To my left, several peasants milled prior to the sun even touching the earth. They gleaned the previous day's battered stalks for lingering wheat. It had been a poor harvest so far. The fields had been thinly planted because of the shortage of men at last planting. Many had died in the war. I paid the peasants no mind, lest I remember my own childhood too keenly, and how we'd always seemed too short of food and too long of lazy men.

There were strangers in the practice yard of Lettoir compound, a lone couple dressed in the browns and grays of the lady, and I didn't even know them. The bulk of the men out practicing wore yellow tunics over black britches, colors of some noble house I couldn't place.

Several young men were clad in peasant tunics and clearly ill at ease while learning their wooden swords. I kept on looking, but after half a morning, I recalled none of their faces. Such was to be expected. Sergeant Hadarm and his Lettoir horsemen were dead or still on the battlefield clear across the kingdom.

Lady Lettoir's great house stood on a gentle hill, well within the circle of pikes, mounds and ditches. Out on the wide surrounding porch, Maid Minari shook out one of the lady's pretty rugs.

From the many signs and smells, only a few horses occupied the stable. The dogs had been turned out, probably to fend for themselves in the fields. It was a sign that even the lady rationed her food for an anticipated hard winter.

The gate guards displayed several odd colors, mostly black and yellow. The gate was better manned than in the past, and, every once in a while, a guard walked by on a lonely and endless walk around the pitifully weak pickets. The duty walking around the fence might have been penance, for it was only the one man, and his face constantly frowned when he was not talking to himself in an angry whisper. I saw no relief for him in the many hours I waited. A sergeant, whom I didn't know, came out to get him at sundown, but no man took his place. Penance it had been.

In all that time I only recognized the maid out of the dozens of people I'd known while I'd lived as one of Lettoir's.

A good scout can wait a long time, though I'd not shown much patience in my training, and I'd never read it in my histories. Perhaps it was a trick bred into me through my Debrecian blood. Perhaps it was something I'd also learned by observing the Debrecian scouts when they'd been my enemy. Or, perhaps more likely, it was just that Yellow Eyes and I had hunted a field of groundhogs and spent the previous evening making jerky and hard cake. Though he'd eaten more of the meat than I'd flamed, our bellies were fat. We had ample provisions and were in need of the rest offered by lying about on the fringes of the meadow.

A full squad on horseback left at dusk, nearly emptying the stables. Their horses were not common to Lettoir, nor were their uniforms, these latter being foreign, the black and yellow color of hornets. A couple soldiers wore breastplates, and a handful wore chains, as if minor cousins of some middling noble. My day of numbering proved interesting; there were at least three score still in the compound, and a handful of those showed some good training. I'd not expected professional footmen, especially so many. The last time I'd been graced with word, Lady Lettoir had been making handfuls of peasants footmen and was not well blessed with horses beyond those I'd stolen for her on the field of battle. That had been a score of horses at best, most of which had been returned to us when Sergeant Hadarm had reinforced us just prior to the last battle.

I decided there was no other way to learn about the many mysteries than to ask the lady herself, in person. I was going to see her anyway, a small diversion before going on to find my mother, whom I was certain had good knowledge of the Queen. But first, I owed Lady Lettoir an explanation regarding my sudden departure from her guard. None had ever been kinder to me, and thus I couldn't pass her holding without this courtesy.

I asked Yellow Eyes to keep an eye on my horse. Yellow Eyes found the chore of horse watching amusing, so I told him I'd be burdened with my stores and slow as a gopher if I lost my horse to gluttony. He wanted to discuss the idea of gluttony, but I put an end to our conversation by telling him the number of night clouds was just barely enough to hide me at the moment. This he understood perfectly.

The pikes were easy to pull apart and replace, while the ditch and mound fencing were even more easily traversed. I had knowledge of many favorite spots for breaking in and out of the compound from my days as a soldier and stable hand. I'd done it every night, so even the greater guard was no hindrance to me. When a good-sized cloud ventured across the moon, I simply walked all the way across the vast lawn and right up to the lady's house. I'd never known the kitchen door to be locked. That night was no exception.

Annie was cleaning up the fancy plates and silver as I gave her my compliments and apologies for barging in at the unseemly hour. She looked at me as if she didn't know me, which was even more surprising to me than the way she held her cleaver as if she thought I might be food.

"I find it admirable that you're willing to defend the good lady, even from the position of my lady's cook, Annie, but you needn't fear me; I've only come to repay my debts to Lady Lettoir."

"You be a traitor, they say. It is true, be it not! Yes, the same eyes, the same hair as that Abe boy. You be cursing us all wit' suspicions."

"Oh. Well then, perhaps I should repeat that I've no quarrel with you or our lady. I have not been made aware of your hardships. I can tell you, there were few courses open to me." I showed her my hands.

"All you murderers be liars. Now stay still so I won't have ta' cut you in too many places." The cook was a peaceful woman in my memory. Still, she came steadily at me. Cooks are particularly handy with the cleaver. As well, she was the heavier woman, and, as she approached from across the vast kitchen, I thought it possible I'd have to nip her with my sword.

"Enough, Annie!" yelled Lady Lettoir. "You may not make a mess of my kitchen by bloodying it with one of my servants!" She stood under the archway separating the kitchen from the manor's dining room.

The lady looked from me to Annie. Then she walked within a foot of me, as bold as any man, and slapped me across the cheek.

She retreated through the dining room door and into her parlor. I shrugged at Annie, whom I thought at least loyal to Lady Lettoir.

Lady Lettoir sat beyond the dining room, in her parlor, rocking a chair. Her head leaned down, weeping into the tapestry she'd been sewing. I sat a little off to her side in a hard, though well crafted, chair made of cherry. There I waited for her mind to catch up with my arrival.

I waited upon her emotions some more, but I felt it unhealthy to wait forever. "I wished to become a soldier in service to a great lady. At that time, the world had no place for me other than early death for my sins or as a broken whore. So, in my heart, I felt called to your service. I had a book of magic, and I knew one spell, which I used to make people believe I was a man of sixteen."

She looked up with red eyes and an angry scowl.

"I told you I was good at lying. Your man, Sir Lastion, was most observant regarding this point. The problem is, my lie was my life, and I don't repent it because truth was death. As you know, Farstand is cruel to women. I can read, I can fight and worst of all, I can dream. You must understand this, for I've now traveled and come to see the kingdom of Farstand beyond my father's little farm, and, in seeing it, come to know its evil. King Falstaff's laws make us nothing."

The lady sighed as if she'd thought many things and couldn't find words to put them together.

"Much has changed here. I'm worried my visit may bring you new trouble. I'll be quick. I owe you two years of service, regarding which I can no longer fulfill my obligation. This has the value of two golds. Further, I wish to keep my horse. She is often cranky, but I've grown fond of her. She's also old and held steady only by the magic of the Goddess, but I'll pay the full price of a pony for her." I put twenty-nine silvers on the table beside her chair.

"I have no use for your money, Abi." I couldn't see the lady's eyes as she dabbed them with her sewing.

"I do not wish to leave your service, a thief. In spite of what they say, my heart is true," I told her.

Outside, things were unraveling. The guards couldn't hide their smell. Having spent time in the world, I now knew my senses were far better than theirs.

I took the extra sword I'd carried into the house and put it on my lady's table. "This is the soldier's sword you entrusted to me. I return it as well. As you see, I still have my own strapped across my back, so I'm not defenseless. Now I own nothing but my heart, and that I will keep in memory of your love for your guardsmen."

Feet banged on the flooring of the vast porch that circled the mansion. Shadows shifted outside the windows. The fools thought themselves stealthy, I imagined.

"I once promised I'd defend you in this very parlor from the attack of the enemy. Do you remember that promise, my Lady?"

She looked at me, her cloth gripped tightly in two hands. "It was most unbelievable. You seemed so naïve." She added after a pause, "You seem so naïve."

"Just tell me the meaning of the men who surround your house. Why are so many foreign soldiers at your manor when the army is fighting at such a distance?"

"They've imprisoned me in my house. The King has told the baron to deal ruthlessly with our fiefdom. They see this misfortune with you as proof that a woman is ill-suited to serve as lord. I have been called a failure. I now lord this house alone, in keeping for Sir Pritchan, the brother of our neighboring lord. He is to be keeper of my lands."

"I should slay him for you." I put my hand up over my shoulder, feeling the hilt of my sword.

"He awaits the first sign of your return. Once you're captured, I shall be taken to the baron's keep and kept as a lady in waiting. Perhaps it is for the best; I have seen no prospects here in many years."

"Ah, I see the depths of your trouble. Now, should I kill them or not, my Lady? Speak swiftly, for I sense they are at your very door."

"No, they do not often come to visit," she said, telling me her ears and nose were not as good as mine.

The door crashed in before I finished that thought.

My sword sang as it swung through the air. I stepped forward instinctively and plunged it into a lung of the first man into the room. With as much force as I could muster, I jumped and kicked his dying body free of my steel and into his fellows.

The next man I had to parry. His sword spent itself when it slammed into the small table, flinging the pieces of silver into the air like snowflakes. I sliced through the cloud of silver. Cutting the swing short, I plunged only the very tip of my sword into his throat, which rendered ample damage and didn't require so much of an effort at freeing my sword for the next swing. With that, my rhythm established itself. Many fell. I felt as if I could take them all as they wedged mostly near the doorway.

"Stop! Please, stop!" screamed Lady Lettoir.

Her command gave me pause. Just then, two men I'd disarmed with deep cuts to their hands and arms rushed me. There was a press of men at their back. This left no room to swing. Thus hampered, I stabbed them both with my knife, but I was up against the wall and soon lamenting the chore of fighting so many in such a little room. If she'd not caused me to pause, I'd not have lost the momentum. There'd been a half swing difference between cutting each of them in turn and being crushed under the weight of their meat.

They soon had my sword, my knife and a good hold on one arm then the other, and, with six of them on my back, it took the rest of them no longer than five or six minutes to tie me by the wrists—though it might have only seemed so long. All six of the ones on me had plenty of scratches by the time they were done. I whispered a curse at them, suggesting their scratches fester.

My legs still kicked well enough, so they took another few

moments to secure them. I soon had nothing left to fight with, other than spit and teeth, though I chose not to use them for fear they'd gag me. In such an event, I'd not get the last word whenever it became necessary to mock their manhood.

They braced each of my elbows. Standing wasn't easy, for I'd strained several muscles and was sure to beat my record in bruises. Blood dripped from a half dozen minor cuts about my person. Most of the blood on me was not from my wounds.

I counted seven dead soldiers, though I'd not remembered getting a really good poke at quite so many. Others sat around the room, holding one limb or another. There were six more with bruises and scratches.

Over by the dining room doorway, Lady Lettoir picked herself up from the floor where she'd somehow ended up after all the sword swinging and knife poking and wrestling. Not a piece of furniture stood. There remained no tapestries or pictures on the walls, and all the china in a glass enclosed cabinet had become pieces scattered near the far corner. Blood dripped down the walls and ceiling. Her floor glittered in smeared pools of earthy red. I'd never seen such a sight and immediately decided I preferred battles outdoors. Nature has her ways of tidying up.

Lord Pritchan made an appearance. He was a strong but dowdy man who probably thought himself too important to do any of the fighting. He sneered as if he'd been the one who'd captured me. I had no doubt that thus it would be sung.

I looked around at the carnage and thought maybe I should be the one doing the sneering. Instead, I remembered the desire to remain un -gagged and decided to look meek, which, when I thought about it briefly, could end up the best trick of the day. In fact, the crone within screamed still, so it pained me to pretend civility. Such was sure to be the biggest lie of my life. On the other hand, it was expected; I was, after all, just a woman.

"Hold her fast," commanded the captain unnecessarily. I felt them clamp even tighter.

"So, this is the witch. You have caused much turmoil." He looked up at me as if he'd just won a boon. He walked around, stepping over a couple of bodies as he did. Some of his men were clearing out the others. This left him increasing room.

"My brother, Sir Gusserin, will be most pleased to discover we've played the right hand in your capture. And alive, no less. Perfect. The baron and King will be pleased to hear your voice screaming in their dungeons. Do you know your worth, foul witch? This fiefdom and the one beside it. Not to mention, a king's ransom in coin. My brother has spoken to the baron. You've killed the duke and the baron's own brother, from what I hear. How did you manage that? Was it poison, or some other trick that slowed their hands?"

I wanted to tell him it had been swords, but all my instincts were needed for my ruse. I said, "Please, fair Captain. It's not me you seek. I have also heard of this evil woman who has killed the duke. It was why I came here, you see, to win the bounty."

"Hum." The captain put a couple of gloved fingers under my chin and lifted my head. "We shall see. Bring in the wenches," he commanded his men.

Soon, they shoved Annie and maid Minari into the room. Minari's eyes became the bigger of the two, no doubt contemplating the cleaning job ahead of her.

Annie held her skirt up by the hem. She nearly slipped on a pool of blood by the doorway. I could tell by her bold expression that she didn't see Lady Lettoir over by the kitchen door and hidden behind a couple soldiers.

The captain stepped back and enquired, "Is this the witch that goes by the name of Abe?"

"Yes," said the cook. "The face be no much different, and that hair be unforgettable. She used to hover by me kitchen for dog scraps. I'll no forget her walk, nor the air o' her. She thinks herself better than most. Never ending talking about this or that. Mostly fighting and trouble. Kinds of things best left to the King's kin. She brought me witch's herbs. I threw 'em away, lest she taint us." I admired how well Annie embellished.

Minari looked at Lady Lettoir, as if for approval. She simply nodded then put her eyes back down so they'd see her as simple.

Annie walked right up to my face and added, "It be her. Now, where be me payment, ser? Am I to not get the reward offered by our King?"

"Ah yes. Your share is on the floor. Take it and make no further mention."

Annie looked at the captain, aghast at having to gather her reward from the blood. She still did not have a good view of the lady. I had a better position, and Lady Lettoir appeared less than pleased with her cook.

Annie had no choice but to get her skirt bloody and pick her silver from around the glass, broken furniture and bodies.

When she came close to my feet, I bent my head down and whispered, "You have enough silver for five years wages, Annie. Then where will you sleep, and who will be your master? Will he call you ugly and beat you when the soup's too cold?"

The captain punched my face. It seemed to be my day for it. I remembered I was supposed to be meek and let myself shirk.

His movement aside gave Annie her first good glimpse of the scowl on Lady Lettoir's face. Annie went pale and then reached around for only one last piece of silver. She broke into sobs and rushed out the door, a few silvers short. If it had been up to me, I'd have insisted that she take every last coin.

Minari looked over to where the lady stood. "I'm sorry for the misfortune, ma'am. I'll start cleaning as soon as the room is clear."

The lady's voice was steady. "No need, Minari. We will be leaving in the morning. I will join the court at Helfax. It seems my estate has been forfeit for the benefit of those who have rendered greater service to the King. I will, of course, require your assistance in packing and making preparations for the journey and as my maid thereafter."

"Yes, ma'am. I'll be pleased to accompany you wherever you have need of my services." She curtsied. For the first time in my life, I found room to admire a meek woman. She must have been horrified by the carnage of this little battle. Her face was quite white, and she trembled against the far wall, but at least she remained loyal. I decided then and there to think, what would Minari do, whenever I was addressed, so as to convince this captain of my harmless intent—

present wounds and bodies notwithstanding.

But first, of course, they had to drag me over the blood pools, across the yard and into the center of one of the corrals. A couple of large men pounded a peg into the earth. They meant to tether me in plain view. A chain circled my neck. The other end locked to the peg in the ground.

My wrists remained tied, but my ankles were loosened. All around me men watched at the edges of the corral fence. At first they threw rocks and dirt, striking my already tormented body, but then one of the sergeants made them stop. Apparently Sir Pritchan had plans for me beyond dragging my corpse to Helfax. No doubt he wanted my confirmation that he'd not brought in the wrong body.

Many volunteers showed up for the pleasure of guarding me. Even during the last wee hours of night, five sat on the fence, looking at me as if I was amusing. There they taunted me, especially when I awkwardly tore strips of cloth off my own clothing, managing to bind a couple of the wounds that I could reach with my bound hands. I had no ointments, so I blessed my wounds with chants. Only then did they pause from their antics and listen.

An order came down early in the morning darkness that no one should talk to me either. I knew this because all of a sudden the chiding stopped, and the silent stares became all the more consuming. Still, I heard them whispering:

"She doesn't look like much. I coulda' took her by myself."

"The room was closed in. You know how a fight with a cornered drunkard can be. Tables and chairs get underfoot."

"Witchery will do that. Make a man slow, they say; turn time against him, move furniture about and such. Send it flying, I hear."

"What's that?"

"You know. She calls on hell. Witches can slow down the world, I says."

"Seems impossible to me."

"Yes, but so. Even the sun stops for her. Only for us do things keep moving. Thus the wench is fast. Banshee, they calls it. Catch her by her arms and her legs and keep her still, they say."

"Bah!"

"Believe as you want! But, I knew a priest. He spoke of it."

On and on they went with their ideas. They had more thoughts on witchery than I'd even imagined possible. I listened, hoping to catch some good hints regarding magic, though the bulk of their notions were pure idiocy.

"I am not afraid of a tall wench. In fact, clip her nails, and I'll have a spell with her in me bunk. She has a good turn of the leg. You know what they say about good turned legs. Leads to the finest pleasure," one man said.

His whisper was weaker than most, and he said this only to his friend's ear. I turned to the sound of his insult and let him know I'd marked him even from the distance. Both he and his friend stopped their conversation and looked away. When they looked back, I was still watching them. I didn't quit watching them until they departed.

I had to remind myself that I was a meek woman, for inside blew a tornado. It was a test of the Goddess, I decided. Why else would she let me be so easily taken? She obviously intended for me to be tested anew and put to some different trial. Well, with only one minor interruption defending the lady's house, I'd made it four days without killing any men; I could make it a day or two without spitting on one as well.

What would Minari do if she overheard such a blatant threat to her womanhood? She'd walk briskly away and hide under Lady Lettoir's petticoats, I answered for myself. Well, the specifics were not the point, I decided, thinking I'd not played that last hand well. The enemy had to be lulled to sleep. It was as if the Goddess had told me this from the minute I'd been subdued. By the time it grew light, I thought myself ready to devote myself to the challenge of humility.

Chapter Three

I fell face first, hitting a horse patty on the dirt road. A rope slowly dragged me until the man driving the lumbering wagon decided he couldn't get away with it anymore. This took some time and much chafing upon my legs and back. I whimpered, as seemed required by my new tactic.

I knew they were slowly thinking less of my power, suspecting their dead and wounded had been because of cramped quarters in Lettoir's parlor. It was a good excuse for them. Personally, I thought it was a good reason why I'd slain so few, that and the way the lady's scream had hampered my rhythm. That is not to say I didn't know my limits. Then again, maybe not.

Several times on that first day, Lady Lettoir came back and commanded I be given water, though she'd been stripped of authority and could do no more than ask the favor. She was going back to the baron in Helfax to face her own disgrace for having hired and overseen the female soldier who'd killed the King's brother. The worry on her face seemed mostly for me though. It was proof that I was still her soldier—apparently her only one. It probably helped that the men I'd killed in her parlor were not her own. In fact, nothing in the lands of Lettoir would ever be hers again. They'd even stripped the parlor out from under her, once I'd been arrested.

The sympathy she showed was spreading though; it was hard to not see a lady in her. Many of the men who had once looked at me with thoughts of murder were turning eyes of brief compassion our direction.

The captain was a different matter. I was his prize and claim to a new fiefdom. His brother had promised him Lettoir, plus half of another fiefdom. It pleased me to know my price was so grand that it would lift a landless second son. In all but final proclamation, the lands of Lettoir had become the lands of Pritchan.

Captain Pritchan was determined that I walk and stumble all the way to Helfax so he could display his coup and make a slow spectacle of me in every village. It was a third of any decent pace, drawing out his gloat and proving his willingness to assist in my punishment while he still had control over my body. There, in Helfax, the baron would chasten the unwise lady and pick up my responsibility, getting his pound of me before marching me to Farstand where the King himself awaited.

Lady Lettoir, though left to some dignity, was as much on display as I. We'd already paraded through a few small towns. I learned the feeling of being mocked. The wet spit and bruising stones were not so bad considering what the baron and King surely had in store.

At first I'd been hoisted into the open bed of the wagon for a spell or two of rest, but then the men with scratches started to become ill from constant itching. Captain Pritchan thought it a good idea to bring along a few of those who'd been only slightly scarred in my capture, as further punishment for the squad's poor performance. He already showed signs of regretting it.

Their conditions worsened. Some couldn't even open their eyes for the swelling, and walking had gotten too painful for most of them to bear. Thus, a third of his score of guards had become a burden.

Though it was because of my curse, I honestly didn't enjoy their suffering. Such had been laid upon them in the heat of my wrath. Now I could clearly see they were much the same as the soldiers with whom I'd served as a guard of Lettoir. The battle between us was over, and I thought there could be no better time for sympathy than in the midst of my own persecution. It seemed the kind of characteristic the Goddess might find interesting, and I was on a quest for such tests of my character, given I'd so often been singular in my approach to trouble. The sword is not all there is to a person, I realized I was doomed to learn.

Still, their itching was just as well. Watching them suffer inspired me toward many related plots and schemes. Ideas were greatly needed, considering the situation.

As the captain came back to see why his wagon had stopped, I cowered away from his stick, and slowly found my knees. With a bowed head and meek voice, I said, "Fair Captain, I'm sorry for stumbling. I fear I'm just a woman. I've also caught the plague of scratches. The itch is a spreading plague shared by many of us, is it not?"

"Huh. You'll get a few minutes rest. I've determined to deliver you whole. No doubt you'll recover from your minor afflictions because I command it. See how easy that was. The baron and King will consider it a favor that we present you alive, or as well as can be arranged. They wish a sound body to vent their sorrow, so fret not your suffering here; it is not too much."

"I do see, my Lord. It's what I deserve for yielding to the dark one's temptations. I repent it with every breath and every step."

He smiled, showing his pleasure at hearing my repentance. "I can see you have some remorse. It is too late for your life, but it is good to bring a sinner to God, even if late."

"Yes, I understand this now, fair Lord."

Lady Lettoir rode back, escorted by her maid. "She can't last very long in this heat without adequate food and water, Lord Pritchan. It's five long days, or three weeks at this rate, and we've only begun the journey. Can we not pace the suffering?"

"Hold your tongue and know your place. I can see her condition without your scolding. She'll be treated as fairly as the law allows. I know you would spoil her as if a maiden of the court. Perhaps this trip will be a lesson for you as well. Don't you see what becomes of servants who are coddled? We have our example—the killer of a prince!"

"I see I have been less than capable in my duties, Sir Pritchan." I did not like the meekness I saw upon her face as she spoke this.

The captain nodded at her. "Yes, you have learned a thing or two. Not for it, but to learn. All of this may turn out well for you, lady. You'll be settled at Helfax court. It was the baron's own fault for not recalling you as soon as you'd widowed. Now things will be set right, and once chastened, you'll see it is for the best. So then, I will send my quartermaster to see to the witch's watering."

I kept my eyes low. "Thank you, my Lord." Dipping lower, my

head found the ground, as if I couldn't stand the swirling of the world around me.

My eyes strained up to see. The lady and her maid looked after him, and then back to me. I thought the lady was going to say something, but both of them had a sense of sad resignation about them that they didn't speak past. They were mourning my death, it seemed, as if something of my legend had meaning to them. This I found most curious, both the fact they'd given up on me, and the idea that a lady could regret the travails of a peasant.

I said, "Do not be overly worried, kind lady. Are you not aware that if I'd not bewitched you into thinking of me as a soldier, the white guards would have surely burnt me as a witch years ago. You have given me the time to make a name for myself. No peasant I know of has earned as much as a mention, for I have sinned and read many books of history. In all of them, I've read not one mention of peasant contributions to the world. So, I feel blessed above all others from my station. And, I suppose the captain will be pleased to know I must repent even that prideful notion. In my heart I repent most of all that the two of you must bear the rude whispers and darker station offered from within the cold halls of Helfax."

The lady bowed her head in prayer and whispered to nobody, "I have lost my lands, oh Lord, though losing them was only a longer time coming than I'd first expected. Now I must watch this torment and the awful burning of one of my servants. Why do I feel wronged, my God, if I've been told I must also feel so guilty?"

I asked, "Well, did he hear and answer your prayer, my Lady? Perhaps you should try the Goddess; she will find you more worthy than the god of men."

She seemed surprised I'd heard her and turned her horse away. The maid lingered a moment longer. I didn't know the reasons for the maid's many glances, but she looked young, and I knew I was a mighty curiosity.

Up at the other end of the rope I was tied to, men in the wagon scratched and looked too miserable to even notice the visiting nobles. The itching was well inside of them, I could see. My curse had worked better than I'd even hoped, surprising because usually my spells took great worrying-over to be effective. I'd not even taken verse from my spell book. Good thing my books were safe with Ella, I thought, but then again, she was with Yellow Eyes and had her own troubles. I hoped that my wolf didn't grow too hungry.

The quartermaster came back promptly. He was a thin man with decent cooking skills from what I could gather. We'd been on the road for over a day, and he'd fed me twice and watered me twice again as often, which was the most allowed a prisoner by the laws of Farstand. He knelt very close to me this time as he handed me a bowl and filled it with the same cold broth he's fed the itching men in the wagon. I wasn't supposed to talk with him, but only Lord Pritchan cared, so I often thanked him and breathed a blessing as well. Each time I'd spoken, it had been with as much meekness as I could muster. Thus it didn't seem terribly difficult getting him to listen to my advice.

"I feel guilty about the itching, kind quartermaster."

He answered in his own whisper, "As you well should. Are you a curse hag as well as a murderess and all the rest?"

"Seem to be. I didn't imagine it would work, but so it apparently did. I repent it. Let me help with the cure and prove my remorse, so I'll not be forced to watch it as I walk on the end of this rope that binds my hands so firmly."

He gave me a cold stare and then carefully asked, "No tricks."

"You have my word as a witch."

He looked at me hard. I shrugged as if to tell him it was all I had to offer.

"Out with it then!"

"The itching is like the itch of nettles. Strangely, nettles are their own cure. Have you not heard of this remedy?"

"I haven't, and it seems a trick. I should have known better than to speak to you. You are a witch and can't be trusted," he told me as he refilled my bowl with some more water. The generosity suggested he remained interested. The water was very brown and had not been well sifted, though I couldn't tell as I drank it. My weakness was fake, but my thirst was as real as it could get.

I chuckled lightly, so as to not make it insulting. He leaned even closer to me. Perhaps he thought his fortune would be in telling my tale; many had made their way as a bard with less of a tale than mine.

"What is so funny, witch?"

"As you all say, I must be a witch. Do you not know that a witch is bound to the earth and can't deceive those she wishes to cure? We know many tricks for the breaking of itches. Ask the men who rode with me into battle, and even the soldiers of Sho, who benefited from my many cures, though I hated them even as I rode by their side. I can tell you how to cure these men, and I can also help keep you from getting the same malady. The crazy part of it is, I must tell you truly, lest I am no witch at all. Of course, I might not be a witch as well. Now that would be a different matter entirely."

"I can't listen to your riddles. I am forbidden this conversation." He took back his bowl. A little of the precious water spilled between us.

"That is true. Do not speak if it troubles you. Just listen. The green berries of the nettle plant can be crushed and put into a tea. They appear as if a tiny row of baby grapes. I'm sure you've seen them. That is best. If not in season – ah yes, they are not in season. Well then, the nettles themselves make the best medicine for itching in the late days of the year. You must be careful in picking them, but, as you know, they're everywhere, particularly close to the edges of the forest. Pick them with a rag. Break the very tips off and soak the rest of the nettle in water. Boil several handfuls three times, twice quickly, then cool, and then boil the last time for as long as it takes you to saddle your horse. Then drink the tea. It will cure the itching from the inside out. You'll see. A witch can't abuse the strange powers of the earth."

"I think I shall. Then I'll feed it to you next time I come with water."

"I see you don't trust me. So be it; your prudence is wise. Feed me first if it suits you, though it does me no good, for it is man medicine—not suited for women whom God has ordained to suffer minor afflictions. When you've fed me some, then give it to the soldiers in the wagon if I stand up against it without harm. You'll see."

"I'll think on it," he told me. As he went, I saw him scratching, though I doubted he had any reason for it beyond the seed planted in his mind. I was left only half quenched from my thirst. A soldier made me get up, and the wagon started in front of me with the sole soldier walking beside me. He soon crept up, talking to one of his friends in the wagon.

I looked back, seeing nothing but our dust. No one truly wanted to be close to a curse-hag, and fewer wanted to smell her wake after three days of constant tension, sores and sweat.

Then, quite unexpectedly, I smelled Ella. I looked around, but didn't see her. The brown and gold leaves of late fall blew from left to right. I dared not stare too mightily into the coming wind, for I hoped she'd stay hidden until I could get to her. Yellow Eyes was with her, which was a mixed blessing.

They'd taken my clothing and put me in rags, which was fortunate, or else I'd have smelled Ella on myself and not caught her scent as easily. I was dressed in a brown dress that had been shorn years back by one of the lady's servants, upon entry into her service. It wasn't fitting for a woman to wear breeches, and it was particularly unfitting for a woman to wear the uniform of a soldier; this they'd told me when they'd tossed me the rags. I suppose it shouldn't have mattered. I'd come into the world with nothing, and spent sixteen years trying my best to keep my tall body inside of one or two endlessly patched tatters. The rag I wore was the best I'd ever worn up to the moment of my sixteenth birthday when I'd been fortunate enough to steal some things decent from a few dead White Shirts.

Now, at eighteen, I felt like an entirely different person who'd been draped in the rags of a distant memory. Flea ridden clothing no longer fit me, regardless of how well the garment covered my ankles.

It was an insult—not just to me though. No, there was something else inside my body that was insulted, something deeper than my mere and singular flesh, something that spoke for many.

I believed that I smelled the scent of Ella. It mingled with the smell of Sir Pritchan's horse, and that of those pulling the wagon. Though it was distant, it seemed obvious that she wanted me to know she was there by the way she lingered upwind. Such intent was not in her nature, for she was nothing more than a dumb horse. It must be Yellow Eyes who was leading her, I determined. I pictured him with Ella's reins tightly clamped in his teeth. Such a thought was, of course, equally nonsense. Ella would rather trample him with her hooves than be led about in such a fashion, and Yellow Eyes had no skill leading a dumb animal about. More than likely, he was chasing her.

With each step I took, I worried at the ropes binding my wrists. I'd decided the best approach was to loosen just one winding and not the mess of it. Little at a time it came, and in order to hide my work, I tucked the tiny loop I'd freed back into the wrappings. Every so often a soldier pulled at my wrists to see I was still nice and tightly bound.

By the middle of the third day, I was out helping a couple of the guards pick nettles while the others took a rest and watched. The chore wasn't easy on me with my hands bound to one another. Another rope around my waist was connected to my hands to keep me from reaching out very far. I wasn't given a rag for my fingers, so I took several scrapes of the nettles as I collected them for my tea. Then the quartermaster set me to the task of brewing it. My instructions had been too specific for his taste, so I showed him the details as I did the work in a big pot. It was my idea to add some honey for flavoring, and, when I poured it, a sprinkling of lucky clovers gave the top of each mug a festive look.

I drank mine with delight, adding a second cup to prove it harmless, but mostly because I was parched from the days of short water rations. It wasn't hard to add a chant of healing to the mixture, though nettle tea is indeed a remarkable cure for the very same itch that nettles themselves create.

My hands had started itching from the picking, but were soon cured. By morning, several men left the wagon, showing sudden recovery. They were glad to be back to doing the soldier duty of guarding me from in front of the dust, which seemed more like they were escorting the nobles toward Helfax than me to hell.

When the guard came to check my ropes, he left satisfied, for the pulling of the one loop free had made the rest of the bindings even tighter than before.

The fifth day I walked with only one man still in the wagon before me. One guard took up the rear. He loped along many paces behind even me in order to avoid the dust.

I disliked the dust as well, but the smell didn't bother me because of how sweetly it mingled with the scent of Ella. My wolfish gifts of hearing, sight and, in particular, smell brought these blessings of companionship. For two days I reveled in it, occasionally sensing Yellow Eyes as well, and then a third smell of an unknown human, though there were many humans near, and I might have been mistaken. I couldn't imagine who might be with my horse. The idea of someone in possession of my animals and book troubled me.

Then the perfect thing happened. A man was sent back to sit in the wagon. He took his right boot off and pulled at the skin on his many blisters. The quartermaster examined the man's feet at the first break. The smell made me glad of the choking dust.

"I know the cure for blisters, and would enjoy the remedy as well, for I've missed my boots and my feet are not made of leather," I told the quartermaster.

"Would it be rocks in poorly fit boots, just as nettles are the cure for their own itching, witch?" he asked.

"No. Nothing as mysterious as all that. Listen… they say that the highest pine cone holds a fine white syrup that will cure any wound."

"So, we should stop again and climb the tallest trees for you?"

"If you're patient, you can wait for it to fall. Just mark it and sit back a while. Witches are known for patience and have been known to clear the cones from under a tree. Each morning, we come out of our hollowed oaks wherein we witches commune with the demons and see if the tallest cone has fallen. Sooner or later it will happen."

"Months of time waiting is a luxury."

Captain Pritchan came back with Lady Lettoir and her maid while we spoke. "What luxury is that?"

The quartermaster fidgeted from foot to foot. "She says that, like boiling nettles for the itch, we can cure our wounds and boils with pine sap taken from the highest cone on the tree."

"Ah, an admission of witchery, there alone," the captain said.

The lady intervened, "That alone is not witchery, Sir Pritchan.

Many wives and barbers use plants to help cure the sick."

"I would agree, but the part about the highest cone on the tree is suspicious," Sir Pritchan said.

"My thoughts as well, my Lord." The quartermaster pressed his lips tight and nodded.

I quickly added, "Yet it really doesn't have to be the finest sap. Great wounds have been cured by simply stripping the pale inner portion of pine bark away and applying it to the wound with nothing more than a rag holding it still. I'd have mentioned it before, but it's common knowledge, known in almost every kitchen."

In truth, such herb witchery was a closely-guarded secret, a vocation of some and a danger in unskilled hands. No witch worth her craft would ever think of giving a patient a strip of bark without at least grinding it into a powder first in order to mask its origins and protect her trade. It was also a service, for the ground inner bark coating was far better than bare bark.

"No harm giving it a try, Ser. It's only bark, common enough," the quartermaster said.

Sir Pritchan shrugged, riding away to the front of the line while the quartermaster found the closest pine tree and cut away a strip. Even before nightfall the man in the wagon was up and walking again. The combination of my prayers and herbs amounted to a quickening of the cures. I remembered back when I'd met the Debrecians in the woods and how they'd spoken of the curing powers of their shamans. It all made sense, for the crone's gift to me had indeed been both that of healing and violence. Curing these men felt almost as good as had been cutting upon them with my blade, I realized.

Then I recalled the other thing they'd said about how important it was for a shaman to have the guidance of a Queen, lest she know only violence. No wonder I felt unfinished. No wonder I felt this incredible desire to find a woman I'd never known.

My best idea came to me a day later, at a time when Helfax was only a day or two away. Some of the men had gone on a hunt and come back with a boar, which they slaughtered on the back gate of the wagon in front of me. I, of course, was a prisoner, and not allowed meat. They dined in earnest by the late night fire. I imagined myself Yellow Eyes, and even heard him creeping up close to our camp where I was tied about the waist, seated with my back to a tree where all in camp could watch me.

I imagined seeing through his eyes and lusting after the meaty bones. *If I couldn't have it, then they shouldn't have it as well,* my wolf mind thought as I watched with great yellow eyes from the cover of the thick underbrush. The meat aged as I slept, my wolf's mind dreaming it rancid.

Later I was awakened by a soldier taking his morning piss as close to me as he could stand without hitting me. I looked up at him with a meek eye, and then glanced away as he turned to show himself more fully.

Before he could turn away, I looked at the meat that had been left to sit on a cool rock. Flies buzzed off what remained of the grey, spoiled mass. It was as if it had been sitting in the sun for a week, I noticed. The Goddess had turned it at the whim of my dream.

I whispered my spell:

"Let them think it unspoiled.
Make them lust after this flesh.
The taste will be pleasure.
May the Goddess be praised.
May the Goddess be lifted.
May the illusion hold to the light of dawn.
Tpunwvw Own"

Almost as soon as I'd cast it, I felt dizzy. It hadn't seemed a very large spell to me, but then again, upon thinking about it, the spell was certain to affect many, and thus in her wisdom, the Goddess had extracted a greater price from the magic than I'd at first imagined. I woke from my dizziness just in time to watch as they ripped into the meat that morning. They ate as if it were the best meat they'd ever eaten.

We took to the road, and, as we walked, the wagon slowly filled with men. Soon we stopped by the roadside, setting up a sick camp. A few of the men could barely move, while most of them simply took more trips out into the woods than were reasonable.

A stake was grounded. My ropes stretched from that and a tree. The stake held an ankle and the tree my waist.

"Why is it you're not ill, witch?" the quartermaster asked through clenched teeth.

"You didn't bless me with the rancid meat," I told him.

"The meat was fine. It was red throughout."

"Then I'm mistaken, but it hardly matters, Ser. It's an ailment of the stomach, and thus I am doomed to watch your suffering, regardless of the origin."

He retched, spewing up water and a bit of the grey meat. "There must be a cure. You have so many and haven't been quiet when not even called upon."

"Ah, there is one, but it isn't easy."

"Say it, witch!" His yell caused him to have to run into the woods and empty both ends.

When he came back, I gave him my answer, "Cherries."

"Bah! I've often filled my own stomach with cherries and on occasion felt almost as bad as this. Now I know better than to listen to all that you say."

"Like nettles, the cure is deceptive. You see, cherries churn your stomach, as you've well stated, fine quartermaster, but they also purge you of the thing within that ails you. It's soon drawn out of you at both ends. In no time at all you are empty and no longer suffer. You see, if the problem is rancid meat, any that stays within will likely kill you, fine Ser. It must all come out swiftly. If not, I'll be left to rot on this tree with no minders to march me forward."

"What good is it? Cherries are early summer food, and I see none about."

"True, and thus the difficulty." I left it at that. He went off to drain his backside again. I waited for his crawling return.

I whispered, "But, there's one idea I've heard of in the absence of cherries. It's not as good, mind you, just as nettles are not as good as nettle berries, and bark is not as good as the highest pine cone, but it serves our purpose, I suppose."

"Out with it," he barked, shaking me about the shoulders while leaning on me for support.

"Cherry leaves do just as well. They'll be long and red and yellow now, just like the cherries, and if colorful enough, they'll hold a similar magic," I explained.

"Ah, I've no strength to look for such a tree."

"I'm tied to one. Have you not noticed the very thing before you?"

He reached up and grabbed a handful of the long and red leaves, and then noticed that half of the tree's leaves were already under his knees, all red and yellow and, in his eyes, perfect for his uses.

"What am I to do with them?"

"The best thing to do is to make a tea. If you had a big pot, and a knife for this rope, I'd be glad to make some for every one of you."

"With all of us so sick, you'll try to escape. I don't think you're all the bards have said of you, but I'm sure you're in some way shifty," he told me.

"Ah, well then just eat them as they are. Three or four will do, if you can get them down. Or, you can take my word that I'll not abandon you to an ill fate. After all, Lady Lettoir is also ill, and I've sworn my sword to her." We both looked over at the lady and her maid. Along with Sir Pritchan, they weren't fairing very well, for each had taken a large portion of the rancid pig with their breakfast.

He lunged for the wagon. Once up, he kicked the barrel of water down first and the big iron pot next. He gave me some flint, and then he pulled out his sword, cutting away the rope that bound me to the tree. I still had ample rope about my wrists but was put to work partially secured. I made a quick fire, belaboring the flint because they were watching me for signs of any magic that would have made the job easier. Soon enough, the water and leaf brew steamed. While it boiled up, I ground as many of the leaves as I could between a pair of rocks and added the bits in liberally.

"We will need all the honey for taste in this one, for boiled cherry leaves are bitter. If we had used cherries, of course, we'd not have the unpleasantness," I told him.

He gave me all we had, and I stirred it in before ladling out bowls of the bittersweet brew.

The quartermaster crawled around, giving it to the least suffering first, and then he took his time with the others. I cringed when I saw him give a bowl to the lady, who was next to last, leaving only the maid untouched. They, being women and of course, out of favor, had to wait before receiving the cure. I took that as the right moment to kick the pot over and offer some advice:

"The cure is a man cure. Don't give her any, for women weigh next to nothing in the scheme of things, and thus all women are made to suffering before Sho."

He stopped spilling the first drops of tea into the delirious lady's mouth, and he looked over at me curiously. I could see in his eyes he'd heard something oddly spirited in the way I'd addressed him. In fact, it hadn't been an address at all, but a commandment.

All of a sudden, he knew. Fear filled his eyes.

I smiled at him, not without some compassion and then unwrapped the rope binding my wrists. It came free easily once I had the first loop untangled. Then I walked over to the captain's horse and stole back my knife and sword, strapping the sword over my back with a good belt that I took right off the captain's convulsing body. The boots were more difficult to find, for I had to go from man to man before I found anything that was not fully worn and that also suited my feet.

Most of the men watched all this, but none were in any condition to stand up steady enough to fight me over it.

I was a few feet from the quartermaster when I told him, "If you were a witch, you'd know cherry leaves are full of the darkest poison. And, if I were a witch instead of a shaman warlord, I'd not be free to feed it to you, for witches can do no ill. Some things are not what they seem. Others are exactly what you've made of them."

He wasn't feeling well enough to answer me back.

The surrounding land was old country, and the meadow was well removed from any peasant dwellings, so I determined to take my time finding the best blankets and provisions that the backs of the three good riding horses would carry. This left only the two nags for the wagon, both of whom I set free and told to go home. They didn't remember how to run, so they started walking down the dirt roadway. I knew they'd lose interest at the first sign of a new meadow full of clover, but it was the best I could do towards getting rid of them.

I was on Pritchan's horse, holding the rope leads on the other two horses and was ready to make my escape when I felt the affliction of a conscience. I couldn't leave the good lady and her maid to die from my poisons. As well, it struck me that Sir Pritchan's men were a lot like the men I'd ridden into battle with. Many had treated me kindly, considering I'd murdered so many of their bunkmates.

Up in the sky, it was too bright for me to find the moon, upon which I was sure I'd find the Goddess looking down at me. She'd be ready to tell me her thoughts, for it was in similar times that she chose to add mightily to my confusion. Oddly, she did not take advantage.

After washing out the pot in a creek, I filled it with water and all the salt I could find on the wagon. I gave the potion my blessing and told it to hurry about its chore, dig deep and rut out all that it could find. Then I went to the women first, forcing them to drink as much as they could, as quickly as they could manage. Lady Lettoir was first. She trusted me the most and swallowed three mouthfuls before looking up with eyes that said she thought I'd poisoned her for a third time. Then she grabbed at her throat and rolled over to the grass, losing what remained in her stomach. It was a beautiful thing to watch because she didn't quit until there was nothing more coming out than a trickle of water.

Maid Minari crept away when I came to her. "Please. Don't kill me too."

"You must trust me. The cure is hard, but I mean to have you swallow as much as you can. My potion is blessed to work deeply and with haste, so do not mind the purging." I crouched while holding a bowl.

"No," she said with all the strength she could manage, which wasn't much. She managed to swallow instead of drown after I pinched her nose. She seemed sure I was killing her, I noticed, and probably hoped my poison would quicken the departure once her purging began.

I was disgusted with myself for having been harsh with her because I saw more in her every day. I determined that humility was underrated and in some women, a blessing.

The afternoon passed slowly as I administered to the sick. I saved my spells of health for the women. The lady was the first one able enough to help, and her maid assisted me soon thereafter. We made a fire, and then we found some oats to make into a soupy meal. Pritchan's men recovered much more slowly. Cherry poison is not something to trifle with, and thus I was greatly surprised to find that all the men were recovering from it, little by little.

It was a good time to leave when I noticed Pritchan himself rise up on one elbow and look over at the oat pot with something resembling hunger in his eyes.

"Well, I must be going now," I told them, as if parting from friends.

Pritchan spoke up quickly as I once again pulled myself onto his horse's back, "What about your soul, Abi? Did you not tell me you saw the light of salvation in your repentance? I ask you, what does death mean if, in living a short while longer, you earn yourself an eternity of damnation and pain? At first I hated you but have come to desire saving you from that fate."

"You meant to earn yourself some land, Sir Pritchan, nothing more. The words you speak serve your interests, just as the God who filled your head with lies serves his interest."

"Not so. Yes, I covet the land, as you suggest, but I also serve my God with conviction. You can be saved. If you come to your senses, I promise to deliver you to the baron unharmed, and will even give you rest in the wagon. I'll tell him of your repentance of this poisoning, and how you demonstrated it by remaining my prisoner. In saving my men, this time you've overcome the demon. It says you're fighting a war within, just as a soldier against the dark one is also his victim."

"Can I tell you a story before I go, Sir Pritchan?"

"You must not go." He shimmied forward on the ground, begging.

"Listen to my story, Ser. It goes like this: Do you not know we are all born of a mother? The Goddess is displeased with you for abusing the ones who have given you life. She says, 'If you do not repent and come to worship the holy Goddess under the guidance and leadership of the witches, then you are doomed to be hung by your privates over a tree in hell for all eternity.' You can be saved from this, Sir Pritchan. All you need do is come to repentance, and let me slowly torment you to death over a pit of flaming coals. Do not worry much about it, for in the scheme of things, I shall torment you only for a short while and the Goddess will have you forever thereafter."

"Blasphemy!" he screamed, though his voice sounded raw from recent vomiting.

"Yes, it is. She is the god of woman." I squeezed my thighs, signaling the fine horse that was my latest spoil of war.

Chapter Four

I went only a few paces along the rutted road before stopping. I needed to sort through the prospects in my head.

I sniffed the breeze, using my wolf talents. To the north were the familiar smells of Yellow Eyes and my horse, followed by the strange scent of the person they'd decided to run with. There was no road there, only trails. Why did they avoid me and yet linger so pointedly upwind? To be always upwind meant something. I should deal with that, I thought, but it would prove time consuming.

Escaping to some entirely different kingdom was another idea I gnawed on. Sir Pritchan would not go long without reinforcements from the local lords. They'd grown more plentiful the closer we'd come to Helfax. My cures worked quickly. Enough distance on good roads would make that moot.

Then there was the rescuing of my mother to consider. I'd concluded I'd go save her from the slow death of her wifely captivity, and together we'd find the Queen. I considered going for my mother last because it felt like the only choice that put meaning to my life.

In spite of the threat posed by Sir Pritchan, my soul was light, knowing I'd not murdered him. The magic of compassion gladdened my heart a little. Why I'd not thought of it much before was as much of a mystery to me as the smell of a human mingling with that of Yellow Eyes and Ella.

I lingered with my thoughts long enough for some of Sir Pritchan's group to sneak up. I unsheathed the sword across my back and turned, seeing only the women. Lady Lettoir and her maid limped the final few steps to where I waited way up high on the peak of my saddle.

When they stopped, they were too winded and weak with fever from the recent sickness to say anything at all. Thus, they spoke to me with their eyes. It was then I thought it likely my newfound compassion was going to get me killed—or more than likely something a little worse.

We rode away towards the former lands of Lady Lettoir and my mother's home. The entire time we rode, I increasingly thought it the stupidest option of my three. Everybody close to there knew the lady. I was in the sackcloth dress that, coupled with blades, boots, horses and the female sex, made me the strangest lady's escort anybody was ever likely to witness. On horseback, my simple sack dress bunched up when I rode. That showed every peasant we passed nearly all of my fair legs, the display of which in itself was a sinful novelty. They'd add whore to the tales of me for years to come.

Still, we rode like flying dragons once the last of the sickness passed. None of us spoke for the noise of clapping hooves and the quickness of our afternoon's passage.

We rushed through villages where peasants gawked in amazement. While a captive, they'd hit me with stones and rotten fruit. The sight of me, the famous duke killer, had perhaps been the memory of their lives, so my return was no small event either.

One town's eyes turned upon us early, but only a few made to stand near our path. Those who were slow or overly bold earned themselves a butting from Sir Pritchan's horse. I learned he had a great desire to be a warhorse. He was fast, tall and inflated with muscles; otherwise, he didn't have the great girth needed to carry armor into battle.

In one town, a man took the time to pick up a stone and cast it in my direction. This afforded the lady and her maid a brief rest just on the far edge of the village as I circled back and used the good stallion to butt the man up onto a porch and through the local drinking parlor window. None of his brave friends was foolish enough to linger on the wooden porch. I would have killed the man, had I not still been fixated upon learning the new and tricky skills of kindness.

That appeased me for a second. But, by the time the porch cleared, I decided it would be best if I found some means of working off the frustration of being too compassionate, so I drove my horse into the parlor itself. I had to duck nearly the whole time.

Six or seven men scrambled at the first sight of my sword. Tables toppled. The man I'd pushed through the window found some fresh strength and leapt out the same way he'd come in. Instead of working around a large chandelier, I sliced through its rope, sending flaming candles and melted wax onto the pretty and polished wood floor. After that, the place proved empty.

They had two whole chickens already cooked for me—my favorite meal—and enough ale to fill a handily provided bladder, all of which I strapped across the back of my horse before I made ready to leave the town with a good memory of the limits of my ability to forgive their torments. It wouldn't be good to leave my legend completely unattended.

I saw many faces in windows, but there was no more nonsense, such as rude men standing in the roadway tossing stones at my horse.

I yelled into the growing late afternoon shadows, "My name is Abi, and I am a Shaman Princess of a great Debrecian tribe. That is not the same as only a witch, for witches are peaceful, solely relying upon such as me to defend them. That I shall do if I chance upon the abuse, so learn some manners.

"Do not forget my visit either, and, if I should pass before you once again while in bondage, do not think it easy to cast stones and spit, for I shall never die, even when I look dead, and my eyes stare at you from beyond the grave. And also, that I have given you the gift of your lives!"

I suppose I was angry because my words sounded all jumbled. "And also . . . well, just you never forget it . . . or me . . . for even my ghost will come back and kill you enough to make you wish you were not living!"

Breathing became difficult from all the yelling, but I'd become extra angry about never being allowed to say what was on my mind, even if it was just to peasants who were busy with their dinners and running away from my sword.

When I got back to where Lady Lettoir waited, I saw a little fear on her face and could even smell it on Maid Minari.

I forced a smile. "I have no intention of killing them, but I mean to have them fear me so we'll have no more of those antics. We don't need any following us and thinking it an easy pot of money at the end of the hunt."

"I understand, Abi, but, as I watched, it seemed you enjoyed it more than is pleasing." That had been the lady's first chance at words with me since she'd joined my swiftly fleeing company.

"Yes. I did enjoy it. You have no idea how much laying waste to their little parlor was needful, so I could settle the thirst for destruction that aches inside. Do you not know I am a shaman, and my spirit is filled with a desire for warfare and the death of my enemies? It is said that with no Queen to guide me, I'm ready to burst, and I believe the saying, for it is how I feel."

I brushed a strand of reddish curl from my face and added, "That's not to say I'm unwilling to meet the new test of compassion that has been laid before me by the Goddess. I left them whole, but things can't be taken to a ridiculous extreme, or my skin will itch, my neck will fill with knots, and I'll go mad with the boredom of my day."

"I suppose that will not do." I could tell she wasn't convinced. In fact, I'd heard a hint of scorn in her tone.

She, of course, wasn't cursed with the crone's gift of a shaman soul, and, thus, how would she know? As much as I honored her, there were still many things a lady wasn't made to understand in her training; training that included speaking about nothing and in circles, sewing pictures of colorful ducks, and wearing pretty dresses that didn't even show her legs moving when she walked. Being made to do only those things, I suppose, was something like suffering, but then again, if she didn't know my sort of suffering, why had she decided to come with me and then complain about it? I didn't have the time to ask that particular question, for we had plenty of dusk-light to help us see ourselves farther down the road.

We rode slowly until we were out of sight from those mingling in the streets of the village left behind. I recalled the next village was just on the other side of a creek. Instead of crossing it, we went up the creek, avoiding notice. There we cleaned our bodies from the smell of sickness and abuse. This was work and not pleasure, for we were women, and it isn't in our nature to brag about unpleasant odors among ourselves.

Our new path skirted past the back gates of some village gardens. We then found a less traveled farmer's road where I had us get down and walk beside our horses because we couldn't ride them endlessly and still have use of their services.

The lady walked as close to me as she could in the cart-wide lane. I sensed her building up to a speech. I didn't know why she'd chosen to come with me, nor did I feel comfortable with the ample sorting that I felt had to be done regarding the nature of our changing relationship. Perhaps this was her problem as well and why it took her so long to formulate a starting place for the discussion. I could almost see it swelling up like a fat plum in the middle of her mouth.

She was short and wore her dark hair long, as was the fashion. It was full of curls that were undone, falling across her back. The locks blew in the occasional breeze, and they threatened to get tangled into every overhanging tree we passed on the poorly tended cart road. I thought her pretty for a noble, and, in a way, I felt sorry for her for the starch in her blood.

Once, she glanced over at me, as if ready to say her peace, but then she looked back down the road instead. I wasn't happy to see her look away. Her eyes were so deeply green they were nearly gemstones, and her face had some interesting turns around the mouth. She was older than a mere maiden, but I thought the wrinkle or two beside her eyes attractive. One more thing: she held a wealth of gentle wisdom within her, part of which I envied.

If I were Abe again, and of noble rank, of course, I'd probably desire a better and longer look at the lady under some blanket. She wasn't so old that she was of my mother's generation. On the other hand, I was no noble, and I knew certain thoughts between women were impolite, regardless of rank.

She'd have made a merry childhood friend, I thought. I never had one my own age in all of my own miserable childhood. They say girls make fine friends for other young girls. I wondered what two girls played at? I'd seen some with dolls in their clutches, so perhaps they played with dolls. Then I could think of nothing whatsoever to do with a doll other than to pull it out from under my skirt and start feeding it and carrying it around in order to save myself from the misery of listening to it wail. Such was the state of my life at that moment.

Of course, I could also talk to it and tell it how to grow up. I had plenty of things to say to my doll, I decided. For one, I'd tell it how to fight and how to keep still until it grew up and was big enough for its fingernails to scratch out an eye.

I looked back at Maid Minari and then over at Lady Mayran Lettoir, and I decided there were probably a few things I'd also want to say to my doll that were less violent in nature.

My mother had taught me more than how to fight, I realized with some more reflection. She'd taught me how to sew and how to keep the stew pot fresh and how to make jerky and candles and even how to keep quiet at night so as to not arouse the anger of the men. Almost all of my witch skills were my mother's gifts. Ah, lots of other things too, I came to understand, once I'd thought about it even more.

She held me a lot, mostly without saying anything at all, though I think we both were saying something just by holding on. Thinking about it, I sensed just then, on that road, that maybe she hadn't been just holding me, but maybe she'd also been waiting for something. It was like she'd been safekeeping me in hopes of feeling it when it came.

"Oh, Goddess," I moaned. "Let me see her both quickly and in good health! Together we'll go and find the Queen. Then we can hold each other without being afraid, and we can talk to one another too, for nothing now holds our tongues; not men, not even the gods.

I sensed, with all of my being, that the time for us had come, and yet it made no sense. Why hadn't my mother laughed with me like we were just little girls, in all of our lifetime? There'd been plenty of occasions for cheer. The men often left us to tend the fields for days on end while they went off thieving or whoring or maybe doing even worse things that were unknown to me. Goddess knows there were plenty of things in the world I'd never heard of before! Particularly, it seemed, all the pleasant things.

But, something had held her beauty back, and it was my greatest hope that, when I found her again, I'd find out what it was and murder it.

"Compassion is for the best, Abi," whispered the Goddess. I fell to my knees because her words had me giggling so hard. My horse walked on alone, a few more steps. My reaction to the Goddess's absurdity must have seemed strange to Lady Lettoir. Perhaps she thought me mad for laughing at seemingly nothing at all.

Scowling, she leaned right over where I rolled. "I'm sorry. I only said, 'Can we stop here for a rest, Abi?' If it's no, then fine; we can walk a little farther."

I stilled. "Oh, I'm sorry. I must have misunderstood you."

"What in the name of God did you think I said?"

I got up and brushed the new dirt off of my skirt. "Well, my Lady, I thought you, or in truth, the Goddess, said, *'Compassion is best. '"*

She went behind me and brushed the back of my hopelessly soiled rags. "Well, I suppose your conscience is speaking to you and not to me. But, I might have also suggested it."

"Here, my Lady, let me get that." Minari came around and was soon brushing me off as well.

I said, "By the Goddess, do you two have any idea how long you'll be doing that if it is to become even noticeably better!"

They both stepped back, and then Minari started laughing. I turned to resume our walk while the two of them got it out of their systems. *Hum, I thought; maybe this is what it's like to have women as friends?* I knew I had become the butt of the joke, but the easy feeling among us wasn't such a bad thing. I thought about turning about and telling them a joke. When I'd been magically male, my fellow guardsmen were always laughing at jokes. Some of them were even funny. Then I realized I didn't know any that were appropriate for ladies and thought better of it. Could it be that the only things funny were things that ridiculed women?

I paused while they caught up and then asked, "Do either of you know a joke? You know, one for women? I've never heard one, and I think maybe there is no such thing as a joke made for the ears of our kind."

The laughter stopped, replaced by their pondering eyes. The lady even looked like she might cry. I realized she was an overly emotional woman. Well, of course, it had been a hard day, and she'd still not told me her festering thoughts.

We rested for a few minutes and fed our horses in some tall grass. Ella was close, as was Yellow Eyes, but for some reason they were shy and didn't come into our camp, perhaps because of the smell of strangers.

Finally the lady spoke, "I do know a joke suitable for women."

Ah, I'd been on the edge of my rocky seat wanting to hear her tell me why she'd decided to tag along. Perhaps there'd be some revelation in the joke. "I'm eager to hear it, my Lady."

"Fine then. Well, there was a lady from the keep who was out in the fields on her masterfully bred mare. She intended to hunt her falcon. The great bird soared into the heavens, and then upon spying prey, dove faster than an arrow into the field. Perchance, the falcon came down too hard and landed directly upon a great boar. The boar gored the dazed bird before running into the nearest hedgerows and disappearing there forever.

"The lady rode to retrieve her bird, and, when she did, she saw he had both feet in the air and his eyes open. He was very still. She gasped and raced back to the castle.

"There she implored her husband, the great baron. 'My husband,' she said, 'my prize falcon has fallen and been gored by a large wild pig with mighty tusks. What should I do?'

"The husband graced her with a thoughtful expression. 'Go back, and make sure the bird is truly dead.'

"The great lady had not thought of that, and so she ran out the castle door. She quickly mounted her horse, but then she remembered something and got back down, returning to the castle. 'My husband,'

"'What now, woman?' the baron bellowed.

"'May I borrow a bow?'"

It took me a moment to understand. Then I got the giggles, which the maid was now catching. It was a truly funny joke, but then when I'd settled myself, I had to ask, "Is that not also a joke on women? Was she not daft, and did her husband not yell at her as if she were an inconvenience?"

"It's just a joke, Abi," said the usually timid Maid Minari.

It had taken some courage for the meek maid to scold me, so I nodded to her and smiled. Then I thanked the lady for the entertaining joke and spent the next hour of riding repeating it in my head so I'd never forget it.

I changed a few of the words in my head and wondered if it would make the joke less amusing if I had the baron bowing to the great lady and asking her if he could be of service. Then perhaps he was the idiot who offered her the bow instead of her asking for it. Maybe he was the one out hunting the falcon? Then the whole rest of the joke could stay as it was, with him bothering the baroness instead of the other way around. Ah, I was taking it too seriously and ruining it, I came to understand. It was just a joke. Nothing of the real world was meant to be in it.

The farmer's road was perfect for our uses. When others neared, I walked into the woods, and the lady and her maid stood aside. The peasants were always startled to see a lady standing aside for their passage. She was without a guard, as well, but they could obviously see Sir Pritchan's horse, and it was enough to keep them moving, probably thinking a knight was in the fields answering the call of nature. Night fell on us while we were still on the clear roadway, and so I insisted upon moving on, staggering our pace from walking the horses to a good trot and then back to walking them again. Thus, we made several times the progress we'd made on the trip out of the lands of Lettoir.

The farmer's road was so good that it was the first hours of morning before we stopped to sleep. The lady and her maid were draped across their horses' necks, and they were dreaming more than riding, so I laid out their blankets and bedded their horses for them. There was no need for a fire because they were dead to the world before I could even unsaddle our horses and set them with long ropes in the fields.

That's when Yellow Eyes showed up. He stepped around the sleeping women, and then stood before me as if nothing unusual had been going on for all of a week. The bandage around his wound was gone, and, from the look of his belly, he'd not suffered from poor hunting. I, on the other hand, was all out of fat on my bones, and he sat there laughing at me as if to tell me I was the one who'd starve if it weren't for the pack.

I agreed with him, if for no other reason than to get past the gloating. It had been some time since I'd had any sleep, and it wasn't a good moment to play with my emotions. He seemed to sense this and didn't press his point any further. Then he didn't know what to do with himself and wandered around sniffing at the sleeping women. Tiring of that, he sniffed at the horses, none of which were so soundly asleep that they didn't notice a wolf in their midst. They started stomping and neighing up a ruckus, like mules. That threatened to break their ropes or maybe even a leg.

"Cut that out, Yellow Eyes. Nobody has had any sleep in days, including our horses, which we will need if we are to keep ourselves clear of the men who wish to put me to the torch."

He told me he'd protect me while I slept through a perfectly good night—when the hunting was clearly the very best. Just as clearly, I needed to be out hunting, and together we'd find enough to put some fat into our bellies. Then we could sleep during the day, which any decent pack member did except for ignorant humans. While he didn't say that into my head in exactly that way, he did look out into the field and howl with a couple of short grunts, which meant the same thing.

"Guard me anyway, for I've not had the convenience of picking my days and nights lately, given I'm being chased by rogues, nobles, priests and peasants alike. And besides, I need to discuss things with you about my horse and the stranger, so keep watch over us, and we'll talk about everything at the first sign of daylight." With that I went to bed on a piece of ground that I'd not taken the time to even prepare with leaves or rushes—just a blanket.

He was standing over me when I got up off a rock that had spent the short night under the small of my back. Even though it seemed only seconds later, the sun was up, and I guess I'd managed to sleep enough to bore him a little. I think he was worried the strange women might wake up before I did because he didn't know them, didn't trust them, and he suspected they didn't know how to talk without screaming at the first sight of him. Not only that, he suspected they'd be worthless at the chore of hunting.

I told him if he didn't stop complaining about food, I'd throw a stick and have him fetch it.

He stood up straight and tilted his head before telling me only stupid dogs did that.

I told him, *"I know only dogs chase sticks, but such is the point. It is, after all, just a wolf joke, and thus nothing of the real world is to be found within it."* The explanation was wasted on him, for he wasn't happy with much of what he'd stumbled upon since entering our camp.

"Here is a better topic, Yellow Eyes. Who is this person with Ella?"

He answered in my head: *She's your ghost. A while ago, I noticed she was wary of me. After that, I got suspicious, but, when I followed her, she didn't chase me away. My curiosity grew when I realized she'd found you and was stalking your every movement. She hunts as she moves, seemingly without effort, and leaves her bones, some with good meat on them.*

"So, she wasn't frightened of you? And, apparently she won you over with a few half gnawed bones."

He didn't answer, nor would he look at me. No wolf enjoys being thought of as a scavenger, even though they take every opportunity.

"I'm only fooling with you, Yellow Eyes. Thank you for your report. Things have gotten complicated for me, and I've needed your news. It's good we're both cunning. Your diligence is a sign of a great leader who has lived long and who knows better than to meet every challenge with his teeth. I think we're both learning these new skills together, hard though this is."

He looked back at me with a serious face before leaning over and gripping my wrist with his teeth. He left a couple of minor punctures in the skin, and, when my arm was sufficiently wet, he let me go.

I thanked him for the compliment. Then I worried about the things he'd said about his mind having been clouded and thus made to believe for a while that the strange woman was me. Such a muddle upon a wolf's mind is wicked witchery.

I'd been so distracted by my wolf that I'd forgotten the women. Minari stood in her skirts with her dress clutched to her bosom. She looked as if she wanted to scream but was terrified to do so. The stick she held was pitifully thin, only useful if the chore was swatting a spoiled child's behind.

Between her feet, the lady found her morning eyes while still in her blankets. They also lit up like daylilies when she saw my wolf.

"It's a fine thing to see we're all awake, and there'll be no dickering over slow risers when we have many miles to cover." I picked up my saddle.

"That's a wolf!" said the lady as she crawled out from under the shaking legs of her protective maid.

"Ah, yes. Yellow Eyes is his name, and don't try to pet him. It's an insult to treat a great pack leader as if he's a pet. He comes and goes as he pleases, and pretty much eats the bulk of any rations that meet the sunlight. Just so you know the rules, my Lady. Otherwise, he may grow unhappy. Then he might raise a fuss."

"A fuss?" asked the maid. She picked up a blanket and nervously folded it into tidy squares.

I said, "Not that way. Roll the blankets tight, and with the damp side out."

The maid complained, "Is there to be no breakfast for the mistress?"

I began cinching up Pritchan's horse. The ladies started loading their own horses when they realized there was to be no breakfast. Lady Lettoir appeared the more tired of the pair, but she was soon doing as much labor as her maid. They bundled the last of their gear right where they'd slept so as to not move around much and arouse attention from Yellow Eyes.

In short order, we were back on the cart path and making good headway. I told Yellow Eyes he was the best pair of eyes among us and would be of great value as our scout. He took that as a compliment, and the horses did better as well without all their scampering when he got close to being underfoot.

Finally, I could take it no longer and had to ask the lady the ultimate question: "Why have you decided to join me?"

"I am not sure I have joined you, Abi." We'd been on the path for a good part of the morning, and she'd spent it trying to pin up her hair—while ahorse. Every so often, the maid came by and lent a hand, but it was a long strain from horse to horse. Finally, the lady relented, and the whole mess of hair tumbled down. Pins dangled from the many ends.

I had to correct her, even though she looked dizzy from the hairy disaster. "I see you've joined me, and not without some considerable delay in my progress. I had spare horses, and I had a free rein. The skills I employ don't lend themselves well to a host of women in a caravan. Further, I mean to find my mother, and those in pursuit might guess my intentions, so I have an even greater need for haste than I previously enjoyed."

My horse stopped, and the other animals obeyed my lead. I added, "So, if you're not sure if you've joined me, I have to ask you to do me the kindness of telling me where I might better leave you."

Her maid came up and started plucking the many ornaments from her lady's hair, taking advantage of the stop.

The lady replied, "The truth is, I have no good place to go. At the time of your departure, I looked around, and all I saw were Sir Pritchan and his men and then emptiness beyond. They were leading me to a life at Helfax court, where, you must know, a woman without land or prospects or even a sponsor will be taken in as the lowest form of lady in waiting. The waiting part is not quite as enjoyable the second time around, young Abi, particularly as I am now kinless and nearly accused of the crime of harboring you."

"I see," I said.

"Do you? Have you been to Helfax? It's not a comely city, nor is the keep grand. Then there is the matter of the baron's brother and his untimely death under your hand. Just by your having been in my guard, I'm eternally guilty of it in small measure. That, of course, is enough to ensure I never coddle favor among the baron's blooded entourage."

I had to correct her: "Ah. You must know it wasn't I who killed him. It was the great and glorious Debrecian, Beckli Kahnsa. I was tied up in swordplay with Sir Lacellor's dashing young Sir Drake at the time, and I had no part in killing Randolf, nor did I see enough of it, for Sir Drake kept me busy and wouldn't listen when I implored for a delay. He is a master with his sword, and so I could afford only minor glimpses. From what I did see, it was a lovely battle on the part of the great Debrecian ambassador. Did you know she killed our baron's evil brother with the technique of a thousand cuts? It was inspiring. I would have done the same to Sir Drake, just to make a double dance of it, but, of course, such a thing is unthinkable, for the man is too beautiful to cut upon."

"Sir Drake?"

I got down and decided it was a good time to start walking my horse. "Yes, Sir Drake. He's the man I'm married to in my dreams at night. I see him standing by a soft bed. I take his clothes off him, and then I put them back on him, and then I take them off and put them on him again. He's surprisingly patient when I do this. I do it over and over again until I decide to lie down beside Sir Drake. Of course, I'm just a lowly serf, and I fancy he thinks of me as an enemy, for he was greatly disappointed when he discovered he couldn't easily slay me in our last encounter. He even swore an oath in anger when we were parted from our deathly struggle. That isn't the sign of a man who is infatuated with a woman, I suppose. Further, I did his army many harms while riding for you and the baron, and I think they know who did it, for at times I heard they were looking for a woman who was also a warrior. I don't think Sir Drake put the two things together at the time, but I'm sure he has by now, given some counsel."

She said, "So perhaps I came with you due to your inspiration then." We were all off our horses now, and she walked closer beside me.

"I don't understand?"

"Yes. Inspiration, Abi. No matter what they do to me, I can always think of you and know it could be much worse. The whole world could want me dead."

I thought about it a while. "That isn't a kind thing to say to me, my Lady."

"No, it was not. I am sorry. It seemed clever, but certainly there is not much that is amusing about it, now that I reconsider. Please forgive me."

"There is nothing to forgive. I'll always owe you. Still, you haven't truthfully answered my question. Why have you decided to share my path and not some other?"

She said, "If they catch us, I can always say I came to ask you to repent and turn yourself in at Helfax. I could say that, when I did so, you kidnapped me. So, it is not such a big risk for a lady in eternal waiting."

"It is also not an answer." I stopped in the path.

She paused as well. I could imagine the trouble racing around in her head. "Fine then, if you insist. The lowest lady in waiting is certain to be picked up by an old and disgusting noble who in truth only seeks the services of a mistress. My time will be spent spreading my legs in the lofts, followed by shepherding the servants, and in time, lending a hand, increasingly so until one will not know the difference between me and every other peasant. If his wife does not murder me, then I'll be forced to murder myself and thus be doomed to eternal damnation either way it is done. Do you not know the rules of court? Do you think the only place people have trouble is in the fiefs?"

"Where does that leave you? How can life be better by following the likes of me?"

"You will have to go to the rebel lord, Lord Lacellor. Soon you will see the light of it and turn in his direction without need of my goading. There is nothing here for you, just as there is nothing here for me. The only chance either of us has is to present ourselves before Lacellor's court and ask for favor. They will not see me as a tainted lady in his court. In fact, they will thank me for my tiny part in ridding the world of the likes of Lord Randolf and the man you truly murdered, Duke Crestlin."

I laughed out loud at that.

"What is so funny?"

I patted the sword across my back as I answered, "Don't you know? I've personally killed at least a hundred of Lacellor's men and am responsible for many others. Sir Drake knew me as an enemy as soon as he saw me, as did Lacellor's other nobles, I'm sure. We didn't win any of the battles against him, but through attrition, Lacellor can't continue long in this war. He'll not be the first leader to have won all his battles and yet lost the major struggle. Much of that was my work. How can any leader forgive such transgression?"

She said, "You killed the duke."

"Yes. Even though it was just one man, it was an act of treason. Not even the enemy loves a traitor. I once heard one of Lacellor's footmen call me that, and he was begging for his life at the time, making it no small act of courage! I had no choice but to let that peasant live, for such courage is beautiful to me."

"It's not as you think. I will speak for you. He will see the value of your skills. If you kill an equal hundred for Sir Lacellor and this Sir Drake, all will be forgotten."

It didn't feel like her speaking when she suggested killing a hundred men was both easy and right. She'd even said it while looking me right in the eyes; I knew this meant she didn't see the slightest problem with her plan. The nobility were always so naïve.

I said, "Ah, whatever suits you to think, my Lady. It hardly matters because I have to see my mother before we go our next direction."

"I have noticed. There are no lands bearing the name Lettoir anymore, Abi. There is nothing back there for either of us." We started walking again.

"There is my mother. She is everything." I felt no need to elaborate.

We walked in silence for a while, and then the silence felt overbearing. I looked over at the lady, who was now sheepish and very pale. She stared at me and sighed so hard she nearly sobbed. I knew the thing weighing her down was about to come out, and I also knew I wouldn't like the sound of her words when they came tumbling all over my feet. I thought, surely, whatever she tells me will soon render the world a darker place than it has ever been before. I wanted to turn and run from her then.

"Abi," she said before yet another pause. "They have taken your mother to Helfax."

I turned in place, looking back the way we'd come, dropping the leader to my horse. "And you didn't tell me! How could you not tell me?"

Behind the lady, Maid Minari shrieked. Even Yellow Eyes came trotting back, though I did not notice until later.

"How could I tell you? They will have her surrounded by a hundred guards and in the lowest pit. The whole idea of it is to keep her chained up so you will fall into their trap. They may have even killed her by now, and if not, the dungeons will soon do the job for them. Ah, such horrible news to hide, and such horrible news to tell. Do you not understand why I didn't want to tell you? I thought, maybe Abi will become too distracted by her struggles while escaping to even have to be told. Now that you know ... well ... you know what they want you to know. It's as if I have betrayed you by telling you they have her." By the time she'd finished, she yelled almost as loudly as I'd yelled. Later, I had to at least admire her courage, but it did nothing for the sinking of my heart.

I moaned, "Ah, yes, I was right. The world is a much worse place than just a minute ago."

I ended up crouched in the road. There I tried to find the place where my heart had fallen. I sat over on my elbows. Finally, I leaned farther and put my face into the ruts. I couldn't sink far enough, and I couldn't find my heart down there anywhere.

I'll just breathe a while, I told myself.

Then, heart or not, I'll go to Helfax and kill everything alive: every man, woman and cow.

I got up, found the saddle on my horse, and turned us around.

After all, what need did I have of anything but my sword?

Chapter Five

The fires of the mightiest forge raged within me. The blaze asked more than even a great warrior could quench, so I gave it its head. Not enough water existed to put it out anyway. Oh, how I wanted someone to stop me. Oh, how I prayed for someone to stop me.

As for the lady and her maid, they did all they could just to keep within sight of my dust.

As I kicked my horse onward, I did not notice the great tree across the path. That, my horse leapt. Nor was I dissuaded by the creek we dangerously forded, it having swelled to flood depth without a cloud in the sky. The grass fire left me choking when I found my way through. I should have realized that something beyond nature had stood up and taken notice.

It was at the next creek that I finally understood these things as signs. The bridge had blown over and fallen to pieces. Parts of it floated down the stream toward the great and distant river. Other parts poked out of the shore, as if picked up by a giant's hand and spiked at odd angles into the mud. The posts were torn, not cut; ripped in two and speared about. The grounded ends stuck up with a thousand splinters.

This creek was wider than before, though shallow; I knew this from our last crossing of it a day earlier. Oddly, it wasn't swollen, as if the invisible storm that had swelled the last creek hadn't reached this tiny distance to even touch the one before us.

I heard the lady gasp when she stopped. She and the maid looked about frantically, obviously terrified upon sight of the destruction.

Lady Lettoir took out her handkerchief. She rubbed her face clean of the soot from that grass fire. Her actions reminded me of the many oddly coincidental hazards we'd passed in only a short time.

Her horse's tongue was hanging. We'd nearly run our horses to death. I looked up at the sun and realized how long we'd ridden hard. Ah, I was a bad soldier to have forgotten myself for this much of a whole morning. Still, I couldn't breathe a whole breath. I didn't think I had a heart, but something was beating inside of me a thousand times a minute. I couldn't get to the chore of killing the baron fast enough.

A stranger took hold of my lips: "Oh, please, dear Goddess, stop me."

"Amen," I heard Maid Minari add from behind. Her voice was both tired and serious, conveying neither humor nor scolding.

"Why are you following me? Don't you see what I'm about to do?" I turned my horse to face them, and then back to the front again as if I had no time at all to even hear their reply.

"Oh God, help her," I heard the lady pray.

When I heard that, I felt shamed. I lost my heart a second time and fell from my horse so I could rush to the chore of weeping in the roadway. There, with my hands on my knees, I bowed, as if in prayer, but I couldn't pray for all my crying. There I came to know I was only one person, and as mighty as I might be with my sword, I could be cut to the heart with the simple and the innocent.

A word.

A prayer.

A kidnapping.

An act of mercy.

An act of cowardice.

An act of kindness.

All these things left nothing but confusion and utter weakness.

Was my soul as easy to sweep away as that? I thought back to all the histories the crone had forced me to read and wondered about the many great cruelties of previously lost battles that might have motivated the great warlords of old to act harshly and without good thought. Oh, yes, the good ones put the heartaches behind them. It's one thing to learn from pain, and another to have it take over a life entirely. Well, all that thinking fit into my head nice and squarely, but there wasn't any more room in there for my heart.

I got up and walked to the edge of the creek. There, I pulled my sword out of its sheath and hacked at the broken piers, adding to the ample splinters on the ground. When my arms ached too much to hold my weapon, I thanked the Goddess for rendering me useless. It was all the mercy the world was going to get, just a moment's pause, I determined. I still felt eager to murder the first person who crossed my path and didn't immediately kneel and kiss the toes on my stolen boots.

That, of course, was the precise time the Goddess saw fit to appear. She stood there in the middle of the creek. Her face showed her grave concern, and perhaps a bit of disapproval. She wore her long white robe. Golden hair flew as if the wind was greater than it felt. Her bare feet skimmed the surface of the water.

"I know what you're going to say. Well, I'll not leave this alone. I'll kill the man who has stolen my mother and any of his soldiers who stand in my way. That part of it is not open for discussion! And, quite frankly, I don't see why you feel the need to disapprove!" I shook my fist at the Goddess.

"Is this how you pray to your Goddess?" she asked.

"No!" I put down my fist, using it to beat my breast. "This is how I tell you my heart. This is how I speak truth to the mighty. Let the liars pray as they will, but I'll speak loudly. Let the whole world see my soul and know I passed their way!"

"Ah, Abi, you are truly mine. We gods tire of servants who scurry about our feet and sit upon our laps like kittens. They plead for scraps. You demand the banquet and would steal the table if left to it. Abi, there is nothing but greatness within you. I hold your soul in my hand, and show my treasure to the gods. They gaze upon it with envy. But, this table is too big and sudden."

The Goddess smiled as if pleased with how everything had gone so far. How could she be pleased by how things had gone so far?

"That is all a bunch of fine things to know, my Goddess, but there is still the matter of my mother. I know you and she have had a falling out, and I'll not pry regarding its nature, but she is my mother, and I'll either free her or kill the man who has touched her. This is between us mortals, and this will be done!"

"So be it, if you will. Now that we've agreed upon the matter, do you refuse my help?"

What did it mean to refuse the help of a God? Oh, how I ached to do this alone. It was so very, very personal. Yet, had I not just admitted to myself that I was only one person? There was much left to do in my world. I simply couldn't do it alone, and perhaps I couldn't even do this one thing by myself. I wept, shamed to know that I had to ask the Goddess for her help in such a personal matter.

"Good, my child. It is not weakness to feel as you do. Great leaders put the world across their shoulders. The best see greater things than themselves, and these great things they cannot bear alone. Don't you know you are not the only one suffering and powerless to change much with your two lonely hands? Can you not see the need is not for wandering warriors, but for great and purposeful leaders? Feel what lifts us all as one? I shall grant you your request, my child. I shall lend you my hand." She stretched her hands toward me.

"Yes, my Goddess."

"Then here is my greatest gift: Listen to your council."

Even before the words finished, the Goddess vanished into nothing.

My first bitter thoughts were that it is just like a God to offer me nothing. All she'd said was listen to people. All my life I'd listened to people. What was the point in that?

I turned to look at Lady Lettoir and her maid, and they were standing there with astonishment on their faces. Then they stepped back, as if a score of knights were bearing down on them. I turned back towards the creek and saw no knights or pack of bears.

On the other hand, the bridge was completely intact. It stood as if nothing had ever touched it. In fact, it stood as if the nearby village had just finished its construction. I even smelled freshly cut pine. I touched a plank, coming away with sticky resin on my fingers.

Of course, the Goddess was still gone, and, I sensed, not close at hand.

I was still full of fire. Little had changed within. I got up and went back to my horse. I led it down to the water. We'd be unable to ride any of them for hours. I said, "We might as well take a rest."

The lady and her maid followed, and we were soon sitting on the boulders, watching our horses recover with their forelegs in the water.

I asked, "Did either of you see the Goddess?"

The lady replied, "I saw a bridge, freshly destroyed by a great force, and then it suddenly appeared, as if new."

"As did I," said the maid.

"Did you hear my conversation?"

The lady replied, "Only one side of it. Such is strange to hear, but we saw the broken bridge we'd crossed just yesterday, and I was startled when I heard your prayers. Never have I heard one speak so enraged and forcefully to a God."

"Well, it was two of us speaking. The Goddess's voice was clearer and more casual than mine, I suppose. She stood on top of the water, close enough for all to hear. It doesn't trouble me that you didn't hear or see her, for she picks those she chooses to speak to. I should think that seeing the bridge is enough to convince you that there was a mystery."

After a pause, the lady said, "It was enough. It will have to be."

"Good then. Well, the Goddess didn't speak with me long. She is good at being quick about her business, you see. So, there is little that I need to tell you. Let me start by asking if it is all right if Maid Minari speaks her mind?"

"She has always been free to speak as she wishes," said the lady.

"I have nothing to say right now, madam." Minari stood and curtsied.

I gave her my full attention. "You have something to say, and I'll need to hear it. The Goddess wishes for me to hear it."

It was all the invitation the young lady needed. Her whole expression changed from placid to stern. She put her hands on her hips and took a step closer. "Well then, I suppose I should tell you it's rude to run off and leave us tailing behind. I was terrified. I almost fell off my horse when we raced over that log. I've not ridden horses much before a few days ago. And, my skirts nearly caught fire, in spite of the fact they were soaked when I nearly drowned fording that awful creek. Not to mention that several times I've imagined you killing us in a fit of anger. I know you lost your mother, but it isn't our fault, and we shouldn't be made to pay for it! You should show some consideration." She stomped her foot. "Have you even once thought what's in any of this for me? I'm not a wanted criminal, or at least not yet! I've not lost my lands! Even if we make our way to Sir Lacellor, I'll still be a simple maid. You know, come to think of it, I may be just a maid who doesn't know a sword from a broom handle, but my body aches just as much as everybody else's does."

I looked over at Lady Lettoir, and she was looking at her maid without even a tiny bit of scorn on her face for the way the woman had dumped her thoughts before us. I suppose the lady's lack of ridicule toward her maid's outspokenness was for my benefit.

"Fine then," I said. "I ask your forgiveness, even though I don't think I had a choice. It was the hand of fate pushing me. My only excuse is I am fighting my own demons. I didn't kidnap my mother. The demons did it. And, I shall kill them for it."

The maid was not done. "That's not good enough. We go where you tell us. That's our demon! You must do better than to rush us all into danger. Ah, what good does it do, speaking to the likes of you!"

"You don't have to—," I started to say, but then I remembered the last thing the Goddess had told me. There were only two others among us, save Yellow Eyes. Two and a half people were not even enough to be called a council. "I'm sorry. I should have thought about my actions."

The lady looked at me with an upraised eyebrow. "You're right."

"About what?"

She answered, "There was a God out there on the water. I can't imagine you admitting that without some kind of holy intervention from whomever you saw."

I was growing tired of people implying I was hard headed, not to mention that the Goddess was a figment of my imagination. "When we cross the creek, you are free to use her bridge or pretend it isn't there and ford, my Lady."

The lady said, "Or not cross at all. Have you not considered that she tried to stop you three times before she destroyed the bridge that did finally end your thoughtless course? I'm thinking she put the bridge back, not to help us cross, but to fix things back for the peasants' sake. Your Goddess simply does not wish to harm the peasants for your mistake! It's the same lesson my maid has tried to teach you."

"My mother is in that direction. You yourself told me there's nothing left for us back in the lands of Lettoir."

"The manor is mine no more, but I say we go that way anyway," she looked back to the southwest. "We'll find our sergeant who will help us train a few good guards. They will make us respectable. I have some coin with which to pay a small escort. If I'm to become a traitor, I choose to become one with some good men as guard, lending us a little stature in the eyes of the rebel lord."

I shook my head. "Good fighting men are few, and they're in battle on the far side of the kingdom. We'll not find any in the manor."

The maid answered for the lady. "No. The King disbanded the men of Lettoir after hearing about the death of his brother by one of ours. The lady's men are home, scattered and I suspect poorly employed and certainly up to no good. We know where the sergeant lives, at least, and should see from there."

This insanity was the Goddess's doing, I thought briefly. I knew it, both because it made no sense and because it rang of a prophet wandering aimlessly in the wilderness. A sergeant needed a squad or better. Where was I to come up with that? Only the Goddess knew. It seemed that always, only the Goddess knew.

My council had apparently set the path before us, a thin trail with seemingly no end. I was meant to go find the sergeant, whom I didn't trust, and ask him to put his life in great peril as the trainer of traitors, even though he didn't like me much either. Then we would, no doubt, raise a new little army of six or seven. I hoped for one befitting a whole war in Helfax, though my Lady seemed only to want a royal escort of useless and decorative soldiers.

There seemed to be few things in the world dafter than the likelihood of that panning out for me. Unfortunately, it was a worse idea for me to attack Helfax Keep all by myself, and especially while dragging a couple of useless women around behind me as I did it.

I decided I had no choice in the matter. Besides, once we found some help, maybe the help would take the two ladies off my hands.

Then I'd be free to pillage. Probably, that was what the Goddess had meant to help me get done when she'd told me to listen to my council—such as it was. Then again, probably not. The Goddess never did things simply.

Just then Yellow Eyes came down the road. He was dragging his tongue from the hard run, regarding which he'd just caught up. He was not as fast as a horse, but could run nearly as far. The first thing he did was look over at our exhausted horses. He thought one or two of them looked like he'd run them dead, and so it might be a good idea to slaughter one and eat it for lunch.

Instead, I showed him a beaver dam, and together we harvested a pair, mostly for his hunger, given I'd prefer to eat grass and sand than flat tailed water rats. Fortunately, breaking the beaver dam provided us with enough floundering fish to smoke and fill our provision bag before the next day's travels.

We awoke to the sound of otters scurrying in the shallow pond, eating every last fish. I watched them digest several times their weight, happily slapping and sliding in the mud.

The beaver dam provided me with two water smoothed sticks that I cut and trimmed to staff length as we rode out toward the former lands of Lettoir.

At our next camp, I handed one each to the lady and her maid. "You've joined forces with a criminal. Since I don't want to spend all my days rescuing you, I'll have to teach you how to fight."

Maid Minari held her stick away from her body with two fingers.

"Girl, if I handed you a broom, would you hold it with only two fingers?"

Lady Lettoir held hers better, but in the palms of her hands as if she meant to hand it to her enemy. She said, "Perhaps it is not her role to defend the land, Abi. She is a fine maid. That is not a small job in my eyes."

"It's a little job in my eyes. I've never had use for the service. It has been a year since I've even seen a floor. When we meet with rogues, they'll find her a new vocation though. That, too, will not be the chore of sweeping a lady's parlor."

"Still, she can do little more than anger the highwaymen."

"Probably true, but at least her struggle will amuse me."

Amuse me they did, but only a little, for neither seemed suited to fighting. I had to change my tactics. I put them to briskly sweeping rocks out of the next camp with short strokes.

On one such occasion, I walked over to Maid Minari and put my stick in the path of her next sweep as if challenging her stick. I did it a second time and a third.

She threw her staff into the bushes and took up the chore of straightening the blankets over a place we'd already cleared. Even the lady stopped her sweeping to glare.

I waited until we'd eaten our meal of fish and berries. Then I asked the maid what she'd learned about fighting.

"Fighting? We were sweeping, or so you said. Also, if that's a lesson in fighting, then it's a poor one." She spit out a fishbone.

"Well, the lesson is this. Keep your strokes short, well aimed and solid. And one more thing. Do you think I don't know almost any man is bigger than you? If you come sword to sword, he'll kill you. Once you know you're likely to die, you can begin the lessons with new interest."

The lady laughed. "Abi, you are a trained warrior, and I don't doubt your sincerity, but is there enough time to teach us much?"

"It might be useful to teach you enough to keep the man from killing you in the first moment, and then you can scream for help and run for your horse."

"I don't know," said the lady.

I stood. "I'm not a knight. I am just a peasant girl!"

She looked at me hard. It was a secret that had been sitting between us for perhaps as many as two years. No matter what I did, or how natural the chore of fighting came to me, noble blood wasn't in me. And yet, Lady Lettoir had been the one noble among them all who seemed to see things differently when it came to understanding a person's true worth.

She said, "You are more than a peasant to me."

"Uh-huh," I nodded. "I am."

We rode out on the next day with a new understanding. I chanted staff movements as they worked their sticks against the air. I aimed to get their arms sore by noon. In the evenings, we spent most of our time discussing the feet and not leaving their sticks where their opponents could snatch them.

On the third day of stick training, I decided to give them a demonstration. I had them sit on a log near a small glen. There I summoned my mentor's ghost. It had been some time since I'd had reason to summon her.

She came as a thinner mist compared to the more solid shape of our previous meetings.

The lady and her maid said they couldn't see her at all. Still, the crone fought, and the sound of our staffs and bodies pressing against one another was ample proof. It must have delighted them immensely when my crone bludgeoned me off balance and then swept my knees. I spun in the air, all the way around, landing back on my own two feet. I banged her head with an elbow and some wood. The sounds caused the maid to shriek. Even for a staff, that was a killing blow, so the crone's head caved in a little. She vanished, and of course she came right back. A fresh smile grew on her ghostly face.

Enough fooling around, I decided while circling.

The crone seemed to hear my thoughts. She twitched her staff in the air, and it turned into an exact copy of my sword. I hurriedly grabbed my sword. When we met, sparks flew into the air that had previously only been lit by our campfire.

I didn't have the crone's patience as we measured one another for the counter-stroke. I struck first, forward and then outward, meeting her sword with enough force to slide it upward and useless. From there I sprung forward, killing the crone in one precisely aimed thrust. That move I'd never done before, and sure enough she didn't let me do it a second time. It took a great deal more work to kill her again.

I was laughing by then.

Such is always a mistake on the field of battle, costing me a goring. There was even some pain. Her sword passed right through my gut, slightly upward at an angle from down where she'd pretended stumbling. No more masterful a killing could have been achieved.

The women behind me screamed.

The crone pulled the sword out and then jabbed me through

again. She jumped back, right in time to get out of the way of my dinner, which I lost on the meadow floor.

I left my sword on the ground where I'd dropped it, and, when I got up to a knee, I bowed my head to my mentor. She bowed back and vanished.

The lady insisted that I lay down immediately, and the maid came up to help her push me down, so I had no choice but to do as they insisted.

"I'm fine, other than this hour-old taste of dinner in my mouth."

Over by the fire, Yellow Eyes laughed and suggested I lick it back up.

The lady pushed my dress up around my neck. She gasped, "I can't believe it. Twice I saw a blade come out of your back, and the blood spurt out with it, as if from a fountain!"

"Ah, so you saw something of the fight at least." I got up and settled my dress down around me.

Maid Minari shook her head in disbelief. "We saw a horrible fight, a demon—"

"No, the crone's only a ghost. I've fought a demon before. It's very different."

Minari went on, "It was fierce, but we only saw your half of it until the sword came through you. I was sure the ghost had killed you."

I laughed.

The angry maid stood and stomped back to the log. "Such isn't funny, Abi! How do we get on if you die and leave us alone?"

The lady sagged. "How can we ever learn to fight like that? We only saw your half of it until the sword came through you, but it was enough to suggest I'd never last in such a fight."

I said, "My mentor is a master with her weapons, as is Beckli Kahnsa and Sir Drake. Bandits and common soldiers are not so well schooled, and few of them even own more than a knife."

"Let's hope we don't have to find out how well they fight," said Lady Lettoir.

"We will, and soon. We're in the worst parts of your lands, my Lady. The higher up we go, the more trouble we find. I wish Sergeant

Hadarm could be found this side of your fiefdom, and we were not forced to travel through the passes."

She'd once been the owner of these lands, and her eyes told me she felt the same apprehension. Maid Minari, however, picked up her staff and started sweeping rocks.

Chapter Six

The narrowest mountain pass loomed before us. There the wind races through rocky seams in tiny gales, and it is not easy to track the smell of the bandits, for it flies by and sticks to the cliffs where the shadows invite ice. What I know of scouting, however, told me my father was near, and we were not going to make it through without some blood.

As to him, the only excuse I have for not killing my father is gratitude for raping my mother on the night of my conception. I mention this only to say that he had no redeeming qualities at all.

As we ascended, my father finally stepped into the space between two large boulders. He wore some unfortunate lady's scarf for a mask. My women were well behind me. They were as far to each side as I could put them, so they'd have room to turn their horses without getting entangled. I'd smelled him, of course, and had stopped us several lengths short of where he'd probably expected us to.

Two of the bandits held bows, both short and crude, with no fletching on the crooked arrows. Four others were armed with pointed sticks. To the left, a few more men partially exposed their presence. My father had built himself nearly a militia.

He bore a pointed stick and wore the family's knife. The blade had long turned to rust.

Yellow Eyes darted between us all. He didn't attack when he noticed the numbers. He did make a good diversion though. All the arrows and shafts shifted his way.

"Ride," I shouted to the women. They responded well for their first time in combat, and soon we raced down the difficult pass with a few crooked arrows harmlessly passing behind.

Several turns farther, two men blocked our way. Bursting past the women, I skirted away from the man slowly responding with his spear on our left. Pritchan's horse responded better and under my direction, to the right. We hurriedly rode over the second man there.

My horse turned quickly to the business of kicking at the downed man. Letting him do this, I pulled the reins hard so my horse could continue his duty, but also so I'd line him up with the man we'd passed. That man did me the favor of coming forward, but I brushed his spear aside with my sword, and this refocused my stallion's attention. He knocked the new threat to the ground.

One man was blood and bones and no longer in this world. The other frantically crawled then hurriedly staggered into the scrub. I got down and stole their spears, tossing one each to the women. By the time I remounted, the man who'd crawled away had stopped and even taken a couple steps our way. He picked up a rock.

This did not impress me much, so I turned my attention to pointing my women toward the lower pass.

Upon glancing his way before I departed, his blouse spit blood. His arms flew out and then sagged as all life fled. He fell on his face. The fletching end of an arrow showed, standing above his back.

This the women didn't see as they retreated ahead of me and down the mountain. I looked around but didn't see who'd shot the arrow, nor did I see any more bandits other than the few men above us on the trail, working their way in our direction. I decided to let the women lead and instead do some thinking.

"Very well done, Abi." The lady nodded soberly after we came to a much wider portion of the pass. We walked our horses, glancing back and up at the narrows.

"They were just bandits. Such imagine themselves great fighting men, but they're too lazy to study the arts of a warrior."

"I was terrified," the lady confessed.

"You did well. We ran in good order. That is no small thing. And, my father will be furious."

Maid Minari asked, "What are you saying?"

"That was my father," I repeated.

Minari's face brightened. "Your father, you say? What luck. He did not recognize you. You can speak with him, and they'll let us pass."

I laughed at her naivety. "I don't think so. I'm contemplating the best way to work back and murder him."

"The man cannot be so hard; we should go back and ask him nicely." Lady Lettoir passed a water skin to her maid.

"Yes, of course, we should ask him if he's willing to forfeit a fortune. The man has surely heard that the baron will pay him for my body. Instead the baron will hang him as a bandit and keeping the winnings for himself, as is befitting true blood. My father is stupid. He knows nothing of the baron's treachery."

Lady Lettoir reflected, almost as if to herself: "Surely your father is not so cold, nor the baron so calculating."

"Ah, yes, you have been at your manor for some time. No, I can see this whole thing unfolding in so many directions, few to our advantage.

I put an apple up to Pritchan's horse and thanked him for his good work. "And, in the midst of this journey, the Goddess pesters me with whispers about the need to sort things out without great violence."

Lady Lettoir only nodded. Her maid tightened her lips.

I added, "Then there's the arrow that came from nowhere and killed one of the two who dared block our retreat."

"I didn't see any arrow," said the maid.

Lady Lettoir immediately startled. She stood on her tip toes and looked around for signs of the bandits.

"She killed him cleanly. Whoever shot him was good." I put my fist on my chest and pointed with my thumb, as if showing the arrowhead coming through.

"She?" asked the lady.

"Yes, a female warrior. The one who has my horse. Obviously, one of the Debrecians." I looked around as well, seeing nothing but glimpses of distant men coming down the pass.

The maid sat on a fallen tree and shivered. She started searching to our sides as diligently as the lady was to our rear, only from closer to the ground where it was impossible to see more than leaves.

I'd learned as a soldier that the myth of Debrecians was equal to the truth of them, and it was no small myth they lived up to.

I said, "It's a waste of time looking for her. She'll present herself when she wishes, or when I take the time to hunt her down. In time, I may find a reason for my reluctance to do so. Perhaps it's courtesy that compels me to wait until she loses her shyness. Perhaps I fear that the tribes see me as their enemy, and I have come to wonder about it. The Goddess is playing with my thoughts, but I do not think she wants me to kill these Debrecians."

The maid said, "They are mad women. She'll come for us in the middle of the night and slit our throats. Every child knows this in Farstand."

"If the Goddess wishes. Pray to her so she'll convince our friend there's no need." While I spoke, I watched to see if any of the bandits had made it within earshot.

I noticed that a few of the bandits were closer; they were a persistent lot. I knew many were eager to win a fiefdom by capturing me.

"What are we to do now?" I realized that Lady Lettoir couldn't see them coming. Her eyes were not skilled and not as blessed as mine.

"You'll drive slowly to the right while I circle to the left. Here, the pass is wide. Our horses are also faster than their feet, so they've made a big mistake by moving down from the narrowest part. If they follow me to our left, I can recover to the right, and we can ride by on the right and leave them behind."

"Sounds good, but what if they come between and we get separated?" said the lady.

The maid said, "You'd leave us with bandits and that wild savage out there? We might ride right into her. She can't be that far away in this narrow valley!"

I answered, "You fear this one woman more than the bandits? Well then, perhaps she'll capture you and take you as ransom to Lacellor. Your new home will be all the sooner. Thus works the blessings of fate."

The look on her face told me I'd made a mistake by teasing her. "She'll leave you alone. What use is a lady's maid to a warrior?" That didn't appear to please her either, but my mind was preoccupied so I didn't have the time to seek out coddling words. As I left them, I said, "Walk the horses. The Debrecian won't be fooled, but it's best the bandits see my movements and not your own."

I got back into my saddle and guided the stallion through the scrub to my left. My horse pranced, raising clouds of dust like a hen leading the fox away from her chicks. Soon I'd worked as far left as I could without scaling a rock wall of dripping ice and moss. It was fairly beautiful, but I had no time to appreciate the splendor. I drove forward, seeing at once that nearly a score of the bandits noticed my head or dust and were hoping to catch me up against the wall with a widely forming horseshoe.

It was great sport, and the first I'd seen of such amusement since my truce with Sir Barker. I couldn't help the feeling of excitement when I left my horse behind and walked into the throat of their forming crescent. I had a wooden lance, a sword, a knife and a memory of an adolescence so full of hate that I thought about abandoning the weapons as well so I could feel the life drain out of them from under my finger tips.

Thus armed with a hungry and an unusually mean spirit, I was surprised when I stumbled into Ella. She'd learned a new trick of hiding by lying in a crease between some bushes and boulders. As soon as I showed, she asked me if I'd had enough of her hiding and now wanted her to stop lying about like a yearling without good legs. As surprising as it was to stumble across her without any signs of warning, it was even more surprising to realize she was thinking it had been me who'd asked her to hide in such an ingenious way.

No, stay as you are old friend, I told her in her mind before sneaking forward.

There before me was a young Debrecian. She held a beautifully polished, curved-back bow. The nock of the arrow was back to well behind her right ear, held there by two slowly easing fingers. The older boy, a short ways in front of her, was doing a terrible job of sneaking up on a boulder that was of no consequence, other than the rock looked stout enough to hide somebody, and it had one of their own wooden spears up against it so the tip could be seen.

I saw all of this in a moment, also coming to the conclusion that the boy had only one small second of life left in him.

The girl with the bow seemed familiar. I'd seen her many months ago on the duke's road to Dorne and before that in the woods with the mighty Debrecians, Catrina and Gerta. She'd seemed a mouse then, save for some odd beauty I'd sensed coming from her soul.

As I came upon her, the Goddess also walked from behind my heart and stood in front of the anger. I whispered, "Don't kill him. Give him the gift of a little more life."

I'd startled her. The arrow loosed, grazing across the boy's outstretched arm. He fell to the ground, seeking its safety.

The young Debrecian girl turned to see me standing behind her. Her eyes shed the determined look of an archer and widened to those of barely contained fear.

I realized I'd never seen fear in the eyes of a Debrecian before. The fear didn't disarm her, however. She had two more arrows tucked under a thigh, and with an unearthly ease of motion, had one of them armed in less time than I could breathe. She'd turned to me as if she knew I was the mightier threat, which proved she was no fool. Still, she didn't raise her bow, instead choosing to keep it half cocked and aimed low to some spot between us.

Surely, the girl was a mighty weapon. If there are many such warriors, they'd be the same as a wall before a sea of advancing pikes.

She apparently misunderstood the intention of my stare. "Such a contest is unworthy, mighty warrior. I have sworn before my council that I shall not kill you, even in battle, but only keep watch."

"I've not come to kill you, child. I bid you good will. I've only come to mislead the men who descend. As for watching me, I'll abide it no longer unless you join our company."

We were pressed for time and couldn't linger in discussion because of the closing horseshoe. I passed by Ella as I withdrew. She whinnied, showing her impatience at lying about. Behind me, I heard her get up when the young Debrecian caught up to her. I got on Pritchan's horse, and slipped through the southern edges of the trap just before the bandits got close enough to force me to kill them all.

Ella galloped nearly on my horse's heels. Her thoughts were happy, as if pleased that I was back on her back, which of course I wasn't. This caused me to look around at her to see if it was really my horse I'd been listening to in my head. Sure enough, the young Debrecian sat on her, but the horse finally saw me in front of her, and I could hear her saying hello with her left eye's brain, while her right eye's brain was still thinking about the joy of me riding her. Thus is the stupidity of horses.

I led us in a circle to the far side of the pass and the women of my council.

Lady Lettoir and Maid Minari seemed glad to see me for a

change. I wanted to introduce them to the Debrecian, but she lingered behind, perhaps shy of the company, so I didn't press the issue; time was short. With the bandits too far down and out of the narrows, we raced up toward the pass.

There before us, at the very same point, stood my father. He was shoulder to shoulder with the remaining Ranglesons, Devlon, Kip, and their father Dicket. Kip had always been his father's favorite, while Devlon was the tallest.

I regarded the crudely carved lances in each of their hands as we pulled up short. The lady actually shrieked her surprise as she reined up, maybe thinking we'd been caught.

I rode forward a few more paces. "Hello, father. Nice of you to bring the neighbors."

Dicket Rangleson hefted his spear. "Ah, it's not as we suspected. Pretend as this witch might, this isn't your daughter Garette. It's, in fact, only a wee resemblance. Still, she might fetch some prize." He held his lance at ready.

I laughed at him, and then asked Dicket's firstborn son, "How do you see me, Devlon? Am I not the same girl who murdered your ugly little brother Bullor?"

I looked over at Kip and added, "But then again, your father is right; I am new. I'm now the soldier who has relieved your brother Kitchor of his head?"

I glanced over toward the shrubs where he hid, and finished by saying, "And you, Kevin; are you still so full of mourning for our dear hanged brother, that you fail to notice the return of your sister; the one who stepped over his fresh grave in order to win liberty from you and the thing who calls himself our father?"

"You'll show some respect, girl!" snarled my father.

"I'll show you nothing but steel! Where were you when they came to take my mother?" I screamed. I was so full of rage that tears blurred my vision. Even the good Maid Minari jumped while sitting in her saddle.

My father stepped forward. He came within a few steps of my horse. "The old bitch was useless. Besides, I was away on business when they took her off my hands. Now down with you. My men return in a way that won't allow you the same easy escape. I don't want to kill you. I'll need you fresh and easy to identify when I bring you to the lords."

That was when the Debrecian girl rode up with her bow at ready and eased some bushes aside with her horse, causing Kevin to scramble out and join the others.

Dicket Rangleson, turned and saw her. "Ah now, there are two of her. Witchery is clearly afoot. If it were not for the familiar mouth on the sow before you, I'd say this new bitch is your daughter, Garette."

"We shall take them both. Might this double the ransom?" suggested Devlon.

I said, "You five stand between me and my mother. It is not a good place to stand." The sight of my own family sickened me; reminded me there was a hole in my life that I'd never ever fill, even as it threatened to swallow me up.

One of the Rangleson boys started to come up and join my father, but I commanded, "Warrior! Kill the next man who moves." I turned my horse to more fully gain the advantage of my sword hand. "The Goddess has decided this is not the day to end this grudge, but she'll also not let us fall into the hands of fools."

I glanced over at Lady Lettoir and her maid, and saw the shocked look on their faces as they watched the bandits posturing and the Debrecian straining against the string of her bow.

My bet was on the Debrecian, for she had two more arrows in the crook between her leg and saddle. Her soul pleaded with mine for the command to release. I was sure if it came to that, I'd only have the pleasure of murdering two of the men in front of me, for three of them would have arrows in them before I could get that far.

I rode forward, right up to my father who blocked my path.

Kip took a step, and then he fell back before his foot could settle. He squirmed a couple seconds with an arrow through his heart. Devlon and his father moved aside to kneel over the boy's body where Devlon yanked on the fletching. He broke it off with blood coated hands. As this happened, Kip gurgled bubbles of blood, though he didn't stir.

Devlon looked up at the young Debrecian, and then over toward me, the expression bloodlust.

I watched the other men for a sign that they'd rush me, and, when they didn't, I noted that our Debrecian had a second arrow nocked.

"We will pass now." I put my sword away and retrieved my steel-tipped spear. My father backed away under the threats of my horse and weapon. Obeying my nod, the lady and her maid rode through. Then I followed, turning to keep my weapon pointed at the men, of whom only my brother and father were in any position to do us any harm. The Debrecian appeared to be surprised that I motioned for her to join us. However, it didn't take her long to file through, the clap of her horse hooves following those of the ladies as I waited. Back in the wider pass, my father's fellow bandits were coming up quickly.

My father cut his own arm and held it up, showing me our blood. "I'll catch you, now that I know the stories are true. A traitor and a witch; I think I saw it early. I swear, your mother bedded a beggar, making the likes of you."

"It pleases me to think the same, father; though it pleases me more to know I've never loved you."

Dicket stepped up to join him. "I'll avenge my sons. Don't you sleep at night, witch. You'll wake to my knife! Tell that to your witch mother as well."

"Oh no, I couldn't tell her that; she'd come right back and kill all you cowards. I prefer you alive, so you're forced to drain away your lives seeing yourselves as the impotent little men you are."

"We'll have you. This I promise for Keith," said my own brother. Those words hurt. I'd had nothing to do with Keith's death, and yet my own brother blamed me for it.

At that moment, the Goddess sent a moment of inspiration. I said, "Let me give you some help. Tell all your bandit friends I'm going to Helfax. There, I shall kill the baron and rescue my mother. An army of cutthroats will be useful to you when you come to collect your reward for my head. The nobles will want to hang you instead of paying. Not that any of you are man enough to live, face to face, against my sword."

It was Devlon who shouted, "Bah! I've seen you fight, and you're not so much. Come down from your horse."

"You tempt me, but you are little and worthy only as bait. From this day forward, I will no longer trouble my mind over the sadness of my youth." My great black stallion backed, then we left them in our dust.

I heard footsteps behind me, and then the clatter of an under-thrown spear on the rocks, but my horse was riding too hard for a Rangleson to stab me in the back. After a distance, I slowed and looked over a shoulder. There on the trail far behind me was no Rangleson, but instead my own brother. Such was his desire to amend the family ills. I looked at him for as long as I dared, mourning the family I never had. I'd had a mother, and all these men were cattle in my way. Well, no longer did I trouble myself with such.

So, what was this test of compassion about? Maybe part of it was learning what was worth a war as opposed to what was worth the back side of my horse. I felt certain I was still many cold nights away from understanding more completely the Goddess's mind in this strange and twisting trial.

Chapter Seven

I sensed Ella's confusion as she woke from her dreams and realized the one on her back wasn't me. I rode in front of her on my new black stallion. Once I looked back, she said in my head that she'd come to the realization a stranger sat on her, but she was content with it.

I told her I was glad she'd been well fed and combed, and thus had her loyalty properly purchased. Further, I called her an idiot for not knowing it had been a stranger on her back for many days. The horse didn't answer that. She was easily offended by the smallest things. As we talked, I glanced back several times, and Ella whinnied or shook her mane. During this, I once nodded up toward the Debrecian.

She watched me incessantly and seemed fascinated by the way Ella interacted with me. If anything was constant, it was this watching, as if the girl meant to learn every motion of my neck, buttocks and even the kick of my heels. The back of my neck itched, forcing me to continually reach back and rub.

I couldn't be too hard on my old nag, Ella, though, because the girl's magic had afflicted Yellow Eyes too, and he was more than a twig width smarter than a horse.

The smartest thing about Yellow Eyes was his nose. He found good paths around the villages we smelled. This was excellent because the villages increased as we wound our way out of the foothills and neared the broad valleys. Junipers turned into oak forests and forests into weeds and weeds into harvested wheat fields around our path.

We passed a few peasants, but the habit of hiding from every living soul no longer amused me since crossing paths with my father. Instead, I pretended to be the lady's legitimate guard, in spite of being poorly uniformed and female. That met with mixed results. Most of the stares we got were astonishment. I assumed none knew the dress of a Debrecian, but they could all tell that two of us were warriors and not to be trifled with by the time their eyes met mine and those of the archer. Some, I was sure, guessed they'd been visited by Abi, for I was strange and fresh among their fables. This didn't trouble me. We were far from the paths of nobles and their guards.

Which of us was Abi, well, that was probably a difficult thing to figure out from a peasant's perspective, for the lady was in dust covered splendor, dirty—though this was a usual sign of command. The Debrecian wore clothing obviously made for the hard duty of fighting, clearly the warrior among us. Only my height and sword told that I was special, and the sword was often hidden between rolls of goods on my horse's rump. Among us, only I wore the peasant sackcloth, and thus, eyes often swept past me, as if to say, though a hard woman, surely not she. This I found amusing and played to it.

* * * * *

We came up through a less challenging portion of the mountains with many valleys and foothills. Behind a broad village garden, we encountered a curious shack sitting well away from the community. It had several added rooms and two smoking chimneys, attesting to ample space. Up in some hills, the early night grew more chill than usual. The rain was mostly horizontal sleet. I wanted to find the sergeant and get beyond whatever nonsensical delays the Goddess had planned for me, so I could continue my quest to Helfax and rescue my mother. However, I was no longer alone and had to think about everybody else.

We'd all be sick if I didn't find a good place for us to bed the night. We also needed a place to rekindle our female beings after so many mornings waking up on the hard, cold ground. The gentler women with us had gone as long as possible without a fireplace and a pillow, I decided as I stopped just beyond the yard that held the building. Such notions were trouble, of course, for the village was close enough to see tiny figures walking about with occasional lanterns. Still, they couldn't see us in the dark, and I doubted we'd be troubled by visitors with the weather so brutal.

I looked over at the young, blond warrior. She was so young that her breasts were still not ample, and her hips just beginning to widen. There was little meat on her thighs. It was possible she wasn't even ripe enough to breed. She was tiny by the standards of her race, though closer to a woman by local measure. This was deceptive, for much of her was well strung muscles, much like her bow.

Her eyes were very curious and green as the field. And her nose was cute, assuming such a concept existed in the Debrecian culture. I admired the fullness of her lips, which rivaled mine. I thought she'd have the attention of every young man in her village, dowry or not, assuming she could avoid the attention of her father. Such an evil notion, that, I told myself, looking away from her, lest I taint her with my memories. Such recently jarred memories were the source of my malaise. Surely though, the whole world wasn't like the little one I'd been born into.

To be sure, I was in a foul mood due to my encounter with my father, and I knew I was in no condition to properly pity the next man who crossed me. Still, I was patient in my study of the odd dwelling because of my training, and only that.

The Debrecian seemed to share my patience as we watched the poor but sprawling structure for a sign of its inhabitants; this was unlike the impatient jittering I felt from the others in our company. Sitting in chill is always much worse than riding through it.

The patience paid off when we saw the door of the house burst open, spilling out the light. Right behind came a woman. She emerged under the guidance of a boot and landed face-first in the freezing mud. There she lay, though wearing only a short shirt. Her bottom was exposed and allowed no imagination. Hers was an ample bottom for a peasant, I thought, and hence all the more embarrassing for her.

"Bitch! Try an' short us, did ya! Well, ya' can spend some time out in the cold wind. It'll put a freeze on your ugly mouth an' hording ways. Think what ta' say ta' make me let ya' back in," yelled a big man in the doorway.

I saw he was also naked from the waist down, excepting boots. His most private parts stuck out in the cold for all of us to witness.

This was in spite of a thick layer of nappy, black hair that matched his long, ale-streaked beard. The many smells off him were enough to wrinkle my wolf nose clear across the vast yard we peered over. I couldn't imagine cuddling up to such a beast. Nor did I much like any master of whores, for the occupation reminded me of Ranglesons.

Behind him, another woman crawled on a rug. A thin and laughing man was swatting her around the open room with the buckle end of his belt. The door slammed shut.

The woman in the yard remained there, crying. I got the feeling she didn't want to get up before the night froze and killed her.

"What is this place?" asked the Debrecian girl.

I said, "It's the place meant for my life, and it houses the sort of men meant for my company."

"Ah, and I thought your father only wanted you dead." The Debrecian's voice said she was working very hard at keeping her anger hidden, though on the edge of some limit.

Lady Lettoir removed the icy scarf from her mouth. "I have abided such, for the sake of the men, but this is not fitting."

I nodded to the left for the benefit of the Debrecian. When she moved that way, I turned my horse to the right, quietly circling to within a few paces of where the wide-bottomed woman lay weeping.

There, I got down off my horse and made my way around the woman until I was beside the door. The young Debrecian girl took up station at the far edge of the door. She held two knives, causing me to notice she'd left her bow and arrows back with Ella. She was so young and already such a warrior that she knew the right tools for the battle before her.

I whispered, "My name is Abi," though I was sure she knew that.

"I am Princess Batya, meaning strong shaman warrior."

I said, "It's good we go into battle knowing the other's name."

She nodded, the bob of her tied-up hair accentuating the movement. There was the beginning of a smile. The way she smiled reminded me of the crone in her last moments, though Batya was very young.

What, I wondered, was a princess warrior of shaman blood doing out following the likes of me? She was, apparently, of the same lineage. Then again, perhaps there were many like us? The questions would have to wait. I took my sword out of its sheath. The sound of it rang louder than all of our other sounds in the crisp cold night.

This was finally heard by the wailing woman lying in the mud, whom I'd come to think of as both blind and deaf. She turned and stared up at us with round and horror-stricken eyes. I glanced briefly at her expression, and then I tested the door with my hip. It swung open just as the woman behind us screamed with every bit of the air in her lungs.

The combination of me and the young Debrecian in the doorway, coupled with the ear bleeding scream behind us, caused everybody in the house to startle and turn. The big, hairy and half naked man got the look of a bear on his face. He was no more than a pace away.

I took both hands to my weapon, swinging it up at an angle that sent the blade through his bowels. Blood and intestines gushed across his lap and legs in a flood. He leaned into the blow, and his hands fumbled around my blade. His fingers groped at the spilling intestines.

I kicked him as I tugged my blade free of a lower rib. The whore master fell back and did us the service of adding baritone to the screams announcing our arrival.

I looked around for someone else to kill. A good number of women, in various states of undress, stared at me with horror shimmering across their screaming faces.

Beside me, Batya came forward, seeking some business for her knives. The look on her face was glee, at first, and then sudden frustration, for the big and hairy man bled so profusely it seemed likely his light would fade before she could cut on him. I had to hold her back with my hand, nonetheless, for fear she'd start hacking on his corpse.

All of the women were squealing and whimpering, and still I heard the ripping scream of the woman outside as she ran away into the night. Then, all of a sudden, the woman's screaming stopped, leaving us only to the room of wailing women cringing along the corners of the walls and the dying baritone spilling his guts at our feet.

I looked off to the side, seeing one room with an open door. The bed in there was fancy, with a large, hand-carved headboard. The bed was almost too large, leaving no room for walking around it. All a person could do in there was sleep or wrestle.

Another door was closed, and it was towards this I nodded, taking my hand away from the chest of the eager princess warrior. Her eyes sparkled, and her mouth broadened as she walked to the door and shoved against it. She was once again frustrated when it didn't budge.

I watched this with strange sensations coursing through my soul. Had I once been this eager for the chore of killing? Was I still this eager for killing? It was strange to watch such elation from without. It made me think less of myself. The Goddess was wise; killing was not always pretty, even when right.

Sniveling whores drew my attention. I shushed them, raising my bloody sword to my lips as if it were my finger. That settled most of them down to simple crying.

"Oh, thank the Goddess," I whispered.

Batya slammed into the closed door with her shoulder, but backed away, still frustrated.

After nodding to her, I yelled toward the locked door, "Thank God, the bandits have left." I added, "Yes, they are long gone now."

I heard the door's brace lift, and then the door creaked open a tiny bit. I stepped forward and kicked it open the rest of the way, allowing Batya the honor of entering without the bother.

There was only one candle in the room, but it was enough to see her work. She used one knife to busy his by catching it with the finger guard. This resulted in both of their right hands locked, crossing one another's bodies. His left was undefended. The second knife in Batya's left hand jabbed and recovered sharply. She'd struck only once, that upward and to the middle of his chest.

The warrior turned her back to him dismissively and walked out of the room with the naked man still standing there. He slowly sat down on the dirt floor. Shock was a pale mask across his face. His arms had fallen to his side from some internal weakness and there, seated on his limbs, he slowly died. Not until some moments passed, and just before death, did he bleed as a river through both his mouth and the tiny wound. Bowels spilled, adding to the stink.

A pretty and naked young whore was sitting on the bed. She clutched the bedding to her as if to hide her sins behind the blankets. Her scream sounded painful, as if tearing out her throat. She started the rest of the other women again.

Such sickened even me, and to this day I don't know why that one little death seemed so different. Perhaps it was the quickness of it. Perhaps it was the childlike youth of Batya, and how she'd done her duty with such eagerness. The smile on her face had been the very sun. I think, however, it was because it reminded me of Bullor, the pudgy Rangleson who'd been my first murder. This man had done even less than Bullor to deserve his fate. Both deaths were unworthy of mighty warriors, lending to us their petty and pathetic taint.

Before I could think on it too much, my remorse was spared by the appearance of Maid Minari. She and the lady had captured the screaming woman with the ample and uncovered bottom. They'd done this with only the help of staffs, so it was no small success. Even the warrior Batya nodded her head approvingly when they came in and closed the door.

"What have you done?" asked Lady Lettoir as she entered, carefully working her way around the body by the door. She looked at me with disbelief on her face while shaking her head. "Was this necessary?"

"Not now!" My blood was up, and so I probably said it harshly.

She said nothing more but kept looking at me as if nagging my conscience.

I turned my attention to the whimpering heap of whores. "You'll each take an arm or leg and help us toss these men out into the weeds behind the shack. This warrior will see that you return with water to clean the floor. The two of you remaining will build a better fire and make haste with hot water for the barrel."

Everyone sat or stood, frozen.

I scolded them: "Do you not know you are favored with the presence of the great noble, Lady Lettoir?"

Lady Lettoir stared at me as if I'd gone completely out of my mind. The other women looked at her, however, and then at the maid, perhaps wondering which one was the lady. Our many nights on the road had rendered the lady bedraggled.

Still, the required labor was done, and the lady was first to take advantage of the water while Minari tended the horses and Batya guarded against the intrusion of any customers willing to brave the rising chill. All the while, the whores looked as if they were certain they lived on borrowed minutes. Between chores, they huddled together on rugs pulled into a corner. I did nothing to dispel this fear, for I valued their attention.

The water was cool and brown when I finally bathed. By the time I finished, the lady and her maid were sleeping soundly on the big bed with the headboard, and the young Debrecian had pulled blankets up to the door where her body kept anyone from entering or leaving. She was so unafraid of the seven whores she snored in no time at all.

I used my time on guard duty to sort through the belongings of the women. I took what seemed useful. There was even some money, so I felt obliged to take that as well, though we had a fortune in the saddlebags.

All of them had at least one colorful dress and several others that were more pretty than practical. I separated the colorful ones from those more commonly colored.

There was also an interesting collection of undergarments. Those didn't seem to have any practical use, and some were so confusing I felt sure there was no way to put them on at all. There was almost nothing they owned that could keep a person warm against the weather. So, I decided to have the whores strip some of the dresses into panels and then sew the panels together to make layered garments. The new clothing was finally much better for sleet and wind and apt to draw the smallest possible attention to skin.

The whores kept busy, but they wouldn't cease crying their way through the labor, as if we'd invaded their home instead of their prison. Some scowled whenever I pitched something of worth into a travel bag. It struck me that, if they thought what I was doing was stealing, they might want to look at their lives as examples of real thievery. I didn't say as much—making comment on it would have only been redundant. The whimpers got worse when I fed the useless undergarments into the fire, mainly to get rid of the clutter.

When I'd grown weary of their cowering, I assigned a new task to them of splitting all the newly layered skirts down the middle, making fat legs of the lower portions in order to make the clothing easier to wear on a horse. By just a few hours past midnight, there was no more thread in the shack. We'd finished a few good garments and retained a sizeable bundle of cloth that I had them make into rolls. The collection of remaining rags amounted to nothing more than what could be used for cleaning. I was eager to trade up to two of the better garments in exchange for the course and thin peasant rag given to me by Sir Pritchan many days prior.

The skirt I chose as an outside layer to my new britches was plain and brown, and bunted three layers thick. The whore with the wide hips did most of the tailoring, though time was short and the stitches tacked or overly spaced.

I ripped leggings from the fanciest orange dress in the house, finding the act of ruining the pretty thing into handwidth strips strangely satisfying. One of the whores watched me with an unusually sad face. A linen undershirt fit by simply tearing the sleeves off a good shirt. Time was short—we needed to be practical, not fancy. Over all of that was a new tunic made of two dresses roughly batted together with rag stuffing.

By morning, I'd gotten a few hours of sleep, as had the whores. I woke to no guards at all, though I imagined Yellow Eyes out there somewhere keeping an eye on the distant village while rounding up field mice. For just one wee moment, the house was silent, the only noise being the cracking of coals burning out in the last of the fire.

It was then I heard the Goddess whisper the most absurd thing she'd ever told me.

Shaking my head, I answered, "No! My Goddess, can't you see these women are worthless as cattle?"

One of the whores stirred with wide eyes of fright.

The Goddess was most insistent, however, and so I settled, again left with only the snapping of the last of the fireplace coals and a room of snoring women.

After a while, I got everybody up. We tied everything valuable onto our horses. The whores watched this thievery horror stricken, for we'd either burned or stolen everything. Even the clothing on their backs had been taken and much of it fed into the fireplace. It surprised me a little to see how shy they were about their bodies while standing around in nothing more than what the Goddess had given them upon their birth. After all, they were whores, and I'd thought nakedness was just a natural part of the profession.

Some resumed their wailing. All of it was meant to teach them a lesson in humility, for they'd apparently not paid attention while lying on their backs.

Then they appeared greatly relieved when I bid them dress in one of the new and better made outfits; they'd managed to sew just enough to go around. Those without good outdoor shoes were given bark slabs and ample bindings for their feet and legs. Then, once again, they lost the look of relief when I dragged the two corpses into the house and splashed their walls with grease. This had the added effect of emptying the place. I had no trouble setting the house aflame with a simple spell cast toward the fireplace.

"Listen up. You are now my Lady's servants. You will go where we tell you, and do as the lady requires. Even her maid Minari is set before you. If you despair, I shall leave you behind."

The fear that I'd kill them had undoubtedly been replaced by a new and maybe deeper worry. This they took up between themselves. They debated as if they had many possible paths. Their eyes looked to the village, the woods and even to the lady.

We had no time for it, so I lied. "Know also, I've written a note for the distant posting board. You've confessed a hand in the deaths of the two men who are burning. This shall serve as your contract of service, lest you imagine a better fate than that of our lady's servant." Finally, silence met my ears.

"They will know we are not at fault," said one of the whores. Some of the others stepped away from the woman, not willing to make trouble so soon after hearing their lives were to be spared.

"Yes. Our best chance is here." She pointed toward me and continued. "This woman is known for murder, and she has no right," added the prettiest one as she defiantly stepped beside the first woman.

"True, I have no right. This I've known all my life. But, neither do you. None of us have rights; for it is written in the hearts of every man and woman in this kingdom: We have no rights, whatsoever."

Batya followed me as I nudged my horse with my knees. Together we set out for the nearby village as the lady and her maid waited with the whores. The lady, from what I could see behind us, was speaking to the women, and this had the result of some preparing near the north path.

Batya and I stopped at the edge of the main street. We watched for early risers. The village was lazy, so I was able to post my message on the board without being seen. The message had not said what I'd told the whores it did. Instead it read the words the Goddess had inspired within me when I'd left my father: *You will soon find me in Helfax!* I'd signed it, Abi!

This village looked so much like the one I'd grown up near that there was no need to knock on doors and ask for directions as we rode our horses into the only stables. It was beside the only house with two floors. There we found four nags and a very nice looking mare.

We didn't have to ask the waking stable boy to saddle a pair of horses and put blankets on the other three. He took one look at us on our warhorses and decided it was a good idea to be useful. We even helped ourselves to several bags of oats that were sitting around for the taking. He said nothing, only quickening his service in keeping with our demands. The boy took off instead of watching us torch the hay, however, and we didn't begrudge him that. He'd been most helpful, and we were through with his services.

I thought it convenient to torch the village's largest house next door as well, which was well separate from the others because of a useless yard of grass. Burning it was justice. It was so large I was sure the man who owned it couldn't have possibly earned the right to own all of it without having stolen the money and toil of countless peasants. The stable boy was doing a good job of arousing the town, so it seemed unlikely that anyone would burn up.

When we got back to the blazing whorehouse, I sorted out the whores who'd walked only a little ways down the back path.

"I've decided the two who've complained can stay and enjoy the attention of the community. The Goddess has only provided five horses, which I take as a sign."

The woman with the wide bottom appeared the most eager to leave. She climbed on a horse best fit for pulling plows.

The town took on the appearance of a kicked ant hill. Some had armed themselves with farm implements and were coming our way, so it was good that we departed by the back path Yellow Eyes was eager to show us. I looked back at the two whores who'd complained, and saw their considerable uncertainty. They glanced at the back of us, and then the women looked toward the town. With nothing in their hands, they ran in our direction. I wouldn't have them and instead spurred us along the path as fast as we could go without the inexperienced whores falling off their horses.

I wasn't the only one who noticed the two reluctant whores.

When we slowed to a trot, Lady Lettoir said, "We should bring them with us. They've no chance back there."

"They've no chance with us," I told her back. "We're nine women and a wolf. Most of us can't fight, and we are slow enough."

"Have you no heart?" asked Maid Minari.

There'd been moments when my very survival had depended upon the lack of the organ. I did not answer.

For me, Batya spoke to the two for the first time. "The tribe can't survive if our breeders don't listen to the wisdom of the warriors. This is most true in times of battle. They challenged a great princess and warrior. They did this as she stood on the field of war with an offering of mercy. I've been told your leader is a proven warlord and most promising. If any of the breeders in my tribe had spoken to me as these women have, they'd have been left corpses in the dirt. And I am but one who is yet to be tested."

"Abi I understand. I have seen her father. You, I am simply afraid of," said the lady.

There, it was out, reminding me we had many mysteries between us. I was eager to delve into them around the next campfire.

Batya said, "You and your servants have no need to fear me, Lady Lettoir. The council has ordered me to do no more than observe this warrior. I know not why. I asked, 'To what end?' I asked until they shunned me and turned me out from my people. They didn't even tell me what to look for, or even if I should return to them. I begged for the honor of my test as a shaman princess. Not one of them offered me a quest, preferring to turn me out for this simple chore. I fear they've grown tired of my persistence, and they see me as too small for the blade. The only gifts I have are those of the arrow and one spell that helps me see the world through the eyes of the one I track."

I smiled. "Ah, thus the illusion. Many say that, when they look at you, they see my face."

"Yes, though I can't speak to your horse," she answered.

Lady Lettoir yelled, "Don't either of you care for the lives of those women back there?"

Batya laughed. "Are their hands incapable of holding a knife? Are their legs bent and unable to run into the safety of the woods? If any man in this kingdom comes for me, I'm free to fight. I'll not die a shadow."

I nodded. "Well said, though you should know they have been taught to look at the world through the eyes of sheep."

"Not so with you, who was raised in the same land and by the same shepherds," Batya answered.

"No, not me, though I've had the hand of the Goddess on my head since birth."

"So I've seen," said the young Debrecian. Around us, the whores were spellbound by our conversation, having seen us as one horror the night before and apparently just becoming aware of the diversity of our several situations.

The lady asked Batya. "What about me? Do you see me as a person of no worth?"

"I've hidden in the trees and watched you. You are a weak warrior but not a shameful woman. Many things trouble me about your circumstance, and you seem to have some unknown worth for a breeder. I await, as do you, the outcome of this and upon our shared fate as outcasts."

The maid scoffed, "Ha! A breeder? I've never heard anybody

refer to my Lady as a breeder, young lady."

Batya glared at her sternly, which caused Minari to look sheepishly back around to the front of her horse.

I had to interrupt. "We're all one tribe for this. Let's not spare honesty, even warrior to lady and maid to warrior, be the words cutting or kind. It may not be the way of the Debrecians, but it's practical here, for we've nothing but one another, and our skills vary greatly, both in war and in conversation. The world is set against us, so we'll not want for enemies. Don't you know I've set before these women the task of serving as my council?"

Batya thought about that some, and then she decided, "It's good that we share enemies. And, I agree to this unusual arrangement. As a warrior I'm a failure, and it's fitting that I humble myself and converse with breeders, as long as they have honor. After all, I've been cast out by my own people who refuse me the test of a princess of war and am thus unworthy."

"I see no unworthiness in you. Did you not say you have a gift? Didn't you tell me you were sent to watch me? Everybody was perfectly fooled into believing you were me. Now that is a handsome trick."

"Even this I failed, for I've been discovered."

"Hardly! You watch me still." I smiled into the morning sun.

"It's not the same."

"Of course it isn't, but then again, maybe the Goddess doesn't have the usual set of tricks in mind for your life. I'm certain she has many mysteries in front of me. Nothing has happened in a way that I at first imagined it should. Have I told you of the year I spent judged unworthy by the guards of Lettoir? All I did was attend their horses."

"The Goddess can't be understood. What fool would deny you such a low honor as a Lady's guard?" She joined me in watching the sky.

"My point exactly. You see, already we've come to an agreement that wouldn't have been discovered if we were unable to speak to one another. It's best that you were discovered, for your council didn't say that you may not be discovered, only that you watch me. You remain worthy. You know, it was only through the application of all my many skills that I found you, and only after many days of your successful stealth. And yet, even you know me as a mighty and tested warrior who has the nose of a wolf." I showed her my wolf medallion. I didn't have the heart to tell her I'd blundered across her in my haste to tempt the bandits into going in the wrong direction.

This, at least, had the effect of setting her straighter up in her saddle.

I finished our conversation by telling her, "Be heartened. The Goddess isn't finished with you yet." This I firmly believed, for I felt her soul and could also plainly see she was as near to a child as she was a woman.

Lady Lettoir looked over her shoulder at us. "I'm glad to overhear your conversation, Batya. I see there's no need to fear one so concerned with issues of honor. Still, two women will die for the simple sin of indecision; I can't help feeling responsible."

Ah, I thought; the lady knew more on the subject of kindness than any I'd ever encountered. Just then I felt the curse of my anger towards my father lighten. It was as if the Goddess had put Lady Lettoir in my camp for the reason of teaching me one of the things I'd always found elusive—kindness.

That isn't to say it saved the two we left behind, nor would it have saved them earlier, for they fell well below the compassion even the most blessed among us dared afford. And I was not that blessed soul. Mine was weighed down by a stomach twisted with frustration over wandering in the wilderness while my mother rotted in a Helfax dungeon.

* * * * *

At the next camp, I introduced the five whores to sticks and set them beating on one another under the supervision of Maid Minari and the lady while I rested. Batya came in dragging a mountain goat behind her horse, which delighted Yellow Eyes for he'd played a part in smelling it out and was considering eating all of it in one setting, even though by weight it was twice his size. We cut the hind quarters off and tossed the rest into the glen for Yellow Eyes to contend with. He ate until he fell asleep and was useless.

By morning, we were well rested and fed, though the whores

could barely hold onto their horses. They complained of soreness in their arms caused by fighting and pain in the thighs because the riding of men was not as much of a strain as horses. That I found curious, given I'd only ridden horses.

We hoped to make camp just above the next village before nightfall. There the lady hoped to find the sergeant. He was sufficiently weathered to have some value, particularly in the duty of training people to fight. The larger we became, the more I felt myself thinned to the many tasks. A skilled sergeant, such as Hadarm, would prove practical, I'd finally determined. Convincing him to join us, well, that was another matter I left to the Goddess.

"I don't understand this technique of teaching these women with sticks?" asked Batya while we rode into the valley.

"It was how I was taught," I told her.

"I see." After some thinking, she added, "but you teach in the style of a great warrior who the Goddess has chosen for the honor of wielding swords. This is a good technique for the likes of you. You're tall and not a breeder."

I answered, "In the lady's cavalry, all the men were swordsmen, though not all were good at it. Still, up on a speeding horse, even a glancing cut can be fatal."

"Ha. This I noticed and reported. Your company fought skillfully with horses, spears, and in some small measure, swords. I reported these words to my council: "They have little effect on the war, but when their great woman warrior leads them, none are better. It's good they're too few, and their leaders don't follow her tactics. We should find a way to kill them, so their leaders think their tactics poor.""

"You've been busy. My captain said there were no Debrecians around. Even I saw few signs of you."

"This is as it should be. We're not yet at war, and it's a great discipline preparing for the honor." Batya held her head up high, and her smile was almost sweet.

"Haven't you learned the sword?" I asked her.

"Well, in my tribe, I've long pleaded for the teaching, but I'm too small. You see, the sword must reach well beyond the flanks of my horse. The longer it is, the heavier it becomes, and thus I'm unsuited to the weapon. I fear it's another reason the council has kept me back from my shaman testing. It's rare in our history for a woman to be sent on the trials of a shaman princess with only the skills of a bow, you see."

"That bow is highly effective. It's far better at hunting than any of my weapons, and you've shown you can kill bandits before they're close enough to even cross a sword." I spoke as we found the valley road.

Lady Lettoir looked up and down both directions, and then she set off for the path leading mostly east and downstream. Her eyes were not those of a scout, but it was good that we all made the effort. I smelled the wind; it carried the scent of miners. Soon we were passing the spoils of many claims that had been played out. Then the valley widened. Ample village smoke rose in the lower distance.

Batya waited until we were more steadily on our new course, and then she raced forward to scale a hillside and look down at the approaches. Soon she was back, and, as if the long interruption hadn't happened, said, "No, the sword is the weapon of a great warrior. These women should be taught in the arts of the bow. As soon as a man comes near enough to prod them, they'll be useless as fighters. They must hold their distance."

"You think so?"

"I am sure of it." She nodded with a smug look.

"Well then, my goal wasn't to make great warriors of them but to give them some small skill, enough to keep them from dying at the hand of one lonely bandit."

She thought a moment. "That is good. I'd not considered it. No Debrecian is ever worried about one lone bandit. But, now that you mention it, I can see the use; the women in these valleys are weak."

"And, you're not too small," I told her, sharing in the spirit of understanding.

"I am. I'm smaller than Gerta, and even Catrina towers above me. Not to mention, the meat on their bodies is more than mine. You, great warrior, are a full head above me. It's plain even to me I shouldn't have been born with the soul of a warlord, for it is wasted on my little bones." She looked up and down my body, as if to show me by the action that her reasoning was without question.

I laughed at her.

She said, "Yes, now you see the folly. In the next battle, I'll be left in the back with the breeders, suited for nothing more than lofting arrows in the direction of the enemy."

This sorrow I understood. The only glory found in a battle was that found on the back of a horse, leading a charge. Of that I was most certain.

I said, "Don't you know my teacher was a great shaman warrior? Oh, I didn't know it at the time, but the Goddess has opened my eyes so I can see it now. That little woman gave me my knife and sword. Before that, she taught me with sticks. At first I was a mite, just like you at your age, but never was I tinier than she. The last time I saw her alive, she was busy murdering four mighty warriors out of a company that had her surrounded with steel. This she did with an iron sword that was crooked and held the false weight of a full claymore."

"Ah, to have seen it. What happened to her?" The girl's eyes no longer scanned the roadside for signs of soldiers or bandits.

"She fought like I've just told you, at an age that must have been three score or better and with a leg that limped. She died at the hand of a company of White Shirts, men who are better trained than many. And yet, my teacher was the happiest I'd ever seen her when they came for her. The glory of battle filled her with joy. When she died, she gave me the shadow of her soul."

Batya's mouth hung half open. She couldn't even speak for a while but then said, "What an honor to be so touched. Ah, and that's a great story as well. Her story sounds much like tales I've heard of my own grandmother, who also was short and had a gimpy leg before she left us. That was before my birth. Excuse me, but I should've asked. How'd you fair in this battle?"

"I was shoved under her cottage, where I was left mute and frustrated. As I should have said, she was a great shaman in all ways, not just war, but also good with spells, though I didn't know it until that very moment."

"Ah! You were not shamed though." She paused before adding, "It was a plot. Then what? Wasn't there a council to send you on your trial?"

"Only my mother and the hangman at my back. I think the Goddess's trials are never what we expect."

Once again, the young warrior took some time thinking. She then said, "I'll be watching you. You don't mind this?"

I told her, "As I've said; if you do it by my side and if it makes us friends."

"Sisters," she told me, though it sounded more like a request.

"Sisters," I answered with a smile. We were both very pleased, so I pointed with my toe at Ella. "As a sister gift, I give you Ella. She seems to have taken to you anyway."

I could almost feel the wheels in her head spinning before she said, "Ah! I've nothing equal to give, save my bow, and I am naked without it."

I laughed. "What a waste of a weapon, sister. Instead, here's how you'll repay me: Teach the whores bow skills. You're right; most of these pretty whores are small and weak women, even for breeders. They'll be useless with a staff or sword beyond pushing away the first bandit. We've no need for useless servants."

"Ah, if I can stand them."

"They're no more than the end of their circumstances."

With some reflection she said, "I see I'm now sister to Beckli Kahnsa." Then she rode forward to scout for a well-shielded camp in the pine-rich foothills above the upcoming village.

My heart was alive. After such a compliment invoking the great name of the Debrecian Ambassador, Kahnsa, well, I'd have given her Sir Pritchan's horse along with the other.

Chapter Eight

Newbrook was a mining town in the fiefdom of Sir Pritchan's brother, Sir Gusserin. As we grew near, I wondered how Sir Pritchan fared. Perhaps he was waiting for me in Helfax. If he knew I was riding into the mountains, he'd no doubt think I was on my way to a winter haven. A smart man, he'd await my return to the valleys. I could only imagine his surprise, once he learned I'd descended right away-- and into the adjacent valleys of lands owned by his own family. The fact is, my mother was in torment, and I was impatient to move beyond the Goddess's plans for me. I didn't have time to linger in havens, even in the name of safety.

After a short week's rest, we came walking down from a mountain foothill, me, Lady Lettoir and the whore Marci. The latter was the whore with the wide bottom. As we passed, men whistled, miners mostly, going for gold nuggets and silver veins. They lived in tents and clapboard huts along the dirt and rock-strewn roadway that paralleled a once prosperous mountain creek on the very edge of Newbrook.

A couple pranced about our bottoms, dancing fancy jigs like they'd not seen a woman in years. One leapt in our way to show off as we wandered by his camp. Marci caught the worst of it, ending with a pinched bottom, which attests to the value of a slower and bigger derriere. I sent icy smiles their way as we wandered onward, though it was the end of my staff I wanted to send them instead.

My urge was to retreat, dress in my best warrior clothing, and come charging back in on horses, cleaving the offending hands one by one. On the other hand, I kept reminding myself that my father was behind me. He'd never been honest enough to be a miner. I struggled to understand the hard work and isolation these men endured, and, when I put my mind to it, I convinced myself to bear no grudge against their simple and flawed humanity as long as they meant no great harm and maintained a sense of appreciation. Of course, once or twice I scolded and cast an eye, giving us another hundred yards of easy walking until the following camp.

My forbearance was the value of a long week of riding and another in camp with the lady, who was always telling me about the value of patience. Thus tested, we walked further into the serpent's mouth.

The lady's face was red. She was clearly thinking she'd fallen far in class of company and was taking the play of the miners worse than Marci or me. I worried I'd need to stop somewhere between tents and repeat to her one of her own lessons in patience.

On the tail of one good patting, I rubbed about my bottom. Marci, who'd had some breeding, but who'd also fallen upon bad times, said, "Such would be a perfect place for a business. If only I'd known the state of the camps just over the ridges, for it's not far from where I've spent my whole life serving so poorly."

"Surely you don't still see your former vocation in good light?" I asked as I tapped my cane a little too hard.

"I make mention only of the need. Here, such service might seem charity. The desperate men in this camp, upon receiving the blessings of a woman's touch, might also view it as good tidings. After all, not all men are pretty and easily wed."

The lady scolded, "Under a good husband is charity. Perhaps someday we'll all find such work and feel better about being born women."

"Ah, what a state we're in when we see making babies in a shack as our better prospect." I said this in my quietest voice as we walked in the direction of another small group of miners lingering in tents along the cart-wide road. Of course, I immediately felt bad about stating my thoughts on motherhood, recalling how many babies Marci had said she'd lost. As well, Lady Lettoir was a widow, and she always seemed a little sad, sadness perhaps born from a marriage lasting too short to bear fruit.

Back in our camp the previous week, my council had been joined by Batya and Marci. Marci was the eldest whore, and in spite of her humiliation during our first moments of knowing her, she gleefully took to her new situation. It seemed her despondency upon our first meeting had been only one of many conflicts she'd had with the management. We'd caught her at a bad moment; she'd determined to lie down and let the elements take her, rather than endure further life as a wicked man's whore. Such an excuse I understood, and I came to admire her for it. Thus she stood in our good graces.

She had many complaints, including the loss of several children through the sin of having had them stolen out from under her and given to married women who couldn't bear. There was an even greater abuse of having been forcefully prodded with a stick upon one conception. She could no longer bear children and was both tormented by it and relieved. With each telling of her torments, I was less and less troubled by the killings a few days back and disturbed in an entirely new way by the memory of her lying in the freezing mud, awaiting death. Already dead in her mind, clearly the Goddess had led us to Marci's shack at the moment best suited for her death, burial, and in our case, resurrection. This, more than anything else, proved to me the Goddess had a hand in our seemingly aimless journey.

Allowing her into our council was also a welcomed sign among the other whores who'd joined our troop. They'd held various views regarding their attendance, some imagining themselves hostages. Their voices were heard, even from the back, though I often had to shush their mouths when they made a mockery of our war council by complaining over trivia, such as rashes and the choice of meat brought in by whoever hunted that day with Yellow Eyes.

At times I had a mind to hunt them a miner. I imagined their potential complaint when I dragged one in with a rope around his heels and a severed spear showing through his gut. I often lingered in my telling of this fantasy, including the many details of tying a naked man onto a spit and applying herbs to enhance the taste by soaking him in such a flavored bath. Of course, that sort of thing would be simple murder, though they imagined me capable of anything morbid, and upon the very first moment of promoting this idea, I heard no more complaints about the taste of groundhog.

Itches, however, saw no end to complaint. This I fixed by having each of them shear the other's head, freeing the camp of their ample lice after an application of my Lavender oil remedies. Marci was saved this disgrace, for the shearing of heads was often a punishment for those caught in the art of whoring, and thus bore a price of honor. The cost of one full head of hair was high enough, taxing her friends with many hours of picking over each and every hair, preceded and then followed again by the application of oils too fine for lice feet.

They didn't like that one of them had been singled out and given special treatment, but I told them their hair would grow quickly, and it was because of our plan that we needed one good head of it among them. This they couldn't dispute.

To convince them of my sincerity, I applied tea dye to my own hair, temporarily browning it so the peasants couldn't see the fire and know my true name until I was done with Newbrook's hospitality.

Thus the whore Marci added her plain looks and slightly wider bottom to our smaller two as we walked into town wearing common brown homespun. We were pinched and prodded by the otherwise hard working miners, but our true names went undiscovered, even as we entered the center of town. It was as if we owned land rights among the domestics, though Newbrook was not so large that we could pretend we weren't entirely strangers.

As soon as we found the boardwalk in front of several businesses, where there were several curious town-folk, Marci announced, "My husband is tired of me sewing everything in the camp with thread borrowed out of his tunic. I'll have to find something, lest he go the winter showing his middling parts."

"Some fine cloth as well," the lady then added, as if an afterthought, "for my husband."

There was a refinement in her voice that was hard to hide, so I'd insisted she refrain from sentences longer than four words. Still, I imagined I saw heads turn upon hearing her noble lilt. These heads were attached to good candidates for town gossips.

I added, "If we have coin for it. Otherwise, we'll have to make due with more awful tanning and what little is left in our dowry chests. Mine is down to river rocks intended for buttons. I shall have to put something else in it, just to maintain some dignity around my husband's mother."

"First we must have thread, and then perhaps the store master has some sackcloth that is spare. Even a little might help shore some hems." Marci smiled while nodding conspiratorially.

The lady chimed, "So excited."

"Oh, I can't wait either. How rarely we get to shop." This was true, for I'd never shopped in my life.

"We should sight-see the whole town." I wished the lady would stop.

"As well as the clothier. I like seeing their ideas. They inspire me to copy." Marci turned in a circle, showing the gossips a genuine folksy excitement.

"I insist, but for most of the town, we can only look in, not buy." I hid my excitement.

Marci sighed. "Don't fret; my good man says we'll luck upon silver. Then we shall shop every year."

I dreamily looked up with my hands cupped as if in prayer. "Or better, perhaps live in town and tend a shop for our husbands, like these good folk who are clearly so blessed by God. I have a certain skill with candles and have often wondered if the scents would sell."

Both Marci and Lady Lettoir looked at me as if I'd gone crazy. I shrugged.

The gossips turned their eyes away. It must have been the things Marci had said because the lady and I were hopeless. I'd thought my pious remarks good because the idea of selling candles bored me.

We'd prepared somewhat; each of us wore cloth thought the least worthy. None dared guess that hanging from my hidden wolf necklace was a coin pouch bearing enough money to purchase half the businesses on their boardwalk. Neither was it known that the price of some miner pinching me in places other than my bottom was apt to be a knife in the gut. Least of all, none imagined the price for my head equal to their lord's entire fiefdom.

Soon the lies became truths, as we had many things we needed, spreading our purchases among any and all eligible merchants so as to not be known wealthy by any single one. We had far more coin than we dared part with, and once I learned the art of bartering from Marci, I was tempted to spend as much of it as I could.

We bought string, yarn and fabric in many practical sizes. Speaking of string, I bought up a store's whole supply of hemp cord, remembering Batya's insistence that we find something better than sinew for making strings on the new bows she was teaching the whores to make out of walnut deadfall. That industry was slow going, with many broken bows. Often those that didn't break were of no more use than for killing rabbits. "Such skills have to be learned slowly," was my sister's answer when I commented on the near-uselessness of the first few weapons.

Slowly I went crazy with the disease of money.

I bought a large set of small knives with wooden handles and three inch blades. I thought them practical for wearing in the belts of my new archers, who were learning the arts of fletching and honing. Some leather on the handles would help make their weapons better. I could see added uses for the knives in battle, particularly after our opponents noticed all the untested bows breaking and started thinking our archers easy pickings.

My eyes were alight with these prospects as I swished a pair of the knives around in front of a startled merchant, ending a feint with an upward jab that resembled the cross tactic I'd seen Batya execute into the middle of the second whore-master's torso.

Marci followed that up with a great deal of public scolding for fooling around with the wares and for having spent the money needed for at least three good milking cows. "Such is not often spent on worthless dining table cutlery, young woman!"

Like I said, she was very good at this.

Then there was a barber in town for the miners. He had several bottles of chemicals, some of which I thought might have uses other than the straightening of hair or the curing of stomach ailments. This sparked more interest from me than was proper, I suppose.

Marci whispered, "Abi, you must stop this line of questions, for only a man or a witch could possibly think to ask such nonsense." After that good warning, I took what I thought needful by smell alone. Marci's advice was sound in yet another way, for the merchant had clearly been misinformed. The hair tonic had the perfect smell of long-curing glue, and the stomach ailment seemed a likely catalyst for arrowhead poisons. I bought one bottle of each.

It was actually Lady Lettoir who restrained my sudden impulse to purchase the wares of a whole army when we chanced upon piles and piles of pre-tanned hides in a store selling nothing but leather and cinches. I proved to them I could cure myself of the disease of money by walking out of there with nothing at all.

Then, when we were several steps farther along, I turned and looked back through the tanner's window as if I were walking away from the beautiful face of Sir Daren Drake. If I were Laucian's wife, I'd have turned into a pillar of stone. Leather was easy, but tanning was always a chore I found miserable, probably as a result of my great lack of patience and lack of a steady home for the pits.

I'd never gone anywhere with the girls before, and in particular, never gone shopping with anybody at all. This was unlike my companions who were probably thinking our ruse a difficult and troubling experience, particularly the more I forgot we were strangers and that we'd be the chatter of the town by nightfall when the merchants closed their shops and went somewhere common to brag. The tally as a whole was staggering. Miners, if they caught word of it, would want to follow us home to see the place our men mined for gold or silver, for surely we were liars about the hole not yet bearing much worth.

I grew certain I'd made a big mistake when we walked by one of the shops, and the merchant came out to tell us all about the many things we'd missed and might want to come back in and discover.

Some of the old gossips out on the walkway took notice, causing Marci to have to say, "We're so sorry, but we are completely out of money. I don't think there is a copper left among us." This didn't appease them much, for our burdens were mighty, and yet another merchant came out of his store and pleaded for our return as well.

"I think I long to go see the pretty houses. I hear some have features of Farstand design," said the lady as means of distraction. Of course, her noble lilt and awareness of Farstand fashion was apt to kill our ruse entirely. The gossips put their heads together upon hearing it.

Then Marci took me by the elbow, and led me off the boardwalk at a brisk pace. We were soon admiring the many houses, some of them with gardens in back and even some with gardens of useless grass in front. We got farther along where the houses were tiny and right up beside one another in spite of the fact there was no need for it with so many empty lots beyond. These houses had no yards at all other than jutting rocks and dirt.

The stream behind them smelled of nightshade, attesting to the difficulty of digging a hole in the rocky soil. I didn't see anybody mining for gold anywhere close downstream.

The lady knew where her old sergeant lived and led us right up to his house. There the straw was holed, needing thatching, and the door was missing entirely. Part of the frame was covered by nothing more than an ugly hide in need of tanning. Sergeant Hadarm's whole house leaned to the right as if a good wind might push it over and wake everybody up with a serious problem that they could no longer ignore. Did I mention it was too tiny to even be a good room for a peasant farmer?

As soon as the lady came close, a woman yelled for her to go away, though the woman inside didn't show her face. Next, a man pushed the stiff hide out of the way, and came out too soon for us to leave. He yelled, "I don' wan' no strange folk on me land."

The way I saw it, there wasn't any land to speak of because the house was almost on the road, and it was stuck right up and nearly next to the one beside it, so, when it fell over, it would surely wreck the shack next door. Out back, no more than three big steps landed a person in the creek, which was apparently the same thing as the community privy. If it rained hard and steady, most likely the whole row of them would be caught in the much needed wash, a fact I was personally hoping to see soon, given my great sense of smell was sometimes not a blessing. Maybe if I prayed to the Goddess, it would go ahead and happen, so we could all stand there and watch the excitement.

Then a toddler came out, followed by another, neither of which was old enough to talk to us, and both of which looked like they had different daddies, neither of them Hadarm.

In the mean time, the man shoved Lady Lettoir without any provocation. She'd been backing up anyway, and only had to fall to end up right back on the road beside the peg end of my staff.

The staff came up, racked the man on the knee, twirled, and then staved his nose in so it blossomed like a big red rose in the late afternoon sun. He started to complain about it, so I smacked him across the head a couple times with the same heavy end of my staff, putting him to sleep. The brute sprawled across what I suppose he claimed to be his entire front yard of dirt. This might have happened of my staff's own volition, but that part of the story is probably my imagination, given I was drunk in the head at the time from having done so much pleasurable shopping.

That set the babies crying and running back into the shack. In the meantime, I don't think I even had to move my feet, which put me in just the right place to help the lady up. She apparently had missed seeing the excitement, saving me from hearing any complaints about my lack of patience and kindness and other similar traits.

"He just fell. I think he's been drinking." I said this as she noticed that the man who'd attacked her was lying in front of the flimsy shack. To my surprise, Marci backed up my obvious lie with a nod, and the lady chose to be gullible.

Some of the neighbors were watching, but, when I scowled at them, they looked away. They clearly were not very worried about the health of the man in front of us. These attitudes left me feeling almost as good as shopping. No wonder so many of the soldiers I'd fought with had insisted that going to town was fun.

Sergeant Hadarm wasn't in the shack, but there was a lady who said she was his wife. She was also the whore to the man out in the yard, and, from what I guessed, anybody else who could sneak in when any of the others weren't close. She could have been pretty once, but none of us could tell it from her many sores.

The lady politely asked the woman about her husband, to which she said she'd seen him a few days ago, but she didn't know where he was at the moment. I could tell she was lying because fibbing was one of my own better talents, and I had no stomach for anybody trying to give the skill a bad name.

I looked over at the two toddling babies who were squalling on the dirt floor. They inspired me to say, "My name is Abi, the one made immortal by slaying the King's brother. As you may suspect, I have a talent. I can murder your babies for you, if you like. That way they'll not have to figure out what to do with themselves once they've become orphans."

This took her a minute to understand, but I think the scorn on the lady's face and the pasty pallor that had fallen over Marci's finally registered the words in the head of Hadarm's unfaithful wife. She moved back on the log she used as a chair and soon had to jiggle in order to keep from falling over it backwards. This she did anyway, upon witnessing my next trick.

I reached up under my skirt and extracted the Debrecian knife gift given to me by the crone over two years previous. The blade shined sharp and beautiful even in the darkened room.

* * * * *

We were soon walking farther down the valley road, this time past the last of the shacks and houses, and onto a long trail that led up a foothill. Up ahead, I noticed a tiny thread of smoke coming from the direction the whoring wife had given for Hadarm's whiskey still.

"You had that poor woman scared completely out of her wits, Abi." I was coming to realize Marci spoke her mind freely, regardless of her company. This I had to will myself to admire, both because her words scratched across my grain and because these same words were usually right.

Lady Lettoir added, "Yes, I could have gotten the truth out of her without all that. After all, we have plenty of coin, and she was a good candidate for charity. Have some mercy." She hiked her skirt over some boulders that had probably been placed on the path to discourage visitors.

"I had mercy. When I made the offer, I hadn't considered sparing the mother, and you see we have left both the mother and her babies in their familiar state of misery. It was only because of the woman's pathetic begging that I reconsidered. Even now I think we should go back and correct the error, but I smell the sergeant ahead and am thus inclined to put it behind me."

"You can't think this way, Abi. None know the will of God." Marci's face suggested she took that seriously.

The lady nodded. "Yes, you cannot play at God, Abi. Leave to God those things that are God's. Now we leave a certain gossip behind. Soon the whole town will know who we are, in spite of the woman's many promises and fainting last demeanor."

"I see I am stood corrected by my council and thus will have to reshape my thinking." I saw they weren't convinced I meant it. Marci, most of all, looked confused, given nobody had ever truly listened to her before. Well, I had promised the Goddess I would honor the rulings of my council, even if such rulings weren't consistent with my better instincts. Regarding this I was determined because it was consistent with my need to learn all the new burdens laid upon me, such as compassion and patience and not letting the crone's shadow rule my life. Never before had I met such a difficult challenge, and, therefore, I knew its worth, for most things easy have no value at all.

We'd gotten to the end of the path. There before us was a one-walled shack made out of sticks and hemp. The whiskey still smoldered over a dwindled stack of wood. My first observation was that the kettle was too tiny to be worth much. With all the miners up the valley, Sergeant Hadarm could have been making big money with a more industrious operation. Instead, he was lying under the end pipe with his hand in the drip bowl.

* * * * *

Marci went back for Batya with the order to break camp and bring the horses around on the foothills. In the meantime, Hadarm woke up. As soon as the bowl was full, an eye opened, and he sat up just far enough to drink it. I wondered why he even bothered with the bowl when he could have just as easily put his mouth under the drain and not had to wait for anything to fill.

Though we sat nearly in his lap, there was no recognition that anybody alive was anywhere near him. It was as if we were as invisible as the air he breathed. I know that to not be the case because the air he breathed came out too foul to have come from any of us. Just about the time he passed out again, the horses came.

I had Marci help me lift him belly first over the back of her stout mount. To keep him from falling off, we tied him hands to feet.

Then I put Marci on my own horse, and told them to make some progress down the valley and into some secluded encampment near where the creek met the river.

The sun fell off the edge of the world as I walked back into the mining town of Newbrook. There, I stole two horses and a mule, but not before sneaking up to and putting my post on the posting board. It read: "My name is Abi. I shall meet you in Helfax." It was my hope that the promise would stay the baron's hand long enough for me to ready those things the Goddess saw fit for me to ready before I fell upon him with all the might the Goddess saw fit to place at my disposal.

Chapter Nine

"How long do you intend to torment him?" asked Lady Lettoir. The sergeant yelled his hundredth insult. The last one had been truly amusing, right from the gut and punctuated by gasping vomit. The vomit had been mostly for show—water and a little pinkish blood.

His breeches were across a rope, having been creek washed along with his shirt. This was convenient, for it wasn't only his stomach that was purging itself from the poison of too much liquor. To be honest, I more pitied the horse he'd been tied across. The horse was innocent, but his nose and ears were large and close to the continual outpouring of smells and complaints.

The lady persisted: "It is not his fault. He has fallen so hard. The man was a great soldier, and it was all he knew. Then the baron had him tossed aside like the kitchen's spoils. What was he to do when he went home to his unfaithful wife and had no prospects for a decent trade?"

Batya said, "Our tribe will not abide a mate who does not respect his warrior. He must be honorable and give our children a trade."

"That is well off the point, child. He is sick, and this is no way to treat a man who has earned my trust."

"Ah, we've only been in camp most of a night," I said. "Surely he can endure his penance until the sun is more than a tease on the horizon."

Batya started laughing. She didn't tell me why, but I suppose our ways were different from hers, and thus the humor. As to our ways, I thought leaving Hadarm belly first across a horse for a whole night was the minimum necessary to teach him the folly of too much drinking.

"Oh, for God's sake!" said the lady when I smiled in the midst of my thoughts. When she tossed aside the last bite of her breakfast biscuit, I picked it up, brushed it off and thanked her for it.

This got Batya laughing again, only harder. When Hadarm yelled, the harmony woke up one of the whores. She'd gone to bed hearing the same commotion, and thus upon hearing our chuckles, looked over at Hadarm's naked buttocks. She started laughing until tears came and were soon falling so fast it was clear she was depressed and not happy. We were all left to wonder about the range of emotions that dredged both laughter and tears up at the same moment. This seemed to happen to all of us from time to time, leaving us in poor moods, often at the very start of the day.

That's when I woke up everybody and brought forth the many blessings of our shopping trip. Even that didn't brighten many of the moods until I told them to get busy mending all that needed to be fixed before their archery and field lessons. A busy woman is a happy woman—or at least it's the state we find most like home. Breakfast helped as well, and I had more biscuits from freshly stoned flour to pass around.

The time came to cut down the sergeant, which I did with one quick slice of my knife. He fell to the ground, transforming into a groaning worm. Rather than unbinding his hands and feet, I slipped a money bag over his neck.

I told him, "This is your first month's salary for reenlisting in the lady's happy guard. You are retained with the rank of sergeant, putting you now above all but me and my council. If you don't like it, you can go back and serve the wench in Newbrook."

This he didn't seem to understand, so I left him to figure it out. After a while, he came to one of his senses and, instead of moaning, asked for something to drink. I was ready for the request, handing him some of my best purging tea.

He took one smell and noticed it reeked. The bad smell reminded him of his usual, I suppose, for it suited him enough that he took several deep swallows. Then his eyes widened, and he tossed the cup at me with all the meager strength he could muster after his joyful night across the back of the wide horse. He was soon purging some more, satisfying me that there was nothing remaining between his mouth and his anus other than those things the Goddess willed remain.

* * * * *

I thought a few guards in the grey and brown of Lettoir might appeal to a rebel lord. This had always been Lady Lettoir's plan anyway. Sir Lacellor might see value in raising her among them and perhaps even thank her for bringing some useful guards to his realm.

My plan was similar, but not exactly the same. If he were pleased, perhaps he'd lend me some harder soldiers to help me rescue my mother.

Men shunned us, but we found women who were willing. Creating this force as we moved towards the lands of Lacellor was costing me a lot of time and energy, however. Further, I had no idea how these few women could possibly be of any use in a war. The Goddess had seemingly set me on this course, however, and I knew obeying her was not in contention.

As we passed villages, I invited the world to Helfax. I had no secret plot but hoped the baron would find out about my stated intentions and spare my mother until my arrival. I also imagined my enemies in one place, so I could kill them together. In my dreams, I rode among them, and with just one broad swipe of my sword, cleaved whole rows of heads from their bodies as they stood on the boardwalks screaming, "Traitor!" Such had no logic, and I knew it, but the lack of logic only confirmed my belief that I was directly on the path set before me by the Goddess.

Fortunately, there were always new things to do now that I had others under my charge. For one, we were becoming a mob of women. We were certainly not good with arms, but this didn't bother me yet. Finding recruits and then feeding the growing family did. It was one thing to live off the land when we were ten or twenty, and yet another when we were several companies. This didn't take long to be the case, and, in fact, arrived well before we had to consider putting down for the winter, which I foresaw as another ghastly delay forced upon me by circumstances.

Hunting for all our food was soon too much of a chore, for we had to move steadily toward the safety of Lacellor. We also had training to do and were diligent at it now that we had a sergeant. My solution was to separate the better fortuned farmers, monasteries, and minor noble holdings from some of their goods and all their livestock. We chanced upon one town where the local lord bred fine horses. That was a good find. I left them with nothing, lest Pritchan's guards learn of the raid too quickly.

The whore Marci had an idea that added greatly to the swelling of our ranks. The ruse lasted a good week before we became too famous and started to feel the pressure of Sir Pritchan on our tracks. Marci walked into the towns and made an offer for the least pleasant and ill-suited girls among them. Those just near or just past marriage age were what we wanted. Big and bony were best. Those found to be unpleasant, even if they were discarded wives, were perfect.

She'd say, "My lords seek headstrong and difficult women, good for heavy labor and in need of being taught their proper place in society as a result of their failure as obedient women. They have no need for good women found in favor by their fathers."

This met with delight. Everybody in town knew just the right girls, and runners often left in good haste to spread the excellent news of how a noble's agent had come to deliver them from the unloved.

Some were ugly and even more often spiteful as they were led to her recruiting table, sometimes with their fathers' fingers clamped about their ears.

In no time at all, Marci had half a score lined up in nearly every unsuspecting town or hamlet along our path. She inspected them for suitability to hard labor in the mines or fields. She left them no dignity, making each step behind a curtain tossed over a rope so she could more properly inspect every part of them. In public, she made rude comments about the state of their teeth and the uncomely meatiness about their limbs. Whenever one of them cast a disrespectful glance at an elder or her father, Marci's hand was swift at reddening a cheek. Regarding this, the elders often nodded, eager to show their agreement with the treatment.

Whenever Marci found one to add to her chain, she put a collar on her and screwed in the lock so the hapless woman knew of her selection even before the fee was settled with her father or next of kin. I knew that, if I were one of the women, I'd have been planning Marci's murder ten steps past the very first bend in the road. Such was the beauty of it.

Usually near the final selection, the lady rode in with Hadarm at her side to make the payment. All could clearly see her noble demeanor at a glance, and thus any concerns about how Marci was going to manage were instantly put to rest. It was noted that the lady was the one with the gold. All the haggling was pushed aside, for even the parents couldn't recant the decisions of a true-blood noble.

I occasionally watched the ruse from the woods. The unwanted women sagged. Their eyes frosted over. Spirits were crushed. They'd been betrayed, chained, paid for, and now put into the hands of a noble and her sergeant, doomed to a short life of hard toil.

Later, the lady often told me how it amazed her to see so many of the fathers eager to part with their grown daughters for the mere sum of a gold coin. I didn't remind her that this was a year's taxes, and most families had to pay dowry to rid themselves of their female offspring. An incompliant girl had the habit of ruining a family name, and she lingered around the cottage for a handout far past maidenhood. They often died from the elements or from some hard moment involving someone else's pleasure. In Farstand, it was no mystery why so many daughters never made their early winters and why so few lasted without the proper disposition of a marriage.

We took a half dozen from even the smallest village. The men went away grinning with the joy of their newfound fortune, while we went away noting the direction of their travel, so as to not miss the chance of a personal visit to retrieve the coin.

I recall one such occasion. As soon as we'd finished the raid, our new servants were led before the group and made to kneel while still in bondage. They'd been made to run many miles, putting good distance between ourselves and those we'd just rid of their new wealth. The evening's lamb was already slaughtered and on a spit over the new fire.

My warriors surrounded the terrified women. Our best ten warriors were flush from their successes. It was something to see the new servants' eyes as they knelt before archers and women holding pikes, some with blood on them. To the new and disoriented, a woman with a week's worth of the sergeant's training was a campaigned mercenary. A good look at one of Batya's more closely selected archers was enough to still a weak woman's heart, but not because of the archer's size; it was due to Batya's insistence upon iron discipline among her chosen.

The smell of leather and freshly run horses swirled around us all. The last raiders remained on their horses in the back rows, a bit of drama advised by none other than Marci, who seemed a master at all sorts of orchestration. All of this, over two score strong, made us look mightier than I knew us to be.

The chain bore seven maidens, two of them bone ugly; one of them was temporarily fat. Another was strong and wild, but otherwise not well in the mind. She didn't have the good sense to be afraid and instead spit at anybody who moved too close, including my sister Batya. When the woman spoke, the words made no sense to my ears, other than I knew them to contain insults. I wondered why Marci had picked her.

I could see they all wondered why we had bothered with buying them when we could have captured the more lovely and acceptable women among them for slaves. As well, we might have done so for nothing. Or, so I assumed they were thinking that because that was what I'd have been thinking. They had no way of knowing physical beauty, and slaves were not what we wanted.

Yellow Eyes sat beside me as I took a seat before them on the only chair among our provisions. He was gnawing on one of the sheep's half-cooked limbs, well content, though only I seemed to know it.

Batya paid no mind to anyone at all. She preferred to walk right between me and the spitting woman, going about her business. The Debrecian set a pot by the fire. Her hair was bound up like a yellow flame. It reflected the light with every toss of her head. I could never get over the style and imagined what mine might look like tied up like hers.

I thought my sister perfect and beautiful. As well, such detached behavior made her all the more frightfully lovely in the eyes of the new women.

Lady Lettoir didn't attend these meetings, nor did her maid and the sergeant. They would have been no help.

The one woman kept spitting on Batya's back. It was truly amazing, and all eyes were watching this, including those belonging to Yellow Eyes, who laughed, though again none noticed it as such, for I have found that few know the moods of wolves as well as I do.

Batya turned slowly and looked at the woman. Then she embraced her and kissed her on the cheek.

This even I didn't expect, nor did I understand it at all, but the effect was sudden and startling to all who witnessed it. I said, "Such an embrace is a mystery to us."

Hearing that, Batya let her go. The mad woman sat back on her haunches and ceased her ill behavior as if bitten by a snake. Batya stepped away. She put her knife back into her belt, though none had seen her draw it. There was no blood on the blade, which was perhaps the biggest surprise of all. Having finished with her chores of love and terror, Batya left our circle to observe from the edges.

I laughed. Then I whispered into the unnatural stillness of so many women, "The gods still fight over our little souls."

This gained the attention of the mad woman with the rude spitting habit, and she got up out of the dirt. The silence only deepened. I'd felt the Goddess's will when my sister had gotten so close to the woman. This inspired me, so I left my chair. I drew within inches of the woman's lips. Her head turned up and all the way back as she looked at me with new and proper fear.

I took the young woman's lips in mine and kissed her. My tongue slipped deep into her mouth, such that we tasted one another. When I was sure I had her full attention, I whispered into her ear, "I have many souls. Would you like to see one of them? *Kavete oas ux elpuvn. Tpunwvw Own.*" I spun my fingers between us, kissed them, and touched them to her forehead.

She didn't know I couldn't give her one of my souls, but I could feel how thoroughly her own soul was healing, and how it seemed to her that I'd passed something on to her that was foreign. We both could tell it was nothing like the old and tired one she'd been born with. That soul had suffered under too many ugly memories. I knew her myths, and thus, if she chose to see it as a demon fleeing, so be it.

There was no angel to replace him, but the part of her that remained was enough of an angel to appease the sense within me that allowed me to see such things when others failed to notice.

I unlocked the collar from around her neck and then led her to some food and water.

When she was settled, I stood before the other six and asked them, "Why did six of you allow this one woman to spit on my sister? Do you not know the spirits continually commanded the warrior within her to kill those who do not show her honor? Do you not know my sister is a shaman princess who is soon to be tested and has thus been made hard in spirit by the Goddess herself? She is to be respected if you wish to live even a short time more on this earth. For this crime, I'll starve you to death if I'm not later convinced there is some use for you, and you will not eat today so you may think hard on why I should love you."

I told the ones who were minding their chain to keep them locked together, and to put them out of the camp where I wouldn't be forced to see them.

We did feed them, however—purging tea. The purging was not unlike that given to my sergeant, lasting well into the morning.

In the morning, we listened to their many suggestions regarding their own worth. Some fancied themselves good cooks or seamstresses, while others implied they owned green fingers, or could sing capable lullabies. After listening to the useless suggestions, I gave them to our sergeant, who as usual, complained that some things were beyond possible as he issued them some freshly whittled spears. The sergeant always complained; it was a sure sign things were going better than expected.

The six new spears had been made over the night and with the very hands of the mad woman whose soul I'd healed the evening before. It seemed nobody had actually asked her to do the work, and nobody knew even where she'd found the knife. A quick check of the camp found none missing.

I went to ask Marci why she'd chosen such a mad woman, and she could come up with no sound reason.

I asked the girl for her name, but she'd grown mute since the touch. The only words she spoke were the ones she spoke with her eyes.

We spent one more night in that camp, as much time as we dared in any. On that night I held a meeting of the council. Lady Lettoir came into my tent and sat beside me. She looked at me funny, and then Batya came in and looked at me even funnier.

"All right, what's the problem?"

"That girl," said the lady.

"Ah, the crazy woman." I shook my head.

Batya nodded as well. "I've not yet seen her sleep. She lives in the woods closest to your tent. Perhaps I should have killed her the night before, if for no other reason than to understand her better."

The good lady shrieked. "You can't understand a dead woman once you've gone that far!"

"That's my point. Once dead, understanding is perfect. Also, when she's dead, there's less worry," explained Batya.

Maid Minari started arguing on the side of Batya, which was at least a fresh alliance and unexpected. Marci took the side of the lady, though she showed some reservations when she said, "The girl's my fault. I should never have picked her. She had good bones and meat on her, and for just the right moment she was still. Maybe we should just leave her behind?"

"For that matter, why so many women and not two or three good men?" asked Lady Lettoir. "We can pay them, make good uniforms and present ourselves to Sir Lacellor in a way that convinces him we are nobles worthy of rank and shelter."

"These women are the mirrors of my life. Is this not noble?" I waved my hand toward the rest of the camp.

Lady Lettoir sighed. "I'm sorry. Of course, you are right. But, this crazy one is a danger to us all. I see no need to kill her. Why not set her on her way?"

I nodded before addressing my whole council. "The tally is two to two, so I get to decide. In fact, it wouldn't matter if it was all of us against her, for the Goddess has shown her hand in this matter. Don't you know I've seen this girl's soul, and we've bartered together under the light of the Goddess? It's not madness you see but rather determination to never return to her former condition."

Batya sat back and seemed troubled upon hearing my words. "The Goddess has spoken directly to you then?"

"This time she whispered, starting from the moment of your kiss on the woman's cheek. You can never tell how she chooses to speak to a person. Do you remember the night we first met, a year ago, before we were reintroduced? That night she was sitting on top of the moon? Now that was as clear a conversation as any I've ever had with anybody," I told her.

"I didn't believe you. I looked up when you mentioned it, but nobody was there; I saw only the blemishes on the moon's face," my sister said.

"Ah, just as it was on the battlefield. There were thousands on the field, but both she and Sho were present, and only I heard them. At that time I wasn't sure if it was a curse or a blessing. I still have times when I'm convinced it's a blessing and then next, that it's the other."

"I've never heard of a shaman who can speak to the Goddess. She gives shaman and others of lesser gifts magic, but by custom, the Goddess only speaks openly to the one who leads us all. This is a rare and beautiful omen," Batya said.

"I don't understand the many details of being a Debrecian. All I know is the Goddess has seen fit to show me this girl's soul, and thus it is not right to ignore her will and cast aside her gift."

To this they all nodded agreement, though the lady and her maid showed some hesitation regarding my choice of deities.

* * * * *

From that moment onward the issue was settled, and from that moment onward the girl slept just outside my tent, both her mysterious knife and a freshly made spear ready, following only the instructions of her freshly clean soul. Ah, the only perfect soul among us, I mused. No wonder we all thought her mad.

On the morning of the second day, we were breaking camp. Only the rear guards were not busy. Theirs was the last duty of cleaning up the underbrush by raking and laying fresh leaves upon our departure. We kept our fires to one small circle, hoping to leave the impression we were no more than a half score. When we marched, we rode in no more than groups of ten and sometimes cleared some tracks with brush dragged behind our horses' tails.

Such was also the case in our raids, employing no more force than necessary. I knew from my readings on war that knowledge of the enemy was of great value. The greatest advantage in the clash of armies is numbers, and the second is might; I didn't have the second, so I could ill afford to lose the first through lack of caution. Since no king is ever willing to allocate a whole army to a mere handful of peasant brigands, I hoped to not be at a disadvantage when first confronted by a decent force.

As a mighty scout for the enemies who pursued me, I'd always been amazed at what an army willingly exposed to my scouting. I determined, and drilled daily into my warriors, that this wouldn't be our folly, for we were weak enough from lack of experience, broadswords and thickness in the shoulders. I came to start every tactical lecture with the saying, "We raid Pritchan's towns for food and horses but do not mistake the ignoble chore as proof we are an army."

* * * * *

I stepped out of my tent. Many were busy before the sun, showing great discipline, so I gathered my own gear, eager for the road.

Ah, what were we doing? The quest for the Queen seemed all but forgotten. My mother rotted in a Helfax cell. And, here I was, tending a growing body of women, already nearly three score. This is where fate and listening to my council's advice had brought me. I couldn't wait to deliver the entire burden to Sir Lacellor and get back to the things that mattered.

As soon as I was clear of the tent, the crazy woman busied herself with my stakes and roping. She bound the canvas as tightly as any trained soldier. Then she fetched my breakfast, as well as my sister's. We Debrecians sat, quickly eating, discussing the deployment and also watching the mad girl load our horses, this, too, better than expected. Her own horse hadn't even been introduced, and yet she found it, and put upon it nothing more than her blanket, for that was all she had in the whole world other than the clothing on her back and her meager weapons.

I wasn't used to being coddled and found my hands wandering about my hair and buttons in idle confusion.

All these chores happened the very moment after I thought of doing them myself. It made me certain something of my own mind had been shared between us on the night of passing souls. Finally, I had to ask her to stop before someone discovered the secret and mysterious nature of her service.

I took her aside and said, "I don't know a good name to call you. I thought I'd call you the crazy woman, but I fear you'll take it as an insult, and the other warriors will scoff at you. Instead, I'll call you Angel, in honor of the Goddess who sent you, for it's said that between the gods and man are the angels."

She was overwhelmed by my compliment, though I had trouble getting her to lift her broadly smiling face and look into my eyes. I had to add, "You're not a servant here, but you are a soldier, which is harder. Your purchase was a ruse to help us recruit the right sort of women for our company. We want the castaways and those who aren't happy with the domestic lives picked by our fathers. So, when you look at me, look at me proudly, for here things are different. Here you belong. Here you needn't look at the feet of any person who hasn't earned your respect honestly. We shall start with the sergeant, a man who has earned my trust, and then if you're worthy, with my sister, a woman who is of my blood. Then when you're done with enough training to be good with that knife, you can break my tent and pack my horse and even kill my enemies...but only when I'm too busy to do it myself, and only with your head looking at something other than my feet."

The girl nodded her head. Then her face broadened even further into the biggest smile I'd ever seen in my life. She turned, and, with her head up so high I doubted she could see the first flakes of snow, she walked on, awkwardly climbing up on her new and unfamiliar horse.

After some wild kicking about at his neck, her horse was more confused than helpful. Mostly by accident, he found the right direction so the woman could report to the sergeant.

She didn't talk to him either, but then again, neither did he talk to her. All he did was shake his head at me. I could almost hear his brain talking. It was complaining to itself about the quality of our recruits. Such reminded me of my first day in Lettoir manor. He'd made the same mistake with me.

Chapter Ten

Sir Lacellor's border was five days away. We'd skirted Helfax, leaving it two days to our rear. The farther we moved from Helfax, the more my heart fluttered. If not for the many charges now under my wings and the guidance of the Goddess, I'd have been unable to withstand the temptation to turn my horse and charge through the baron's gates.

Thoughts of the rebel, Sir Lacellor, filled me with additional dread because the last time his men had crossed me, I'd been his enemy. The thought of going to him was in itself more delay than I wanted. I determined to get there, rush through the diplomacy, and get back with a decent army as soon as training, fortune and earliest spring weather allowed. Even if my mother were dead already, it was as good as written that Helfax was due a harsh visit. I was no longer going there in a suicidal fit, but I was definitely going there.

All of this, of course, assumed Sir Lacellor was capable of forgiving me for having killed so many of his footmen, which I imagined was no small forgiveness.

In the meantime, we were once again going in the wrong direction. We'd come down out of the mountains, riding upon the first snows of winter, using every minor path.

We couldn't go a mile without bumping into a dozen shepherds or farmers in their fields. For that reason it became even more critical that we move in only groups of ten, coordinating our movements and coming together in camps that were somewhat loosely connected and well hidden. Thus any given peasant could only say he'd seen us and we were less than a company.

We trained on the road. A few of the women learned quickly, so we gave each one good skill so they could teach the others as they moved from group to group.

Once we had our system in place, I was left almost completely out of the training, given that Marci, Lady Lettoir and I had the duty of holding an army together. Such was more about mending, feeding, rounding up, praising and scolding than anything else.

Necessity dictated that our soldiers spend much of their time concentrating on the skills of scouting, message running and a few formations with one or two weapons. Some women knew only the spear, for wielding one while remaining ahorse is no small chore. Batya sorted through them for archers, eventually holding back no more than a score in her personal ranks of better fit and generally tiny hellions.

Once she'd settled upon the best, she taught a couple the art of the curved-back bow, which was an unusual instrument of sinew, horn and birch, yielding nearly twice the power of a regular bow. The problem, of course, is only a few were made because of the skill required and our shortness of time, so most of our bows remained the cumbersome longbow, mostly of lighter weight and crude construction.

I longed for Lettoir's corrals, and even the wooden swords, for in our haste, if it couldn't be done on a horse, it couldn't be done at all. Among us was no more than a score of iron weapons, mostly crude and conquered from town guards as we passed through. Those had been nearly all old soldiers, their weapons no better than bludgeons. I'd have given two dozen mounts for a master blacksmith and two weeks of his work over a decent forge.

The good side was my women were beginning to know how to run horses and every one of them thought of themselves as part of the best squad under the lady's flag. I let them think themselves mighty, for the lie was good for morale.

Even Angel thought of herself as a fine warrior. She did so from the moment she managed to climb on her horse without falling off the other side. No defeat deterred her sense of accomplishment.

She was quickly the favorite benefactor of Sergeant Hadarm's shaking head. If the women were made to poke at a tree trunk ten times with their short pikes, Angel poked at it a hundred. I often watched the sergeant take the others on to another exercise while

Angel persisted at the old one, seemingly oblivious to his insistent screams for her to join the others. Ninety-nine of the times she was terrible, and then the Goddess touched her and she struck perfectly, always when the sergeant was no longer looking. Then she marched happily over to join the others, sometimes when they were three or four exercises removed from the one she'd just finished.

Angel still slept outside my tent, though the sergeant always asked her to join the others. She got away with it because she was mute and crazy, and mostly because I told the sergeant the Goddess was putting Angel where it pleased her.

What he didn't know was that, as soon as he finished with her training, she sneaked off and caught up on all the parts of her training she'd missed.

One day she came back to my tent well into the early morning night. I watched her with my blessed wolf eyes. There was a second knife in her belt. I had the sergeant ask around, but once again none had come up missing.

The bad side of doing most of our training separate and on the run was that I'd lost two messengers to brigands and another to a Pritchan patrol, which told me he was on our trail again. At times we lost contact with whole squads for as much as two hours before they found one or the other of their sister groups. When it came to a real fight, I'd have to bring my fragmented army together with a level of proficiency I'd never read about in any of my histories. On the other hand, at least we were practiced at the mistake of being splintered.

Yellow Eyes came running in, skirting the northern wood-line. Like the others, he scouted the pursuing cavalry of Sir Pritchan. They'd been joined by some White Shirt knights. From the way my scouts described their leader's bearing, my old friend, Captain Barker, had joined up, explaining why Sir Pritchan had managed to unravel our constantly shifting course.

A good field commander knows when a thing is inevitable and turns to meet it before it runs her down. The time came upon us only a month of wandering out of Newbrook. So much had changed about us in that one short month, I was unsure of the hand I held.

Still, I commanded Batya to bring our forces together and meet at a woods climbing to a great, mile wide meadow. Such land might be a place we'd stand a chance against the more experienced men of Sir Pritchan and Sir Barker.

I chose to camp where we'd have the advantage of long lines of sight for our arrows and some hope of controlling our forces. We had no skill with blades and little enough with weak arrows and wooden spears. There wasn't as much as a shirt of mail in our ranks. We had better numbers but needed open land in order to maintain constant movement and control. My women were utterly doomed if the battle stalled into a melee.

"Two score. They be many, a dozen in light armor, and not a man be without a shield and sword. These are no town guards," said the first scout to give me decent details. The girl was excited, as if she expected a miracle the moment she told me her news. I would surely save them all by kissing upon their foreheads. She was also out of breath, as was her horse, but, as soon as she gave the numbers, she rode off to the west to help find a wandering group. Only forty of us were on hand. We had just under a hundred in all; half that if you only counted the women among us who could last toe to toe with a man for longer than half a minute. It was time to pull Batya aside and consider our options:

My sister said, "The good thing is the sun is falling. Pritchan will have to camp well short of battle. Then we'll set the field. I doubt he knows where we propose to meet him, nor does he imagine our numbers."

At that moment she looked as young as I'd ever seen her. Her face was pink and flushed. All she wanted was a fight.

I said, "Here we have a battle where I can feed our one hundred women into the teeth of two score experienced soldiers and watch all of our women perish in the greatest folly in human history, and all you see is an opportunity to loose your arrows and stick your spear. The field is perfect, but you and I both know that among us are only three mighty warriors. Have you ever struck a copper vest and felt your bones shaking sore enough to wonder if you can still hold your weapon and do it again and again? Can you imagine these poorly trained women finding out the limited reach and aim of their wooden spears on such a battlefield? Pritchan is a fool, but he stands with Barker, who is a fool as well, but a man who has proven he can fight."

"Ah!" grumbled my sister.

We looked out across the promising field, now both seeing it for the death trap it was. Another group of our women came riding in. There was cheer on their faces as they met friends, all of them anticipating a mighty victory. They looked tiny, and their lances were mere branches. Both the lances and the women who held them were as thin as month old saplings, for few had grown enough muscle to bear more stout weaponry.

"A posse of forty is a large number when well disciplined; enough to guard their flanks and maneuver their horses with ease. They can even make every possible mistake and still defeat us," I mused.

Batya said, "Yes, I suppose these breeding women might not last. So, what if the count was one score? My archers could punish such a group."

"Ah, yes, but they're at least twice that number. It's our ill fortune that Sir Barker has met up with Pritchan at just the wrong moment. One or the other we might have taken. You should know, the white knights love nothing more than the murder of strange women, and Barker has personally promised to meet me with the best of his murdering kind."

"Well then, that only encourages me. Perhaps we'll make do if we're made to fight harder," said Batya.

Finally, I saw another group approaching. This one had Lady Lettoir, Maid Minari and the sergeant in it. I felt the need for some help impressing upon my sister the righteousness of pessimism. And here it came.

Sergeant Hadarm jumped down from his horse first, and while walking up immediately complained: "You can't be serious! There are nearly two score professional men at arms out there, some most likely born on horses. I'll have nothing to do with this slaughter, Abi!"

"I hear you, Sergeant. Tell me your plan," I told him.

"Well, we leave. We split into squads and run. The border's not a week off; half that if we sleep on our horses. I'll put the best riders with the lady and—"

"Half will be run down; another quarter lost on the trails. Among our disadvantages are many horses fit for no more than plowing. What kind of leader lets half her soldiers die with a pike through her back and without a decent fight? And then when we get to Lacellor, what will he think of our great and fancy contribution? How will he greet the great Lady Lettoir, escorted in by weeping tatters? And, if I can't do this, what can I possibly do at Helfax with parts of his army? All will ask these questions and be right to spit upon us."

Sergeant Hadarm gave it some thought, but then he decided, "All that sounds like a trough load of pig dung to me. A good commander weighs the situation and saves what he can. You put this company into the field and we'll all be wishing we'd run a day sooner. You'll thank any God you can find for the tatters."

I looked at Batya and said, "Now you'll do well to consider; our sergeant is long on experience and he is no fool. These considerations are what must be weighed before a warrior fights her army. It's not enough to set soldiers on a field. You must also see your army leaving it in good order. As it stands, the sergeant has shown us the only clear choice. We save half, or we save nobody at all."

She kicked at the ground, not liking it one bit. "If it were ten from my hearth I'd neither run nor die killing such a small number of my enemy. And to imagine, we have them more than two to one."

"Yes. Beckli, Gerta and Catrina; the woman with only one leg, the scout who shows great caution and three more like them; I can see it as well, but we've a different company and have given unto ourselves the chore of their masters. It's not just a duty of honor and glory, but one of responsibility."

She started laughing. When she wiped her tears away, she said, "And here I thought my only duty was watching you. Is that not how it started? Is this how it ends?"

I said, "Then watch me, and while looking at me, tell me what we shall do to save our army, for that is the only task before you. We are poor sisters indeed if we live only for our longings. We guard no crossing. We protect no towns. We lay siege to no man's castle. Tell me only how you'll save my army, my sister, or say nothing at all."

With that the discussion was over. We had no plan, but by morning I'd have an assembly of all those we reached out and gathered. When Pritchan marched across that field, he'd either be met by a hundred foolish women or know we were running.

* * * * *

That night I couldn't sleep. Batya rested by my fire, but the sergeant and others of the council were in their tents. Guards had been posted, and only two of our scouts were still probing at the edges of the enemy camp. Word came that the last squad would make it to us before dawn, which was the only reason we waited. It looked as if all was settled until the rising of the sun.

Then, very late into the night, the Goddess sent us our Angel.

She walked in from the direction of the enemy. In her belt was a third knife. Across her back, worn in the fashion only favored by myself and a few of the Debrecians I'd seen, she wore a sword. It was no trinket either. Her sword was steel, not iron. Its hilt was crafted of metal bracing around richly-oiled rosewood. This I found out later, but at the moment I could clearly see her sheath was green leather and steel. A fancy wool strap served as binding across her chest. Judging from the hilt and sheath, the sword didn't compare to my own, but it was far better than most. I remembered seeing one just like it hanging from the belt of one of Pritchan's better soldiers. In fact, it had been the best sword among them that was not Pritchan's.

She sat across from me with a smile on her face, but with her eyes cast toward the flames as if she meant to tell me she was here by my grace and wished to not disturb me.

When she was distracted for a second, I tossed a small stone over to Batya and my sister opened her eyes as if she'd not really been asleep. Then I nodded toward Angel. She didn't think as highly of Angel as I did, but I could see her impression change in the few seconds it took her to count the steel hanging off the young mute's body.

"Tell me, Angel, where did you find such a nice sword," I asked.

She looked around sheepishly, and then shook her head with great vigor.

"Ah, don't be troubled. I know you've not stolen any of your knives from our camp. Nor have you taken them from the poorest peasants. I also promise to not take any you don't see as spare and necessary to share with your fellow soldiers, some of whom do not even have the first knife with which to save their own lives."

She thought about that some, then reached into her belt and put one of the knives on a stone by the fire. Her tongue went out of her mouth, and it stuck there on a spot above her upper lip.

"Why thank you. I shall find someone who has none and give it to her, being sure to tell her it's a gift from her sister, Angel."

She shook her head no, bordering on the edge of terrified, it seemed.

"Yes. Don't you see, you're mistreated by some of our women through ignorance? They don't know you yet, for there's much you can't tell them. But, one will get the gift of your knife, and then perhaps two will, and then three and maybe even four someday. When someone speaks ill of you, these will say, "Ah, she's strange indeed, but did I ever show you what she gave me out of the goodness of her heart? Is it not something? And, have you not heard she is called an angel by Abi?" Then others will see you differently; strange still, for I'll not deceive you, but you'll be their strange sister. In battle they'll stand by your side and kill any enemy who might do you harm."

She stopped shaking her head and sat as if frozen by her thoughts. Then she took a second knife out of her belt and set it on the same rock.

Batya spoke next. "That's enough. A warrior should always have two good blades."

Angel, who never smiled at anybody but me, looked over at Batya and nodded. Then she smiled, and all was as it should be.

I asked, "Now Angel, can you tell me where you got your fine weapons, for we've use for more of them."

She looked around as if looking for something and then stood up. She spun around. When she slowed, she crouched down a little, heading off a few steps toward the edge of our woods that abutted the fields. A mile over on the other side of the fields was the enemy camp, they still unaware of our close proximity.

The three of us walked over to the field's edge, stepping a few paces into the high weeds. Up above, a sliver of the moon gave us its smallest light, sprinkling the tops of the weeds with a melancholy haze.

I said, "An enemy without a sword is only an enemy with a spear, much as we."

Batya said, "This is true, but if we had swords, we'd be no better off. None among us has trained with the weapon."

I turned and looked at her. She was tired. Her eyes were puffed up and wet. "So now you are the cautious one."

"I have many years of listening and have added this day," she said.

"What else?" I asked her, feeling something more might be made of our lesson.

"Men without swords and without horses, now that's something," Batya said.

"We could never pull it off. The horses are well guarded. Forty horses is a great number. They'd have no more than five or six to a rope-line." I waited to hear a rebuke.

"Are twenty swords and twenty horses a great number?" asked Batya.

I looked over at Angel, and she appeared as if she'd only been half listening. Then she shrugged while still looking toward the far end of the field.

"Is it too dangerous to ask you to go get some more swords? I mean, without a fight. I don't want to send you over there just to get you caught."

Angel looked around as if trying to see if anybody was going to catch us plotting. She made walking signs with her fingers, followed by pointing to the distant woods.

"How many?" I asked.

She pulled at her finger, and then stuck up three.

"Damn. We need twenty to make a difference," Batya said.

Angel stuck up two more fingers.

"Three or four are better than none," I said. "Besides, thieving is dangerous work. I did this sort of thing in the last war. No soldier worth his horse sleeps more than a hand's reach from his sword. Gathering what's stumbled across is difficult; doing it from a shopping list is impossible."

Angel clapped her hands. The sound startled us all. One of our guards came out to the edge of the woods to see if everything was all right. Once Angel had our attention, she stuck her hands out in front of her and walked around as if she were carrying a four hundred pound baby.

I asked, "Do you need someone to help you carry the swords back?"

She clapped her hands one more time and then nodded her head with no small amount of energy.

I looked over at my sister. "Let's get some people out of bed."

* * * * *

I waited alone in the field, save for my wolf and mount. I had all I cared to own on my horse's back. At my left hip was a shield. Two knives were within easy reach in my belt. The sword I craved to hold was across my back. I had the only steel tipped spear among us, gripped so it stood up in my holder.

I felt as if nobody alive in the whole world could stand against me. My, wouldn't it solve all our problems if the enemy saw me one by one and took their turns. By sunup, we'd be finished with this.

Pritchan's tents were directly in front of me, no more than a hundred paces, if that. Many of them were camped in the field itself. Without a better moon, I knew myself to be virtually invisible to the enemy's weak eyes, though if it had been sunny, not a soul could have missed me. I had better eyes and ears than anybody, so I knew none better than myself to do the oversight in case something went poorly.

A mile behind, most of my women were ready as well, their things packed on their horses, but not so loaded that they couldn't drop some bundles and fight instead of run.

There I waited while Angel and two others infiltrated the enemy camp. I couldn't see them, but once I noticed the high grass parting to my left. That had been quite some time ago, I reflected as my horse snorted impatience. Perhaps he smelled Pritchan. I patted him on his neck and whispered a lullaby into his mind.

Again, to my left I saw the tall grass sweep out of time with the breeze. I was amazed I'd not heard more than the slight movement of the guards yet. I'd come to offer myself as distraction, should the three brave women be discovered. They didn't even bring their horses. A mile is a great distance to run bearing swords and daggers, and with armed men at their heels.

Then, just to my left, Angel stood up. She waved at me. When she saw my dark shape turn, she leapt for joy. She seemed a childish bundle of happiness. I made a sour face at her, which she couldn't see, and waved her to run back to our camp before she was discovered. This startled her, causing her to fall to the grass. Steel hitting steel told of her swift movements. I felt certain she'd wake half the camp. With great relief I watched the grass and weed stalks shift along, telling me she and the other two were making some headway below the slightly more distant stalks. At least two of them had more sense than to celebrate while a stone's throw from the enemy soldiers. Then, near mid-field, they stood and ran.

After a fair wait, I turned and slowly rode back across the field. Sergeant Hadarm met me well short of our woods.

He said, "I don't believe what they've brought back. That crazy girl of yours brought in nine swords and a bag full of knives. She's back there handing them out to her squad like the solstice fairy. No wonder her village sold her to us; she might be the most vile thief in all of Farstand."

"Unbelievable, but Goddess sent," I said to him.

"As I said. So, which is it to be? Would you have us move these women out of here? Perhaps the theft of a quarter of their steel is enough to persuade them to be cautious? A more deliberate attitude from them doesn't serve us well in a fight, but a hesitant enemy is perfect for running."

I laughed. "Barker will talk to his God and his God will scoff at the idea of piddling about with such obvious signs of near success. I can see him rushing across this field like the rising sun. It doesn't matter if a man is without his sword if he can murder you just as easily with his lance. I'd wished for twenty swords, though expected two, and marvel at the effort to get our nine."

"Fine then. Perhaps you're right. Still, we risk much with our archers out there alone. They could be cut to pieces. Archers make decent rear guard. Pity to lose them."

"And my sister," I said in agreement. With his reminder of our stakes freshly renewed, I turned my horse and soon found myself right back where I'd been while doing oversight. I was in better spirits this time though, knowing we'd had half a success and that my role in the other half was going to be more personal.

I yelled, "Captain Barker! Are you still sleeping, or have you risen early to call upon Sho and ask him where you might find me?"

There was movement to both the right and left in the field. These were the newly alerted sentries, I assumed, though they'd moved back a step or two and not towards me. Soon the soldiers who'd camped in the field came out of their tents, and some of those in the trees followed. I laughed when so many of them appeared confused and always looking around themselves as if unable to find something precious among their possessions.

"Ah, so there you are," said a voice. I found Sir Pritchan's shape when he stepped out of the trees. A proper sword dangled from his belt, though he'd only had time for his britches and boots. All of them were still a good seventy yards in front of me, but they now knew where to look and some had eyes good enough to eventually find my dark silhouette.

"Sir Pritchan. Delighted to meet you again, but didn't I tell you I intended to keep an appointment with you and the baron in Helfax? Don't mistrust my word, for though I'm a liar, I can't lie about something so dear and sacred to my heart."

"If so, then why do we find you raiding in a direction decidedly away from the baron's city?" I could see him waving and nodding to his soldiers, all of them apparently thinking I could see no better than they. More men arrived, even as some fell to their knees below the level of the tall grasses.

Over to my right, I sensed a few soldiers crawling closer in the weeds and grass. Some thought to surprise me. My attention was certainly diverted, so it might have worked had I not had my good nose and eyes, as well as those shared by my friend Yellow Eyes.

"Would you see to that for me, my friend?" I asked my wolf. He trampled off in the direction of the guards sneaking toward my right.

I said more forcefully, "Only a small side trip for supplies, Ser. Helfax is a certain visit in my near future, for I know the cowardly baron has stolen my mother. Is the witch finder, Captain Barker, among you? I seem to smell the odor of White Shirts, the evil killers of old and harmless women."

"Yes, and it seems true that he can lead me to you. Now, I have had a great and terrible time tracking you down, given you've wandered to raid so many fine noble holdings. Surrender, and we'll give you the same offer as before. You can repent and be blessed before meeting God in the afterlife," Sir Pritchan said.

"Oh, goodness. I'd completely forgotten about that. It was a good offer, one that would end so many of my current miseries, but I hope instead to make a better offer to you, Sir Pritchan."

"Any offer from a witch is an offer of deceit!" a familiar voice said.

"So nice you could join us, Sir Barker. Was your time with your woman as pleasurable as I promised?" He came out of the woods, also strapping on a sword. It was good that Angel hadn't fleeced these two. Some chores I yearned to do myself.

"My woman is my business. I also notice you didn't answer my accusation. Is there not deceit in your intentions? Will you put us all to sleep, claiming it lasting? Well, it won't work this time. I know witch-magic to be least effective on the devout and short lived upon the holy," Barker said.

"Sir Pritchan, you should listen closely to the captain. He's more right than wrong on most occasions, including this one. And yes, again I do come before you bearing a great and mighty lie. Perhaps he's right; perhaps I am a witch and can't help myself."

Just then one of the men flanking to my right stood up and spun around. He twirled in a circle, looking into the grasses. The man tossed his spear into the weeds, and after having disarmed himself with a poor throw, ran for the cover of the men lined up nearer the trees. Yellow Eyes paid him no attention, circling around some more, spooking his fellows. They didn't run but were making no headway at all because of his torments.

"Did you see that man, Sir Pritchan? He must have seen my vipers. Don't you know all witches have command of the serpents? It was the serpent who gave one of us the very first pear, you see. Sir Barker knows much about these things and can explain it to you better than I, for I'm just a woman and deep thoughts about the myths of men don't suit me, I've been told."

I noticed that, over to my right, the tops of the weeds and grasses were shifting again, this time back towards the wood-line. Suspicious signs of wolves were one thing – snakes yet another.

The nobles didn't answer, which meant they were plotting, so I had to give myself some time, fibbing, "I didn't come here to fight, but to negotiate the field. We are angry and dissatisfied women. We hope to fight you on this battlefield in the late morning, when the sun is well up and near noon. If you have any courage in you, you'll wait and meet our challenge when we present our lines to you."

"I'll make you an offer in return, Abi," said Sir Pritchan. "Surrender the women you've deceived and we'll spare their lives and even see they are tended as good slaves under the guidance of a benevolent master in a foreign land."

"As is more than decent, given their taint," added Sir Barker.

Pritchan had a desire to be thought of as a statesman, I'd long come to think. Barker, on the other hand, had seemingly lost what little understanding we'd fostered together during the last campaign.

I had to brag. "Don't you know I have five hundred sisters, all of them well armed and born on their warhorses? When we practice, I am oft unable to earn a decent stroke with the wooden broadsword."

"We have tracked you long and hard and seen the destruction of your feeble banditry. You have ten to a score at best, all without good arms, and, if you choose to lead these worthless women to their deaths in the morning, then so be it, but it belittles us all to listen to your sinful lies," said Sir Barker.

"Would you dare face twenty women such as me? I have never

lied to you about one thing, Sir Barker. I can fight, and you've seen it."

This drew no response, for there was a distraction to their rear. I heard shouting and the sound of tree limbs snapping, mixed in with the rush of hooves.

I said, "I thought not, for you are cowards in your souls, and I am Abi, Shaman Princess, warlord, and Debrecian by birth. There is no fear within me, but now I invite you all to listen to the quickening of your own hearts, save Sir Pritchan and Sir Barker, who shall sleep for me and the Goddess, short though the nap may be." I twirled my hand in the air and said the magic words, *"Tpunwvw Own"*

I lowered my spear. Kicking Sir Pritchan's great black stallion, I drove forward towards the line of men even as Sir Pritchan fell and Sir Barker staggered.

My head swam as well, for they were men of the God Sho, pulling much from my magic. I'd tried hard to limit the power of my spell, but I knew little about how the Goddess's blessings worked. I managed to charge on, right up to the point where I broke to the left and rode over a man crawling in the weeds. He screamed, causing many of his fellows to rush to his aid and toss spears behind my path.

My horse and I rolled out of that, and then we headed back into the middle of the field. I looked back at the confusion. Nobody was giving orders, and yet a good score of men were in the field where I'd attacked the left. A few others attended to Pritchan and Barker. Still, and far more importantly, a trickle fell back into the woods, running towards their own horse lines. That alone displeased me.

Then, in the distance to my right, a woman on a horse burst out of the trees. Behind her trailed a leader attached to six horses. That wasn't all, for behind her came another woman, she leading a string of five -- then another with three, and another, until I counted over a score of horses racing across the great meadow and towards our lines. After that was a longer wait, after which twelve archers on horses burst out of the same trees. I picked out my sister, telling her figure from the way she rode. She rode one way, but shot her arrows in the opposite, aiming for something in the trees. None of my women could shoot while running, but to Batya it seemed as natural as walking.

I rode off to join her. When I was halfway, four men on horseback burst forth from the woods, explaining what she'd been shooting at.

I yelled at her, "Keep running. Look after your archers," as I raced past, toward the four men on horseback.

They had swords and spears, but apparently hadn't had time to strap on saddles. Thus they couldn't turn quickly and were awkward with their weapons as I rode my horse right at the flank of the very first man. My spear was wasted through that man's chest. I couldn't help but lose it. I reached over my back for my sword, and raised my shield up with the same hand that held my reins. Then I was on the next man, whose lance bounced hard against my shield and sent me cantering too far away to get in a good swing.

I had to turn, and did so just in time to see Yellow Eyes leap on a man and drive him off his horse. That spooked his animal. It started running back the way it had come.

The man who'd been impaled by my lance fell over. Then his horse slowed to a standstill. I noticed Yellow Eyes had the sense to ignore the man he'd knocked down and find cover in different weeds. This saved my wolf from the momentary attention of one of the remaining two horsemen.

I rushed up to another enemy as he pulled hard on his horse's mane. His turning proved convenient, allowing me to jab his horse's hip. The stricken horse screamed as I attacked the last man. He was busy trying to pick up the man who'd fallen from his horse.

The last horseman dropped the man he'd started helping up and drew his sword. Our swords crossed with a mighty clang, but I had the speed and angle. My horse nudged the head of his. That turned them enough for me to get in a second swing. That too clanged, but I was in good position to bring the edge of my shield across and push him off balance. As he fell I slid my sword across his middle.

He screamed, landing in the field alongside his fellow.

That was enough, I thought, for others were likely to come if I remained as bait. I grabbed the leader on the horse I'd just attacked and took off with it in tow.

My horse hadn't taken ten strides before I passed my sister. She'd circled back just that quickly and stood high in her stirrups with an arrow in her bow. As I passed, she shot two arrows toward the three men still alive. I heard one sharp yell.

She quickly turned and joined me in our flight across the field. Neither of us bothered to look back.

As soon as we got to our end of the field, I had Sergeant Hadarm lead a score of guards and ten archers to make a picket against any foolish pursuit. When barely into the woods, I counted our winnings. We'd lost one archer, but killed at least four of the enemy. We had half his horses and a good handful of his weapons. This meant half of them would be on foot and the others in need of reorganization.

As we took measure, our picket caught five of Sir Pritchan's scouts rushing towards us. A good volley of arrows dissuaded them, sending them back with the likely report that we held somewhat better strength than previously imagined, though many of us were within the wood-line, disallowing them an even larger count.

We remained on our horses as we counted the new odds against us, for my decisions were coming quickly. If I dismounted, I'd be the only one on my feet.

My sister was excited from being in the raid and from throwing back Sir Pritchan's scouts. She said, "This number we can fight. Even your old sergeant can see it."

"No," I told her. "This number we can run from, particularly with so many fresh horses. That way, if they're foolish enough to come for us, they'll not have their newly demoted footmen at all. Pritchan will wait for us to meet him in the field. That will give us even more time. Then he'll have to contemplate leaving half his men. He'll have to argue with Barker over this. Barker's man will ask for all the good swords and all the remaining horses. Pritchan will hesitate to put all of his men on their feet in favor of a full score of mounted White Shirts, not wanting to give up on some credit for my capture. By the time they're done squabbling, which may never end, it'll be too late, and as I've said, with these few good horses, we're now faster than we were and will have no stragglers."

"Ah! I wish to kill them now, taking advantage of this confusion. Then we'll be done with it," said my sister.

The sky was turning grey, the first sign that the sun was close to the horizon. We could see one another more clearly. I reached over and touched her on the arm and said more gently, "As do I. But we can't. I have come to my decision. Listen to me. These women are not yet warriors. Imagine them as they might be after two more months of hard training, wearing leather, on horses with iron-tipped lances and even wielding swords in the worthy hands of women grown strong of arm. Imagine us meeting these men then! Don't you see that battle, my sister? If we come at them now, many of these women will die before they can become what I see in them. That would be a sin. But later, well, that will be something."

She bit her lip, but then she eased and looked over at the women lined up and waiting on their horses. Every one of their faces was eager to get at the men across the field.

I noticed her making just that observation, and it was then that I said, "Don't you see yourself in their eyes? Now, look at mine. They're the same as all the others. The only difference is I see a little farther than just across this meaningless field."

"Then we'll come back," said Batya. "I can't disobey you. Besides, you're right. Still, they've killed one of my archers. You must give the promise of returning, for the sake of my heart."

"Yes. And then, all the way to their keep."

I rode over to my sergeant and told him it was time to share out the spare horses and set the women to a well disciplined trot for the border. There was no longer a need to spread ourselves out into squads, or wander in raids left and right, for we'd roll over whatever came before us, and leave those who opposed us in our wake.

I watched until all my women left the camp. The last thing I did there was take a piece of paper out of my bags and pin it to a tree on the edge of the forest trail.

It read, I shall go and make ready, so I might soon meet your baron in Helfax. I signed it, Abi.

Chapter Eleven

Lone women in Farstand ate the grass in the fields like cattle. Many were widows of war. As we got closer to the border, there were scores of them living in front of burned out cottages. In last year's battles, their men had been conscripted, handed pikes, and slaughtered, sometimes all within the course of a single day. Many widows were cast off their holdings by greedy male relatives or taxing lords. They favored the crossroads where they begged the beggars.

These women looked up as we raided. They pleaded with anyone they thought might lift them to their feet. We couldn't stop, but instead only glanced at them as we rode by. Occasionally our council deigned to pick one up, and someone would grab an outstretched hand, lifting the poor soul onto a rump. These occasions, I later discovered, amounted to many times more than were within sight of my counting.

One trouble was finding them young enough and strong enough to hold onto our backs as we galloped the horses for an hour and then walked them another. It was a gauntlet, not of enemy, for we were too mighty to be opposed by any town guard, but mostly of guilt regarding those women we couldn't grab up instead of leaving them to their fate.

Thank the Goddess for the noble holdings we raced through, stealing food, blankets and, most importantly, enough horses to keep us all ahorse, though many were doubled up and nearly all were by the time we made the border at Redwater River. Whatever we thought useful for weapons, including the kitchen cutlery, was prized.

As a consequence of this run, it was a greatly confused crowd that crossed the ford and entered the lands of Lacellor. Most were glad Sir Barker and Sir Pritchan hadn't caught up. We looked more like refugees than a genuine guard of a great lady though. The last two hundred new members were starved and sickly women who'd yet to be tended by any form of healing, or even introduced to us. This taxed every experienced soldier I had, just to keep order amongst the mob until we literally fell from our horses' backs.

We all entered into a great slumber the minute we could no longer see the border's river at our backs. This fell upon us such that we didn't even know ourselves enough to post guards.

When I woke up, the place looked like a battlefield full of the dead; it seemed as if more than a few were wounded when they twitched in their sleep. Women sprawled everywhere, and without any order. Never had I seen us so ill prepared. None had even bothered to pitch a tent. Half the horses wandered about with their leads unhitched. Not ten of the animals were unpacked. If Sir Pritchan or Sir Barker, or anybody from either the King's or Sir Lacellor's camps had come upon us, we'd not have even been able to surrender, for it looked as if none of us could get up.

All the burned and abandoned cottages added to the illusion of poverty. War had made its mark on this place for two decades, scaring away all the people.

I found two women wearing the colors of Lettoir, and managed to get them to set us some kind of loose guard by at least resting out a ways toward the river. Then I started gathering up the horses myself and tying them into lines behind the deepest canopies. We'd accumulated nearly two hundred of the beasts, but all were hungry, saving me from having to chase them. By the time I was nearly done, some of the others in colors noticed me working. Watching me do everything apparently embarrassed them. They quickly helped by pulling down the packs.

Yellow Eyes walked into the camp and sneezed. The smell was worse than anything he'd ever smelled. Then he told me there was another pack around, and the leader didn't like him much. I told him to ask the leader to come speak with me if it came to trouble. That was such a little problem it refreshed me, restoring some of my resolve, for I knew the wolves in these parts.

When I was done with the horses I could catch, I determined it was also time to get people up and doing something before an army came along and did something else.

* * * * *

Batya was sent out right away with ten of her archers to retrace our steps and scout out the King's side of the river. We'd moved too fast to know the enemy's intentions and were in dire need of cattle, sheep, grains and fabric, all of which I intended to steal from the King rather than rob from Sir Lacellor's fiefdoms. It was a bold move. I hoped to catch them off guard at first, establish our herds and industry, and not need the raids so desperately thereafter.

On our side of the Redwater River, I put Marci in charge of husbandry. She took thirty of the most unlikely soldiers under her wing. These were put to mending fences or rope lines for our horses and hoped-for domestic animals in the abandoned border fields. This was no man's land, we slowly came to realize, and thus barren of the peasantry, which pleased us all. Being by the river, the fields were fertile, and I had an army to defend them, giving me an advantage the missing peasantry probably had not enjoyed.

Marci's women also sorted through our meager provisions, giving account. Five cooked continual meals in rows of large pots, while five more boiled every article of clothing, as well as employed bark and nuts to dye half of every outfit grey and the other half brown.

Several of these new women were pregnant, and some were found hiding toddlers and babes. This didn't make me happy at first, but then I noticed many of my soldiers playing among them at meals and by the campfires. The women smiled at them when they gave them the last bites of their rations. All these children came to us half-starved, making it impossible for me to eat as well, without finding one of them and giving a baby a bite just to see the infant happy. No doubt they ate better than any of the rest of us, but the way these children restored all our morale and made us more determined in our work was a greater blessing than any I'd seen even from the Goddess.

Minari endlessly inspected the rows of housing, most of which were little more than sticks leaned up against tree trunks to ward off the wind and a little of the rain. When she was done with that, she inspected the soldiers we were making. She ensured that each of them clipped her hair and was lice free, followed by seeing to their clothing by exchanging rags that had been freshly dyed for the faded ones on their backs. Any woman not training and found sitting about dirty was sent straight to the creek to both bathe and fetch wood or water. Minari's training as a maid in a great lady's house was perfect because the job had required great fastidiousness and tireless oversight.

We made twenty squads of new soldiers, eight to nine in number. Each was overseen by one who'd been a soldier for at least two weeks and observed at least a day or two of my training on the march. All these squads were rotated into the care of our sergeant. He engaged each in short-pike exercises to both build their muscles and body awareness. Training on the horses was more difficult; this took closer attention and squad-sized formations. He started with how to put a blanket on one of them. Then it was how to get up on top, and even how to not fall off, particularly if the horse was rider-shy or chose to actually move.

We formed eight squads from the better women. These showed they could sit on a horse and point their pikes in roughly the right direction, no small matter with their thin arms. All of these needed training, but I had them do it on their own because our sergeant was too busy setting twenty less experienced squads into decent riding order, which I insisted upon, even though we were short horses.

The following was the accounting of my older soldiers: Batya had ten of them out across the river, and considered nine more as part of her personal archers. I left these in reserve so she'd have fresh soldiers upon her return. I needed ten more to guard the camp and scout the area. Three squads made a screen out on our side of the river by making that land their quarters.

When all of this was counted, we only had a half company of barely decent soldiers left for the guard of Lady Lettoir and myself. Each of these two squads was led by a whore. The horse-soldiers didn't know it, nor would I ever tell them. Instead, I made it clear that it was a great honor to be led by women with nearly two months experience.

One of these squads was better equipped than any in my army.

Angel had given each of them at least two blades, some of them swords. These were the only swords among us. Thus it was natural for me to take both squads out into the woods and set them to chipping limbs to make practice swords. In two days time, I'd taught them enough to block or slide the enemy's first thrust away, saving themselves for at least a few seconds of battle, whereupon maybe somebody else would stab their opponent in the back. It was enough to inspire them and make them imagine themselves almost as blessed as Batya's archers. A steadily increasing number of women wore the practice swords across their backs, getting the feel of a real one's weight. They even sharpened them, imagining them metal.

I had them take the wooden swords off on the fourth day and give them to another squad in need of similar practice. A week passed, after which I stole six of Batya's archers. Thus it came to be that the lady and I rode towards Lacellor's castle with six archers, five women wearing swords and wooden spears, as well as five more with only spears.

I need also mention Angel. I couldn't make her stop her endless smiling upon realizing she was a soldier assigned to my side. Neither could any person on this earth keep her from following me to Lacellor, so telling her to come along had not been spoken.

I insisted on the best horses, all wearing saddles and blankets. We were grey, brown and clean, as well as stiff from recent training. We were not soldiers yet, but these women were all proud to be something other than what the world wanted to make of them, so few we passed noticed our lacking skill by appearance.

What they did notice was our sex. The villages on this side of Redwater River looked little different from the ones on the King's side. Men stood on the edges of the roadway, pointing and debating us. Others openly laughed. Once I stopped and stared at a drunk until he fell into the gutter, but as always the lady was at my elbow, telling me it wouldn't be diplomatic to murder the peasants even before I'd been introduced to their great and rebellious lord.

It was with a raging soul and non-diplomatic demeanor that I entered Norfaton, the city of Lacellor. These people were used to armies, but not us. Here it was worse than in the towns, as they jeered and gestured close enough to touch. As we got near the keep, the roads became crowded by houses and the guilds. Soldiers lined the roadway, mostly near inns and places of entertainment. Some came close, as if to threaten us. They did not know our colors and rudely asked.

One captain insisted as he stood in our path. He said he'd not let us pass without some details. I showed him the detail that mattered by pulling out my sword and resting it across my pommel.

"Brave Ser, we intend to introduce ourselves only to the great Lord Lacellor," I said. "We will do this by riding calmly up to his castle, or we will do this by cleaving ourselves a path. I have much to do, and have no time." Behind me were six archers in two lines, each of them with an arrow nocked and loosely aimed toward each side of the roadway. I had no idea what Angel was doing, but I could see many thin reflections of sunlight bouncing off the panes in the storefronts.

He swallowed, and maybe decided I couldn't be reasoned with. He asked the better dressed woman beside me, "Do you come to us with peaceful intentions, my Lady?"

"Oh surely," Lady Lettoir said. "And, do not be hardened by my captain's rudeness. You see, this woman is a Debrecian and thus short on patience, no matter how much I have tried to teach her better manners. Such people are good in a fight though, as I'm sure you know, and thus I wouldn't be without her. She is the best with a sword I have ever seen, and much deserving of her station. I can assure you reasonable behavior from her, as well as her sincere apology if you will escort us to the great lord so we may pledge our allegiance."

She leaned over, as if telling the man a secret. "Her mood and our condition can be attributed to months travel and no few skirmishes." She brushed off her ruined skirt as if further explaining.

That apology part didn't suit me, but I put my sword away.

"Ah, so you are foreigners come to join our struggle? And the awaited Debrecians as well—"

"Not all, just the one, though she seeks help in training these others to her standard," interrupted the lady.

"Ah, that explains it all then, and tells me why these foreign women are armed and on horses, I suppose. Let me find my mount and have some of my men clear the path for you, Lady...."

"Lettoir. And you, kind ser?"

"Sir Finley, my Lady. I am honored to serve a woman of true character, and I—"

"The honor is mine, kind ser. Lettoir is a distant manor, with few as kind or noble as you in attendance, so you see I mean it when I tell you I feel honored. In any event, I have been deposed from these lands because of some unfortunate alliances favoring Sir Lacellor, and been put into even rougher circumstance by making the cut cleanly. Still, I bring some guards and two hundred horses to the great knight's aid, come what may of it. I fear I have nothing beyond that but trust."

"Lady Lettoir, lands or not, your nobility and beauty any man can see. I, Sir Finley, am at your disposal." He bowed his head slightly.

The man finished with the formalities and mounted his horse. A rude crowd had formed around us during the discussion, and it was with some hesitation that I put my anger behind me and followed the man. Several other soldiers came up as escort, seeming to me more like guards, though if they thought themselves such, they weren't enough.

Every so often Sir Finley looked back at the lady, glancing at her bodice and legs. I'd been so long in the saddle that I'd not even thought about the fact that none of us rode sidesaddle or that we'd all split our skirts. Some of us had outright tailored our skirts into britches. Finally, small cloths had long been abandoned, and with it, the rest of our modesty.

Just to spite them, I hitched my britches up to the knees, giving them all a fair look at my many bruises.

Oddly, Sir Finley didn't notice I was showing more skin than a bar maid short her evening tips; he was still glancing back at the lady. I looked at her, and saw something on her face that got me saying, "Oh, for Goddess sake, just go up and ride with the man."

She looked at me nervously and then collected herself. "It wouldn't be proper. We've not had formal introductions."

"You must be pulling my leg. What was all that back there?"

"It was informal, and there was nobody to speak for me."

"That's ridiculous. How are you to get on? You have no kin in these parts, and other than Finley, no friends either," I told her as we found a main boulevard and could finally see the castle in the distance.

The lady spoke: "Then some higher lord, perhaps at the insistence of his lady. Sometimes the king or a baron, as was in my case, will make a suggestion. That's how most are betrothed in our rank."

Finley looked back, too far ahead to hear our discussion, but he saw our eyes on him. The lady smiled as if she'd not even been speaking to me.

"Being a noble is for idiots," I had to say.

"Then you shall be in good company, soon enough, and be judged through the same glass as well." She dropped her smile the second the man looked away because he had to avoid running his horse into some women crossing the street.

"Oh no, not me. I know what you're saying. Don't confuse me for a noble."

"Really now? Whose army do you think I claim as my guard? Do you imagine it is mine? Oh, surely I'll play my part, but there is no denying who it is Angel defends with her knives. There is no end to the wonder in Batya's eyes when you as much as suggest a new technique for teaching those with pikes. And these archers, though they've been given over to your sister, well, did you miss how quickly they jumped to join you on this trip? They all volunteered, and those left behind grumbled. No, this isn't my army, Lady Abi. You've loaned them to me for this occasion, only so I might also lend them my name before Lacellor. And, when you finally make them into decent warriors, the ruse we play will be both redundant and well into the open. Do you forget I am in your council, not you in mine? Also, I am not the last to learn your title of shaman carries with it the title of Princess. A princess is no small noble in any land, regardless of how loosely akin."

"You should be the princess. You play yourself too small. Of all the nobles I've met, none are more worthy nor are any as kind. The men of Lettoir were lacking legends as fighters only because of their numbers and the jealousy of your lessers. This was much to your credit."

"Ah, and thus the need to find a good husband before I've none under me regarding which I can pretend to be benevolent and wise," she agreed, though it sounded like something else to my ears.

However, two can play the tedious game, I decided. I yelled forward, "Sir Finley. May I make the formal introduction of Lady Lettoir. It seems I was rash upon the occasion of our first meeting, and neglected the duty. I'll not have it go unattended, nor said that she had to speak for herself due to any deficiency, for she has none in my eyes, nor in the eyes of any who can properly see."

He turned his horse, allowing the few paces to close. When we came abreast, he said, "No harm came of it. I have to at least admire your sense of duty to your mistress, Captain." I could sense the word captain was hard on his tongue, but also that he was trying to make a gesture.

I said, "I thank you, Ser. Now, if you will escort her more closely, even better. I have the need to inspect my soldiers as we march closer to the castle. We're not much in appearance, but it serves us all to do our best with what we have."

"Quite true." Sir Finley's words sounded brighter.

Just as I turned my horse, I had to add, "Oh, and incidentally, I'll be the one determining when I'll make my apology. Let us save it for the battlefield, where there I shall apologize by slaying the men besetting you and your fellows."

He watched me leave and, when I was well away, I could hear him laugh. Apparently he'd thought I'd stated a joke. Perhaps it was a joke; I'd not yet determined if I wished to join Lacellor all the way to a battle. He did tend to lose a lot of footmen, and I'd not yet seen him fight light cavalry, nor had I seen any women in his ranks beyond the much promised and even more absent Debrecians.

We came to the castle where we were told to wait. As soon as the captain turned to cross the bridge, I tended my soldiers. One was sent with three silvers to secure an inn. Another pair was put in charge of our long list of needs at the local clothier and markets. Wagons filled with goods needed to be purchased with our raiding money, no small investment. Others were detailed to find the names and situations of all blacksmiths and their apprentices. The time here was not to be wasted, for we were all aware of the condition of our camp.

Finley came out to tell us we should find an inn for the night because the affairs of court were many and the chamberlain had no spare room on his schedule. I smiled at him. "We have already done so. As to chamberlains, I have determined that whatever one of them does, it's worth my while to do the opposite."

I retained Angel and one of the archers. Together with the lady, we marched across the drawbridge. Finley protested in favor of prudence, but he'd been half cowed by the lady, and was the other half cowed by one look from Angel.

"Maybe it is best if we . . ." the lady started to say, but, by the time she'd gotten that far, she realized it was a waste of breath. Even the guards at the gate were confused, seeing the captain and the Lady and then the way I told them with my eyes that I wasn't in the mood for any nonsense; indeed, they'd better be sure they knew what they were doing before they made a big mistake and got some noble angry.

We managed our own way up the stairs and directly into the grand chambers where, sure enough, there was a session of court in progress. One of the pretty guards, thinking I needed suggestions, stepped forward, but I brushed past him and then so too did Angel, and then the nobles. That is how we all passed him, right up to the front of the audience. A knight sat before us. He was only a little older than a boy, a few years older than I, though his forehead was wrinkled, body thin and attitude tense upon seeing our interruption.

He had an unruly shock of brown hair, pageboy length, but wore the breastplate of a ruler, perhaps so they might recognize him among his more stout fellows. The further down you went, the more practical the lords dressed, ending in wool britches tucked into a pair of thick black boots.

I nudged a pair of pleading merchants aside. Somewhere behind us a guard banged his pike on the floor, which we heard even over the shouts and chatter of the audience.

"What is the meaning of this!" yelled a wide man holding a book of records.

"Are you the chamberlain?" I shouted.

"I am, and I note your party is not on my ledger."

"The last chamberlain I encountered was also an idiot. I spent the better part of a year wishing I'd killed him the moment we met." After that, the audience murmured but at last grew silent.

That's when I realized the Lady and Sir Finley were bowing. I glanced around, nodding for my archer to keep her head up.

Angel seemed to be enjoying herself as she looked around at the statuary. One in the corner particularly caught my eye. It was a woman cut from wood, but painted regally. She had a leaf in two fingers of her right hand. She seemed bound in the wood and I didn't think her nearly as handsome as statues I'd seen in the duke's castle, but the artistry was still fun to look at.

I asked, "Would that one be the Goddess?" But nobody answered.

I was too busy to enquire further, having to reach down to the Lady and pulled her up to her feet. I told her in a clear voice, so all could hear, "From my experience, when speaking to the floor, even the gods sound like fools."

Her face reddened, and I don't think I'd ever seen anyone nod to nobles, as deeply as she did at that moment, and still be standing. I suppose I was embarrassing her. I sighed in exasperation.

Just then the boy stood. I realized he was older than he first appeared. Perhaps his many troubles played a role in aging him oddly.

Beside Lord Lacellor were much bigger men, including Sir Drake. His face was much easier to read. Only protocol stayed his hand on his sword; protocol being such that it was. Farther along the front were several other knights. I thought it a waste, thinking back to how much work my one sergeant had to do and how much help these men might be if put to the honest work.

The boy said, "At the risk of setting my knights upon you for rudeness, I suppose I should ask your intentions before my court?"

I realized I'd accidentally presented us poorly, and thus I had to drudge the image of the great Debrecian ambassador, Beckli Kahnsa, up in my head before I said anything terrible.

"Ser, I thank you. We have a pressing need or we wouldn't have bothered you. Since I am better with my sword than my tongue, I'll not delay introducing Lady Lettoir. No kinder lady can be found in all the land of Farstand."

"I do not recall the name, Lady Lettoir," said Sir Lacellor.

She cleared her throat. "This has not gone as we intended. Perhaps another time will be more appropriate, kind Ser."

"Oh no. Nothing has happened this exciting in this court in some while. Please continue, Lady."

"I thank you, your grace. To begin with, I apologize for my captain. She is a Debrecian, and, of course . . . ah, endlessly I must apologize for her. Yes, it seems I must say this everywhere we go."

The people surrounding us found that funny and interrupted with some laughter.

The lady waited patiently, but then continued, "But, she is the best with a sword I have ever seen, and is magical with her soldiers to the point where anybody who has her under wing would be a fool to part with her services. As you might have noticed by how solidly she applied us before you, Lord Lacellor."

This too the court found amusing. I shrugged, not finding much amusing.

"I see." Sir Lacellor said. "And what of the woman with the knives? She seems most threatening still and not the least bit professional."

"Oh, that would be Angel. She is an amazing thief of enemy wares. When she first came to us, she was full of evil spirits, spitting and swearing at all who came within range. Our princess cleaned her soul and claims her service. Since, she has not sinned, nor spoken a word."

Some mumbled words. I didn't feel comfortable telling these strangers tales of my magic, and so I gave the lady a glance.

"Who might be this princess?"

"My Captain, my Lord. Abi is a servant of the Goddess, and from what I have learned, been tested and judged a Princess of the shaman blood. She holds magic in the eyes of some from her tribe, I'm told. Shaman is an honored title bestowed upon Debrecians who are found to possess the spirit of a great shaman warlord. The details are vague to me beyond that, for I confess confusion regarding the gods. I am led to believe there are those among you who know more than I about the Debrecians and their many princess titles."

"I see," said Lacellor, seemingly not impressed. A knight came over to him and whispered into his ear. Lacellor looked over at me and then returned his gaze to the lady. "We shall save this for later. What is your purpose before this court, Lady Lettoir?"

"I came to place myself before the great knight, for I too have been shunned by our neighbors without good reason. Also, I have come with three hundred refugee women who sought my party's protection. They are camped just this side of the border, and their provisioning is beyond our means. Still, they do not come begging. Some homestead the spoiled border lands. Others already fight as raiders across the Redwater. We hand picked them all with an eye towards making soldiers of them, imagining an army of light cavalry made solely of womenfolk."

The crowd laughed with abandon.

My voice was not as sing-song as the lady's when I shouted, "When I crossed the river, I thought it was to a better land where women could be free. Do not mistakenly think women cannot fight. And we will do so without the useless armor of knights. Be it known that in the last war, my cavalry struck down six hundred of your foot in the battle of the crossing, and they were no more than a score of light." I had to stop myself from saying more. At least the laughing died.

"Is this true, Captain? Tell me what you saw of it," the rebel lord asked.

"Our colors were the lady's, dark grey and brown. We rode with the hated white guards—not by choice. When we were asked to stand under your arrows, I was made to watch my sergeant die. I could no longer tolerate the waste. We rode forward, cleaving at the edges of your left-most block. Soon the battle was lost to the duke's forces, but so too were a quarter of your footmen, denying you the ability to follow up at the duke's castle in Dorne. You may ask the handful I let depart that field, for they will swear a woman in the colors of Lettoir defeated thirty times their number, bearing little more than small arms."

"And, what will you do with our help? Do you intend to murder more of my forces?"

I remembered Beckli again, and turned so the crowd could see me. "I will take my women to Helfax and kill the fat baron who has insulted us both."

"There are many barons in Farstand, Captain. Why this one?" asked a man standing a few faces off from Lacellor.

I looked at the man who'd spoken. "The Goddess has chosen Helfax, Sir Drake. As well, she has commanded that I bring an army, but it would please me no-end to murder them all by myself."

"Why would this Goddess wish that a handful of women on horses do this impossible thing?" Sir Drake persisted.

"I didn't ask her. All I asked of her was to assist me in finding the Queen. For this it seems we must go to Helfax and rescue my mother."

Sir Drake turned his great and beautiful body. He looked at his lord and said, "You see what this is, don't you? This is a woman who wants to rescue her mother, plain and simple. My guess is she has lied about her part in the crossing, lied about her ability to create this force, and even lied about the Goddess speaking to her. If she's a princess, I'll eat my chain-mail."

I felt the nerves in my hand wishing to grasp my sword, but then my hand thought better of it. "Ask your wounded shoulders if I'm a liar about my skill, Sir Drake. I trust they've healed, and if not, I shall do so for you in person when we're done, though I think I'll use slow herbs and not trouble the Goddess with any of her magic."

"Ah, even there you've been found out. The woman I fought was different. You bear only passing resemblance. She was taller and even had a longer sword. Still, it's good you're not the same woman, for the one I fought was known to be a traitor and a coward. I should have just hanged her," Sir Drake said.

The lady smelled the tension and broke between us. "This is not about my captain. We have women with babies, and horses with no shoes. While we practice with wooden swords and no shelter, we have the dreaded White Shirts and agents of the King seeking our destruction. We don't ask for much beyond the things we need for our immediate self-protection, and in so doing will grow strong and support the general rebellion."

"Which one of you is the captain, which the princess and which the lord?" scoffed Sir Drake.

"Can you speak more kindly to the lady? Your manners say I should hate you, but instead I find you appealing, so I'll only ask."

"So you see, it's about common desire after all," said Sir Drake.

"Ah, Sir Drake, yes, you are beautiful to my eyes, I do confess this. As for passion, I'm yet a virgin, against all odds, and though I have longed, I've been too busy to miss it as much as a good woman should. The only thing I truly miss is fear. It should be apparent what these two things had made of me, and if not, you shall soon see."

"No," he said, "for, I do not know you and suspect you a liar with a mouth full of pretty speeches.

"Then you see me as a coward still? Must we again duel to see one another better?"

Sir Lacellor interrupted, "There will be no fighting here. Coward or not, I judge Lady Lettoir's intentions true, at least to our cause. However, light horsemen are of little use to us, save as messengers and diversion."

"Help or not, I'll prove otherwise." Then I spied the big bearded knight with the huge axe. I couldn't help but remember him fondly. Our eyes met, and I smiled when I recalled our last meeting.

"For the gods, I know you," shouted the man. "You killed my horse!"

I said, "Now here is a steady man with an axe!"

Lord Lacellor put up his hand, stilling the ensuing uproar. "I see we shall have to take this up in private. It has dwindled into idle boast. Come lady, and without your captain, to my private war room. You and my trusted circle shall consult regarding the services you might render the revolt. Don't expect much in return, for your captain has already tried my patience. I put it off to Debrecian heritage, for we all know them to be difficult women; for us, saying much and doing little."

I started to say something, but the lady put her hand in front of my face and I decided to not bite it off. Instead she accepted graciously, and the rest of us were not so politely asked to leave the keep.

Before I did, I looked back to the statue and found the female God was no longer holding the leaf. Instead she had her right hand over her heart. I didn't know what the lady God meant by that, or even if the statue was the Goddess, but I knew the missing leaf was peace, and the heart was passion. Both seemed distant to me at the time.

Leaving the place was fine enough with me. I hated keeps, and was looking forward to the inn. I'd never slept inside of one before, but had heard it was a pleasure.

Chapter Twelve

It was a long two days of worry over Lady Lettoir's negotiations that drove me before the grandest mirror I'd ever seen. I glared at myself in a tailor shop where I also discovered the finest cloth imaginable.

In spite of the splendor, my mind wasn't with me in the mirror. The lady had sent word only once and only minutes after I'd left. She'd quickly jotted that negotiations were ongoing, which I suppose meant the nobles in the castle were socializing and that she imagined them falling under her charm. Goddess knows I didn't like the wait.

Well, that was what I guessed was going on, given that, if any serious aid born of quick and sound thinking was to be forthcoming, it would have happened already. Thereafter came two days of nothing—nothing two more days of my mother suffering in a dungeon.

Instead of relying on the unknowable, I'd already come to the conclusion that all things worth having were had by the works of one's own hands.

On the very first day, I'd put the archers to work buying five quality dresses suitable for well married merchant wives. While still fastening buttons, the five of us roamed the city, looking nearly normal.

Over that time we spent most of my stolen money on things needed in order to build an army from the very ground. By ground I mean iron, wool, linen, nails, saws and seeds, all intended to amplify the value of our silver through our own industry. These goods were bound up by our other soldiers and put into the wagons we purchased.

An idea struck me that all I needed was to find eating parlors close to the guilds whose services I coveted, and there ask for the names of apprentices who'd not quite satisfied their masters. We paid cheaply for the names, a bared ankle or filled cup. This is how we found a pair of young men who had been cast out from the blacksmith guild for charging too little and offending the master. We did the same thing when looking for carpenters, armorers, cordwainers, and a half dozen other skilled laborers.

In just two days time, I'd put together eleven masters. Here in Norfaton, they'd never see their names on any door and they knew it. I promised them two silvers per month, and after two years labor, the full rights to their own shops in a new town. No need to mention that the town was not yet built. This half truth inspired them to help us purchase the right supplies. With these things we filled a second and third wagon. All of this awaited departure.

With that moving along, I still had one more order of business. In order to fill this final need, I had to dress in the finest clothing available. That's what I was looking at in the mirror. It was bright yellow with even lighter yellow flowers embroidered in swirls all the way to the bottom. The neck was lace, as were the wrists and a fringe at my feet. The material floated over several petticoats. They'd tried to add a little hat that tied under my chin, but it was too much. Everything was so expensive that the guilt-ridden owner of the clothier insisted upon adding powdering for my face, pink for my cheeks and red for my lips. I tasted olive oil and rose hips.

Before me in the mirror stood a lady I felt sure Sir Drake would never recognize. Then there'd be three of me he could say he'd never met. Was my face so lacking it wasn't even memorable? I thought it a good thing he'd never seen me as Abe, or there'd be no end to his confusion. Mostly though, there seemed nothing of me in his head. Each time he'd seen me, he'd only imagined someone worth sticking with his sword.

I puckered my lips, thinking them perhaps too full. Or, maybe it was my nose that was wrong; I'd always thought it too tiny. Then again, I'd also known my cheeks were too flush. Even my eyes were too round and light green wasn't a popular color among the locals. The red and straw-colored hair was certainly an imperfection and implied a wild and foreign character. Well, that last part I wasn't too sure about, but clearly the other flaws were hard to overlook.

The archers behind me in the mirror, however, did their best to overlook the obvious defects. They nodded their heads in approval and slayed me with kindness. Angel even cast an extra-wide smile meant to set me at ease. I knew better, knowing myself no beauty, judging from the reaction men gave to my every word. Otherwise, why such overboard approval from the competition—were we women not always rivals in such matters, and thus inclined to tell each other the opposite. Such was only natural and not necessarily intended as wickedness.

I had to say, "This will never hem out to make a proper uniform."

That's all they let me say before the women surrounded my body and stole my money purse, paying the merchant every silver he asked without even bartering the dress down to a decent price.

Then they took me into an alley, and pulled loose my warrior's tail. Angel came at me with her knife and trimmed the bottom edges of my hair straight, while an archer wetted a comb and raked the other side of my head until my skull ached. Pretty and painted wooden pins were set above each ear, and the front locks were cut so my hair fanned across my eyebrows in a way that still allowed good vision. They'd soon gone too far and turned my red hair into silk. They claimed it needed a fine rose-oil sprinkle just to stay in place. I was thinking, if this is what it takes to be a lady, then I'm glad I was born naked and a peasant.

They put the strange, tiny and totally useless hat back on me and tied it neatly in place. A fat lily was pinned over my left breast, (My bosom had been bound up and featured the edge of a stoutly strapped small cloth that laced in the back). This caused the lily to rest at an angle, as if it didn't even need the pin to stay put unless I bent over. The women stood back, nodded and declared me done and no longer ugly.

Good thing I had my old boots on, or all of me would have felt ridiculous, but the many under coats were so wide I couldn't even see if my boots were fastened correctly or even if I had them on.

I'd never considered it before, but I became unsure how anybody wearing such an outfit managed in the privy. I determined to get on with it before the subject became important.

An archer nodded to the closed carriage driver we'd rented for the hour, and he got off to offer me his hand and help lift me up as though I'd been rendered crippled by the outfit. After having to hold up the dress in order to get into the back and also manage to close the tiny door without catching the skirts in the frame, I came to feel lame indeed.

Angel handed me my staff through the tiny door window with the black, rolled-up shade. The peasant weapon had been painted an insulting color of pink and only roughly had the look of a lady's cane, though also overly tall.

I thought, I could have bought half a horse for the pleasure of this ride, and then poked my head out and forced myself to say up to the driver, "To the keep, kind ser."

My small escort of women followed on foot, hoping, I assumed, to remain as close as possible so they'd be the first with news of my result.

All the guards nodded when I walked across the drawbridge. I wondered if they'd still be nodding like idiots if I had a hundred warrior women all come in, one after the other, each dressed just so? So much for the defenses if they were all Debrecians determined to raise a ruckus.

I even hailed a guard. He rushed through the hallways and stopped at attention. "Fine guard, would I be interrupting your duties by asking you to deliver this message to that new woman. What is her name? Oh, now I remember, Lady Lettoir."

He bowed, and upon looking at me overly long, seemed to lose his train of thought for a second while he studied my face. I felt sure I'd been found out, but then he said, "I would be delighted, my Lady. Do you wish to await a reply?"

"I will be out in the training yards, I think, enjoying the sun. Would you be so kind as to find me there when the lady sends a response?" He nodded. I wondered if noble ladies thanked common soldiers.

"Might I suggest the garden in the inner court, if you'll forgive my being so bold? The men are oft uncivil when they train."

"If they fail to charm me, I shall be in the garden. Else, I do wish to see if our men are ready to defend our honor against the evil might of Farstand. It troubles my dreams when I imagine them unready." I did my best to keep my eyes orbs and like those of an innocent fawn, reflecting the saying: "When ugly, at least make a presence." After all, there had to be some reason why my archers had decided to darken my eyebrows with charcoal.

"Ah, I understand, my Lady. Well, it will be an honor to devote myself to tendering your reply, and I will spare no effort in finding you wherever you may light, good Lady." He lowered his head and crossed his body with an arm.

Of course, he didn't move until time dragged out. I awkwardly nodded and walked off. The man had seemingly been struck stone with the look of me. I knew myself to be an odd girl. Being so tall, full of bosom and flame of hair, but I'd thought I'd cleaned up fairly well and wasn't such a poor sight that he had no other choice than rude gawking at my face and hem-covered boots.

Such wouldn't do, so I mouthed a small prayer to the Goddess for the gift of a more appealing look to my face and body. I hoped she'd see it for the necessity and not some silly plea appeasing vanity.

Next, I took a turn in the vast hallways and found myself nearly to the back exit. Just when I thought I'd made it, a young lady in a pink and black dress that nearly rivaled mine stepped out from a room. She saw me and stopped.

I was caught for sure, I thought, when she said, "Oh, no. Not another new one. Have you no men where you come from? Must you set upon ours, ruining it so none will ask for a hand until we are all past seventeen and well into our old maidenhood?"

I completely forgot myself once hearing the insult, telling her, "How rude. I'm not so ugly that I will turn your men against all of womanhood." Then I stormed off, as I suspect any decent woman would do after having to endure such criticism, regardless of situation. Worst of all, she was right about the danger, for I was as old a maiden as they came, well into my eighteenth year and without a single prospect, not to mention I had much to do before I could even indulge the consideration of finding somebody desperate enough to have me.

Just outside the back door, I had to pause. Here the air was better, and so I thought to look up into the sky and beg once again for the Goddess's intervention, lest my deception come to no good end. I even twirled my fingers into the air and tried to fashion my spell in a way consistent with those in my secret book of shaman rituals.

Soon, I felt sure my face flushed a little, and imagined a small blessing. It restored my faith enough to allow me to make my way down some back steps made of granite.

I walked up to a stone fence by a host of well-trimmed bushes and old oak trees. There I looked over at some of the nobles competing in their small shirts. It was winter, but the sun was high and the lowlands not particularly bitter. I confess I admired the view of sweating muscles and steel, even though the latter was stained wood. This was especially so since I no longer had to deal with the restrictions upon watching men that I'd felt while disguised as Abe. As a woman, I suppose I was allowed a gander.

At first they didn't see me, the axe man, Sir Drake and others, as they practiced with great intent. They employed wooden swords and other faux weapons, such as mace and a well carved axe. Oaths, grunts, moans and rude words issued between heavy breaths.

Then one of the younger men, who'd been knocked aside by the axe man's shoulder, turned his face towards mine. He paused. Pausing is not a good idea in battle. He got knocked across the head by the great wooden axe, even though the axe man was clearly trying to slow his swing as it came on surprisingly uncontested.

The axe man saw me too, and ceased an oath, regarding his friend's lacking attention, in mid-word. I'd murdered his horse, I recalled. His face went slack, and he ended up staring at my nose and eyes and every corner of my mouth, ending with a fixation on my overly large breasts. His stillness caused the rest of the yard to fill with eyes and a great slowing of the action. One inattentive man remained about his chore, thumping Sir Drake across the thigh with a sword. It had virtually no effect on the mighty warrior's muscles.

I twisted myself a half turn. This left me hidden behind one of the large oaks where nobody would be forced to look at me.

Instead, I faced the back wall of the keep. There, a story up, towered the high windows of the room where I'd pleaded our case two days earlier. I knew the wooden statue was there just beyond the wall. I counted the windows over. Instead of more block, there hovered the great wooden statue of the female God whose name I still didn't know. It hung in the air, an impossible feat. I guess the Goddess wanted to make sure she had my attention.

Her hand was still over her heart, the sign of passion. She even cast a shadow, as if to let me know the miracle wasn't my imagination.

I knew what she was thinking, and so I answered her thought with, "It's hard to feel such a thing as passion when one also feels so unlovely. Ah, it was a bad idea, this ruse. I'm much more comfortable as a soldier, where I'm expected to be hideous, which is often an advantage among the others. Can you help me? I can't win them over if I'm not greatly improved in appearance."

The statue laughed at me. She then said, "This is an issue of passion? The heart is not to be played with, my child. Such spells cannot be as easily undone as the one I blessed you with before when you joined Sho's army."

"You know I have given that god up, so do not tease. Now listen to me, my Goddess. I don't ask for love, but simply something closer to beauty."

"Twice already I have so blessed you, though never have you had need. Do you not know that you have always been most fair among maidens? Such added blessings might cast a glow that is uncommon."

"Well, my Goddess, clearly it is not enough, for all who see me in this dress look at me and cannot look away. Can you not see how I have turned so many of them to stone? Nothing could be plainer than they are aghast, and thus I have to insist on a further blessing and one in no small measure this time. Otherwise I'll not be appealing enough to trick them into playing to my tune." I added, "Please."

I heard her sigh. The wooden figure started shaking, and then gave off a straining creak, as if this sort of ordeal was harder on the gods than the slaughter and mayhem of war. Finally, the statue cracked completely. A split started in the wood, running from the square base of the statue's hem to just under the ample and half showing breasts. A few brown shavings fluttered out of the crease and into the breeze. The wooden statue disappeared back into the castle where it belonged.

Her violent sigh was still in the air. It turned into a wind that blew through the leafless oaks and well trimmed hedges. When it was done playing in the yard, the wind blew across my body, lifted my hem and flew the edges of my hair. I gasped, breathing the last of it in.

Such was clearly a sign, so with a little more confidence, I turned and showed myself to the men who had gone back to their task, seemingly not having heard or seen a bit of the mysterious conversation with the statue. I supposed they were intent upon not glancing in my direction either, unwilling to take a second glance at such an unusual woman.

They practiced in slow motion, as if teaching one another the proper angle of arms and legs and weapons. Sometimes that was useful; the crone and I had done just that on some of the harder lessons with my staff.

Then one of them looked at me and bowed slightly before going right back to the fighting. Others did as well. When this happened, each of the opponents followed the lead of the first so it looked more like a dance than a contest of blades. I soon realized they weren't actually teaching one another in slow motion, but were in fact just being lazy.

I assumed this was also a sign that I held sufficient allure, and thus was at last able to move forward with my plan. Then again, perhaps they acted this way in front of all the lady nobles, regardless of beauty, it being mostly an issue of politeness.

The big axe man thumped his opponent on the head again when the man with the sword chose the wrong moment to glance at me.

He said, "Sorry, good Ser. Here, let me show you how to better hold your sword in order to shield against such a blow from such a heavy and manly weapon as the axe. If you will be so kind?" He moved the man's arms around to put him into position for a demonstration of how the curve of the axe blade shouldn't be allowed to pull the sword blade into the hilt where a simple and effortless twist of the axe could unhand the other man's weapon.

That I didn't even know, so I found it interesting in ways that had me wanting to ask questions that were inappropriate.

"Oh good knight, you are mighty with that axe. Do you mind if I watch? I shall be no distraction," I said while moving over to the gate and finding my way into the much trampled practice yard. As I came, I made to slightly limp, explaining my pink and homely staff.

The bearded axe wielder said, "Why, I thank you, my Lady. I

should get you a cushion. Let me do this. I can send a squire, and it will be seen by all my fellows with jealousy."

"No need, it is a minor twist, and I see no need even for a proper cane, given it will be healed shortly. I thank you, nonetheless. I wish only to admire our warriors who have sacrificed so much for our noble cause."

All my time with Lady Lettoir had given me the seemingly foreign language I spoke, but never had I felt as much a liar, mostly because of the flowery and prissy lilt off my tongue.

But then again, I wasn't the only one speaking with an awkward dialect. Sir Drake's opponent managed to back up enough from the fake swordplay, ending up within conversation distance. It was a younger knight, perhaps only a few days from the station of squire, and so he naturally thought me his equal due to how the powder made my face seem near that of an infant.

He stopped, bowed, and caused Sir Drake to also have to quit. "I am the knight, Sir Allen Lindie. Would you grace me with your name, my Lady, for the gods have frowned and previously denied me introduction?"

I wasn't used to the attention, but collected my wits and answered well out my backside with, "Let there be some mystery, for I hear it customary to not give a lady's name until another speaks it for her. You might call me Lady A, if for no reason other than it eases conversation." Then I did a tiny curtsy, the first good one in my life.

"Then at dinner tonight I shall scout for any who might speak on your behalf, as I fear will many, though my heart insists that I be found true among them." The boy was handsome, though I didn't think him much of a sword match for Sir Drake, nor did I find his tender complexion to my liking.

I could see that only Daren Drake was not pleased with my complete disruption. He didn't exactly frown at me, but, judging from the way he probed his fellow knights with his eyes, I didn't have to be blind to see I was less than welcomed. I'd have felt the same way, were these men my three hundred barely-trained women. The thought fortified me.

"Have I offended you, fair knight?" I asked, Sir Drake.

He bowed. "I'm sorry if it shows, my Lady. It is a crime to offend your beauty, and I too wish to learn more about you, but I feel bound to better prepare these knights for battle, lest we come again upon the field with too few ready knights. As you can see, many of these are young, and have only recently been raised to the level of those worthy of a warhorse and better armor."

"Ah, that I did notice. Also, the lacking skill. Still, I meant you no intrusion, Sir Drake. My only intention was to see how things go."

"Do you know me, Lady A?" Sir Drake asked.

"Ah yes, great knight. I was different then, I suppose; when we last met, I mean."

"Yes, we all grow up, and in tender young women I always find the change surprising if much time has passed," Sir Drake said, showing some kindness at last.

"Yes, some little time has passed. Nor did you think much when looking upon me last. So many changes have occurred in our disposition that it startles a heart to imagine them all," I told him. Several of the men were looking at my bosom, but when I swept my eyes past, their faces rose and smiled.

The man with the axe huffed, but then smiled and said, "I am Sir Casar, my Lady. The lacking skill among the younger knights … well, I can assure you, it is mainly caused by fear of unsettling the lady's … person."

"Ah, then what about the others?"

"The others ma'am?" Sir Casar asked.

"It didn't seem that any of the fighting was really all that difficult, including yours. I've even imagined myself in some armor, trying my hand at fighting for the rights of our people and gods." I took my staff up in both hands and pretended to strike an enemy up and to the side.

Sir Casar said, "For that you would have need of a lady's sword. My grandmother had one made of silver and pearls. I will show it to you one day if you come to the lands of Gristle; even if you don't, and I can find you somewhere else."

Sir Drake said, "Else, if any man lends you as much as a wrist-cuff of armor, I shall slay him myself for offending the purity of women. No offense, my Lady, but to lose such beauty is beyond the will of any God." That interruption I'd not expected, causing me to look up at his face and forget my true intentions.

"Well then," Sir Casar said playfully, seeing something unspoken in the pause.

I said to Sir Drake, "When I was young, they allowed me out and not always bound by corsets and hats with no purpose other than to attract attention. I was a rowdy child, full of what the peasants call spit and bitter ale. I was often scolded for it. Since, I have gained some small measure of refinement, but am not fully cured. This perhaps explains why you can't remember me from the last times we'd met. Things were so different when we were only a little younger, Sir Drake."

"Ah, now I am curious and see the excuse for our missed practice," he answered.

"I think even in this ghastly dress I can take any three of you in a tussle. What do you say to that, fine knights? Here I have a cane, like the peasants and servants use while playing at war. Let me see if I can match your wooden swords and great wooden axe."

Sir Lindie told me, "That would not be seemly."

I had a new trick learned from the women in my pitiful army. I pouted. "Oh, come. Let us play. I'll not be hard on you. One pass to see how life must look from your eyes, and then I shall be off and leave you to your tasks of getting better."

"Better? We are already very good, my dear," Sir Casar said, pushing his chest out so it was greater than his stomach. He was the kind of man who was impossible to dislike, I discovered. I gladdened when I recalled I'd not murdered him in the last fight because I'd run out of time trying to do just that.

"One pass, and then you shall be rid of me and my playful insults, good knights."

"What will it take to satisfy you, my dear?" Sir Lindie asked.

"Sir Drake?" I asked the man I needed the most.

"Fine enough then," Sir Drake said, "just for a moment, and then you must promise someone will make a formal introduction at the high Lord's table."

"We should find a dry spot, so as to not spoil your lovely dress, my blossomed child," the axe man offered. He also offered his hand and led me to a place leveled off with flagstones.

"Oh, this is so exciting. I feel like a little girl again with this staff as my weapon and filled with anticipation for what little movement my bodice will allow me at least."

"How shall it be then," Sir Drake asked. All the other men filled the space around the stretch of flagstones. This left the three knights I'd been conversing with as contestants.

I suggested, "Well, let's suppose I am a grand knight and am attacking the castle of an evil Farstand lord who is intent upon keeping all the captive ladies in Lacellor's company and making of them his servants."

Sir Lindie put a stern face on and said, "Such will never happen. One look at you and even vile King Falstaff will alter his plans and put a new Queen on the throne instead."

I ignored him. The boy clearly had a grain hunting mouse in his pocket and wasn't a difficult conquest.

I continued, "The three of you must pretend to be the enemy and defend the castle moat. Thus, I shall have to rush through the defenses as one of you might in real life, and see things as if I were there on this great occasion of victory! Do you not see how I long to experience a moment of your glory? In this small way, perhaps I can imagine your sacrifice and duty as I await your return in some dreary keep or lordly manor."

Sir Casar said, "Ah, I see the reasoning here. It is a noble idea, once one wraps one's head around it. Yes, my Lady, I shall stand here with my axe in the middle, and act as if to bar your way." He walked to the middle of the flagstones, and turned to face me.

"And you, Sir Lindie, if you will please stand a step or two closer than the mountainous knight. This leaves the great knight, Sir Drake, to defend the very castle door." I tittered. I didn't know I could do it, but somehow I made the sound.

Soon the three of them were lined up before me. "Now there should be a wager. All the ladies make tiny bets as tokens of sport. What little thing should we bet on, my good knights?"

"Who is to sit near you at next meal," offered Sir Lindie, as if the thought had been pasted on his forehead by night shades.

"That seems fair, and to the man who holds you back the longest without losing his good stance," Sir Casar said.

"Death to the man who soils your dress or bruises your ivory skin," Sir Drake said, finally in a good and jesting mood. It was well out of character for him, I noticed.

"Such tender mercy would insult a lady, Sir Drake. We are not so fragile as all that."

The crowd of men around us all found the exchange amusing, and so my plan was going easier than I had expected.

I got to the point while the harvest smelled ripe. "Suppose we make any man I pass untouched by blade into the trainer of my guard for the season. That way you shall be by my side often, sharing the comfort of all my meals as you come to know me more closely than you can even imagine."

"This wager seems unfair to me, my Lady," Sir Lindie protested. "Under these conditions I should have no reason to fight you at all, and I fear I will deny you the feeling of a valorous knight forging through the enemy's defenses."

I laughed. "But sir, do you not know that, if you win, you will still win the right to be my servant; as well, you shall earn the right to kiss me in the shadows on winter's most festive day."

"Ah, Sir Drake," Sir Lindie looked across his shoulder, "you may have reason to murder me, for it is likely I shall have to later repent bruising this astonishing lady with the flat of my sword or even cause her to stumble, gods forbid."

"You should be waiting in line behind my axe and not before me."

"When you both let her slip by, no doubt because of the way your pricks have consumed all your blood, I shall simply grab her and save us all from suffering the wait until the nearest holiday," Sir Drake proclaimed.

I put my hand to my mouth and pretended offense by making my mouth round and my eyes saucers. I said, "Please Sir Drake, do not take advantage, lest you forget me again and I be made to return in some years and make yet another anonymous introduction, perhaps as lady B next time."

"Oh, dear lady, should I win this contest, a day may come when I have you to myself, and then I shall forbid you another such display as this. As well, by then you will no longer have need of these amusements for recreation."

I looked past the others, and into the great knight's too distant eyes, saying soundly, "I think I have been insulted, but I am not entirely sure."

Sir Drake continued, "If you took that as an insult, fine lady, then you do not know your own beauty and have no talent for seeing into the hearts and dreams of all who surround this charade."

"Well, with that I suppose I shall have to begin my quest, lest I drain the entire day of blood."

It took me less than another half breath to pop my stick between Sir Lindie's legs. When I extracted the wolf's end of my staff from his groin, I hit the bone on his wrist sharply, and then had no trouble picking his wooden sword up as I stepped nearly over his kneeling body.

"Oh, I am sorry. I couldn't resist, for that seemed an overly large target. Is such a strike even proper for a noble in gentlemanly warfare? Oh, and now it doesn't seem right that I should so easily advance." I said the last to Sir Casar as I looked back and forth between him and Sir Lindie.

Lindie got up. He suffered from the raining chides and laughter of his fellows. Even huddled over and in pain, the man managed a smile. His fellows noticed his good nature and slapped him on the back as they welcomed him into their surrounding fold.

"I think Sir Lindie wishes to tell you such is barely fair. He might expect some later favor in recompense," Sir Casar explained. He added, "Unfortunately, it is my hope that you shall be preoccupied, denying him the chance."

"Oh, then I suppose you intend to come at me with your mighty axe. How can any person stand against such a weapon, much less only a little lady."

"Well, once there was a woman who survived it, though some contend she was no lady." I had not expected his confession. The men chuckled.

"So the memory of the encounter is still with you? Was she a ghost? Does she haunt you still? Perhaps it was a witch or one made mostly of the mist?" As soon as I said those words, I couldn't help but feel guilty about it. It was the crone's shaman soul in me that made me say such things.

"No, she was just good. I was better, but ill prepared to face such a mystery."

I laughed then. "Fine then. Let me see if I can escape your kiss, though a bearded face so kind should not go wanting." It did occur to me that I was slowly losing much of my ladylike banter, but the goal was so close I felt it hardly mattered.

He smiled at the comment and stood with a wide stance. Then he put his axe forward as if to ease it my direction and thus force me to the side or perhaps even down on my knees. Like he'd just shown us all, I put my staff into the lean of the axe's bottom curve. I slid my staff to the handle of his mighty axe where he'd have all the leverage under the good sun. Then I braced the other end of my staff against the heel of my planted boot.

Sir Casar smiled, seeing my mistake. He tried to twist his heavy wooden axe. This time, however, it didn't budge due to the way I knelt, planting the end of my staff into my heel. All he managed was to get himself stuck trying to puzzle it out for a second, which was enough for me to reach up and stick him in the gut with Sir Lindie's sword.

A great gush of air escaped him, so while he sorted his breathing out I scampered past him with tiny little lady steps that had them all wondering if they'd truly seen what they'd just witnessed.

"Ah, how exhilarating. I find myself at the very castle door, and here confronted by the old King's most mighty and handsome warrior. Is this not like Marcol and the giant in the Gospel of the Vinnie?"

Sir Drake said, "It does seem so, but mostly I am unsure of my vision so far, so do not ask me to think so deeply."

I tossed aside my staff, and instead put my sword out in front of me in a two handed warrior's stance of great power and surety. "Well then, trust not your eyes, and instead meet me as you might one on the road to the duke's castle. There you will find a likeness of me that you have long forgotten, though I do not choose to return there with malice in my heart, nor revenge in my soul. I simply wish to return there . . . to meet you once again and remind you of it as you swear to train my guard in the coming season."

"What is this?" He warily raised his own sword, matching mine.

"No more than a simply born woman who laments that you can't meet my eyes and long for me as much as I have your handsome face, good knight." I touched his sword and then circled it perfectly.

"Yes, somewhere I remember you, Lady A," he confessed, though his face looked even more confused than before.

"Then this further reminder, after which I think you shall need no other." I brought my sword around in a wide and sweeping strike that I knew he could easily counter. Our wooden blades banged together violently. This I bounced off and worried my blade into his shoulder. Then I came around again, but stopped short of the slap, instead coming under his guard to stab him in his second shoulder.

I could see his recognition, and then his slow, growing anger. The contest could easily get out of hand under such circumstance, so I tossed my sword aside. "I declare Sir Drake the victor. This means, of course, that you three shall train my guard for the season, and that you, Sir Drake, have the obligation of giving me a kiss on the occasion of winter festival."

I picked my staff up and walked away from the silenced lot of them. They had a nice bench on the far side of the fence. There I sat, fussing with my dress and awaiting word from Lady Lettoir.

After a short while, I was pleasantly surprised to see the guard coming out of the castle with a note in his hand. He came and left, soon replaced by the presence of Sir Drake, who seemed still angry with me. I folded the note and got up to greet the great knight with a curtsy. His friends were at his side, and in spite of the continual eyes upon my body and face, I noted thoughtful minds.

"Who are you really, my Lady? I have reason to suspect some witchery because of the chatter about earlier meetings."

"It does not matter, Sir Drake. You have sworn service. My lands and needs are a hard two-day's ride. I know the details of my offer were not forthcoming and somewhat under false pretenses, but I do intend to hold you to your promise because it is needful beyond the simple will of you, your friends, or myself."

Sir Casar said, "I'm sorry to tell you we can't go far from the great knight, for we have sworn our allegiance."

"Well, this has been handled as well, good Lords. Lady Lettoir has secured the promise of Sir Lacellor that, if any knights should prove willing to help us train over the upcoming season, then I shall have rights to hold them to that promise. Sir Lacellor's hand has signed this letter as his only concession to the great lady. Of course, I don't imagine he thought any would accept, but as you know, some already have pleaded for the honor of helping me create a swift new army of light horse. My women have such need of your skills."

"Ah, Lettoir! You must be the sister of that awful and hostile woman who goes by the name of Abi. This is trickery," Sir Drake protested.

"No, good knight, I am not the sister of Abi. Abi's only sister is a Debrecian warrior who goes by the name of Batya. She is also warm on the eyes and lovely in spirit, but Batya won't put up with insults that offend her honor, for like me, she is a shaman princess of great power and influence among the heavens."

Sir Drake conceded, "Then it has been you all along. One of your many deceits is to constantly trick the eyes of those you wish to punish."

I stood. "I wish to punish the priests and nobles of Farstand, and none other, least of all you. Just be ready with all you need for a long winter encampment and possibly many encounters with the enemies of Sir Lacellor. Be so by first light. If you miss our departure, our wagons shall be easy to find on the road south, leading to the border where one must use both skill and trickery to survive the world that has been set against us."

I stormed down the path and into the back door of the keep, not awaiting any answer, nor did I bother to pick up the tiny and useless hat that flew from my head and settled on the great back steps of granite.

I later learned that such was done by another.

Chapter Thirteen

Batya's horse fidgeted, as if sensing her anxiety regarding what was about to come. She and I were alone on the road and looking toward a distant hill on the road farther north. She said, "For a month, they've shunned you. They do no more than their duty. When was it written that respect—"

"Stop worrying, sister. Let the three knights of Lacellor sit back on their mighty war horses and watch. Consider, if Sir Drake and his friends were to help us in this, they'd go back to Norfaton and say the only reason for our success was two swords and an axe."

She spun her horse around, putting the distant knights to her back. Personally, I felt glad they were so far away. If they showed themselves, they'd ruin our plans.

My sister wasn't as easily content. "They have good horses, and the companies have trained a month following them in these maneuvers."

I reached over and stroked her horse on its mane, then said, "Our new sergeant will have to apply what she has learned today. Better now than a month ago when you were so young and eager, you and I alone leading my horsemen."

How odd to speak of age. My sister couldn't have been more than fifteen, and yet she led my army. One couldn't tell her youth by the fire in her eyes, but from a distance it was sometimes hard to see her power for her large horse, my old horse Ella. I'd heard some of the enemy had come to call her a ghost through the fame of her raids. Possibly many of them mistook her for me, though I was tall and red and harder to miss.

My sister's raids had kept us going, allowing my soldiers the time they needed to train and get better. I had two hundred who were fairly steady on their horses now, and another hundred in the first of their training. Some of the two hundred were even good at one or two skills, allowing them the ability to do more than lose a pike at first brush with a solid target. How many, we'd find out shortly.

Batya said, "This will not be the same as a raid, and they don't seem to know it. It's good to respect the enemy, even if he is a fool and has split his cavalry off due to overconfidence."

"Wisely noted. Caution is the difference between a warrior soon in trouble and what is needful," I agreed.

"Yes, I feel like a mother setting her daughters on their first ponies," said Batya.

"Then go and set them gently. I've sent the Goddess before you, my sister."

She looked at me. "You look better with your hair about your ears, a clean shirt and the pretty skirt of a breeder."

I smiled at her. "Thank you. You look better coming back to me with your life so you may spy upon me."

She smiled, and then rode her horse into the wooded hills to the left of the roadway. I wished she had a sword, but as always, my sister sold herself too lightly and only bore a bow and short lance.

I looked to my right where two sat on their horses just in the canopy of trees. At my nod Angel stayed, but Sergeant Sasha disappeared forward into the rightmost woods. I should have asked Angel to go with the soldiers as well. Such a request would have proven useless. It was all I could do to get her to hide in the woods a few strides away. She was my shadow even in the shadows.

When I'd asked others to take her under their wing for a spell, they'd just laughed and told me they were comforted knowing I had such a dedicated bodyguard. Sometimes I didn't feel like their leader, but instead their prisoner regarding certain things.

Angel looked tense. I noticed the whiteness of her fist around her short lance.

One of our scouts came toward me from far down the road to the south. She was galloping swiftly, and only when she was half down the slope did she ease her way into the woods to my left instead of coming to me. If she'd ridden right up, the signal would have told me things were not going as expected.

The battle would happen quickly now, regardless, for I doubted even the quick action of myself and Batya would be enough to reach all my forces before the enemy showed. I knew from experience that communication in battle was critical, both having as much of it as possible, and knowing when it was useless, or even deadly when hurriedly misused.

Fresh dust was already rising beyond the next hill from which Batya's scout had come.

Then a standard.

And then an enemy scout's head.

Finally, I saw Sir Pritchan's face and two other nobles in mail.

They stopped at the top of the hill, looking across the long sag of the roadway to where I rested in my saddle a half mile away.

I unbuttoned the top buttons of my pretty blouse, and then adjusted my cursed corset.

There was no pike in my hand, nor did I wear a sword. In fact, I was dressed as comely as a noble lady, complete with a white lace shirt, a colorful array of skirts and a bright wool blanket under my saddle. For this occasion, Pritchan's stolen black stallion was also disguised as someone else. I'd painted him with some fancy white spots, to include one on his face. He wasn't happy with the decorations, but just as is the case with all horses, forgot the offense the moment I presented him with an apple.

As might be expected, I pretended to not see the coming knights and their hundred orderly men on foot. I got down and instead looked at the heel of my horse. It was all I could do to keep my skirts up out of the ample dirt, bunching them up high with a hand while bending and holding some of the material between my knees. The stallion looked back at me with one eye, curious about his legs, not mine.

They came down as one, the three knights on horses first. The scout retired to the rear. I was glad my reports were right and only four were on horses. The scouting reports suggested as many as a hundred professional footmen. At a distance, I saw files, marching over the rise in near perfect stride. I knew that on long marches such spit wasn't preferable and was in fact overly tiring. Someone must have ordered the formality for the sake of a noble woman on the roadway.

I did a quick count of them as they came half the long distance, soon entering the bottom of the road's dip. There were just under forty per column, two columns wide. I wasn't so greedy as to not think the smaller number better.

It wasn't until Sir Pritchan was half way up the rise, and a hundred strides from me, that I lifted my face and dropped my raised skirt in seeming surprise. I saw his eyes drop, and realized he'd been drawn to the sparkle of the necklace resting in the lee of my low-cut blouse.

I struggled to get my foot into the stirrup, which, given the absurd quantity of skirts, was almost not pretend, and then after three poor tries, awkwardly pulled myself into my saddle, belly first. From there I shifted as if uncomfortable until I sat.

"Hail, lovely lady! There is no need to flee!"

I turned my horse, but then turned him again, coming around in circles two times before getting him under control, as if I were not accustomed to handling a horse properly. I ended up facing their direction.

I showed him a hopeless face, held a hand closing my buttons, and shouted, "Have you not done enough? Are you intent upon killing me as you've done my guards?"

"Say not, dear beauty. We have no desire to harm you. We are not the raiders, but only some of those sent to cross the river and put an end to the banditry of these same whom I suspect have also accosted you," Sir Pritchan said.

"Why have you waited? My guards have failed their duties to me by dying too easily, and my dress is as much as ruined!" I yelled back in what I imagined to be typical noble form.

He'd piqued my interest, and I wanted to hear all I could about this new plot to waylay my forces; otherwise, I'd have already sprung the battle with a whistle. As it stood, I couldn't imagine my women holding. The soldiers were lined up in perfect order before us, mostly along the lower portions of the roadway.

"We knew nothing of your plight, but now we're here. All will be safe," he said while riding toward me. I didn't have the good sense to feel vulnerable. In fact, I'd forgotten I had no sword and was indeed defenseless should he recognize me. And, of course, why should he not, for I was not so different. All my women had recognized me without much comment upon returning from the castle a month ago, in spite of the many spells.

"Is this all you've brought? They are as many as a thousand and everywhere, I hear." I spun my horse around once more.

"This is enough, but we have some White Shirts on horses assigned to us as well. They are swift and scouting to the west. Our cavalry will join us at the next river. Two score experienced men on good horses. Do you think that not enough?"

"Against a thousand!" We were now only thirty yards distant, and I was almost out of time in the collection of my information before my curiosity became a problem.

"My lady, of course they seem many because of their swiftness, but these are only women who raid us and no more than two score at best. We certainly have --" He stopped in mid word. His eyes had wandered briefly and settled to the side where there was nothing but trees.

I was worried that one of my soldiers had shown herself, but instead I saw the snout of an old friend, Golden Eyes. Beside him were several of his pack.

From a few yards closer to me, Yellow Eyes ran from the cover and across the road between me and the knight. He raced right up to Angel, who'd apparently gotten concerned and brought her horse too far forward.

Sir Pritchan followed the streak of my wolf, and his eyes came right up, meeting those of my bodyguard. She had her short lance pointed forward, and there was no doubt she was tired of waiting and apparently found that he'd come far too close to me for her comfort.

It was no use pretending any more, for I'd gathered all the intelligence I'd needed anyway.

I whistled into the woods.

Suddenly a number of experiences happened all at once. Some of these I can only tell because I'd pieced them together from conversations around the campfire. This is because Sir Pritchan had more quickly pieced his own little situation together. From the look in his eyes, I could tell he still didn't recognize me. Yet, he'd clearly come to the conclusion that I wasn't the innocent lady he'd first imagined.

I instinctively reached over my back, finding only my own loosely fashioned hair. Of course, at my belt was nothing more than ribbons and lace.

Pritchan was studying the horse between my legs, and from the shorter distance could clearly see the white spots were only paint, and the horse had once been his own.

The man swiftly pulled his sword out, alerting the other two knights and some of the footmen as well. Four of the closest footmen came running. Both of the other knights reached for arms and kicked their horses.

The roadway between those on horses and the four footmen filled with wolves. They appeared less than eager to attack so much steel, but instead snarled wetly, causing the footmen to retreat and one of the horses to rear up wildly, nearly throwing the knight.

Angel had come down to the road, aiming for the broad side of the three men on horses. One turned with his shield up, splintering her short lance, though not without the impact nearly toppling him and his horse, for both staggered.

The last knight recovered from his horse's terror. He quickly swiped his sword at Angel as she flew by. I sat frozen, seeing the blade sweep across her back, and was more terrified for her than my own circumstance.

The last I saw of her was when she wheeled around, again aimed at the two sword and shield bearing knights. She'd turned her horse using only her knees, for the reins were not in her hands, but instead two long bladed knives. Even I didn't suspect she'd gained such skill as a horseman. Still, I saw it as a mistake, for she'd left her better sword sheathed and useless across her back.

Such a timely but terrible distraction was just what I needed when Sir Pritchan came at me with his own sword ready, and mine so very far away.

The best I could do was turn the black stallion to face his charge, keeping the horse's head between myself and the man's steel. He maneuvered his horse, frantically sweeping his sword, but frustrated with its limited reach and clearly reluctant to nick the feisty black horse he recognized as his own.

I didn't have time to thank the Goddess that the man was so short and his sword equally stubby. Instead, I backed my horse a couple steps up the road, angling back towards the wood-line.

All this happened over a few small seconds. I had no delusions that I could hold him at bay with my horse's head long enough to escape under the canopy, and wasn't even sure if the canopy had anything magical about it that would save me either.

It was Yellow Eyes who gave me the chance to find out.

I was so focused on the sword that nipped close and snagged in my skirts that I didn't see the great wolf's charge.

Sir Pritchan ducked over his horse's neck when the horse reared. The horse reached around with his teeth, biting at the wolf sliding down his hind quarter. Yellow Eye's claws left fat and long cuts in the flesh before he fell off and rolled in the roadway. Pritchan's horse kicked frantically, somehow missing my wolf enough to give him time to find his feet and run away into the opposite woods.

I rode into the closer woods, picking the direction because it was where my horse's head pointed and I had no time to waste on turning.

Just before I ducked into the canopy, I saw the dirt road stretching out below us all. It had filled with the chaos of a great and terrible battle.

* * * * *

This I heard from our new Sergeant Sasha, many days later around a late and somber campfire.

Sasha does not speak as eloquently as this telling, but this was her meaning.

Sasha's story:

Trees blocked much of my vision. I saw the reaction of the footmen as something up the road drew their attention. A few even broke away from their loose files, scattering even farther to the side. Something in me feared for Princess Abi. There is nobody better in a fight. I had to consider that and do nothing, for I had half our force under my command.

For more seconds than I dared count, we'd been in perfect position for the ambush, but received no signal. I was determined to hold our ranks. I remembered the many warnings: Anticipation of battle distorts a soldier's thoughts. Even a poorly made command was better than undisciplined warriors falling on the enemy in dribbles.

We were too far into the trees to see much. Men passed in front of us in bits and glimpses. Thus, not too far to be discovered in kind. So, it was with enormous relief that I heard the yell across the road, "Loose arrows!" I'd not heard it, but apparently Abi had whistled.

Arrows burst up out of the tall tree canopy. They came halfway to where we waited, then fell upon the soldiers. I saw what seemed like all of them sticking out of the dirt around the soldier's feet. This made me think our opening salvo was a disaster, but then one of the soldiers in front of us fell to his knees. Another walked across my view, screaming about an arrow sticking out of the top of his shoulder. Since I could only see a score, this didn't seem as bad a result as I'd at first imagined.

Many of the soldiers moved into the far woods and organized a line as they went. As soon as they started this, I saw some of the ten decoy archers. They bravely came out on foot. These few shot at them from less than thirty paces. A couple of those arrows came right across the roadway, hitting the ground and low limbs where we were waiting. As far as I could tell, none near me were hit.

The soldiers in the roadway were not so fortunate; two or three more of the ones in my sight seemed punctured. Men now ran toward the fleeing archers.

The archers disappeared into the trees. The other row of enemy soldiers kept good discipline. This, I learned, told of solid sergeants in their ranks.

As soon as the first half came abreast of the far trees, I motioned for my soldiers to advance on their horses.

Some of us had to move their animals on foot, while several others could ride them with a stoop. Thus we came out of the trees in less order than I'd have liked. But, the plan was to not hesitate. I was to be the first. Each beside me came out a bit later. Later still, on down the line, such came on the enemy. We were a wave, the point of which was my own lance.

I charged directly, having a good path to the roadway, and was the first to strike one of the enemy. Because of the distraction, it felt a good solid hit that pierced the man's back a little. My run was short and I didn't have enough momentum to run it cleanly through him.

As soon as I got to the other side of the closest rank, I turned my horse, a tactic meant to ward short swords away. I hesitated, attacking nobody until I felt two or three of my women near.

My lance flew out of my hands when we advanced again. The second man's pike deflected it. I didn't have time to worry about the miss, going directly to my sword.

The count was no more than four or five seconds. We quickly swept the line of thirty men. And butted them with our horses, and slashed the few that outlasted our lances. By the fifth man, others in our broadside came through with me. All the men nearby fell to our steel and wood. So I put those beside me abreast. We wheeled. We aimed up the north road. Others of our women ahorse mingled in our path. Some we went around. A few were helped out of small troubles. Every man now fought in two directions. They became even more scattered and utterly at our mercy as we rode against their grain. My group drove over them one by one so that we didn't need our weapons. A crowd of women with nothing to do filled my roadway in the end.

I wheeled us south, four ranks deep. We were treeline to treeline, like a mountain cliff. Some of our archer's were still being hunted in the forest by a handful of men unaware of their doom. The mass of us started southward, bearing upon the last score of soldiers. Many of these dogs discovered themselves disorganized between the road and the archer's trees. One man was bled and trampled. Then another. And another. They were like lambs already roped and ready for the evening's meal. A couple ran into the woods. Wounded men from our first victory limped and crawled, seeking ten who stood in a group. These defiant readied pikes, short swords, and a bow. One fled south, down the slope of the road. One ran west, from where we'd come in the beginning.

I never reached the ten. The last third of my women caught them in a wave from the woods. They charged this offering, yelling the name, "Abi!" Those who stumbled north or east were trampled by my ranks. I yelled for everyone to stop when the last man fell under the hooves. Women soon mingled in place. Teams were assembled to scour the forest. I passed on the eastern edge of the roadway. And thus we were a river of horses mingling in a pond of blood.

Before we were more than a third of the way down the roadway, I saw the vanguard of Batya's raiders. They came out of the woods to the far south. They'd already shot the enemy scout. His horse ran unridden. It raced away, up the rise to the south. Two of Batya's archers split off, chasing the animal down. Batya must have seen that the battle had already been won. I laughed, imagining how annoyed this must have made her.

Still, the great Debrecian warrior came down the road toward us, a force of three score women on horses and with enough fresh spears. Even the great Batya had a spear. Having the run of the roadway, she led with all the momentum I'd lacked in my short run from the wooded side of the roadway. When she drew close, she tossed her spear right through the chest of the last man running away.

This everybody on the whole battlefield saw. A roar of victory filled the air with the name, "Abi!"

My forces raced ahead, meeting Batya's. I was quickly yanking on my reins to turn around once again. For a moment, I was useless in the press.

We all gathered, faced north once more.

The road was blood and bodies. Some wreathed. Some crawled. One or two stumbled into the woods. There, the teams of archers finally came out. They shot the dying with whole quivers of arrows. I went there in the end. Three were dragged out of the woods and tossed into the ditch.

There'd been too many of us. Their foot had become scattered and disorganized when we'd split them. It was almost as if the whole force of us had fallen on each of them one at a time. For this error they'd paid with complete annihilation. They could not touch us.

Seeing what had come of Abi's plan filled me with pride I'd

never known before. Thus I came to understand what we'd become.

I determined to learn my lessons from Abi and her sister. I knew I'd never want to be on the other end of what they taught me.

It took a while organizing women. Gradually I wandered all the way north. There I saw many of our women lingering over bodies. The wounded were given no quarter. We all had long histories of abuse at the hands of Farstand's men.

Batya ordered the bodies dragged into the trees. She yelled, "Much of our strength is in what remains unknown."

A few wolves stood around near those trees. As soon as I came near, they disappeared into the underbrush. I didn't know them. Princess Abi had one that was friendly to her, though.

Only two women perished, while three more tended their serious wounds in the grass by the roadway. Some women helped, and others made litters.

I remember thinking, it's over. Then there seemed nothing to do. Like a ninny, I awaited orders. But, I was now a sergeant. I made commands to others, but do not remember what.

When everyone was busy, I looked farther north. There, up on the distant rise, three horses stood. Two of them belonged to the nobles. The other I'd last seen under Angel. Under the horses lay three grey lumps. None of them moved.

Without delay I kicked my horse and started up the slope. Every time my horse took another step, it seemed I'd gotten nowhere. Then, beside me raced Abi's sister. I looked into the eyes of the young Debrecian warrior. We became a team and realized I'd never before actually seen her afraid like she seemed at that moment.

When we got there, two knights and Angel lay dead in mud the color of blood. There was no sign of dust down the far slope of the roadway. Batya worked her horse, taking several frantic looks around for signs. We found broken tree limbs on both sides of the roadway. We looked at one another. Our eyes agreed. I went one way. She went the other.

* * * * *

I learned those details of the battle through Sasha, around the campfire. At the battle's beginning I still worried about the ability of

my ready cavalry. Equally, I hoped to get back to the roadway, find a
weapon, and lend assistance to Angel, whom I feared already dead.

Instead I was unable to do more than worry about the probability
I'd soon join her as a ghost. Sir Pritchan seemed determined. He
would have had no chance of catching me had he not been so short
and able to duck under the limbs. My dress continually caught in the
branches and I had to pick my way, while he needed only to set his
horse's nose upon the tail of my own.

Then there was the matter of my left leg. It bled just above the
knee, enough to soak the fabric of my skirt. I put my hand over the
wound as I rode, increasingly aware of its sting and the fact that my
skirt had a long gash in it, all the way through the petticoats as well. I
suppose I'd been so distracted in my efforts to ward off Sir Pritchan's
sword that I'd gotten myself soundly sliced.

The wound was deep, and the effect of it made me lightheaded at
the time when I needed all my faculties in order to maneuver under
the many low hanging branches.

I wanted to turn us south. In that direction I had more than
enough help, assuming the battle was going well, but there was a crag
barring my way. It wasn't steep, but it was still too high for my horse
to manage in so much brush. It guided my horse northward, always
into the wilderness and away from the help I needed. Behind me I
dared not look, but heard the brush breaking and the steps of a noble's
steady horse.

There was a point at which I realized I had to do something other
than run farther from the battle. I drove my horse over by the crag. It
was easy enough to fall off my saddle and onto the shell top. I came
to my feet on the new plateau where I switched directions, using the
same cliff to guide me southeast.

Sir Pritchan rode by. He paused, but there was no good place to
run the horse up, and so he cursed and went on.

My leg was nearly useless. The knee wouldn't stretch completely
forward and buckled with every few steps. It was also prickly, as if
going to sleep. I knew that was a sign it needed more blood. The
needed blood was still flowing freely out of me, and so I had to tear
some of my hem off and tie the fabric around the leg even as I limped

ahead. Tending to the leg while moving in leaps cost me more time than if I'd stopped and done it more quickly. To make matters worse, the tree cover was not so low here, but the weeds higher. Pushing my dress through it was miserable and a skill I'd never practiced.

I tore at the strings behind me that bound my dress to my waist. This cost me more time and was also no help toward the effort of moving through the weeds. Finally I stepped out of the dress and its many skirts entirely. With one sweep of my fists on the collars, I ripped the buttons loose on my shirt and left it and its useless and overlong lace sleeves behind as well. Now at least I could move, but the trees thinned the farther southeast I went on this new ground. It was slowly changing into more of a field than a forest. The sparse trees again thickened before breaking at the roadway, but I knew I wasn't going to make it that far with Pritchan on my back.

All the while, I looked across the ground for a stick. There were all kinds of them, short ones good for kindle, long ones the length of a house, fat logs felled by lightning, and limp roots sticking up out of the ground like snakes.

Over my shoulder, I saw that Pritchan had somehow managed to drag his horse up the crag a few yards farther down from where I'd crossed. Such was his luck that day. He'd make the distance I'd just covered at ten times my speed.

Just when I thought I'd have to try begging my way out of death, I saw a stick. The thing was much too thin and coated in green slime. It angled with a dog's leg and a finger root wobbling on one end. I didn't imagine for a second it would survive the first cut of a sword.

Knowing that, I picked it up anyway, and turned to stand my ground against the knight in mail on his well-bred steed as he bore down on me at full gallop.

He tried to ride me down, but his sword was in his right hand, and I leapt to the other side of his horse as he rode by swinging it. I barely missed getting trampled. Instead of trying that again, he rode up more cautiously until I was made to back up in order to keep a distance. Then he got off his horse and looked me over at sword's length.

His eyes looked down my body. I was naked from the waist up, save for the corset that didn't cover my breasts. Below the waist I wore a small cloth and some dark gray stockings I'd taken in a raid near Helfax. The hastily tied bandage was whitish and dripping red. Blood leaked down into a boot. It squished wetly as I stepped back, matching his every movement.

He said, "I see I've captured something of a beauty. Now I am glad I haven't killed you. Yes, I can see you understand me. I shall be merciful and keep you as a slave for my bed if you answer my questions completely. What say you, wench?"

It struck me that he didn't recognize me. This I hadn't expected. Had I changed that much in such a short time? I decided to play on that little hope, swinging my stick awkwardly, as if I had no experience in weaponry at all. I answered, "Please, my Lord. Do not hurt me. I was told to deceive you, and was threatened. I am a woman of noble birth. Your own eyes saw how the raider burst out of the trees."

"At your whistle, girl! You'll answer my questions, and then I'll tie you up and put you across the rump of a horse for later spanking. That is certain, so quit lying to me at once!"

I backed a step at a time toward the woods surrounding the roadway, but it was a long ways away, and I knew I'd never make it. Another thought occurred to me though; he'd not seen the battle forming on the road below us because of his preoccupation with me. I wasn't sure if that was going to help, but at least I knew more than he did about the broader play at hand.

He saw me looking around for signs of help, and said, "Your fellow raider is dead by now, and any others just as surely. You are alone. Yield wench, and I shall not be too harsh with you."

I had no answers, and instead stepped back another step. I held the stick close in front of me, between my breasts as if protecting my virginity.

"Yes, you will do, once properly bedded. I like them timid. I'll teach you better manners in time. Now tell me, where did you come upon that horse? And, I don't like lies, so prepare to tell me all you know about the raider's camp."

I decided to tell him the truth. I knelt down in the weeds and pleaded, "Oh, please do not torture me. I'll tell everything I know.

The horse was given to me by a woman named Abi. It is she who leads them, I suppose. She has a camp just beyond the river. That's where you'll find the raiders. Now will you let me go?"

"How many of them were with you?"

I put my stick in the weeds under my fists and sank even lower. To him it might have seemed like a bow, but the wound in my leg had truly made me weary. I said, "There are nearly a hundred and fifty of them on this side of the river."

He stepped close and tapped me on the thigh wound with his sword. I winced. "Ten thrashings with a cane for you for that lie. Now, how many of you are there, both here on this raid, and back at your camp?"

"One," I said as I swung my stick into his knee with all the force I could muster. The stick shattered.

Sir Pritchan fell over with his sword still in his hand, but so too did I, from the strain of it. My leg had weakened me beyond good use.

Still, I rolled up and, by jumping on one leg, grabbed onto his horse's mane. I put a leg over his back. My mind screamed *snakes* into the horse's mind.

I wasn't truly on it, and had only enough strength to hang from the horse's hair with one fist while my foot slipped off the animal's back. I was dragged beside him a few strides. My knees and feet bounced off the ground. Something in my arm tore. In less than a dozen strides, I'd been beaten enough and fell into the field. The horse managed to accidentally kick me in the ribs with a hoof as he flew past.

My mind dropped into something like a mist thereafter. Sir Pritchan hovered quite closely above me. Next, I felt mud on my cheek and hands behind me tying my wrists. The pain in my arm was what woke me long enough to know this. I screamed in agony, and then looked over and knew I was dead because I was staring sideways and up at the most beautiful face I'd ever seen.

* * * * *

I learned these things many months later. The delay occurred because Sir Drake was slow in coming to terms with my resolve. Still, these words fell right out of the mouth of the great knight. I'll try to be faithful to his telling, though speaking for him is a little embarrassing.

"I saw what the bastard had done to you, and was not happy with myself for letting my pride consume me all of a month.

"In all that time, I'd only spoken to you with harshness, and even insisted upon the same treatment for you from my men. And yet you accepted this in order to see to the training of a few of your horsewomen. It took that moment for me to realize I'd been a noble goat.

"It wasn't just the sight of you in that field either, but well before it. One look at how your army swarmed over the road was enough to convince me that I'd been empty pride. I looked to the left and right of me, and the same thoughts were clear as sunlight on both Sir Casar's and Sir Lindie's faces. What was the matter with us? We were not men, but fools.

"Then we looked down upon you once more, and saw the last charge of your bodyguard. Never had I seen such courage as then. I'd so often thought of her with a dismissive shrug, and yet I'd never known a man to equal her courage as she dove upon the enemy swords, bearing only knives.

"Then, you no longer occupied the road, but I could see a knight leaving for a trail. I knew you'd left your weapons with the pack animals in order to ensure the success of your deception.

"That was when my heart sank. That was when I first remembered the harshness of my tongue towards you all that previous month. Were you never to hear a word from me in kindness?

"We were so far away from the field of battle due to our stupidity. Yet, we were in the woods before your own soldiers were a quarter through the battle, and I can tell you that all the way down the road we marveled at the beauty of your light horsemen as they split into the enemy without a thought toward the folly of barely trained women against experienced soldiers.

"Seemingly much later, when we came upon you in the field, I witnessed a knight leaning over a bloody body, clearly made so through abuse and beating. You were hoarse from screaming, though

I don't imagine you knew it. He'd just bound your hands behind you, and was rising when we came around him in a circle.

"The things we did next were not chivalrous, so I will appreciate that you not mention it in Sir Lacellor's court.

"And he even told us, this Sir Pritchan, 'Three against one is not chivalrous.' But that didn't keep us all from hacking on him until there was nothing decent left to carry home to his kin. Let the carrion have him.

"When we turned to pick you up, it was your sister we found. She had you in her lap and was chanting for cures to your Goddess. She prayed with a face full of tears until I felt a warm wind and realized the tiny warrior held great sway with someone in the heavens.

"This you might also choose to forget, for she later told me that, if I ever spoke of her anguish, she'd put a hex on my future heirs and send the locust to feast on our fields."

Chapter Fourteen

I, Abi, fought to keep my soul on the earth as I felt a few blankets under my back. Many feet above, a floating cottage smoldered. Tendrils of smoke sifted out in sizzling streams. These formed puffs of summer clouds, cheery as can be in the clear blue sky. As the timbers burned, the coals fell away fluttering in the air around me, turning into butterflies and petite yellow finches.

I heard steel on iron and an old woman laughing above. There came the quake of fallen soldiers landing on her smoking cottage floor.

Up there were a few loose floorboards, allowing me a view of a battle from underneath, and that apparently was the cause of her laughter. Through these gaps I notice, without emotion, the splattering of blood. It dripped in rows between the slats, wetness falling through the fields of butterflies and birds, turning into rose petals which fluttered, but never quite fell all the way to my feet. Here, far below all these things, came a soft summer breeze.

I reached up, but the cottage was suddenly so small that my whole hand covered it when I held it up just right.

I followed my hand upward and became one of the pretty yellow finches. My wings flew me in ways that made up into down.

Below me slept a tall and beautiful woman. She had a lovely white dress on, full of petticoats and wrapped with lace and ribbons. It was hiked up on one side, showing a shapely leg bulging with a poultice under a clean bandage. She had other hurts too, I understood, but the woman rested comfortably on a soft cot, and I felt sure I'd offend the gods if I disturbed her peace.

I was also sure she was familiar. I reached down to move some of her light red hair away so I might see in what way I knew her, for I was sure I did in no small measure, and thought it important that I come to know her even a little bit better.

When I did this, my finch feet couldn't touch her. Rather, they clutched something thin and shiny like a tin needle. I tried to see it better, but my eyes were not on the bottom of my head, so instead I flew around the meadow of flowers with it, looking for my nest. As I flew, the needle between my sharp talons sang to me and I sang back to it. I was a bird, and so the only thing I could think to do with the singing needle was weave it into my nest.

Then I sat there in my weaving of comfortable sticks and sang for another bird like me to come along.

As I looked out over the meadow, it seemed a constant buzz of tiny creatures dancing over the flowers in celebration of the Goddess's handiwork.

In the middle of it all rested the same woman on her cot. I saw it wasn't one woman, but two, and they only looked like one person because they rested in the same place while they shimmered back and forth. Though this made no sense, I was just a bird and only found it a little bit more curious than the flowers and the bees and especially the butterflies that were also miracles, for they'd once been nothing more than tasty worms.

Then I sang for a long time. Nobody came by to share my nest.

I watched her some more, and she wasn't two women, but three shifting around in the same space. One was a dark grey princess and lovely, and one was a pure white virgin and lovely, and one was dirt brown and lovely as well, though they were all lovely in different ways that I didn't understand because it wasn't important to me yet.

I was a bird, and, after my curiosity waned, wanted them to go away because they were a distraction.

There was nobody else like me around, and I had something in my nest that I wanted to show off.

One of the women got up. It was the old woman in brown. She had hair the color of my needle, only not so shiny. The woman stretched her old and tired limbs and seemed continually laughing up at the burning cabin that was hovering just above the meadow, so close now that I thought she could touch it. The other two slept on and didn't see her walking around by herself and coming my way.

I should have flown away, but was struck stupid and didn't even move when she reached up and took my new shiny treasure out of my nest. When she did this, the nest disappeared, and I had to flutter, thinking there was somewhere else I had to go in order to better watch for the other bird like me who would not come.

I also saw this from where I still slept on my cot under the burning cabin. The old woman stood over by a tree pulling my sword out of a bird's nest.

Beside me knelt my sister. She was lying against a bundle of soldier's gear, right beside me with her hand across my stomach. There she'd finally given up watching and had fallen asleep. She'd been troubled about something, which of course wasn't all that unusual. And so I thought all was as it should be and only sighed.

The old woman in brown peasant sackcloth stood behind my sleeping sister. She wore my teaching sword. When she looked at me, she was no longer laughing. Then she bowed as if I were the King of Farstand, which was silly. Only the upper part of her body showed, just on the other side of my sister, and that part of her bowed so low her breasts touched the young warrior's body. Like that, my teacher's ghost face drew so close I could have kissed her old and crusty lips. I could tell most of all that she was as tired as the rest of us and, in spite of the earlier laughter, wasn't in the mood for nonsense.

I looked away just in time to see the cabin in the clouds fall to pieces again and flutter away in a scattering of crows. Then I looked back at the crone and my sister, seeing them both sleeping, shimmering across the same soldier's bundle. They seemed both in the same place now, one nearly the same as the other. One of them was golden and one of them was the color of the earth. Both the old brown and the young gold were lovely, like they belonged together, though I was just a bird and didn't know why.

When I woke up, my head seemed splitting under the blow of an axe. My chest hurt, and I recognized the pain of yet another broken rib. My clothing had gone missing. I wore only a thin shift. The big tent smelled and felt of a nice, warm fire. I had a thick wool blanket, and my cot was better padded with spare clothing than any I'd slept on in many months. When I tried to shift, every joint in my leg protested. I determined to not try that again for a very long time.

My sister's hand moved off my stomach, but she'd gone too many hours without rest and only stirred that little bit. I brushed aside some of my red and yellow hair. That allowed me to see her other hand. It held my scabbard and sword across her body like I'd read a king once did on his sarcophagus.

When I saw it, I wanted it for my nest. Then again, I remembered that, when I'd sung with it woven in there before, no other bird like me had answered my singing. So I left it with my sister as I drifted back to sleep while thinking I had come to know the women in my dreams just a little bit better. I was just a bird though, and thus I didn't know why I was thinking at all.

* * * * *

I woke once more in what felt like the very same night. My sister was gone, but she'd not been for long I guessed. The fire still burned.

The pains inside were still there, though now I also noticed the bottom side of my gown had soaked in cool sweat. My head felt only a little hot, but throbbed. There were bowls around me, signs that my sister had been working on a cure. She was not an herb witch, but only a young and learning shaman. Still, it was clear she'd been watching me and apparently she'd learned something, for the taste on my tongue was that of tea made from rosemary leaves and willow bark.

In order to avoid the wetness, I had to roll over onto my other side. That's when I saw the Goddess.

She was the same old and rectangular wooden statue that she'd come to fancy showing herself as ever since I'd introduced myself to Sir Lacellor's side of the river. The old wooden Goddess was right beside me, looking up at the ceiling of the tent with white painted eyes, not moving or saying anything.

For a while, I watched her, thinking she was dead. I reached over and touched her chest with a hand that shimmered white and ghostly grey because of the effect of the sudden movement on my drugged eyes. Gradually I felt the wood rising and falling, though slowly and with a heart that quivered as if it were no more sufficient than that in a finch.

The thought struck me that I wasn't as ill as the Goddess. Though she was fickle and often distracted when I needed her the most, she was also a creature of this world and had often come to my aid. I had to repay the kindness, and thus I mouthed a spell over the old wooden effigy. With it went the burning in my body. The heat sank below the skin of my forehead, and then down my neck and torso until it crept along my arm and out my hand. Sparks, like little white lightning, lanced from my fingers as they jittered over the Goddess's chest.

My fever was just as quickly breaking with new beads of sweat and shakes of chills, though I was still mostly warm. After some shivering, I could see a little more clearly. Beside me was not the Goddess at all, but only an angel. She was naked and covered in bloody rags. Even where there were no bandages, there were crushed bits of purple yarrow flowers mixed with some good brown mustard and many signs of stitching.

Both of her legs were straight, and her arms had been placed neatly to her sides. I had never seen the woman nearly so white, nor so still. It was as if all the blood had drained from her body, and she lay ready for the undertaking.

There were as many spent bowls of cures around her as myself though, for which I was thankful. I found her hand and took it to my body, holding it closely to my womb where I curled around it and made it warm.

She startled in her sleep, and then went right back to the chore of resting. Her stone cold hand warmed such that it felt as if I'd linked her life to mine. For this we were not two women, but one flesh.

Sure enough, there, a little between and above us, hovered the chilling face of death. I watched him, a warning in my eyes. The face had the look of Captain Barker, but it also was similar to Sir Pritchan and even the fat old Baron of Helfax. He seemed very disappointed, floating there with a sour face. I would have laughed at him, had he not been so near.

Death was all about his business though. He leaned in and out, following closely our every shallow breath.

* * * * *

Some years later I came across the chronicle of Batya. In it I learned this regarding the occasion of my sickness:

When the man, Lord Drake, bore her in, I saw a dead woman in his arms. He put her body on a cot. I sent out all but the most severely wounded and two midwives.

I prayed ceaselessly to our Goddess as the cures in my hands were mixed. I never saw our Goddess in the ways Abi spoke of seeing her with her very own eyes. Still, I felt the great God with us in the tent. Some of the less ill felt her so strongly that they grew fearful. These weak in spirit departed. Others were comforted. Those were the ones most in need of the sick tent. Thus was the power in there and the strange spirits that always surrounded my sister.

When the night was not half over, Abi's scars had almost vanished. I could tell her fever was close to breaking, and the great red swelling in her chest was almost righted. It was a miracle the likes of which I'd never seen.

This wasn't true of her bodyguard Angel. The woman should never have been taken to the tent. She was there more as an honor than a cure. I had the midwives clean and sew her many wounds, some of which were all the way through her. She'd been gored several times by the knight's swords as she'd flung herself upon them with her knives. I didn't mind the useless chore of tending her, for she didn't have the soul of a breeder and deserved my attention.

She never woke, which was a good thing. Then she died. This took far more time than any of the healers expected.

I went out to find someone to help me carry the brave and crazy woman to her grave, but upon my return with two strong women, I saw my sister curled up around her arm and Angel breathing once again. One of the midwives brushed back Abi's clothing to show me something. I couldn't believe my eyes. All the cuts and bruises on my sister's body were healed, but in their place were long and ugly white lesions. Each of these new marks was in the same place and direction as those across the body of Angel.

Abi's breathing felt shallow and her fever returned. Not even in the worst of moments before had she been so ill. Angel, however, nearly glowed pink.

Word spread of the miracles surrounding my sister. Soon, women lined up outside the tent, hoping to see in. I had to shoo them back several times during the night. By morning the line contained all of the camp. Not a thing was getting done. One of the midwives had convinced them all that something worth seeing was hidden by the tent. This miracle was also the grave illness of our leader, Abi. It was hard on my soul to continually berate the women who honored her, for they came out of love and to see the one who was worthy.

Lady Lettoir was still with the man, Lord Lacellor, but I held council with the honorable breeders, Marci and Minari. Together we decided they couldn't be turned away. We opened both the front and back flaps on the sick tent. The women filed through one by one.

Today we have testimony. Over four hundred women witnessed the miracle of the healing of Angel. They also saw the price of such magic. We'd put fresh wood on the fire. We unbound the clothing to the waist of both women. Every woman in the camp saw the matching marks on their two bodies.

I had to cover the breasts of my sister when the women were done. Last in line were our sergeant and the three loyal knights. They too couldn't be turned aside. All three of the knights had seen Abi when she'd fallen. They knew the miracle of her cured wounds. As well, they mourned the new wounds across her body.

Sir Drake led the men in prayers. They prayed to several of their gods, including Sho, for the sergeant still hadn't chosen any other man to pray to.

Lord Drake finished his prayer by leaning over her body. He laid a fancy noble woman's hat by her pillow and then kissed my sister on the mouth. I heard him whisper, "It is winter's holiday. Did you not make provisions? Well then, we shall have to look forward to the next one." I hadn't seen this in him before.

When they were done kneeling at the bedside, Sir Drake came to me. He said, "I am sending Sir Lindie and Sir Casar back to Sir Lacellor for a rest. They will bear a message. It will read, *The gods honor this woman like none other! Do not turn any of Lady Lettoir's requests aside without considering whom such a denial might offend.*"

As time has passed, I too have grown to understand the fruits of this miracle. It sprang from a small act of love. The seed of it became a tree reaching into the sky like a soaring bird.

At the time, I wasn't pleased when we put the flaps of the tent back into order. I knelt there alone, seeing the newly saddened condition of my sister's body. I considered taking the sword in my hands and severing the arm of the brave and mad guard beside my only sister. Then I considered, what would such an act do to the magic? So many things were not mine to determine. I'd never felt so helpless. Even my bowls of herbs made no difference in the condition of either woman.

In the end I couldn't stand it and found Ella. I leapt on her back. We raced into the forest.

There in a clearing I hacked on a fallen tree. My arms ached, and I fell from exhaustion. It seemed that days had passed since any good sleep.

Upon my last nap by her side, I'd found my sister's sword in my lap. How it had gotten there, I had no idea. Abi had certainly not gotten up and fetched it.

I looked at it, hoping I'd not chipped it in my senseless fit of rage. It remained unscratched.

There, over the sword, I cried and pleaded to the Goddess to save my sister. Instead of the Goddess speaking to me, my sword started to sing. It had the sound of my mother. She'd failed her test of a shaman, and I'd not known her long enough to remember her face. Then the sword called me granddaughter. I'd not known my grandmother at all, for she'd left us to search for the missing Queen.

I tossed the steel on the ground.

It couldn't be; my grandmother had vanished from the tribe years back, nearly a score ago, well before I was born. With her had gone the last spirit of a fully tested shaman among our tribe. She'd left us all to be led only by our council, since our Queen was also missing. How did the soul of such a mighty warlord get to be in my sister's sword? I asked her this.

She answered with a song. She sang, "I am not in the sword. I am in you. Pick up the sword, and let us walk together, my child."

I said, "This is not my sword. It belongs to my sister."

She disagreed. "The sword belongs to nobody. Pick it up and let us walk together, my child."

I couldn't disobey my grandmother. The woman was a fully tested Shaman Princess of great power and she had spoken to me from the land of the dead. Even without a body, I could not disrespect her. Such a woman, even in spirit, was equal to my sister, also a tested warlord and not to be trifled with. I took the sword in hand and fastened its sheath over my back.

Then my grandmother stood before me, a ghost that I could see through. She also had a sword, though it wasn't pretty.

The first thing she did with it was hack my neck nearly in half.

I got up from where I'd fallen, realizing I was still alive and not even in pain. Still, it hadn't been a pleasant feeling. This time I put the sword out in front of me. I was never a tall person, and so I had to hold it in both hands. I felt her blade hit mine. All my bones suddenly buzzed like they meant to shake apart.

That's when the teaching started.

Chapter Fifteen

As time passed, my wounds healed and so too did my resentment of Sir Pritchan. In fact, I came to miss him. He lived by the rules of his world, which were often in conflict with mine, but he was not pure evil. For example, he would have liked to have seen me repent before he turned me over for torment and execution. As he saw it, the afterworld was longer lived than this tiny one, and he'd intended to save me from damnation. The problem was, I didn't believe in his heaven, and didn't think for a moment that living there among his men and priests would be a pleasant way for a woman to spend an eternity.

Equally, when he'd seen me as a misbehaving maid cast among some brigands, he'd thought well enough of me to want me. That was certainly better than where I'd started, a cast-out from my family with no prospects at all, save hanging or bedding in a whorehouse.

I glanced at Sir Drake as he rode alongside, and I wondered what he saw in me. What were his designs? The man had been acting strangely of late. For some reason, he'd not let me out of his sight since I'd woken up from my sickbed.

Even more troubling, what were my intentions toward him? Sometimes I had to sort out my missions and had no time to number him among them. I had to put my army and their new lands in order. I desperately needed to find my mother and save her from the pits. Had I forgotten I was searching for a Queen? And, more immediately, I had to do something about Sir Barker's cavalry, for it dogged my rear and occupied my sister's every waking moment. She ceaselessly pestered their evening camps, to small effect.

All of this had been complicated by my slow recovery. Everybody had wanted to tend to me, especially Angel, who'd somehow recovered from her wounds so quickly that she was the first one to help me to my feet. Of course she didn't tell me how she'd managed such a quick and scar-free healing. I had to ask others. They conspired, only telling me it had been a miracle and leaving me in confusion.

I looked over to where the group, Minari, Marci, Sergeant Hadarm, and Sir Drake, sat upon their horses. I said, "The time has arrived. We shall deal with Sir Barker."

"That's what I've been telling you," said Marci. "Batya's been using that spell to make Captain Barker think she's you. By nipping at him, she's been keeping him away from our camp—and of course, such can't go on forever."

Minari added, "He only has two score. I say it's a good day to settle it, now that Sir Drake has brought us a score of his own men at arms."

"I suppose I shall have to quit asking, what will Minari do, when I find it strategic to pretend meekness." She gave me a confused look. The woman was slowly becoming a part of my army. Though she still wasn't much with a weapon, she was masterful at keeping all the details of supply and billeting in order.

Sir Drake said, "My men were only peasant born messengers a week ago. I brought them to train and see what could be done with this new idea of light horses. They've just started to learn how to ride in formation. I'd prefer a squad of your women at this stage of their training."

It surprised me that he had any confidence at all in my soldiers. I said, "Have you come to think of us that highly, Sir Drake?"

"I've seen what they can do when properly led and when they outnumber four score men on foot by three to one," he confessed.

I nodded. "Do you think them capable of taking two score experienced soldiers in light armor and on good horses?"

"Probably, if we have a good field and put enough women into the attack. It's not like attacking footmen though. I've seen this Captain Barker's men. His horsemen will fight, and with any kind of order to them, shift the field quickly. Thus the question becomes, how many can you risk losing in such a meaningless battle?"

"And you, Sergeant Hadarm?"

"We've both fought beside him. Don't ask me what you already know." I could always count on my sergeant to point out the obvious and to do so as if still speaking to his recruit.

I said, "I agree. My mother continues to rot while we play with him. I must get to Helfax the moment the weather breaks. Goddess willing, spring is upon us. And yet, if we confront him, our losses may lead to further delay."

Sir Drake said, "If you are intent upon this folly in Helfax, he will continually be in your rear. There's a rule of war, is there not? Such is not acceptable."

I glanced from face to face. "Your advice is that I attack him, and that I am wasteful and irresponsible if I attack him. Are we all agreed then?"

Sir Drake said, "I shall send for some of Sir Lacellor's knights and professional forces. He can send troops to mop up this intruder on his lands. Sir Finley, in fact, has shown an interest in our cause, hoping to win the favor of Lady Lettoir, whom he courts."

I found those thoughts interesting, and I also found it interesting that Sir Drake showed more than his usual passing interest in our affairs. I asked, "If we ask this favor, Sir Drake, what do you imagine will be the tales regarding our worth in Lacellor's court?"

"You have proven your worth in battle, and already shown the worth of a quickly-trained light cavalry," he said.

"Then none will take this as an opportunity to say, 'Ah, they were good at raiding a few poorly led soldiers on foot. Such has no real merit.' And, they might be right, for I wonder as we grow, do I have need of this favor?"

He glowered at this. The man nudged his horse closer to me and then leaned in until his lips were next to my ear when he whispered, "You don't have to prove anything to me, my Lady. This man has a personal grudge against you. Until you are fully well, I forbid you near him. Even after some healing, I will have to insist upon handling this for you, if not with an army, then personally."

He took his time guiding his horse back around and regained his original position among our circle of horses.

I should have been offended. I should have reminded him that I wasn't some lame breeder, as my sister would say, to be told every little thing to do by a man. And yet, his discretion had thrown me off guard, not to mention his obvious concern for my personal safety. And here I'd given up on the idea of wooing him. Suddenly I had no idea what I'd do with him if won. *Best to not linger on that.*

Here was a man who'd been reluctantly pulled into the chore of training my women. And now he was threatening to come between my sword arm and the business end of the enemy's metal.

As for my sword, I had a good one across my back, but not the one given to me by the crone. That had somehow fallen into the hands of my sister. Since she'd never shown an interest in learning the sword before, I was reluctant to ask for it back. There was something of the Goddess's work behind that. I'd even told her: "The thing has a teacher's magic within." From the look on her face, the revelation hadn't come as a surprise.

After some thought, I said, "We have two hundred here on horses and will encamp in the rolling hills to our west. I have told my sister to bring Sir Barker to me there in three days. By then we will be ready."

"Foolish and wasteful," Sergeant Hadarm said.

Sir Drake agreed with my sergeant, once again playing a demon's advocate. "Their horses are heavy. They have more armor, and their pikes are both longer and better made. Oh, you will kill him sure enough, but, by the time you reach him, half your two hundred will litter the field."

"Then I shall not reach him, Sir Drake."

"Simple minded," the sergeant scoffed.

Sir Drake's mouth opened then immediately shut. I nodded, and we returned to the task of reaching the open hills by nightfall.

* * * * *

From up on a good hill, I looked over the rolling plains. Sir Barker and his men were supposedly a few hills beyond the dust of my sister's archers. Batya had more than a squad with her, the few easily outpacing Captain Barker's heavy horsemen and his several strings of supply horses. His strategy was simple; he imagined dogging her until she made a mistake. Hers was simpler; she never made a mistake. Now it was simpler still, as she raced in my direction with enough lead to ensure Barker ran straight into our field.

"You are intent upon this?" Sir Drake asked.

I nodded. "And you are intent on playing my minder instead of tending to your new light cavalry?"

"Precisely. I've grown fond of studying your strategy. Arrogant though you may be. You have a way of testing my patience."

I laughed at him. Even Angel smiled, perhaps hoping to see a fight.

He displayed a face suggesting no offense. "These tactics—have the Debrecians taught them to you? I find them most unusual. If so, was it your sister who advised you on these dangerous techniques?"

"No. They are from the Tartans."

"Oh. I've heard of them, a fading people well to the north, but know little of their customs."

"Well, from my readings—"

"You can truly read? I thought you were stretching the truth when I heard it said. Hasn't the King declared it illegal among women in your land?"

"Lady Lettoir reads. I've also seen to it that several who lead us know some words," I told him.

"You would change the world. This is just another way in which you are a criminal, my fine and dangerous lady." Though, as he looked away toward the coming dust of my sister's horse, I noticed a smirk. Could it be possible that Sir Drake was becoming accustomed to my sinful nature?

"As to these Tartans then?" he asked after a pause.

"I see much in their limitations that we share, Sir Drake. They had no stout bloodlines in their horses, nor were they rich enough to carry many spares. They were often called into service at sudden notice, bringing only farming tools as weapons. The hunting bow, short pike and common axe were favored. Few Tartans owned a shield."

Sir Drake said, "Ah, I can see the similarities. So, good tactics befitting their lack of arms and horses are hoped to gain an equal chance on the battlefield."

"No. Not equality, Sir Drake. In one battle alone, four hundred Tartans took their leisure destroying six thousand knights, mostly while running away from them."

His face suggested it was unbelievable. He asked, "And, you read this in a book?"

"Yes."

"Well, perhaps that explains it. Some books are not to be believed," he told me.

"That is true, fair knight. Still, what choices do we have?"

He smiled at me and answered, "You called me fair. I am compelled to be most agreeable at the moment."

I didn't know what he meant by that, but I was spared the need to ask by the arrival of my sister. Her horse was out of breath, having been run hard. Sir Barker's white knights showed plenty of dust of their own by then. Soon they'd appear over the last small hill.

I told her where our forces were positioned, where to place her archers, and where she could take up a position leading my main forces. Just that quickly, she departed to our rear. Only Angel and Sir Drake remained at my side.

A long distance forward of my position were sixty light archers and spear bearers. They sat in their saddles, two deep; the second score and a half were archers, the first spear bearers.

These women were not entirely fresh, for I'd worked them tirelessly over the past two days, teaching them a few new skills.

As soon as Captain Barker's cavalry rolled over the hill, he saw them, and strung his soldiers out in a double line on the opposite side of the field. This was very polite of him, as I'd expected. We were formally positioned, so his noble training implied that he should do the same.

From the looks on their faces, these thirty were pleased at the prospect of finally meeting my army in formal battle, even at two to one odds. Pausing before their assault was one of the weaknesses of the nobility. If it had been me leading Barker's force, I'd have ridden right over my poorly armored women.

I motioned for Angel and Sir Drake to stay a few paces behind me as I slowly rode down the hill and past this presentation of women to speak with Sho's knight. Captain Barker came out with two of his own to speak with me.

I noticed that only a few of the soldiers behind him were from the previous encounter. These new men were solid warriors, some of whom I'd run with a year ago. There were no faces resembling highwayman hired to fill some hole in the ranks. Instead of sloppy edges, they all had at least mail and helmets. Their tunics were the official white ones that ran nearly to their knees. Below that were good black boots that did reach all the way to the knees. Blankets were neatly rolled behind good saddles. I imagined none of their swords were pig iron, nor did the hilts on their steel lack leather and quality engraving. Pikes were steel tipped and leather handled. The horses were large, their eagerness for battle clearly judged by the look in their eyes and the steadiness of their necks. I imagined smoke blowing from their nostrils

The enemy's faces were also steadier than any I'd seen in a Farstand company. These were the best men of Sho, I understood, come to pour vengeance over the witch who'd made a mockery of their God.

Thus I felt compelled to make a mockery of them.

"Sir Barker, I see you've not seen the wisdom of relenting."

"The Lord is unrelenting, witch, and before you think to cast another spell towards these men of God, consider, I've put wax in their ears and also chosen them for their steadfast diligence in prayer. They are immune from witchery."

"Well and good for them, Captain. It relieves me the guilt of slaying them then, for they are as prepared to join their God in your imagined afterlife as ever they will be."

"It is good you see death before you," he said. "However, do not take too much pride in the number of women you've fooled into dying for you. If so, then you shall die with the guilt of having killed many women. Two to one are no odds against battle-hardened men of God. Instead, surrender to me, and I shall only take their horses, leaving these misguided creatures to the lust of Sir Lacellor's army."

Sir Drake rode up from behind me and said, "I represent Sir Lacellor. If you've grievance with him, then let us touch steel to steel and in that way end this forever." He pulled his sword out and showed it to Captain Barker.

Captain Barker wasn't so easily swayed. It was a tribute to their training that neither Barker nor the two beside him drew swords.

He said, "I've seen you before. You are a good man in battle, but this is not your fight. If you choose to make it your fight, then so be it; we are already at war with Sir Lacellor, and my men are prepared to destroy you along with this rabble."

I had to hold Sir Drake's horse back by leaning over and putting a hand on his harness. I wouldn't have us break the protocol of negotiation, nor would Sir Drake fight our battle for us. This was no longer a battle between me and the representatives of Sho's White Shirts, but rather, it was to show Sir Lacellor that we were allies to be taken seriously.

I said, "We'll fight, Captain Barker. Let it also be known, I've asked my warriors to not aim for you, and instead leave you to a lesson. This way the Baron of Helfax will hear you and be compelled to listen. He will know I am serious about meeting him in his hall. If he wishes to avoid dying under my blade, then he needs only return my mother to my warriors."

"Foolish bitch!"

That comment I wouldn't answer. Instead, I rode back up the slight incline. Sir Drake followed me, but, as we passed the lines of my three score horses, Angel slipped from my side and joined in the first rank. She'd not trained with them, but, of course, she'd been ever watchful, and telling her that this wasn't her chore would have been, as always, a waste of my time.

From up on my hill, I saw there wouldn't be the usual joust to get the other side to attack first. A horse came out from our side, burst across our front, then returned to the ranks. One of theirs did the same. After the show, we took the initiative. Sergeant Sasha's command, "Forward!" rang clear and high pitched.

Our first thirty trotted toward Sir Barker's pike-braced line at a steady prance. The white guards tightened up their lines, shields up and long pikes forward. Then, with only one short bark from a squad leader, our back rank arched a volley of arrows, sticking several shields and only one horse, though the animal didn't falter. At least half of the arrows were weak and short due to our lack of training and our varied quality of bows.

The closer spear bearers lofted their spears into the enemy's face. These women were larger and hand-picked for spear duty, but the range was too far, and any fool could see it.

Our heavy ordinance fell short. Only a few spears made it to Captain Barker's lines, but one struck a horse, and one man was temporarily removed from his horse when two spears hit his shield simultaneously.

A couple of the white guardsmen broke rank to avoid spears, and had to return their horses to the line once they'd passed at knee level. The man with the wounded horse fell back and quickly changed to a spare horse, made ready because of quick thinking and good training. Captain Barker was intent on watching my soldiers spend their spears for a few minor losses. He saw he wasn't within good range and that we were disarming ourselves quickly.

The line of archers shot another flight in a tall arch.

Before the arrows fell, the first line of cavalry pulled their spare spears from the lacing holding them in place. They advanced a pace more and tossed them at the enemy, disarming themselves entirely.

The archers, having quickly reloaded, sent a third thirty arrows nearly straight into Barker's soldiers. His men found themselves shielding against arrows and spears coming at them from both overhead and the fore, though once again, most of the arrows and spears fell far short.

One more of Captain Barker's men fell from a horse, this one dead or seriously wounded, and several of Barker's horses fussed from the sting of arrowheads.

Sir Barker had a handful of men also armed with short bows, but they were few and shot sparingly due to the need to continually man their short shields. One of these, in fact, was the man who fell, given the shooting of arrows caused him to hook his small archer's shield on its saddle mount, and thus hampered his defense.

When the wood stopped flying, my spear bearers had no good weapons other than a few crude swords and knives.

Captain Barker had to realize we weren't going to press forward and close at all, given we were out of spears entirely and half of my warriors were defenseless. One of his men was on the ground, and less than a handful of horses were hurting, but still on their feet and eager to charge.

He'd suffered all the losses he would take. Our attack was finished, lasting no more than a half minute.

A command was heard over the constant din of hooves. Sir Barker's horsemen lurched forward.

This instantly broke the order of the first line of spear bearers. They weren't the only ones to turn away from the oncoming lances. Soon, all three score of my women fled in utter disorder. One line merged with the other at about the same time both lines became a scattered mess.

Some were too slow in turning, not having enough experience on horses to turn and get them going, but the bulk of my cavalry fled in a mob, first backing away towards my hill, and then tracking across my front and to my right. Our horses preferred the relative flat land, as even the horses sensed the panic.

This left me and Sir Drake exposed, should some of Sir Barker's horsemen choose to turn our direction and climb our hill. Otherwise, the enemy raced on slightly rested horses at the heels of our stragglers, seeing the victory before them as the grander prize.

They overtook one woman on a tired mare. She fell even with the steel pike heads. My heart sank when I saw her poked and then cut in turn by several enemy swords. Her horse slowed, and then stood in the wake of the enemy with a bloody body slipping from the saddle. I'd seen many deaths in my life, but ones such as that are unforgettable.

I decided I had no choice but to withdraw when a few of Sir Barker's men split off, and so Sir Drake and I broke along a parallel path, keeping to the small heights of the grassy hills and paralleling the battle below.

Our horses were fresh and well bred, and thus we had no trouble gaining ahead of the two groups of soldiers. Those who'd come for us saw our speed and veered back to their ranks.

We stopped several hills beyond the first clash. There, we had a good view of another pair of small rolling hills close to the river. Our three score raiders drove their horses over one last rise. All of Sir Barker's horses charged over at their heels.

They were met by the remainder of my forces. I had Batya's archers at the top of the hundred yard wide funnel opening. There were three score of them now, and all were on our best horses. Behind the archers was a row of women holding long pikes, the best in my army, with many months of training. Down nearer the river were nearly a hundred women with iron tipped spears and braced pikes, supported by a handful of superior archers, all mounted and forming the other half of the funnel. Farther up the hill, Sir Drake's new light horsemen waited in deep reserve.

The far right neck of our funnel consisted of several rows of experienced women. They were well within danger from crossfire where the neck tightened. Here, my archers had been told to shoot at angles leaning in towards the wider portion of the trap, a far more effective manner of getting past the enemy's shields anyway. Even if a man were directly in front of an archer, she was trained to shoot at someone else, making use of an angle and trusting her neighbor to return the favor.

The brave and mostly inexperienced women who'd led my enemy into the ambush filed through the neck of the funnel. There, planted in the ground, were fifty long lances. They plucked the weapons out of the ground as they rode past. Sasha formed one decent rank of ten, closing the end of the bottle behind the hooves of our last warrior. Archers from her group circled around both flanks, adding another row of archers to those manning the funnel's walls.

Sir Barker's leading five crashed into these, toppling several of ours holding pikes. As the horses and bodies slowed their charge, spears flew and arrows reached for lightly-armored men and horses. They bogged near the back rank, and after that, one by one, fell.

As the trap reshaped, we walked our horses down the hillside, closing the distance between ourselves and the fight.

Some of Sir Barker's cavalry, bunched behind their stopped lead in the breech, organized and broke to the side. One of these sliced clear through two ranks. A small contingent of women with spears circled, ran him from his wounded horse, and prodded him ceaselessly when he fell.

This second assault to our wall stopped at our back rank, slid off, and returned to the dubious safety of the center. Sasha turned from where she'd stopped the first breech, took three women with her, and charged them into the wall where the one man had slipped through, trampling two fallen men and defeating their fighting mounts. A single horse, one of ours, freed itself and fled across the hills.

Those men who remained searched for a weakness, taking hit after hit. Any way they rode seemed to take them closer to a new deluge of arrows, increasingly exposing their backs. Some of these men made runs, finding single women too far forward or unskilled with their weapons and mount. Yet, more men died at the end of our reaching lances and no few arrows, all at close range and coming at them from deep ranks and concentrated units of our better warriors. A cork of dead horses soon completely blocked the funnel's narrow end as well as the former breech to the side. Barker's few defended against three pressing sides as we reduced intervals and closed ranks several steps.

This gave Sir Barker and his remaining handful no more options as we squeezed the wide end of his field. He chose to form another attack on the same flank as before. Doing so, of course, exposed every man's rear, as well as side, to lethal flocks of well-aimed arrows shot at angles intended to defeat their remaining handful of shields.

Such vital organization took precious seconds, and we gave him none. Nor did circumstances allow him to regain command of his men, as two broke from the charge. These attacked Batya's archers, each now armed with curve-back bows and ceaseless training from my sister. Those two died riddled with wood.

Our long lance bearers rode up and met the last weak charge. I'd given orders to favor their shields and not lose their lances, nor overly press an attack, thus allowing the archers to do the hard work of killing.

It all happened as if from the hands of the Goddess. In fact, it was over nearly before it started. Almost as soon as the first few fell in the neck of our bottle, Sir Barker's strength was too little to cause a breach.

I saw my forces bend as required, but hold until the last man stood. These peasant breeders sat on their horses in lines that would have made any knight proud of their discipline. Batya was at liberty to ride up and down the ranks, inside the battlefield, insisting on good order at all times. If not for the blood, I'd have imagined her on a parade field instead of within the midst of the enemy forces.

Between the corralling ranks of women warriors, a few lone horses wandered, most limping over the field of red-splashed grass. One dragged a corpse around by a foot in a stirrup. Most of the enemy horses were dead or dying, casualties of our excessive munitions. With so many pikes, spears and arrows, the degree of carnage was unavoidable.

Across the field, five or six men crawled as if away from their own bleeding bodies. I'd corrected our previous error and ordered that anybody able to leave our battlefields would be allowed to walk home and lay witness to our power. They'd not be believed anyway, and so I doubted the enemy would intelligently use their witness against us. In any event, the chance of any of these men walking home was remote, for every one of the wounded was riddled with arrows. Those in the heaviest armor had been singled out by design as targets for our spears.

Only one man still sat on his horse. He had an arrow in his arm, but was otherwise unscathed as he wandered across the battlefield cursing at the lines of women who by then had even closed the fat end of the funnel, and were thus his captors.

Batya rode toward him. Her sword—my sword—was sheathed across her back. Its sheath was crossed by the wood of her bow. In her hand she held a spear down low and with the ease of a Debrecian born to the weapon. Her eyes were alight with the delight of a warrior in the midst of a battle of her own making.

Captain Barker raised his sword, threateningly, but Batya worked her horse expertly, keeping his threats well away without even bothering to raise her spear. None had ever been better on a horse, and Ella was in her glory.

He soon tired. The wound in his arm took a toll.

Batya asked, "You are the man my sister calls Captain Barker?" She was still young, I was reminded. Her voice was girlish and thin and with no small amount of Debrecian accent. Still, I heard it clearly from halfway down the slope I was descending.

"Cowards! Is this finally the much promised Debrecians? How did you find so many short ones with brown hair and brown eyes, and also so weak they must murder in a swarm? As well, unwilling to meet my soldiers in a respectable charge?"

"There are only two Debrecians among us, knight. These women here are not Debrecians, but breeders. They are she-spawn of your own king, sent back to haunt him, trained by the Goddess who spits on your God. It's Her voice that guides them now; that at least like the great tribes."

"I know no such she god, nor such a voice," he raged.

"You know the voice of my sister, Abi, well, I hear. It's through her we hear the words of the Goddess. Yet, for some reason she imagines she owes you a life. Some foolishness about service together in the last war. Well then, take your life home with you, but do not do so without first promising me that you'll no longer hunt my sister. If you don't make this promise to me here and now, I'll end your time on this earth, for I and my soldiers have not sworn that we shall spare you one more breath with which to spite my sister. I'll honor my sister in all she commands, save for this!" She rode around his horse as she spoke these words, troubling Sir Barker to have to turn his horse to continually face her threat.

"You are a child!" he said.

I kicked my horse, racing farther down the slope, hoping to put an end to my sister's challenge of the great and experienced knight.

When I got close, my sister commanded, "Close those ranks!" The women I'd intended to move through shifted their horses such that I couldn't pass. I turned, hoping to find another place to make my way through in order to stop the battle I envisioned my sister losing. The ranks moved forward, soon two horses deep everywhere and allowing me no quarter.

I screamed at them to move aside, but it was as if my voice were the wind, for all the women were heeding only the words of my sister. Never had I seen such insubordinate behavior from my women.

There, just ahead, I found Angel and tried to wedge beside her horse, but she just looked back at me and smiled. I saw blood on her pike and lines of more blood on her britches from where she'd wiped her knives before she'd put them away in her sheaths.

Sir Drake came up beside me again, and I felt his hand take hold of my reins. I shot him an angry look, but he wouldn't relent, and I didn't have the heart to fight him, for there seemed great purpose and resolve pasted upon his face.

"I hear the witch now. Let me settle this here and now with her, as is proper," Sir Barker said.

"You're unworthy!" my sister screamed. Up some on the grade, I witnessed her stick her spear into the ground, and pull forth her sword. That filled me with terror because, though small, she was an expert with a bow or a spear. *Could she possibly match the skill of Captain Barker with a sword?*

"And if I kill you? What then girl?" Captain Barker asked.

"Then you'll have to kill her." My sister pointed to Angel. Angel drove her horse up a half step, as if to let him know she was more than willing to be next. Instead of her sword, Angel drew her knives. My mind painted a picture of her diving upon his sword, being run through as she pinned him with a knife in each of her hands. Captain Barker couldn't possibly imagine this madness.

"And if she also fails?" he asked.

Upon hearing this, another of my warriors rode her horse a half step forward. She only had to wait a half breath before several more nudged their horses. Soon, the circle surrounding Sir Barker and my sister was a good bit smaller.

Captain Barker looked around at the women. "This is without honor."

My sister answered, "Where was the honor in chasing my sister around all of Farstand with two score men? I'm compelled by the Goddess to kill you. She doesn't speak to me as she does my sister, but I'm certain of her will. Don't trouble yourself regarding the rest of my warriors. I'm a shaman princess, and won't be long in killing you myself."

"Batya! Let me do this," I shouted into the circle.

She couldn't ignore me, but answered by speaking to the captain, "My sister doesn't know these small things are no longer her duty. It falls to her warriors. In this, all her voice means is I grow short on the time I need to kill you." Upon saying that, she circled with her sword. Their swords met with a strong sound of metal on metal. My vision was hampered somewhat by the heads of my troops as the contestants moved to the side.

"Your sister has taught you some." He withdrew his horse a step after only a couple strokes.

When my sister didn't back up, he added, "I'll leave. There's no honor in killing a small female child." He put his sword away, but when he turned, the women around him made no room for his escape.

My sister insisted, "You'll swear to your pitiful God that you'll no longer seek the blood of my sister, and that you'll return to your home. Then you may retire!"

"All right then. I swear to the only and true God, Sho, that I shall not personally bloody your sister!" It seemed to take a lot out of him to say that.

My sister wasn't satisfied. She added, "And you will not lead others against her."

"I'm still a knight under the rule of my King. Would you have me denounce all dignity just to save my life, child?"

I had to interrupt. I said, "No. We'll not ask that, Sir Barker. Leave us now!"

"No!" my sister insisted. "This is my duty, not my sister's. Listen to me. You'll not lead any men against my sister, or you'll die here. As for war, you're free to follow your King in any battle he chooses. That way you may retain your small honor, but you'll no longer pretend it's an honor to hunt my sister as if she's a dog. She's proud, too proud for her own safety, so the duty falls to me. Hear this: I am determined to kill you here. And I swear to you, she will never be alone and free to meet you in single combat."

I was angry, riding around the outside of the circle. What right did Batya have to defy my authority and make such claims on my freedom? Sir Drake's hand was still on my reins, but the result was more of him being dragged around than me being restrained.

The wind suddenly descended on me and my horse. This breeze slowed my horse's stride until he stopped. I kicked him hard, but the black stallion refused to move. I felt the wind warming around me even more. I tried to speak, but was struck mute when a gust filled my lungs.

We'd stopped still as stones outside the ranks, my soldiers' attention inward. I could see that Sir Drake felt it too. He took his hand off my reins as if he'd been touched by fire. Then he watched my face with alarm as I felt the presence of the Goddess fill my soul with warmth and a numbing contentment, against which I immediately struggled. It wasn't natural, but my anger was tied in a knot, and though my concern for the safety of my sister had not lessened, I knew it was no longer my place to keep her from declaring the final course of this battle.

I had to obey the clear will of the Goddess. I shouted, "The Goddess is with us," and though it pained me to say it because of my sister's disobedience, I was compelled to add, "She sends her blessing upon my sister." It only added to my anger, having to say the words the Goddess had placed upon my lips.

"Bah! More godless talk! Fine then! I swear to not hunt this witch. We will enjoy all-out war soon, and on the way to decimating Lacellor's rebellion, all of you shall be in our way. You will not last, for you've camped on the battlefield."

Upon declaring me a witch, Angel nudged her horse forward another step, and I thought for a moment that all the negations were coming to a violent conclusion. Instead, my sister restrained herself and the others. She commanded some to make way with their horses, and then waved Sir Barker away with the back of her hand.

His gaze lingered some on Angel and then on my sister again, but he took advantage of the offering and left the field. Two others among his men found their feet and managed to drag themselves up on a pair of barely living horses. Those wounded soldiers followed the nobleman, and were allowed to leave, though I knew they wouldn't last the road.

The rest on the field consisted of the dead and the dying. We robbed the enemy bodies of their possessions, then collected our own eleven dead, as well tended our wounded.

As we finished, night fell like a curtain. We didn't camp there, though we were tired, and the grass was soft near the bodies of our enemy.

Chapter Sixteen

I would never get used to the hollow sound of great halls. Even whispers feel lofty in such caverns, though as I aged, I came to understand that most great words were uttered in much more humble places. Such was my pessimism as I stood in the center of Sir Lacellor's grand hall.

My sister endured my question: "Why did you defy me during that last battle?" We waited for Sir Lacellor's appearance after breakfast hour.

She whispered, "Have I asked you to forgive me?"

"No, you haven't."

She said, "And, I will not do so now."

I looked at her curiously, and noticed she wasn't scoffing at me, but had meant it. I asked, "Who is the leader who is first among us?"

"You, of course."

I asked, "Well then, have I been remiss in my discipline?"

"Oh, that's easy. None dare cross you. Do you know the way our women fear your punishment of having them miss training by standing to the side of the practice fields for a week of penance? Some have told me, 'If she were to have me flogged, I'd miss but a couple days in the sick tent.'"

I said, "Still, you disobeyed me."

"No, I don't think so."

"How can you think such a thing?"

"Didn't you tell me you felt the Goddess's breath? If it's her will and if you are her voice, then it's your will as well."

"How can that be sensible?"

My sister didn't answer. After a little while she asked, "Can you tell me how you came to your test of shaman warlord?"

"Are you asking me to explain things regarding your culture? I'm a Debrecian, but in blood alone, for other than you and the two women who raised me, I've only seen Debrecians in passing. You, however, were raised in the tribes. I should be asking you that question."

She laughed. The sound echoed around the vast hall. Several nobles and petitioners were present, and thus we were even more of a curiosity than ever, for the nobles watched us continually for signs of wildness as we stood in the center of the grand aisle.

She asked, "Didn't you feel something change within you?"

"Ah," I said, "my soul is constantly changing inside of me."

"Well then," she asked, "what was the feeling you had just before you mentioned to Beckli Kahnsa that you had passed your tests?"

I thought about it a moment, but all I could think to say was, "I felt as if nobody in the world could touch me with a sword or pike or even a catapult, and, if I willed it, I could gather the women of the world around a rag on a splintered pole as long as it bore my name."

"Yes," she said. "I have recently felt this soul. And before, in the form of my grandmother, who was once a great shaman."

"When did this first come to you?"

"The night of your injury. It was also the night when I awoke with your sword resting in my lap. Later, I met my grandmother in the woods. She told me she'd taken up residence beside me. She then cleaved my head from my body. Since then I've wanted nothing other than to learn the sword and kill your enemies."

"Ah. Soon thereafter I awoke with only two tormenting spirits -- and a new contentment, for the crone's seemed silent. I've not missed her endless anger."

My sister added, "All your dreams were troubled. You'd taken to yourself the wounds of your bodyguard. It was as if the Goddess were one of the midwives, walking around the room with many duties, not all of them healing."

"Then you chose to defy me on the field of battle because of all that?" I needed to get us back to the point.

She answered, "I've given it thought. Though I am little in the Goddess's sight, it is said, a high shaman cannot be easily recalled.

This is most true when the Queen is threatened and in the midst of death."

I thought about what she'd said, and determined, "War should not come with ease, even for leaders. Perhaps, even for Queens, for not only is a Queen the leader of her people, but she is also the mother of the dead. Perhaps, when we find our Queen, she'll show this worthiness by talking to those who've fallen."

My sister nodded. She stood beside me, dressed in a dark leather skirt. Her vest was made of steel chain and under that was a well-tailored tunic of light brown. Such was a compromise, we'd thought, between us and their knights. She bore my sword across her back. Her hair was up, bound by several wraps of cloth in her usual fountain. She was going through a growth spurt as well, already taller than the local women.

I wasn't much different, though my dress was full, fine linen, fringed in lace and almost as much in fashion as the better-born women who were slowly making their way in from the wings. I bore no weapons. Well then, I suppose I was very different, but I'd let my sister put my hair up in similar fashion to her own. That way they'd know us as a pair, given I'd never seen the fashion on any other than the Debrecians.

I heard the banging and boots near the doors. Sir Lacellor and his knights filed in, followed by Lady Lettoir and her maid Minari, both in splendid gowns befitting nobles and their maids. I'd discovered the convenience of Minari as my spy, them seeing her only as the lady's servant.

The first words out of the rebel knight's mouth were, "Why do you never bow to me, even slightly? Do you have other loyalties?"

I said, "We are more allies than servants. To be sure, these women have had enough of low service, and present ample worry upon their table, without the interruption of formality."

"And yet you live on my lands. Is that not enough excuse to offer me allegiance?"

"The lands we live on were abandoned as a result of war and no knight's willingness to abide them. We do you a service by living there and giving fair warning of invasion, come fighting season. How much would you pay to have others guard your border, were we to leave?"

He sat down on his throne, looking exhausted, even though it was still only dawn. "Clearly, talking to you will not be any easier the second time around. So be it then, let us get to the point that hampers our negotiations. According to the refined, and gladly tactful, Lady Lettoir, you seek a mission beyond Dorne, in order to invade the remote and rather poor baronage at Helfax. You wish to invest in this simply to gain the release of your mother, whom I've been told is a peasant—not meaning, of course, to offend you by mentioning her low birth."

"That is correct, Sir Lacellor."

"Why?"

I realized I'd spent so much of my time trying to prove the worth of my women that I'd not considered the new line of questioning. Sir Lacellor denied his help because he lacked faith in us, I'd solidly imagined. Now that I'd shown us worthy, it seemed there was another consideration. I wanted to say, "Because she's my mother," but he'd already established that as insufficient.

I said, "King Falstaff of Farstand has determined she is worth a cell in Helfax. I am led by the Goddess to think she has hidden value. My hope is that she has knowledge of the whereabouts of the lost Queen sought by the Debrecians."

"You expect us to empty the castle of knights in order to discover an imagined treasure?"

Sir Drake leaned toward the grand knight. "Your grace, I'm as uncertain as you that this venture is worth the cost, but surely there is more to this than the release of a peasant mother. If Lady Abi has determined the Goddess sees worth in the battle, then it is as she says, for this woman is no common reader of palms. The air grows thick around her as she communes with her God."

Sir Lacellor then said, "Well then, I suppose it may be a matter of one God versus the others. So, let me ask you this: What do our gods gain when you find the missing Queen who serves your God? I have been told that if the Queen is returned to the tribes, then the Debrecians have no more interest in our cause. This leaves us without allies when we face our enemies. It is in our interest that this Queen never be found."

I was speechless for a moment. This I hadn't considered. I finally said, "It will not be the men of Farstand who give this Queen to the Debrecians. It will be through force of armed women that this will be done. I shall personally rescue her, and with the help of the Goddess, we shall bend the Queen's will so she will see the common worth of your cause."

He disagreed, saying, "If after all this time the Debrecians have not declared war on the enemy, then how am I to think you can convince them after their demands have been satisfied and through no cost in the conflict at all?"

"It will be done because it's the will of the Goddess. Even in this room I've seen her. May I ask, Sir Lacellor, who is the wooden God who decorates that wall?" I pointed to the statue of the woman off to the side and high up the wall.

He looked over, as did all the guests in the great chamber, and said, "It is only a symbol of fertility. She goes by no other name than the god who blesses our women."

"Such is appropriate, Sir Lacellor. It is through her common, unnamed and almost peasant presence that I've seen the Goddess here three times. Each time I've spoken to her, she has made it clear that my course is predetermined. Be it known, I shall find my mother, and through her I shall find the Queen, and, when the Goddess is satisfied and the Queen recovered, then we shall talk of other matters. Let it also be known that the God of the Debrecians is the same as the peasant adorning this temple. For your servant and my Queen are one in the same."

"Then go," said the great knight. "Find your way to Helfax. What need have you of us?"

"The Goddess has requested that I ask your assistance."

"Again, why?"

I looked at the people in the room. "So she might test you and see if you are worthy."

"I am unworthy?" shouted Sir Lacellor.

I said, "Such is not prophecy, Sir Lacellor, for I am not a prophet as is Beckli Kahnsa, nor am I eloquent. It's instead, simply the will of the Goddess, insisting that I ask for this assistance. What will be the will of the Goddess if you refuse? Have you not once wondered why the Debrecians wait, lending you only watchful assistance?"

He said, "They are splintered and indecisive, that is all. In time, perhaps too late, and when we are no longer fit as allies, they will see the threat to themselves and have no choice but to respond."

I wanted to laugh at his folly, but was determined to not lose the moment. Instead, I looked at my sister, who was listening to me most intently, and, though I was speaking to the great and rebellious knight, my face didn't turn when I said, "The Debrecians are not fools. They want to know if Sir Lacellor is a better man than the King of Farstand."

He scoffed, "And the tribes of Debrecia have told you this?"

I looked away from my sister and told him, "Certainly not, Sir Lacellor. Yet, look to the wooden statue. She is all I need to listen to when I want to hear the will of the Debrecian tribes. Do you not know we share her thoughts in these matters?"

He didn't know the answer to that. Instead, I heard the whispers of his knights, most of them saying it was a good time to once again lose themselves in some back room where they could discuss my needs endlessly and into the eternal well of procrastination, while my mother continued to rot in a Helfax hell.

"Perhaps?" came a plea from well to the side. There, Lady Lettoir stood beside her courting knight and freshly recovered maid. When the murmurs ceased, she restated, "Perhaps she can take those who are willing. As before. It didn't seem to cause any great harm. In fact, from reports, there was much learned, and a few new tricks of arms established."

Sir Lacellor looked at his knights, perhaps seeing the commitment and wondering how far to push against the tide. Surprisingly, the man relented to the lady, saying, "I will have to insist on no tricks. Last time she forced the participation of three of my knights through deception." He looked around the chamber, seeing a few smiles.

I could see by the smirks and whispers among the warriors that some recalled my visit to the practice yard with amusement, but most also had the look of men who felt the great knight had bested me in diplomacy.

Then I was surprised again, for Sir Drake stepped forward from where he'd stood close to the side of Sir Lacellor and said, "I am willing, as are some of the knights of my baronage and the new professional fighting peasants I am training on horses. This list of the willing also includes Sir Casar of Gristle."

"I, as well, and those fighters of good blood I have recalled from my lands," said Sir Finley as he stepped forward from the side of Lady Lettoir.

"I will also go," declared Minari. She was in a delicate gown with many skirts. They swam as she stepped forward from the farthest right reaches of the assembly before us. Her declaration was clearly odd, considering the setting and her lowest of all stations as Lady Lettoir's maid. All of those even in the lesser wings outranked her.

As soon as she spoke, the room hushed, and then one man in the back laughed, causing the whole room to erupt in riotous jeers.

The great knight Lacellor appeared to be the only man not amused as he raised his hand and called the people to order. His attention was on the maid, upon whom he cast an angry glare. I was certain he was contemplating her punishment for speaking in the presence of a noble's assembly.

As soon as the room was nearly hushed, I beat his words by saying, "And we shall need another fifty good horses, a hundred steel tipped lances, and provisions for two hundred horsemen on a month long campaign. Also, a map of Helfax: the best one that can be had from your spies. When you secure it, Sir Lacellor, you should give it to my Chamberlain. She will have to help you make arrangements for the transfer to my soldiers of all that is needed within the week." I nodded to the maid, letting my nod linger so it was clear to everyone here that it was the closest thing to a bow they were likely to see from me in their hall. Many curious eyes now fell on the humble personage of the lady's maid.

The great rebellious knight withdrew his attention from the maid and let his eyes settle on the leader of his heavy knights, Sir Drake. I could almost see him sag in resignation. He said, "Fine then. I see I cannot fight this madness. But, under one condition. This Queen and her tribes are of no use to us as things stand. Therefore, I have determined that we have nothing to lose, be she lost or returned to her tribe. When you find this Queen, you will plead our cause to her and do so unrelentingly. Perhaps she will see reason. As you have said, we are allies. You betray me if I lend you my property for this wasteful quest and then you do not also make a case to the leader of the Debrecians for our common cause. Further, you will need to return my men and horses by fighting season."

I nodded to him then left the assembly. Every eye in the room trailed me and my sister. We passed Angel, who had been ever watchful in return, as if she trusted none of those around us. Such was her Goddess-given nature, allowing me the freedom to enjoy a much more diplomatic disposition.

Chapter Seventeen

We raced through Farstand with strings of fresh horses and all the provisions we could steal or carry. Screaming widows of landed lords sang in our dust for two weeks, but they were never troubled with us twice, for we ever pressed forward before the enemy forces could catch up.

Late in this campaign, I found myself riding towards a hidden and little-used valley near Helfax. Sir Drake, Finley, Casar, and nearly a score of knights waited for my arrival with provisions and extra horses. Keeping an eye out for any intruders to their secluded camp were a score of Sir Drake's common-born horsemen. A few at an outpost were disguised in the blood stained coats of the baron's field troops. Two of these we startled out of a noon slumber as we raced past too fast to give warning.

I dismounted and then walked to the table that was set up with our map of Helfax anchored under six large rocks. The map was the best ever made of Helfax Baronage, thanks to the many marks added to it by our women who seemed to have been raised in every nook of Farstand.

I picked up some colored pebbles and marked the towns we'd attacked. The pebbles stole the attention of my knights, belaying their wishes to voice many grievances. Nothing is worse than a warrior made to wait.

The marks had grown into two large arrows, one well to the north of Helfax and the other to the south. Both arrows were steadily moving westward of the city; forming a horseshoe of destruction around, but well clear of, the baron's city and keep. Such warfare, I'd learned, both isolated and drew the full attention of Helfax.

I said, "I've ordered Sasha's group to rest out of sight for a full day. Batya's group knows to do the same thing in the north on this date. Obviously, the distance between us makes the last of the northern marks a guess. We'll hold tonight here . . . and here.

"It's not wise to rest that long. You'll give the baron's soldiers enough time to group a large force ahead of you," advised Sir Drake.

Sir Finley leaned directly across from me. He studied the map. "That's yet another reason why we knights should be leading these raiders and not a bunch of inexperienced peasant women. This Batya knows her weapons, but is too young to lead. She was sucking at her mother's teats only a few winters ago. As well, where did you get Sergeant Sasha, and what is her breeding as a warrior? None, I've heard. She is but a farmer and widow at that."

I'd determined a week ago that I'd not murder Sir Finley. He had some good moments, and as far as he could see things, imagined his words useful. Besides, if I murdered him, who would the lady marry?

I said, "There are several paths in each area, and we'll slip by the enemy best if we hold a while and let them get established in the next large holding where they imagine they can ambush us," I explained with my finger on the last crossed-out town on the map. "However, instead of attacking the next town, where, as implied by Sir Drake, many enemy troops and half as many bandits await, a few of each group will bypass the next two and lightly resume our attacks beyond. This will cause the enemy to race even farther away from Helfax. I want them reorganized so as many as possible are doing that."

Sir Finley sighed heavily, and then said, "Splitting your forces yet again is idiotic. At best, you can only harass them now, and you are never enough to meet them on a field of honor. When your scattered forces are caught, they'll be slaughtered, and justly so for fighting in a cowardly fashion." Several of the other knights nodded agreement.

I shook my head no. Pointing at the map, I told him: "We'll not linger along these arrows, nor will we fight beyond, where the enemy is strongest, Sir Finley. Our diversionary forces will hit them, quickly disappear, circle, and then belatedly meet with Batya and Sergeant Sasha near Helfax. In their place along the route of the enemy knights, I've invited every bandit in Farstand to keep the baron's expeditions busy. No decent person loves bandits racing through their town's street, particularly in the early spring when the silos are low.

This already plagues them. These legions of bandits are my gift to Helfax, and men like my father will linger here long after we are done."

Sir Finley said, "Ah! Even more dishonor. We don't see eye to eye on fighting. Let's move on to another concern: I have my own scouts. Would not setting flame to the villages add to the confusion?"

"And that is honorable? We've thoroughly raided the holdings of many landowners. Those are the ones who support Lord Eron Prescott of Helfax, and such men don't concern themselves with the plight of the peasantry, one way or the other. I'll leave the peasantry alone, unless it proves needful."

"It's not honorable to attack noble holdings without—"

"Good then. If you see it as uncivil, so too does the baron. The man's outrage will empty Helfax Keep and send even more of his soldiers three days in the wrong direction."

Sir Casar was beside Sir Finley, leaning on his axe. He asked, "All I want to do is fight. My axe itches. Just one day there, and we can meet this southern group before it moves away. We'll get a little fighting in and scat on before the whole of them can hit us." He pointed to a marker.

I explained, "We can't linger in war. Once the baron assesses our true power, he'll have rights to call for help from the King."

"Hum," mused Sir Casar.

"So, here is my plan. Let them move farther from Helfax keep. Three days ride is enough."

Sir Drake, showing his head for strategy, asked, "Then the time has arrived for Helfax. What do you plan for us, Lady Abi?"

"As you say, to move directly toward Helfax tomorrow. In less than three days, your knights and light mounted will race down the main street from the east, torching the guilds engaged in the business of war as you go, and stopping short of arrow range, just outside the keep's walls. I want your men at the gates with the first rising of the sun."

"And you?" Sir Drake asked.

"My sister and I plan on turning our forces, bringing all to Helfax on the same night. We'll rest until an hour before sunup, then secure the city on your flanks; north, south, most of his men, still well west. Just before that, I'll personally assault the keep from within. Once I see the first signs of your torches, I'll see what can be done about opening the gates." I looked up from the map, studying their eyes.

Sir Drake stepped close to me. Words were on his tongue and concern on his face, but instead he closed his mouth and only nodded his approval of my plan.

Sir Finley was not satisfied. He asked, "You only have two hundred women on horses. How do you intend to breach the walls of a keep with lightly armed women? I doubt you have as much as a single ladder. On one hand, you refuse to defeat the enemy on the field, and next I hear you intend to attack the baron's keep with mosquitoes."

I smirked. "I don't intend for my women to assail the walls, Sir Finley. Most of my women will meet you in the streets. We will lend aid, harass the city, as well as cover the perimeter of the keep, but otherwise remain in reserve. If we need to force an entry, you knights will do nicely as the advanced force, considering your good armor. Helfax keep has been emptied, is not large, and a good score knights are sufficient at the gates if it is lightly held and has been opened from within. If the gates remain closed, Sir Drake will be free to determine the proper course. Once the mission has succeeded or failed, Sir Drake will rally and return our forces to the safety of our borders in the north."

"This isn't war; it is lunacy," declared Sir Finley.

"You're right, Sir Finley. This isn't war. My only goal is to free my mother. Perhaps we'll have our war next."

"I still don't understand why your mother is so important," Sir Finley said.

I ignored him once more. There were too many people on the march to stop now, and I'd been waiting forever. What could I tell the knights that would make them understand how important her information was? Then I wondered, was finding an old Queen really why I'd been so insistent upon seeking my own kin? Couldn't it just be that I was doing this because the woman in the baron's dungeon was my mother? What right did I have to sanction all this killing for only one woman? They all had their own hardships, and no few of them had their own kin suffering under the curse of Farstand.

Yet, it was my mother. I longed for her caring touch and to hear her insane babble and to even withstand her quick and harsh rebukes. I knew why she'd been so hard on me, wanting to make a man of me; the world we lived in only has room for men. Well now, here I stood, wearing a sword across my back and as good with it as any man. I'd become just as she'd wanted, leaving only the desire to scream her name and fall weeping into her arms.

Sir Drake apparently saw the gnawing conflict on my face, and yet he said, "I'm afraid I can't lead these knights against the gates of Helfax Keep."

I looked up from the map and wondered at his sudden betrayal.

He added, "I'm going into the keep with you. You'll need one solid man at your side, and Sir Finley is as good as I am at charging keep gates. He may be full of questions regarding your leadership, but he's no coward, nor is he a fool in battle. I've never known him to be disloyal to any cause he has taken up. Don't think harshly of his honest enquiries."

Sir Finley nodded, his face determined and made agreeable by Sir Drake's kind assessment.

"As well I," said Sir Casar. "Woman, I don't know why you want your mother back so badly, but the hell with it. Include me in on the plot to open the gates. Besides, you'll need someone with some meat on him. They don't make gates out of quilt batting, you know."

I couldn't think of a good reason to say no, and so I told them, "You'll have to leave your noisy armor behind. We'll be leaving as soon as you can saddle your horses."

* * * * *

The Goose Breast Inn was a quite common boarding and drinking house, a good place for soldiers and peasants alike. It only had two rooms upstairs, both occupied, but a fine repast and better stables than anywhere else. It was thus a good place for us to hide our horses. Most of the bottom floor was devoted to tables and a bar. We sat at a table near the side wall, looking out at both the street and the other patrons.

I was thinking about all the things I needed to be doing with my people. I had two hundred more women training under Hadarm, not to mention as many nearing us at Helfax. Many others were in support or awaiting hoped-for slots in our training cycles. Sitting there watching the men gabbing over their ale was not my idea of a productive evening.

Of course, I was dressed in the most disgusting outfit I'd ever worn. Not only Sir Drake, but also my archers, had insisted on the insulting clothing.

The short-tailored hem and low cut collar attracted the eyes of men in search of any whore willing to go around back. That would be in the stables and for the sum of a full copper or less. I suppose adding a bit of beauty was the point of dresses like the one I wore. No decent woman would be caught near the place I'd entered. Only whores were not shown the door by men intent upon teaching a lesson to the good-wives.

One young man across the room, and wearing a grand uniform of the keep's own guard, sat looking at my upwardly pressed and nearly naked breasts. He did so ceaselessly. I suppose he was waiting for the men at my table to leave or drag me off and be done with my services so he could pounce. Worse, there appeared to be nothing appropriate that I could do about his staring. My profession dictated that I be flattered by it.

My dyed hair was down, fake brown, loosely curled and settled so a curl or two dangled upon the skin of my chest, as if pointing to one of my nipples. I itched from where my cheeks had been powdered, my eyelids coated with strategically applied ash, and my lips painted the same color as blood. Every time I took a bite of my bread, I swallowed some of the lip paint, the contents of which I had no clue because it was tasteless and had been bought by one of my archers. I couldn't even fume at my archers for the painting, given they were settled in at a nearby stable and awaiting their chance to join the main assault.

Sir Drake and Sir Casar chatted ceaselessly, thinking themselves blending right in due to their boasts of large farm stock and amply endowed women. They faked big gulps from their tankards as they ate full plates of black bread. Neither man, to me, fit the setting, in spite of their loud efforts and near rags for clothing. The livestock they spoke of seemed too many and too well-defined by breed. Beards were too trim, and language far too precise. Even the way they sat in their chairs made their breeding obvious to an idiot.

Once, Sir Casar made the incredible mistake of paying for his bread with a gold coin. He ignored the startled look on the serving wench's face as she picked it up and went back to the kitchen to get advice on how to make proper change out of the thing. The bread had only been two copper slivers. Even more surprising, she returned with the change, the head cook in tow, probably to make sure the serving wench didn't quit the job and walk out the front door with the fortune.

Sir Casar just nodded, but he didn't even break his conversation about sickly pigs and wormfoot, as the woman put his change on our table in nine neat piles of ten coppers, one of nine, and another consisting of eight slivers; when properly put together, these latter would most surely not have made a decent half copper.

To say this drew attention is to say rainwater is wet and apt to ruin the late harvest. Sir Casar acted as if it were too much trouble to notice his change and scoop it up. He drank nearly half a new tankard of ale before the young guard across the room stopped looking at the money. Sir Drake was no better, laughing at Sir Casar's joke about how many wenches it took to poach a nobleman's prize pig, as if such public talk regarding nobility were not a crime out of the mouth of peasants.

I didn't dare mention it, given I was supposed to be nothing more than a woman and sitting there for the men at the table to admire as they talked about things important to what seemed to be the world's most prosperous peasant farmers. On the other hand, the men in our group could afford to be misunderstood. They could explain that they were third cousins to some lightly landed noble, given over to farming better than normal holdings. Conversely, Angel and I knew enough about whoring and womanhood in general. We didn't have to pretend much.

The serving wench came around and offered more ale, as well as another round of tea for Angel and me. Sir Casar absent-mindedly pulled another gold coin out of his purse, but, before he could put it down, I touched his arm and pointed to a man out the window who was prodding a cow down the main street with a stick. By the time everybody looked back, I'd placed the eight skinny copper slivers into the serving girl's hand, almost hoping to hear her protest that the slivers were too thin to pay the bill proper.

Then I spilled my tea on the rest of the coins and, in a fuss to help clean it up, systematically stuffed the piles of coppers into Sir Casar's bag. As I did this, I leaned over to scowl at him, not caring that the bending was indecent. That startled the man. He huffed, as if to say to Sir Drake that women could never be truly understood, even as he watched my pink nipples dangling inside of the loose top.

"I think this maid wants you to keep your money safe, Casar! The more you keep from thieving hands, the more she thinks will be her tip. The wench needs to know that her tip may feel like metal, but is much more pleasant," Sir Drake said.

When Sir Drake made this comment, I was still leaning over the table, delivering my scowl to Sir Casar, so my rear end was up off the chair. This gave the great knight plenty of flesh to slap.

I giggled appropriately as I sat back down. I have no idea if it was convincing laughter. Hidden under the table, my nails dug furrows into the man's thigh. Somehow, Sir Drake's smile never faltered, even though I was certain my raking nails drew blood.

Angel was no help either. Though she preferred to remain mute, she managed a soundless heaving.

This distracted us all enough that the young man wearing the livery of the baron's guard stood behind Sir Casar before we noticed. The guard had his eye on Sir Drake, and not at my breasts for a change.

"Sers. I do not mean to be rude, nor to ruin your evening. Yet, I see you have negotiated the attention of two fine woman of pleasure. I'd thought I'd seen them all, but you have clearly procured fresh ones, and of no small beauty. It has been my hope that you would bed them early, but since you intend to linger, might I make an offer for their services?"

"Then all our time charming them will be for ought, sir," said Sir

Casar without bothering to even turn. I could feel my own eyes bulge. He'd thought something charming?

The soldier tightened his lips.

Sir Daren Drake, however, wasn't in the mood for a fight. He raised his hand. "Let us not be hasty, Casar. Hear the good man out. He fights for us. Let him speak his mind."

The soldier smiled again. "Well then. I see you have just started fresh ale and are not yet ready to bed the wench. I'll pay for yet another round. While you drink, I'll relieve my curiosity regarding this fair maiden, paying both your party and the maiden a good copper each for just a few moments of pleasure in the stables. Upon my word I'll return her to your table before you've even completed your drinking."

"Seems like a fair offer, but for wetting the wench, I'll ask two coppers each," Sir Drake said.

"Ah! That is a hard bargain. I've never paid more than a copper in my life, and no more than two for the whole evening. Already the deal is up to four. Still, she is possibly the most beautiful woman I've ever seen. Make it one to the wench, and two for your table, and we will be agreed."

Sir Drake nodded. "Seems I gain two coppers in either event. Also seems right to share. However, see to it she is returned to us promptly, sir; sound and not too terribly soiled."

The guard gave all three of his coppers to Sir Drake and then kicked my chair around, even as I still sat on it. Picking me up by an arm, I was yanked across his shoulder where suddenly the room turned upside down. He rotated toward the back hall. I swayed over his shoulder like a freshly killed lamb.

Before he was more than a pace down the back hall, I saw Angel's tense body and Sir Casar's hand wrapped around her arm as if to steady her. I had again insisted on wearing no weapons, much to Sir Drake's disapproval, but I was certain every crevice on Angel's body stored a knife and maybe even a short sword strapped to a thigh. One never asked; one never needed to.

Then I also saw where Sir Casar had his other hand. It was clasped around the wrist of Sir Drake, and even from my upside down position, I noticed that Sir Drake wasn't pleased to see my kicking legs disappearing down the back hallway. I'd not imagined him so fond of my chastity. But then again, perhaps Sir Daren Drake had some small feelings towards me, even though I was of peasant blood and a continual pain in his backside.

All the way to the stable, I felt the sensation of the guard's hand stroking up and down the meatier portions of my thighs. He wasn't a bad looking fellow, I had noticed, but this was certainly not a good way for me to lose my virginity, even though I was too old to still covet it.

An odd thought struck me while I was being carried across the adjoining grounds to the ample stable: Would the secret parts of me even work after having been made to wait so long for their discovery? Such a thought terrified me, for I suddenly imagined myself forever a virgin.

The thought was brief, for the moment of truth was quickly before me as the man tossed me into a stack of hay and started unbuckling his trousers. He threw his knife on the straw, and on top of that went his sword belt. When his trousers fell, I could tell he was as ready as any man had ever been for a woman, and to boot, was amazingly well equipped for an adventure into my nethers.

Eighteen or not, I was suddenly certain that for this I was not quite ready. It seemed to be coming at me much more suddenly than I'd at first imagined.

When we'd invented it, the plan had seemed simple. I'd let myself be taken out back by the inevitable frisky guard, and, once he was rid of his fancy uniform and in an unwary state of mind, I'd murder him with one of his own weapons. After all, he was our enemy, and I was a mighty warrior who had killed many such as him. I wasn't at all unaccustomed to the sudden brutality of warfare.

Then we'd take his fancy guard uniform that would have been set aside for the bedding. It would hopefully be free of blood and untoward knife cuts. It was more colorful than the ones we'd captured from the baron's field troops. With the clean uniform we could more easily gain entry into the baron's safest haven.

My only concern up to that moment had been that I'd been

certain any man in uniform would want Angel instead of me. Then he'd discover all of her weapons before he even left the drinking room, for I thought it impossible to actually disarm her even if we all tried and had her help. The men had laughed at this observation on my part, and Angel had soundlessly joined them with smiling heaves. They'd not even let me further discuss its possibility before we'd arrived at the drinking parlor.

I was at the point where I was supposed to grab his knife and murder him, but I hadn't counted on the guard's happiness and seemingly great boyish joy as he paused to admire me up there with his legs spread and his manliness wobbling up in the air, which I also found most fascinating. Then the soldier knelt, straddled one of my legs, and pressed himself against my thigh. The organ between his legs throbbed wickedly with every beat of his heart.

His knife was at my hand, but I thought I might have just a few more moments to ease my curiosity before I had to kill him.

To make matters considerably worse, the man leaned down and kissed me gently on the lips. I'd expected him to rip my bunched-up clothing from me, but his kiss lingered, gentle, as if he were afraid of breaking my bones if he leaned too far against my body. I'd not expected the way these new tactics made my body want to surrender. I knew many women who'd been raped, and grew increasingly aware that this was not the same thing.

When he knelt back, he smiled and said, "I've watched you all evening. Tell me that you love me or are at least my friend. Then tell me where I might find you again when next I'm paid. For the sound of a kind word from one as lovely as you, I'll be left a pauper and subject to water alone in the guard mess for two weeks of penance until the next visit from our paymaster. Such is no sacrifice at all if I can have something to remember you by, even if it's no more than the memory of how your words fell from your lovely lips."

Oh well, I thought; that was charming and yet another part of the unintended bargain. Now I was going to have a terribly hard time killing him. In fact, I wasn't certain what I was going to do with him, and was mostly troubled with how long Angel and Sir Drake would remain patient regarding my results. Then again, I did have a duty to dispatch him promptly and properly, I thought, weighing my options. Distracting him was no longer a problem, nor was reaching his knife or sword.

I was slow to answer as I considered all that, but then I managed to say, "I'll need your name if I am to call you a friend."

His smile widened even more. "My name is Niko. I am seen with some favor by the captain of the guards. Someday soon I'll be a sergeant, and then I'll want to marry you. Of course, that is if you will have me and are not content in your current profession."

"Isn't a proposal a bit sudden, Niko? I am afraid I'm not as I seem in your eyes. To make matters even worse, I am embarrassed to admit my father will not be forthcoming with a proper dowry." I don't know why, but somehow it seemed important to me to be brutally honest with him about that one point. After all, he had proposed to me properly, and I'd spent my life convinced that no decent man would ever grace my ears with the few moments of courtesy.

"That doesn't matter, for my heart has fallen for you, and I'll suffer all the rest." The soldier leaned over again and started kissing me about the neck. A little of his kisses went a very long way, so I confess I kissed the top of his head back.

He'd lost much of his haste, preferring instead to spend some time enjoying my body. This worship seemed to me to be very respectful of womanhood, considering it was coming from a man of Farstand. My face flushed, and my pulse quickened, even though I was lying down and not racing across the meadows chasing rabbits.

I was acutely aware of his hardness as it slid across my smooth thigh, soon no more than a small measure away from the flower of my womanhood. There, my legs trembled, as if betraying me and wanting me to lose all reasonable resistance whenever he decided to kick them apart with his knees.

I wondered, was he like this with all the whores, and was asking the whore's hand in marriage also a part of his usual attention. Even more, my mind wandered to the thought; would it be anything nearly as good as this with Sir Drake? Would he make me feel this much pleasure, such that I moaned his name, "Daren."

That last thought startled me, as it did the guard named Niko. He asked with a soft moan of his own, "What? Did you say something?"

And so you see, I had to will myself to come up with an idea that would rid me of this wonderful distraction from my duty, for it didn't seem that killing him was still the answer. I said:

"The fluttering birds.
The trembling bees.
Two by two, hand in hand.
Singing and humming in their nest
It is alike in the heart
By the will of the Goddess.
Sigh to me with love.
And bind thee to my will.
Tpunwvw Own."

I spun my finger in the air above us, and watched his eyes gloss over and hair fly back as if his face had been hit by a sudden winter's gale. He sagged just as suddenly. His lungs emptied all at once over an enormous sigh.

I choked, the spell having taken my air and made me dizzy and gasping. It might have done worse; I had no clue how harshly any given spell might deal with me, and the goddess had given me many warnings about magic of the heart.

It may have been my imagination, but, when he next looked into my eyes, I thought I could feel his flesh harden even more than before my spell. It struck me that there was much I didn't know about the male intruder, and that perhaps it had no end to its capacity to swell, and, if pushed beyond reason, might even explode.

The book of spells had so many love spells in it that I wasn't certain I'd cast the right one in his direction. On such matters I wasn't well experienced, given I'd reserved my magic for more noble matters, such as killing and deceit. Nor had I time to contemplate the whole list of spells I might have cast on him. It was the part about binding him to my will that had made me decide upon the spell I'd cast, and that alone, for that portion seemed the immediate need.

I decided to give the binding a try by saying, "If you love me, you will wait for my treasures and do as I require. Doesn't Sho ask for sacrifice, claiming it is his due, as well as proof against false devotion? Well then, so too is it with the heart of a woman. A good man will wait for his pleasure, and thus prove his love by showing he thinks more of her than a moment of wetness."

On hearing this, he bit his lower lip. Then he sat back in the hay and scrambled to pull his britches back up from where they'd fallen to his ankles. Before I knew it, he'd recovered his sword and knife, fastening them about his waist. Without a doubt, at least the obedience portion of the spell was working.

He put his hand out, and I took it. I soon stood beside him in the large stable cell, uncertain whether the lack of a bedding was a good or bad turn of events. I brushed my dress free of straw and tightened the laces at my cleavage.

When we were proper, he told me, "I'll prove my worth. Tell me any task, and it shall be done, if no more than to have an excuse to see you again when I've something to report. Only first, tell me your name so I may tell others the name of the woman I intend to marry."

"Oh, don't be too hasty. I may have many other suitors," I lied.

"Not when I am through courting you," he told me. Obviously his confidence was not in the least bit shaken.

"Well then, my name is Abi."

"A common enough name, though lovely. Of Helfax? Which part, and what is your father's surname?"

"Of The Wells, and I have no father."

"Thus your lack of dowry and an unfortunate profession," he said, as if offering me an excuse for wantonness. He added, "Tell me, where is this place called Wells?"

Time was short, for my companions had not been entirely happy with the plan and wouldn't wait forever. As well, I had to come up with a new way to get his uniform, and yet he kept on talking, not giving me any time to do so. Still, I engaged his small talk, saying, "The Well is a worthless place at the end of the world, well up in the mountain passes of the lands of Lettoir. I do not miss it, nor do I still call it home."

"Ah then, you might have known of the witch, the one who leads these new raiders. They say she killed the King's own brother and goes by the same name of Abi."

I paused, and then thought to say, "Yes... I know of her. She isn't as bad a woman as the stories say."

"Ah, it is something; to know one so notorious, evil and monstrous. Perhaps you can tell me about her childhood. The men would envy me this knowledge because of her fame. You know, we hold her mother in the keep."

I felt as if I jumped from my skin when I quickly asked, "Is she well? You have seen her?"

"I have been on foreign duty and leave and am just now reporting back, but last I saw, she was as well as one can be for two seasons in the pits, where stale bread and water are standard penance and the chill of winter sends as many as not on to the judgment of Sho. Do you know her as well?" asked Niko.

"Some."

I couldn't believe it. I glanced at the stable door, wanting to rush right out and go to her; look into her face and tell her I was sorry for having left her to my father's cruelty and the baron's persecution. My mother was only a few blocks away from where I stood, and not yet a corpse as I'd truly feared likely. Oh, of course I'd planned to rescue her, but I suddenly knew for sure that she was in the keep, and still alive. It was almost like standing right next to her and not reaching out to touch her face.

Niko clearly thought to impress me by going on about her: "I have guarded her myself. She doesn't seem like much, so her daughter must take after her father, I suppose. Is she as tall as Randolf was, God rest his ugly soul? We've been told to be ever diligent against a tall woman with a continual scowl, witches' eyes of black, and hair that burns like fire. Young for a hag."

I had to take a big breath in order to go on with any sense of calmness about me: "Some of what you say is true, I suppose."

"Then such a woman exists, you say."

"Smart of you to keep an eye out for her, for she is indeed deceptive. Tell me, Niko; what more do you know of her?" I'd been struck with curiosity regarding what others in the kingdom said about me.

"Well, she has the face of a man; that's clear enough."

I bit my lip. "And what else?"

"Foul of mouth, quite ignorant and quick of temper. They say that, if we meet an ugly and raging woman brandishing a sword, we are free to slay her early and speak of it later; though the baron has made it clear he'd prefer to catch the horrible wench and bind her with chains so he can prove his claim before the King. The ransom is double for the guard who brings her in whole."

"Ah, I see. Well, wise is some of that. I know that killing a witch improperly will cause the demon in her to escape; best to leave it to the King's priests. A witch's spirit is catching," I told him. Of course, such was clearly true, given I'd caught the crone's spirit over two years past, and had only recently noticed a lack of her anger and less of an influence over every turn in my life. It was as if she were no longer inside.

"It's good you managed to steer clear of her, when young. One so evil would surely covet one so lovely."

Though I was still anxious, never had I come across a soldier so smooth with the tongue. His verbal skills were only equaled by the oratory skills of the tax collector, Sir Irstan. Of course, tales of taxes and holdings were not nearly as romantic.

Contemplating romance had me thinking again of Sir Drake, and reminded me as well of the need to move on with my conquest.

I stepped closer to the guard and said in my best singing voice, "I once saw her playing with a man's swords in the village. Would you like for me to show you some of the tricks I saw her doing? That would be a tale to tell your fellow guards, would it not?"

"Ah, such is not seemly from a woman. Why did the men not stop her?"

"Well, she didn't practice when the proper sort of men were about," I told him while I grabbed his sword and slowly drew it out of its sheath. I did this awkwardly and without haste, as if I'd not expected it to also be so long and heavy.

I sighed a great heave and then said, "My goodness, I didn't expect it to be so long . . . and so . . . heavy!"

Angel appeared just then in the doorway. She had her arms out against each wall of the opening, and her legs braced, filling the space. I'd not seen such a look of displeasure on her face since the day I'd healed her soul from the habit of rage that had marked her life until she'd met me. There were two knives in her hands, causing Niko to jump back and reach for the sword that was no longer in his sheath. I took a step back towards Angel, so he couldn't reach his weapon.

"Stay away from that woman, my love!" Niko yelled. He grabbed his knife, and brandished it threateningly towards Angel. "Don't you see; this is the witch herself, though in disguise to make herself appear less tall."

"Of course not," I told him. "Did I not tell you I grew up knowing the witch, and did you not see me sitting at the table with this woman?"

"They say she is good with disguises, I tell you," Niko insisted.

Sir Casar and Sir Drake stepped behind Angel. They were huffing from a quick jog across the length of the stable.

Sir Drake said, "What is this? Have you harmed our whore?"

He brushed by Angel, who was showing some indecision. After all, I did have the man's sword, and she knew I was no stranger to the weapon.

"Of course not, ser! Instead, I defend her and propose to do so for all my life," declared Niko as he pointed the tip of his knife down. He was no fool; Sir Drake and Sir Casar were both mightier men than the guard, and both also brandished an equally threatening knife.

I stepped between them and said, "Niko has just proposed to me."

"He what!" yelled Sir Drake.

"He said I was pretty, and he wouldn't touch me until he made sergeant and could properly have me in his marriage bed."

"Well, he can't do it!" Sir Drake shouted.

Niko stepped forward as if my champion. "What claim do you have on her? Did you not hear that she has received a proper proposal? I intend to relieve her of her duties as a whore, which by law relieves her of all previous debts in sin."

This appeared to stump Sir Drake for only a few seconds, after which he said, "It's I who have proposed to her. That is who I am. I am the man she intends to marry, and I will relieve her of her sins!"

I stomped my foot at Sir Drake. "No one can relieve me of so much sin, nor have you proposed to me! Not once have you asked me such a question."

He said, "Well, in a way I did. I kissed you on winter's holiday, and also whispered to your heart that we were to be married some day."

"I heard no such proposal. All my women know I slept through all of winter's holiday," I told him.

"So what? It still counts, for the gods did hear me, and they were clearly in attendance."

"No, it does not. It only counts if I am awake and if I give you an answer to your question!" I yelled, poking him repeatedly in the stomach with the tip of Niko's sword. Somehow I was able to restrain myself from drawing blood.

Sir Drake didn't appear concerned about the poking, however, and proceeded to explain, "Well, what good would it do to ask you when you're awake? You have so much to do every waking moment, and every time I come near you, you're telling me another thing that needs done."

Angel did more of that soundless heaving. So too was there a twinkle in Sir Casar's eyes, and his laugh was hearty enough for the two of them.

Niko interrupted us all: "So, as you can plainly see now, it is I who has asked her properly."

"Well, what was your answer?" Sir Drake asked me.

I quit poking him and said, "I—"

"What?"

"I'm busy. I told him I'd think about it."

"Busy? Ah, yes, busy." Sir Drake sagged as he said the last words. He dropped his dagger into his belt in defeat. The man looked even more disappointed with me than usual. I could hardly stand to see him so distressed, now that he'd bared his soul.

I said, "Yes, busy. We must move on with our plans. As for the proposal, Daren . . . ."

He took his sad eyes off the wall behind me and looked back into my eyes as I said his first name.

Once I had his attention, I continued, "Someday it might be said that in her middling years a woman cast a love spell on a man in order to get him to do her bidding. Let it be known by all these witnesses that the woman did no such misdeed with the man she truly loved."

He turned his head like Yellow Eyes sometimes did when he thought I was speaking to him in riddles and that maybe he'd puzzled some of it out, but was uncertain. I smiled at the great knight. His crooked mouth partly opened in surprise at what he saw in my eyes. I put my arms around his neck and gave his cheek a lingering kiss. In so doing, I felt a tear stream down my cheek. I had to brush it away, lest it be seen by the guard who was at my back.

"Ah! What is this?" protested Niko.

I turned and told him, "Should I not thank this man for his proposal? Did I not thank you just as well? Now I have two suitors. You should each work all the harder to please me. As for pleasing me, time is pressing. I have need of your services, Niko. Daren and the rest will serve as my escort, and you will help me gain an audience with the baron."

"The baron?" asked Niko.

"Yes, we are not peasants, but of slightly better stock. A man of your stature must surely have seen through our disguises. You see, I have a grievance to present to the baron, and as you know, his chamberlain is not the sort of man to grant easy admission. Last time I presented my grievances to the chamberlain, I spent most of a day working with the cooks and was not loved when I finally spoke to the baron, who by then stood in judgment because of the chamberlain's unjust whispers."

Niko said, "I can't do it."

"Of course you can. You are hopelessly in love with me, and can't help but do as I ask. All you need is some time to think about how to go about it. In the meantime, the hour grows late, and my companions and I will need to change into better clothing so the baron will not be insulted by our common wear."

"Are you sure you're from this place called Wells?"

I smiled and batted my eyes.

Chapter Eighteen

The streets were empty. The last vagrant had been hounded into his alley hovel hours ago. The watch itself consisted of an hourly crier.

Niko looked over his shoulder anyway. Each time we passed a street lamp, I saw misery and uncertainty on his face. My spell of devotion was working spectacularly, but I was still worried about him. What could be more apparent than my suspicious nature as a young warrior? He was a good soldier, judging from his obvious courage and claim of being nearly a sergeant. Sure, his loyalties and reasoning had been severely twisted by my love spell, but at the time I imagined even a man had a limit to love's associated gullibility.

My men changed to finer clothing. We farmers and wayward women dressed in nobler garments. Sir Drake bore his sword and Casar an axe. Angel stepped into the full gown of a well-heeled wife of some minor responsibility. Once cleaned of straw and my bodice tied up high, my clothing appeared in keeping with a minor noble's fiancé. The knights' weapons were added and displayed more openly, though we women kept our knives under skirts and swords in the bundles.

I was still disguised, in a way. I thought it unlikely that a warlord would appear more poorly dressed than her warriors.

For Niko's sake, Sir Drake made up a tale: "Our part in the war between the baron and these pesky women raiders will have to wait until after we've made our petition to the baron. Once he has passed judgment on our concern, then we'll undoubtedly be pressed into immediate duty."

The excuse was both as thin as the walls on the old crone's cottage and remarkably close to telling Niko everything.

We'd insisted upon an escort into the keep before dawn in order to avoid the scrutiny of the chamberlain. "This ensures we'll be the first at court tomorrow," I told Niko.

I hoped the guard was as terrified of the chamberlain as I'd been while last visiting Helfax. Sure enough, he agreed to take us into the keep before the man awoke.

We sauntered across the drawbridge without a challenge. The stagnant water below smelled a little better than the last time I'd visited, undoubtedly due to the icy chill of early spring.

Great stone blocks, looming above in dingy lunar shade, made up the walls of the keep. They were coated throughout with black and green mold. Vines roped up the sides, stealing chips out of the sandstone and occasional patch of mortar.

Over to the left slept the baron's huge three-story house. It was on the city side of the moat, but portions of the roof overhung the water, as I'd recalled. The roof seemed to reach toward the keep's upper ramparts. Several other outbuilding roofs were nearly as tall as the baron's, straining for space close to the moat surrounding the seat of power.

I looked toward the street behind us. The broad thoroughfare bristled with merchant signs, hitching posts, thin morning smoke rising out of tall chimneys, and most of all, a dark and silent slumber that gave me chills. It was hard to imagine Sir Finley, my sister and Sergeant Sasha, leading two hundred and fifty cavalry through the streets, sacking the merchants of their goods, tossing torches into the many expensive glass windows of the war-making guilds, and all the while charging the keep's gaping gates.

All across the closed keep before us, dark arrow slits peeked down threateningly, though over half had been sealed with timbers against the draft of winter. In spite of the seeming lack of good military order, iron oil lamps lit the entry enclave, making perfect targets of us all.

Soon we were right up to the great gates. They towered three times the height of Sir Drake. They were made of smoothly-planed timbers, secured within by a pair of heavy timbers.

Recalling my histories, I determined they might be burned with oil over several days, even though they were braced with great iron straps. Thinking about the chore I'd left Sir Finley, I realized how little I knew about quickly breaching such obstacles and determined that if I lived through the day, I'd seek out opinions on the subject. Maybe I'd assign the chore of siege inventions to the women among our settlers who'd taken up the job of blacksmith and carpentry apprentices.

For the time being, all this dwarfed us, as if we were nothing against the might of the great baron's mountain. This observation conflicted with my understanding that the keep hadn't been attacked in over a hundred years, and thus no longer knew its purpose. Its defense had grown lax, attested by the intrusion of the city on some of the archers' sight-lines—not to mention the outer wall's general ill repair.

Thankfully, and without undue delay, a guard looked down, returning a wave from Niko. They exchanged pleasant insults, as soldiers often do. A sally port set into one of the gates opened. It was almost too small for Sir Casar to squeeze through. I was glad they used it though, for I remembered that the big gates made an intolerable racket when swung aside and it was best for all that everybody in bed remained tidy.

We were met by two guards. Both of them were half asleep on their feet. They'd been long conditioned to stay clear of the nobles, a disposition I'd shared while dwelling for two days in the keep. Thus we and Niko passed without proper questioning.

Once through the gates, the keep's entry was no more than an open archway ten paces deep and a score wide. There was a second gate to the remainder, but it was always braced open, I'd come to think, and seemed thin enough to breach with no more than a few axe blows. Unlike the duke's or even Lacellor's great castles, the main keep beyond this foyer comprised a single but large, square structure. The first floor barracks and third floor audience hall were single rooms supported by squared, unadorned columns, and thus the defenses ceased to exist the moment an enemy found any way into any part of it. This, of course, assumed us many and them few.

There were not nearly as many men sleeping on the first floor as the first time I'd been there. Clearly, the bulk of the baron's forces were off to either Sir Lacellor's war or my own diversions. Still, a good two score slept about, lit only by last morning's embers in the fireplaces. They were mostly by the distant walls and nearest the two grand fireplaces.

One man got up and wandered to a port where he watered out the slit. I don't think he even opened his eyes to notice five people walking by the stairway lining the wall near the keep's main entrance.

The stairs led up to a second floor that was sparsely partitioned by a few wooden walls. It was reserved for the temporary quarters of men and women of noble birth. It would be mostly empty, I hoped; most nobles preferred the better inns to the drafty, open rooms of the baron's keep. This is because keeps are not made for living. Their use is mostly limited to the official business of court and of course, last defense in times of siege. Above the second floor, the third and final floor, before the roof and ramparts, hosted the baron's audience hall. It was probably empty of all but a guard or two, given the pre-dawn hour.

Before starting up through these floors, my attention was drawn to the steps leading to the dungeons. One glance and I saw that after a dozen stairs, the steps turned back again for the rest of the way down.

"That's where they keep the traitor's mother," Niko whispered from behind me.

I whispered, "Can we visit? As you know, I knew the old woman. She is from my village."

"No. The guards are advised to report all visitors, even those who show curiosity. Of course, I understand your interest, you being from the same town, so I'll not report it," Niko whispered.

"Ah, then where are we to go?" Sir Casar asked a bit too loudly.

Niko answered, even as we ascended, nearing the landing on the second floor, "If I stow you in a room upstairs, then you'll be lost among the other nobles. A good two dozen are in attendance. Only a word or two of confusion will be heard from the chamberlain when he can't find you on his ledger. If you are quick about your business in the morning, then I may get away with this without notice. It will also help if you are well spoken and not overly bold."

"Aye," Sir Casar said as we arrived at the landing. We found no guards or attendants outside any of the chambers. "Our Lady Abi has grown better with words. She is much better than the first time I heard her speak, which was a complete disaster. Of course, the first time we met, she didn't speak at all, but instead, murdered my favorite horse."

Niko looked back at him with a startled expression then glanced from him to me. "That must be some tale. Perhaps tomorrow you will tell it to me."

Sir Drake eased his suspicion by saying, "Don't fret their sibling rivalries, Niko. These two are like brother and sister; always on the edge of some squabble. The important thing is your wise counsel. We will be quick about our business, at first light if possible and without sleep that might cause a delay."

Niko nodded to his rival and finally led us to a second floor room.

Angel walked in first. Her hand was poised at her hip where I knew she'd hidden at least three knives within the soft folds of her sash.

Only one oil lamp was lit, as were a few embers under the flue. My good night vision enabled me to see the room had several soft pallets and only an old noble woman sleeping on one. She occupied the corner, though her luggage took up half the free space and made a stack as high as my shoulders. The lone dresser was out of free space, coated with powders, paints and every type of comb imaginable.

Useless as so many of the same items were, I imagined being able to buy a score of good horses with the pawning of her wares. If I weren't a guest, I'd have taken the better combs and jewelry for prize and done just that with the proceeds.

Then I saw something truly horrible: Over on a stand rested someone's hair. It was combed into curls and awaiting the old lady's head. Other than the sight of my soldiers' bodies slaughtered on a battlefield, I could imagine nothing more repulsive, wondering who they'd scalped to get it.

The door closed behind us. I'd not expected it, but then I realized the men would have their own rooms. Angel and I looked at one another before taking a seat on the nearest cots where we stripped our outer clothing. We added our skirts and dresses to the stack of luggage where they'd no doubt get lost in the shuffle. After all the disguises, I was glad to be in the simple brown and grey of Lettoir. Though we'd enjoyed no sleep at all, I felt refreshed the moment Angel handed me a belt and short sword, which I promptly fastened across my back. She had one of her own, including three knives stashed about her person; bearing blades was truly a gift the Goddess favored her with.

It seemed a long time before I heard Niko's footsteps echoing in the hall beyond our door. I'd not found out where the off-duty guards quartered, and I wondered where he'd be sleeping. Surely his barracks was close, just outside the keep's walls somewhere, though I was just as certain Niko would find a place within the keep to settle for the last minutes of the night. The man might have been rendered brain-dead by love, but the last time I checked, his mind was still somewhere inside his head.

We met the men out in the grand room near the stairway that lined the keep's outer walls. Looking out an arrow slit, we all witnessed the darkness touching grey.

"We go up to the third level, then above that, where we can watch from the ramparts. At the first sign of fire in the distant streets, we go down and open the gates as planned," I told them.

Everybody nodded, except Sir Drake. "What reason will we give the guards? What if someone up in the ramparts also sees the signs of invasion?"

Sir Casar answered, "We slit their throats, both now in the ramparts and later at the gates."

I said, "Yes, as Sir Casar says. There are a host of guards below, so let's start from above and wait to slit the throats of the guards at the gates. Opening the gates without a good reason will be difficult enough, even if the guards are dead."

Sir Drake gave me a look that suggested he still might not know me as well as he thought. Angel and Sir Casar were all for it though.

We crept up the steps, met by no guards at all at the landing just prior to the grand hall's doors. Then, off to a corner, I noticed a man leaning in the doorway of a narrow tower leading to the ramparts. He seemed to be guarding the streets, but I heard a light wheeze in his slow breathing, telling me he'd mastered the art of sleeping on his feet. Such wasn't only common, but somewhat inevitable in the wee hours of a long night's watch.

I signaled for Angel to take a post beside him and slit his throat the moment I got to the other side of the long front wall of the keep. Sir Casar and Sir Drake were sent to the back walls to do similar duty.

Across the space, I found another guard. This one knelt on the steps of a second thin tower leading to the upper ramparts. The light was poor, consisting of only two dim lanterns. The man stood and squinted as I slowly walked up to him as if bearing a message. When I was nearly abreast of the steel tip on his over-long lance, I pulled my sword out of its sheath.

Fright lit his eyes when he realized he was about to make the acquaintance of Abi, the murderer of his duke. He raised his long steel lance a little more, just enough to force me to deflect the shaft with my elbow. The soldier tried to pull the long thing back, but the butt of it banged against the stairwell wall. Once I'd gone past the tip, the weapon was useless, and the close quarters didn't help him.

With another step, I stabbed him just below the last rib then kicked him in the hip, freeing my weapon.

He fell back screaming. The huge and tip-heavy lance crashed to the stone floor. Then the fatally wounded but slow-dying guard flayed at my weapon with his hands. It was a complete disaster, for I could also hear a fight going on behind me from where I'd left Angel, telling me my noisy work had alerted her opponent prematurely and caused her some trouble.

We were too tight for good sword work. If I could have gotten to my knife under my skirt, it'd have helped. Angel had three and, if she were here, she'd have undoubtedly slashed the poor man's arms to ribbons. Instead, I managed to nick his neck and stop the wailing anyway. By that time, I was covered with the man's blood, and had to run back to Angel just to guard the stairs in case anybody heard us from one of the floors below.

Indeed, someone stirred below, and after some boot shuffling, spoke up the stairs. "Is all well to the upper guards?"

I thanked the Goddess it wasn't Niko's voice, then took a deep breath before bellowing down in my deepest voice. "A man fell. Cut himself. Dropped his pike! Is not bad. Won't hamper his duty."

I wanted to kick myself for saying pike. The word was formally reserved for the wooden weapons poorly fashioned for quickly drafted peasant. Still, the man below spoke back, "Well, be more alert then. If you wake me again, I'll see your sergeant, and you'll no doubt be doing double duty."

His heels echoed, fading away down the second floor hall, followed by the squeak of a door. It was nice to hear that nothing much had changed about the lazy habits and poor attitudes of the nobles in these parts, and how any one of them ruled over any one of us without even the need for an introduction.

While Angel went above to scout out the extent of the ramparts above, I dragged the two dead guards into a dark corner and stole their lances and helmets, so as to help disguise our profile until the sun was up enough to make the ruse moot.

There in the gloom of the tower stairwell, I waited, wearing the painful steel hat. Picking up the heavy lance, I realized right away that the weapon was idiotic for the duty of guarding at night. It would be fine if used broadly while confronting a crowd of angry merchants, or standing a braced line against a charge of heavy horses. It was maybe good at poking anybody racing up a ladder toward the ramparts as well—or at least until the arms tired—but otherwise it only made my shoulder ache, just holding it at attention. If confronted, I promised myself I'd drop it instantly and draw my sword.

Before long, the rest came back, claiming the upper floor and ramparts secure. Sir Casar took my lance and helmet and assumed a post near the main stairway. We remaining three went outside, up on the ramparts where we enjoyed the red morning star as it hovered in the east. Soon, the sun would follow. It already announced its coming by the brightening strip of sky showing the silhouette of eastern forest.

It wasn't long before I saw the flames of far torches as well. At first, it was only one or two pricks of light that came and vanished as the riders made their way beyond the many trees and farmer's huts on the outskirts; but then, the sight of a fair number of torches made a line on the northern landscape before turning down a road and again vanishing behind the first of the houses of Helfax.

"Come to me, my sister," I said into the night air. I was feeling the moment closing when I'd be reunited with my mother. I didn't envy any who'd arisen early, and who might stumble into my sister's path, for a good half of her riders were archers, and all fifty of them were at least newly practiced at shooting from a charging horse.

"Look. The east as well," Sir Drake said as he came down the long catwalk to get me. We went over to that side of the keep, and there were more distant torches, these clearly down the main roadway that held the bulk of the merchant dwellings. Once or twice I caught the red reflection of fire off breastplates. Then, there came a dark smudge against the brightening eastern horizon just to the right of the torches, telling me something had been put to the flames and was adding smoke to the horizon. Angel waved frantically, announcing the sight of Sasha's torches to the south.

Out there also were many of the baron's troops, for he favored housing them in the many inns and barracks throughout the city. It was a city of thousands—I hoped my army big enough.

This encounter must be carried out swiftly. We'd need to get right to our business and be off before word spread. Otherwise, we'd have a true war on our hands, and while in close quarters, start taking as many losses as the enemy.

Soon, the guards at the main gates, assuming they were awake, would see Sir Finley's knights and lesser cavalry as they raced toward us from the direct path of the broad and open main street. Timing was of the essence, for we'd need to open the gates before the situation became apparent from their lower point of view, but not so soon that we'd need to hold the gates for more time than the few of us could manage.

That was when a good idea struck me. I turned to Angel and said, "Go down to the room. Tie up that old woman. Then meet us in the hallway with her chests full of fancy dresses. We'll burn them on the stony portions of the hallway. The fire will be a good excuse for opening the gates."

She nodded, and was off.

"Ah, a good plan," Sir Drake said. "I'll get the oil lamps along the ramparts." He was off just that quickly, and so was I, down to collect the two small lamps next to the grand hall.

I met Angel in the second floor hallway. She'd piled the dresses up to a door close to the grand stairway. I poured my lamp oil across the dresses then along the edge of the whole wall. My oil ended where a pair of ancient drapes hid a pair of arrow slits that had been glassed over and made into windows. Soon, Sir Drake came down with his lamps, spilling the oil along the center of the hallway and dresses.

Sir Casar leaned the last lamp onto the oil. I'd expected the whole hallway to go up with a whoosh, but the oil from the lamp drowned the flame. I bent down and chanted a spell, bringing forth a wee spark. The clothing lit on top, seemed to settle as one small finger of fire, but then the oil casually drew the flame down. The oil would burn slowly, which I thought might be better.

I told them to wait while I crept below to sort out the best way to proceed from there. One by one, I pinched out the lamps lining the grand stairway, slowly increasing the darkness as I descended. I was almost to the bottom step when I heard a man up in the open gatehouse say to the other guard, "See. Not far. Does that light not seem like fire? I tell you, it looks like horses as well."

"Ah, you be seeing things," the other guard said, but then he added, "Oh, all right. Step out and give a look."

The guard post was up a set of stairs, between the hall entrance and the main gate, a small tower of its own. I hugged the wall in the main room, out of sight of the two men who descended the steps. Needless to say, I was still in plain sight of the main hall where two score guards slept. One glance in my direction would show a gloomy figure conspicuously hugging the wall. Still, only a faint flicker of our fire above danced at the opening in the ceiling from which my stairway descended.

When the guards came down from their post, they made a fair bit of noise, which was not good. Then the small sally port in the main gates squeaked open, and I knew one of them was outside, far away from his fellow.

I decided I had to chance an errant eye and leapt from the wall while the lingering guard fiddled with the door brace and had his back to me. It was an easy move to put my left knee in his back, my left hand across his mouth, and Angel's knife into his right kidney, just under the chain vest that was an extra layer of uniform for a guard of the gate in Helfax. Blood splashed across my hand, warming it sickly. It was not long before he finished biting near my arm and squirming about. I let the guard down slowly.

The entranceway was well lit, unlike the stairway that I'd plunged into darkness by snuffing out all the lamps. The space was also in plain sight through the doorway to the hall, though most of the sleeping guards were unable to see my exact spot because of pillars and the edges of the hall's walls.

The problem was, there was no good place to put the body, so I dragged it into the stairwell leading to the guard post, and had to leave him so anyone looking in would see his feet and the long trail of blood that seemed a bucket-full and in many puddles across the well washed and white rocks of the main entrance.

There was a slight pause as I contemplated my next move, for one guard remained outside, and the room had not yet come alive. But then, a great number of things happened all at once.

First, one of the chamber maids had apparently been sleeping on a cot just inside the wall that separated the kitchens from the big room on the main floor. The maid came around the room's partition, having traversed the entire length of the keep. She saw me clearly as I stood in the only good light in the entire keep. Only once did she have to rub her eyes before she came to some kind of understanding.

Behind me, the guard who'd been left outside started banging on the small door. The hilt of his sword on the little sally port sounded like a drum. He then started yelling a call to arms. Muffled though it sounded, it was such that every ear on the ground floor couldn't miss the commotion.

Angel was at my side so quickly that I missed her coming. She held two knives, both pointed upright in her fists as if she intended to drive them both into the groin of any man willing. Then, behind her, only halfway down the steps, I heard the much noisier descent of Sir Drake and the axe man.

By then, several in the back of the room stood upright, and no few of them appeared to have slept in their boots.

In an instant, Niko took up the space in front of me, fully clothed and with a sword in his hand. He must have been sleeping just on the other side of the first pillar in order to have beaten every man in the room to the spot just in front of me. This includes the two knights of Sir Lacellor who were still on the last steps. Niko looked around both me and Angel, trying to find something to poke that was unfamiliar and an enemy.

It didn't take long for his sleepy eyes to settle on my body. I no longer resembled a lady awaiting a wedding, I suppose. For one, my dress was upstairs, burning in the hallway. For another, I was wearing loose britches and the tunic of a guardsmen of Lettoir. The wear on my clothing told of long rides in the cavalry of his enemy's raiders.

That's not to say there were not some other things peculiar about my appearance, and, of course, at the moment I didn't have the time to think much on these things, but they included my hair pulled back with a quickly applied strap of leather, a sword braced across my back, a bloody knife deftly held in my hand, and every other inch of my body covered in blood from two of the sloppiest jobs of killing I'd ever had the dishonor of claiming.

I remembered the instinct that caused me to want to brush a strand of loose hair from my face so he wouldn't think me unattractive. I'd done it without thinking, using the back of my knife hand and leaving a smear of blood across my forehead.

"Ah! Who are you really?" yelled the first man who'd ever proposed to me properly.

I told him, without screaming, so as to keep at least one secret from the horde, "I've already told you. My name is Abi, and I am a shaman warlord of Debrecian blood. And this last part too: Come to set my mother free from the pits of Helfax Keep!"

He might have appeared more startled, had he not already been greatly alarmed. "This didn't seem the bargain!" he shouted back.

"Fire! Wake up, you sleeping fools! Every man, up the stairs, and bring your blankets!" yelled Sir Drake. He was right there beside Niko next, sword spanking him across the back as if he were a brother.

Niko turned his blade on Sir Drake's, but they were turned my way and too close for it to seem as if they were fighting when their blades locked. To make sure it went no further, Sir Casar walked by, softly saying, "Should we yell that Niko has betrayed the keep? Or perhaps Niko would prefer joining us in our escape?"

Niko stepped back, bearing anguish on his face. The man dropped the business end of his sword. "Ah, I've been your fool! What is to become of me?"

Nobody answered him, for we were suddenly busy, save Sir Drake, who still stood facing Niko with a wary posture.

Behind the two, men were taking to the steps. The confusion was too great for them to look us over carefully as they scrambled to fight the fire. That would last, of course, only a few moments once they saw the fire's deliberately laid fuel.

Sir Casar, yelling, "Fire!" had the top brace off the keep gates and was struggling with the bottom one, but then several of the men who were late for the fire noticed us better.

One shouted, "Traitors at the gates!"

Another voice yelled, "Forget the fire. To arms! Secure the gates!"

Two, then three, than six men, some without britches and two without as much as a weapon, filled the space at the bottom of the landing. Sir Drake, Angel, and even Niko turned to meet the new threat.

The guard outside was pushing on the gates. That was making it hard for Sir Casar to raise the last bracing timber as it jammed against the iron cradles. We were running out of time, both for the gates and the rescue of my mother. Just as worrying, my sister and the others would soon be outside, waiting for the grand doors to open.

Sir Casar gave up jiggling the last brace on the gate when a half dressed guard rushed him, and Sir Casar was forced to nudge him aside with his slicing axe.

He gave up on the big brace and tossed the little brace off the sally port. It popped open almost immediately. The guard outside appeared in the opening. As he ducked in, I turned to parry his blade with my knife. The man wasn't in a good position to fight, stooped as he was, but even stooped and only halfway in the keep, he probed at me with his sword. This had the effect of blocking our only way out, and upon seeing the men collecting in the main hall, he knew it, thinking himself the hero.

I stuck my knife into my belt, and pulled my sword out of the sheath across my back. So too did Sir Casar lift his axe. We were both about to murder the man twice when his body shook. He dropped his sword before my boots, and then fell into the keep. I leaned, seeing three arrows deeply planted in his back.

"Ah! I'd forgotten entirely about my archers," I said, though the noise from the shouting enemy behind me made it unlikely anybody heard me.

"Ladies first," said Sir Casar.

"Not so, Sir Casar," I answered. "You'll have to be first, for we can't defend you from without if you get stuck in the tiny doorway. And, if you're not quick about it, we'll all perish!"

I didn't wait for his answer, but instead joined Sir Drake, Niko and my bodyguard in the growing melee.

After blocking a couple of excellently parried sword thrusts, I hacked a soldier's hand enough to put him out of the fight. Then I chanced a glance back, and saw the big man shoving the one brace he'd dislodged from the main gate through the tiny hole. After that, he squirmed through the opening himself.

"Niko next," I declared. To be honest, I could tell his heart wasn't in the fight against his brothers, for he only played defense, which was certainly a failing strategy given the odds against us. On the other hand, he didn't heed my call, stubborn as the others in the cause of making me go before them.

I ducked through the opening before Sir Drake. Niko and Angel followed.

It was a close thing, Angel taking a nick on her ass as she dove through the tiny square opening. In reply, I saw my archers kneel and loose a pair of arrows into the little doorway. Two more took their place when the first two withdrew to reload. They did this in rotation until they'd lost half their arrows, and no doubt taken the initiative away from any enemy intent upon following us out.

I heard a splash when Sir Casar muscled the one big door brace into the moat. Then Sir Casar took a turn at the small door, having the good sense to brush the women aside and hack at the hinges of the small door until he was sure it could no longer properly close without extensive repair.

This was all good, but I didn't like the idea of the slaughter that would ensue if I sent my army through the tiny opening one soldier at a time. Doing so in armor, of course, was impossible.

I looked back, seeing Sir Finley was now close, and soon to arrive with his armored knights. The gates were still not open to him. My mission had ended, a total failure.

Over to the north, my sister rode in at the head of a column of archers and women wielding spears. She pulled up to nearly where I stood. Instead of greetings, however, she started issuing a dozen directives to her squad leaders. Her troops fanned out in teams, quickly clearing the immediate neighborhood of humanity. People flooded out of their houses, rushing away from the area of the keep. Some held babies in their arms, others whatever valuables they could gather on the way out, and only a few were wearing their skirts and britches properly fastened.

That's when an arrow shattered against the sandstone wall behind me, having missed my head by so little that I'd felt its wind.

My four archers answered, killing an archer who'd thought himself safe from good aim, just because he was inside the narrow opening of an arrow slit.

Even more men started to shoot from the upper arrow slits.

We had to move back, but not before Sir Casar had done good damage, severing three and nearly the final iron bolt holding the chain onto the drawbridge. I could see that any weight on their chains would certainly cause them to snap loose, keeping the bridge down and useful. I was beginning to think quite highly of the man's axe. At least we'd not have to swim through a hundred years of the baron's night droppings in order to assail the keep's main door.

Other parts of the keep were not protected by the water, but in those parts the walls were seamless. With those cheery thoughts in my head, we backed across the bridge and into the arms of the raging streets.

Sergeant Sasha was there with my horse. She had a second horse with an empty saddle—that one for my mother.

Chapter Nineteen

I determined then and there that I'd not get on my horse until I'd put my mother onto hers.

When I'd called for a guildsman, one was quickly captured by Sasha's women because of his thought to load a wagon with fine silks and printed linens. I should have thanked him for his efforts. We had little time to load wagons and properly affix horses. In exchange, I gave him a small white cloth, as well as a message for the three score holding the keep, requesting their peaceful surrender.

At the insistence of some lancers on horses, the guildsman walked up the middle of the drawbridge, calling forth. A nobleman, still in the process of donning his chain and way up in the ramparts, waved the man in. Our merchant soon disappeared—seemingly forever.

Time passed—our most precious commodity. I looked up and down the streets, seeing some of my warriors loading wagons with goods. Others bashed in shop doors. This looked chaotic, but our discipline had called for a selection of squads to do this duty from a list. We were quite strict about those needed for other, more pressing business. Still, a few of my better fighting women invested the waiting time by completely emptying the baron's fletcher shops and iron smithy.

All the knights were mounted and waiting. Sir Drake had taken charge of his two score. The knights were neatly ordered in their formidable armor, supported by their common-born cavalry. The commoners no longer looked shabby and wore good helms and chain. They were assembled as three mixed units, two in front, a smaller one in the rear, and outriders on lookout for a surprise. They were all ready to attack the keep, should we find a means that wouldn't get all of them killed.

Farther out, lines of my own cavalry guarded the streets of the perimeter. Others, I knew, roamed the whole city in half score packs, seeking out the shelters of those in uniform who might come to the baron's assistance before we were ready to depart. Reports filtered back, telling us of great scuffles, some resulting in losses, mostly near the many inns where nobles, guards and hired swords were apt to bed.

As time passed, the smoke over the keep dwindled, telling me they'd put out the second floor fire.

We found a second guildsman. He was a nobly dressed, short and round fellow who looked at me with contempt.

I said, "Tell them that, if they've not opened the gates and surrendered their arms in two minutes, I shall burn the whole city down around them. They can gaily watch it from the cowardly safety of their ramparts."

He spit on my blood-soaked tunic. "You wouldn't dare burn a whole city!" I had to admire him for his courage, for my first impression of the man was that of a coward, judging only from his roundness and apparent riches, which I noted for future reference as an unwarranted bias.

He'd spit on me, but I wasn't angry, seeing it as meaningless in light of the hell that surrounded us. Besides, my tunic was so covered with drying blood that the spittle was of no consequence. I told him, "I won't like it, but I have already murdered a grand duke. Knowing this, they make me wait upon their pleasure, thinking me a serving wench who fears their wrath, which we all know can't be greater, none-the-less. Tell them I know why they're delaying, and I'll suffer it no longer."

Their answer was immediate, for they didn't even let the man in their tiny door. Instead, after he'd poked his head in and delivered my message, the man fell back from the sally port and onto his large backside. As he retreated across the drawbridge, guards in the short guard tower shot arrows near his feet. The arrow slits along the walls were full of laughing faces as the man stumbled in his haste to make it back to our lines.

I sent him home with one of my archers, telling her to allow him to fill his wagon with whatever goods he could manage in a few short minutes. He was to depart in peace. The man stood there listening as I told her this, confusion and mistrust apparent on his face.

Next I turned to Sasha. "The wind blows from the North-west."

Upon hearing this, the merchant turned and ran down the street with my archer riding patiently behind him.

Sasha stood there staring at me for a few seconds, clearly not happy with her assignment. She didn't know that the longer we waited, more baron's men would come out of the woodwork. I had to burn the city, given our delay, or we'd be cut to pieces.

When I said nothing more, the sergeant sadly nodded her head. She remounted her horse. After provisioning nearly two score lancers with torches, she led them up the north roadway. They rode in tight formation.

Good, I thought; those who see them light the city will know it was done by an army under good command. All this was in plain view of the keep. I noticed no more laughing faces peering out of the little arrow slits.

The chaos in the streets continued as I thought over my problem. For the next few moments, my soldiers worked like a machine, revolving around me and having no need for my interference. Well, that's not entirely true. We were desperate for a plan, but for that I had to contemplate. I forced myself to slow my pulse, sit still and think, becoming the calm in the midst of a tempest. There, in the fore of my mind stood the old crone, leaning over a book on her cottage table, pointing with her knobby finger at some map or telling from an ancient general.

One thing that struck me was how every house and business along the street seemed to have candles burning behind at least one of the windows. This was true except for the baron's house. There, every window remained dark. It was unlikely that not even servants resided in the building. Even more interesting, the door to his house was battered, but still unopened because of ample bracing, I assumed. The windows were also barred and not yet breached, though some glass had shattered, sparkling among the flower beds.

All but the top floor was stone, so thinking it too much trouble, my women had apparently given it a try and then left it, as was prudent in a hasty raid. Of course, there was the issue of the baron, and that was the key, I decided. They would let the whole city burn, but what would they do to save the life of their useless baron? I'd never taken hostages before, not yet having come to appreciate the value of doing so.

When I turned, my sister was standing beside me. She also stared at the tall building that abutted near the face of the keep. Truly a natural leader, she too recognized it as a time to slow down, consult with her general, and come up with something meaningful, lest our resources be wasted upon folly.

"I see you've been busy, my sister."

"And much yet to do," she replied.

I embraced her, and she me back. It felt as if we'd lost one another for years, and this was our reuniting, here in the fragile calm surrounded by confusion between battles. In fact, we lived in the same camps, though our paths seldom crossed. She'd grown noticeably since I'd last been this still and near to her. She was no longer a head shorter. The observation saddened me when I thought about how our duties had made us near strangers.

"You've grown."

"Have I? I don't feel bigger, only more haggard," she said.

"Once again, you note only your insecurities." I looked into her tired but lovely eyes.

"Well, perhaps thus is due to continually not knowing what I'm doing. It was much easier when I wasn't troubled with so many under my charge," she answered.

"Regarding that, I have thought on it."

"Regarding what, my sister?"

"All great leaders feel as if things are beyond their control. I think such is what it means to truly be in control. I think bad leaders are those who feel as if everything is settled. I recall the great duke, inside of his metal armor, up on a mighty horse, also coated with shining metal plates. The man watched over us, enjoying the full attention of his many attendants and messengers. Do you know what he did when his army was dying before him?"

"No," Batya said.

"Well then, neither do I. All I can tell you is I sensed the man never lost his bearing. He thought himself taller than he was. Everything was well in control, to him. A good man would have been worried. A good man would have planned for things not going well and been troubled."

My sister sighed. "This tells me nothing. I'm not a great warrior. My tribal council cast me out and wouldn't consider me for the training of a warlord, and, though I have your sword and train daily with the ghost of your mentor, I shall never be as great of a warrior with the weapon as my sister."

I shook my head, saying, "When I see this council, I shall tell them I know a great warrior, one who is not only my equal at war, but greater than any of us might imagine. I'll tell them of a warlord who has passed many tests and is also my sister. I'll say she listens to counsel. And, when I tell them this, I shall say her only fault is when she looks at herself. She is blinded by her own beauty. This is also true of all great souls, I think; they look at themselves and can't imagine what rests inside."

"I think not," she said.

Still, proving her mind still worried about the battle, she pointed to a building. Two of her warriors immediately responded, breaking in the front door of a shop devoted to fashioning saddle tack.

"I think not? You are young, and yet in the midst of this great conquest, you only have time for worry, which is fitting for one who has grown wise in a few short months. There is something strong and long lived within you that will not let you enjoy the foolishness of a young warrior any longer."

"I think not," she repeated.

"Fine then. Having paused for breath long enough to think our situation through, tell me this: What should we do next?"

Both of our eyes had long settled on the door of the baron's great house.

She said, "It's simple. We should storm the baron's house, and upon seizing him, offer him as hostage against the security of the keep. After that, we should take your mother and what goods we have already secured, and leave as quickly as we can. Failing that, we should take the house, divert the attention along the ramparts with some grapnels to the north, and breach it with an assault from atop the baron's roof, which is nearer the south and comes too close to the keep's ramparts. Once the ramparts and upper arrow slits on this side of the keep are secured, Sir Drake can assault the gates without many losses, save a few arrows from the guardhouse and, of course, the problem of breaching the little doorway. We should leave this problem to Sir Drake, and get about our business."

"So you see, my sister, you are the warlord I imagined, and already a little better at it than me, for I'd not considered the diversion of grapnels to the north."

She smiled. "I've gathered twenty of my best. Ten archers and as many with short lances."

"I can nearly match that. I have Angel, and as you can see, I've brought my new sword."

I went to Sir Drake and explained our plan while Angel sent her warriors to bash in the baron's door with a stout log and a good run. The bracing on the door gave on the first run. Four warriors entered with short lances. It was time for me to go meet the baron once again and offer him my complaint.

The baron had armed his servants, and they assisted four good guards in the defense of the great house, room by room. My women held them off with lances while the archers riddled them with arrows, often shot from arm's length. Some of the servants survived, including two maids, so we sent them into the streets. After that, it was up four flights of stairs. The baron seemed nowhere to be found.

I looked out one of the windows, accessing Sir Drake's progress. As soon as some iron bars were tied to ropes, several men put some good shields over their heads, forded a shallow portion of the moat, and crept up close to the north edge of the keep. They tossed the grapnels up, not far enough to reach the ramparts and with bad aim. Mostly they hid under the shields, which were growing a good crop of arrows as they pulled in the ropes on the fallen iron barbs. At the pace they were going, they'd never get the grapnels up, but then again, such was not the point.

We spent a little time bashing through the ceiling in an attic room. Once we managed up there, I wasn't happy with it. The ramparts were not as close to the roof as they'd looked from below. There was still a good six feet of air between the roof and the keep. The ramparts were another four up, and most of the run up to the edge of the roof was downhill along the slippery tiles.

Angel, of course, showed us how this was done. She cleared the raised edge of the ramparts with all but her knees, rolling to her feet on the walkway. After that, two of Batya's archers managed to grip and pull themselves onto the block works of the outer ramparts. This drew attention, forcing my women to immediately start shooting at some archers who looked back from the diversion on the north edge of the rampart walkway. Several of our archers shot from the top of the baron's roof as well, allowing me and my sister to leap across.

One girl had the forethought to thrust a bench up through the hole in the roof. Once they laid the bench across the space, all of our force found the courage to breach the gap, the last few by crawling. Then it was a fight of mostly arrows, as every bow along the vast rampart square sent arrows flying our way. It was like standing among a flock of startled birds.

Two men fell from around a kettle of oil. Firewood had been gathered under the kettle, but not yet stoked to full flame. We took that position and tossed the injured men and firewood over the wall. It was good that these defenses had no chance of coming to bear upon our future assault across the bridge.

More women gathered on the baron's roof, supporting our archers already in the ramparts.

After a short rest, I wiped my brow and decided the fight for the ramparts had no need for lances and swords. We were only targets, and thus I led my sister and Angel down through one of the tower stairwells. Six with lances followed, as these stairs were undefended and it was easy to move our forces a level lower.

The soldiers there appeared unconcerned with the fight above, or at least not on this side of the building, allowing us to congregate outside the doors to the baron's grand audience hall and very near the stairway leading down to the second floor.

Vision wasn't good there because of the recent fire below and its lingering smoke. I immediately found an archer leaning out of his arrow slit and cut him across the shoulders before he even turned.

One along the far wall turned, seeing us through the smoke. An arrow sprouted in the middle of his chest. The man fell before he pulled his bow. I looked over. My sister nocked another arrow.

Nine of us walked along the wall, panting from exertion, but still in the middle of a desperate fight. I blew out some air, and led us in a rush of the defenses.

Those who didn't see us were stabbed with lances and swords. Those who turned were stitched with one of my sister's arrows. When we were done, a half score enemy lay dead or wounded along the front wall.

We didn't bother with the back reaches where I was sure one or two enemy soldiers stood guard along the far arrow slits that lined the walls inside the grand chamber. This wasn't the bulk of their force, for those only guarded against a possible shift in our attack, or some trick with grapnels that wasn't forthcoming. We chose to leave them be and instead moved down the steps as a body. The halls on that floor were poorly defended by only five archers. The corners were blind to one another, so we only had to deal with two at a time. I put guards behind some pillars near the stairway. The rest of us went about our bloody work without distraction. We were assisted mightily by the great noise of knights preparing for battle below, masking the noise of our own battle above.

As soon as the front wall was secure, I stuck my arm out an arrow slit and waved at Sir Drake. I could taste success now. My mother seemed minutes from salvation if all went perfectly.

Sir Drake waved back, and then every man in his dismounted peasant forces ran across to the middle of the bridge with great balls of flaming rags on the ends of their lances.

Two of Sir Drake's archers came all the way across. They leaned low near the tiny door, shot in, and then ran back onto the bridge where they dueled with an arrow slot in the guardhouse. In the process, one of them was shot in the arm and had to withdraw. The other man continued to fight, his only defense being jerking motions between shots.

During this small but deadly duel with the guardhouse, all twenty of the men ran the rest of the way forward with blazing pikes. They ducked into the small opening, one by one, led by their flames.

Once I saw this, I ran up the stairs. The battle of the archers was still in progress on the ramparts. I decided it was better to let the last, scant, enemy archers shoot at less women, and instead withdrew six able archers down the stairwell, leaving only two to distract the sparse remaining enemy. We raced down another level, leaving two more as a second rear guard. I lined Batya's four new archers up at the head of the stairway. We were in gloom. The torches along the stairwell hadn't been relit, and the smoke lingered, making it hard for the enemy to see us, particularly with their attention focused on the fight before them.

The enemy had set up rows of benches that were serving as capable lines of secondary defense against the brave men who'd found their way inside the sally port. All our men struggled to hide behind two outcrops in the wall and a lone and tiny stone statue. No few enemy arrows pestered their advance. These shot at close distances.

One good shower of arrows from us stopped much of that foolishness, allowing a few spear bearers to hold against several knights, also blocking the aim of their archers. Many of the enemy had managed to don some armor, and I imagined they were quite capable of beating us back once the flames died on the ends of a few more spears.

Instead of everybody pressing forward though, three men lifted the last brace on the great keep gates.

The gates swung open, spilling in the morning light. There was only a brief pause before I heard the sound of hooves on the bridge. Mounted knights rushed by. It was strange to see. The perspective rendered them larger than life and fiercer than anything I'd witnessed on an open battlefield. Hooves echoed sharply on the stones. Shouts echoed, calling yield, some pleas, others commands, all in a jumble.

I had most of Batya's warriors retreat to the top two floors, hoping to press the last archers we'd bypassed in the course of the battle. As soon as they arrived, the enemy archers surrendered. Ten came down with their arms in the air, startling me when I realized their numbers.

A young noble woman, half dressed in her many skirts, came out of one of the rooms. She was wailing in utter terror. I walked over, turned her around, and gently closed the door to her room.

* * * * *

Five soldiers from Sir Drake's peasant forces, none of whom I'd ever met, lay dead just inside the gates as I looked down the last flight of stairs.

Descending farther, I glimpsed out on the bridge. The lone archer who'd held off those in the guard tower lay dying with three arrows in his body. Five more men suffered with wounds just inside, as were several of those who'd crossed the roof with me.

Upon making the last two steps, I glanced out the great door. Others, fighting in the streets of Helfax, were dying still.

The wounded were placed by the wall just under the guardhouse. Their bravery had been without question.

Upon making the ground floor, I had a man hail the wagon with the expensive silks and linens. After tossing half the material into the moat, we loaded some of our wounded onto the remaining soft rolls. Later, the rest needed placed in other wagons, which Batya was already calling up, even as she sent the first one north. Our midwives were already busy as some wounded warriors retreated up the roads of Farstand.

There were, of course, many more wounded enemy soldiers. I let the enemy's women walk among them and sort them out. Only a few of the Helfax soldiers hadn't been at least wounded, so there was much sorting to be done.

All of this happened before me as I made my way toward the dungeon opening. I hesitated some and took the time to attend to needful things, both anxious to run to my mother and horribly afraid of doing so. What if I found her already dead? Never had I felt so torn.

Niko wandered across the bridge after the fight. Behind him, great clouds of black smoke streamed through alleys and across the city roofs.

He approached me with sadness on his face as I edged even closer to the dungeon opening. I noticed he had his sword in his scabbard, though the fact told me little about his leanings. He wore a brown tunic, but it was otherwise clear he'd been forced to change alliances. I knew many of his friends were dead or dying, much of it caused by his poor judgment of me.

I forestalled his first words by saying, "I am sorry, but I've cast a spell of devotion on you. War is one thing; affairs of the heart another."

I added:

"By the will of the Goddess.
Sigh for me no more.
I unbind thee to my will.
Tpunwvw Own."

My bloody fingers twirled in the air.

He said, "Ah, I can feel the release of some strange compulsion. And yet, I wonder why you still hold my heart after all you've done?"

That was the thing that had me so attracted to him in the first place. Even while simple and replete of rhyme, he was poetry. His sad words sang such that they reached all the way from my ears to the thing that sometimes beat inside my chest.

I had to force myself to turn back to duty. Many things were organizing quickly for our departure, and so I didn't have any more time to attend to the needs of the defense, or even to Niko. Instead, I brushed by him and started walking down the steps that led to the deepest portion of the dungeon. Niko came up behind me and grabbed my shoulder. He walked past. "Let me lead the way. If there's a guard, I may know him."

Sure enough, there were several guards huddled along the back reaches of the guardroom. They stood in front of a row of solid doors. Some of the men appeared to have taken to the dungeons as a means of escaping the sudden breach of the gates. I came up beside Niko, we two against a half dozen men armed with swords and knives.

"The battle is over, boys. Yield your swords to the Lady." The men knew Niko, but also must have known of his betrayal. They didn't budge.

I stepped up. "It would please me to murder you all, given chance has placed you in the worst spot in all Farstand."

"You are but a woman," one man said. His words were brave, but his hands also shook. My legend had preceded me.

I told him, "Step aside. Have you not heard it sung that some have been born with an immortal soul?"

Unexpectedly, a weak and familiar voice answered from inside a cell door behind the guards. "And yet, have you now grown enough to know the nature of the soul within you?"

I answered, "I have heard her calling, but I don't know who it is who haunts me. At first it was both she and my old teacher, but I think the old warrior has departed and found a new home within my sister, leaving only one lingering stranger."

"Well then, do you think I'll tell you who lingers in need of nothing more than an embrace? Is that why you've come? Has my trouble grown lazy in her late maidenhood? Does she seek out the ancients for all her answers?" the voice from within asked.

The men between me and my mother seemed startled even more than before. The biggest man dropped his sword, and swore an oath against all that was evil. Niko let him pass. The others, seeing this mercy, also dropped their swords and knives, each filing past us and up, surrendering to the waiting arms of my army.

For me, her voice brought joy, for in spite of the hope given to me by Niko when he'd said she might still live, he'd been away long, and I'd imagined it quite possible I'd come too late.

I went to the first cell, knowing the voice of my mother had come from that direction. There were no windows on the cell doors, only crude, iron-bound wood. A peep hole showed nothing but the dark, far wall.

Niko found the key ring and fumbled at the first door's lock.

Behind me, Angel almost fell down the steps. Her eyes were ablaze with some unknowable wonder. It filled me with uncertainty because I knew Angel was somehow closer to the gods than any in my army imagined, and she could always feel things others took for granted.

I forced myself to ignore her. Instead, I recalled my mother's odd question. "Mother, I've always had this spirit; such is not a current concern. I've a pressing need for answers to other questions."

Niko finally found the right key to the cell and opened it. There was nobody inside.

My mother spoke again. "Well then, my trouble, speak a better question, but it'll do you no good. Don't you know I only have answers to questions you've not already come to know through your trial."

I felt certain she languished in the very next cell. Now I remembered why I'd always thought my mother maddening as I shuffled over.

Niko found the next key on the ring more easily, swinging open the second cell door. Inside, once again, the room proved empty.

We moved to the third cell door. "Can you tell me where I can find the Queen? The King of Farstand is at war with our people, and they have a great need for the wisdom of a leader who will show them the way."

She told me, "The Goddess won't let me tell you. Should I tell you this against her will when she's in the midst of revealing this to your eyes?"

We opened the third door, and it too was empty. I had good ears, better than any person I knew, for I was blessed with magical senses by the Goddess, and didn't think such slight of sound possible. Perhaps it was the way the sound bounced across the dripping dungeon walls. There were only four more doors, and Angel had come to stand facing the last of them. I felt certain my mother's voice hadn't come from so far away, and so I had Niko try the very next door.

"Then I'll ask you a new question, mother." I hoped she'd slip up and actually give me an answer. Too many people had died for the Queen to go undiscovered.

"Tell me, why has the Goddess given me the Queen's book if she does not intend for me to find her?"

"Ah, so you have found the Queen's own book?" my mother asked.

"Yes."

"How do you know it?" she asked.

"Because the first page said none may read it, save the Queen. Clearly it implied that to go beyond is a grievous sin. As well, it charged me with this task."

"I . . . see." She added, "And then what did the book tell you?"

"As I said, I could not read further, for I knew right away I'd sinned and opened the book intended only for the eyes of the one chosen by the Goddess; the one intended to lead her people."

"A sin, you say? Ah, I see. Isn't our Goddess clever."

We pressed open the door to the next cell. Again my mother wasn't inside. I looked over to the last three doors, and decided I had to trust in the visions of someone other than myself. Angel was before the last door, and though my senses told me it was the least likely of the three, I was not the only one blessed among my people. This desire to do everything myself had to end, I realized. I was no leader at all if I could not trust in others and step back just a moment.

I thought, such was apparent, but it wasn't easy for me to fully trust those who had become part of my circle, particularly those whom I'd always thought more common. And yet, never had Angel betrayed me. This was true even though I knew absolutely nothing about her life other than she was always by my side.

I went to the last door. "Thank you, Angel. I should have listened to you from the start."

My mother said, "Yes, you might have saved yourself all this struggle if you had simply stilled yourself and listened. Then again, you were always full of questions, and apt to get yourself confused while out trying to find the answers among the wolves and the world outside your heart. Now your heart must belong to your people, my trouble. Now you must let go and embrace the other soul you find within."

I grew frustrated as Niko fumbled for the key to the last cell door. I said, "Well, it might have helped if you'd answered just one of my questions before I'd gotten involved in all this difficulty!"

"I have, child. Have you not heard me answer your question?"

"Which one, mother? There were many, and I heard no answer to any of them."

She said, "Did you? Asked many, you say? I thought it was one question about a soul within you, and of course, that is the answer to them all."

"Ah!" I screamed, kicking the door. Niko seemed to never find the right key.

My mother laughed at me. "Listen, child. It's my turn for a question. Where did you find the book meant only for the eyes of the Queen?"

I told her, "In a cabin full of my enemy."

"Ah. For me it was on a trail, some days after my very first battle. I've always wondered why we find it in such strange places. Even the one before me didn't know the answer to that question. She must mean for its finding to be as mysterious as its secrets."

"Mother," I yelled, banging on the door. Had I heard her voice fading?

Her voice became so weak that I couldn't be sure I heard her correctly. "My child, it is time for me to go. I fear the time has come for the cloud to lift from your eyes as well. Go now, with my love, and know that many great things have been called sins by those who are afraid of what might be found within."

Afraid? Never had I known a lack of courage, not even on the field of battle. And yet, I was terrified!

Suddenly, the door opened, and that was without a key, for Niko couldn't find it on the ring. There, on the floor laid my mother. The smell was like that of a week old battlefield.

Niko peered in, then hid his face with a hand. I could see tears on the face of Angel, though there was no hint of surprise. She'd known, somehow. Perhaps the Goddess had told her.

I envied her soundless weeps as I drowned them with a scream followed by many wails.

After a moment, I had to stop myself from my lamentations and look at Niko and Angel, just to make sure my first glances of my mother hadn't been something from my imagination.

I knelt, no fell, by her naked and dead body. I touched her with trembling hands, though the skin was cold and slick and no longer hers. In places, the skin had split due to swelling. When I brushed my fingers through her hair, strands came free and clung to my fingers.

I'd come too late, and from the look of her pale and swollen body, by several days. In spite of the swelling, I could see too much bone at the joints, suggesting starvation. She was still in chains, one around her neck. That one was only a yard long and embedded in the wall more than a yard up its face. They'd hurt her badly, and then when she'd died, they'd just left her as bait.

The marks of many recent whippings were apparent on my mother's flesh. Perhaps they'd questioned her about the raiders. Perhaps she might have lived, had I chosen some other means of securing her rescue? I'd never know.

Well, I thought, at least now I know why the men cornered in the dungeon had given up so quickly upon hearing her voice.

When I'd commanded the burning of the city, I'd thought it a sad necessity of battle. At that moment, it thrilled me to know that Helfax had been turned into a raging inferno. Such wasn't even enough—no, not nearly enough.

This was not over.

Helfax had been nothing to me. Now, even its flames left me empty!

* * * * *

Niko came back with the same guards. These men were now his servants. When they came in to take her away on their stretcher, I insisted they not yet wrap her body. I said, "I want her paraded about the keep before she is wrapped in the finest silks and laid across her horse. Let the men who fought to keep her here know why the city burns around them. Let their noble women know their husbands' true hearts. Let the men and women who fought to win her freedom know why so many of them died to set her free."

Niko asked me, "And who will we say they died saving?"

I embraced the extra soul within and answered, "Say she was the great Debrecian Queen."

Chapter Twenty

"We've found the baron. He and his family were hiding in a closet set against a wall. We noticed that it seemed wider than the other walls," my sister said.

Before me was my army. Scouts were out, and vanguards still fighting delays. The fire was close now, and it was hard to see well down the streets for the many streams of smoke. Refugees lined the roads in all directions leading out of the city. This filled me with resolve to carve us a path and be off to the safety of the border.

I commanded, "My sister, lead my army home. I'll be only a short while."

She nodded, as did the knights. They all knew the need for me to do this alone. I saw the last wagons lurch at my sister's command.

A good-sized squad remained beside the house. I refused all but two archers that guarded the steps. Then Angel and I walked back into the baron's house.

Four women with lances and swords held the family within a spacious room. The baron was tied, hands, mouth and feet, fighting bravely against the ropes, though I was sure he'd not be nearly as brave if he managed to untie himself.

His pretty wife was weeping, sitting in a chair by his side. She held a babe in her arms. The baby slept in a blanket, as if all of her world was warm and lovely.

There were four children in all, including a girl of perhaps five, hiding behind her mother.

The boys were older. The oldest appeared maybe a year my junior. In another year he'd surely grow taller than me. He broke free from the archer who held him. Someone had missed the knife he pulled from the back of his belt, forcing me to grab his arm and twist it behind his back. I took the knife then shoved him to the floor. He landed before his mother's feet.

The mother said, "He'll hate you for that."

"Does he imagine growing past this day and becoming the next baron?" I asked.

The boy glared from his place on the floor. "Yes, and I'll kill you when I am old enough!"

I bent down, letting him see me better. "I want you to remember my face as long as you live. Don't forget it. Come for me when you're ready. Then we'll see who has the ear of the gods."

He didn't flinch.

The baron's wife put her baby down on the cushion next to her lap. She reached down and held the heir to her knees. She was smart enough to know me as a spiteful woman who intended murder because of the death of my mother.

I reached over and took the babe from where she'd left her. The woman reached out and shrieked, but I was quick and had grown used to the sound of wailing women.

I looked at the face of the swaddling babe. She looked as much like her father as she did her pretty, Farstand mother, but, of course, I'd grown to not think kindly of people who judged one another by the accident of their birth.

I thought a good shaman warlord would hate every one of the baron's offspring and, without all this talk, offer them all up as offerings to war. Instead, I thought, I'm no longer the warlord of my tribe. No, that was my sister's fate. I'd become someone different, and even already regretted the taunting of the boy, for it was beneath me.

The sorrow I felt for my mother's murder couldn't be appeased by endless dying, as had been my first inclination, for such wasn't in keeping with my new responsibilities. In that way, these people seemed small compared to my mother's memory. There must be balance in the world of suffering.

I nodded when the thought struck: Mercy is only possible when it is undeserved. What the new person inside of me needed even more than revenge, at that calm moment, was life; in particular, life without reason.

And here it was before me, in a blanket.

I thanked them for their daughter. "I shall take this innocent in exchange for my mother's life, which was so carelessly wasted by you. She'll be named Mercy, for this is her gift to both our houses.

The mother screamed.

"I know a woman whose womb has been made barren by years of abuse in this kingdom of hate. Her name is similar to her new daughter's. Despite her former profession, she's a good woman and a member of my council. She'll be happy to help raise this one to be a great warrior against the once mighty kingdom of Farstand."

Epilogue

I did not kill them; not even the baron who'd murdered my mother. Instead, as I rode away on the heels of my army, I listened to the sweet wails of the baron's wife. It blended with the whistling of the inferno as it blew destruction across the city at my back.

Gary is the author of several short stories and the novel *Zombies in Our Hometown*. He is one of the founding members of the Ohio Writers and North Columbus Fantasy/Sci-Fi writer's groups and is a longstanding member of the prestigious Columbus Writing Workshop. Gary has a BFA from the Columbus College of Art and Design, teaching certification from Otterbein College, an MBA from the Ohio State University.

VISIT THE LOCONEAL BLOG AT

www.loconeal.com

Breaking News
Forthcoming Releases
Links to Author Sites
Loconeal Events

www.ingramcontent.com/pod-product-compliance
Lightning Source LLC
Chambersburg PA
CBHW021328250626
47155CB00002B/638